though she now stood close enough to breathe in his clean musky scent. His eyes, however, pulsed vibrantly alive, spearing her very soul. Otherwise, she could have made a good case for an unknown party dropping a statue in the middle of the parking lot, blocking her car.

Gingerly, she put out her hand, gently brushing the center of his chest, and then snapped it back as if she'd been burned. He felt every bit as smooth and hard as he looked but warm to her touch—hot, in fact. She had not counted on the heat. Yep, he was real, all right, and if she told anyone about this, they would commit her and throw away the key chip. Cat believed a certain truth surrounded every folklore and legend. She'd spent hours, in fact, researching everything she could get her hands on concerning the subject, but still...could this really be a mythical spirit come to life?

"You can see me?" he asked.

"Duh. Yes, I can see you; we wouldn't be having this conversation if I couldn't see you. Of course, I've done all the talking. I thought maybe pookas couldn't speak. Uh, you are a pooka, aren't you?" Cat asked, nervously glancing around for anyone who might be able to confirm her sighting. Twin amber-lit pools seemed to pour straight into her center. Such beautiful exotic eyes...

"And the others—can you see them, as well?"

"Huh? Others?" She took a couple of steps back, finally grasping the precariousness of her situation. Cat swung her head in all directions trying to determine the best route of escape. "A fine time for my flight-or-fight instinct to kick in," she mumbled.

"We will take her; prepare to transhift," Zorroc ordered.

Reviews for ZORROC

"ZORROC is a perfect blend of science fiction, adventure, and romance. From alien races, to futuristic technology, to steamy sex—Zorroc has it all."

~Romance Reviews Today (A Perfect Ten)

"ZORROC is a keeper, definitely worth spending a day totally engrossed in the journey."

~Fallen Angel Reviewer (Five Angels)

"Ms. Gibson pens a story with compelling characters mixed into a gripping plot with loads of twists and turns."

~Romance Junkies (Blue Ribbon Rating: 4.5)

"Plot finely crafted—Lil has created a compelling and intriguing world."

~eCataromance (4.5 rating)

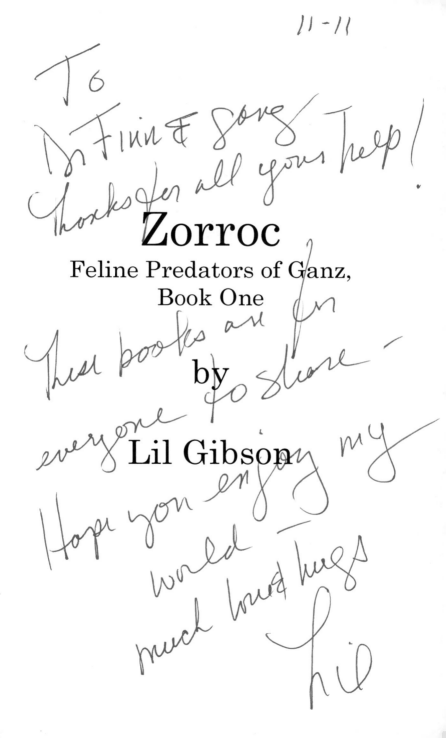

Zorroc

Feline Predators of Ganz,
Book One

by

Lil Gibson

11-11

To
Dr Finn & Sons
Thanks for all your help!

These books are for
everyone to share —
Hope you enjoy my
world —
much loved hugs
Lil

Zorroc: Feline Predators of Ganz, Book One

Cover Art by *Tamra Westberry*

The Wild Rose Press
PO Box 708
Adams Basin, NY 14410-0706
Visit us at www.thewildrosepress.com

Publishing History:
previously published by Echelon Press, 2003,
and by Venus Press, 2006
First Faery Rose Edition, 2009
Print ISBN 1-60154-555-X

Published in the United States of America

Dedication

This book is dedicated to my mother, Connie Shaffer, who forever accused me of having a vivid imagination.
I guess she was right—again.

The Dream

Quiet. So quiet. Too quiet.
He raised his eyelids a fraction to confirm the coming dawn. Nadia's pet tornika should have been clicking happily outside his chambers, the birds greeting each other, and the coming dawn in their individual dialects, and the Apis digging noisily through the brush outside his window for fresh Scarubs. He rose slowly from his mat and moved to the window, then pressed the pad to release the translucent covering. The dawn broke, surreally muted, as if a layer of gauze had encased the House of Ra. It was not the mist that rose from the lagoons with majestic eeriness, which hung no more than a few calabrays from the surface. This mist was falling from the sky. Only that was impossible; Gattonia had been free of pollutants for centuries...
He started at the sound of pounding feet barreling toward his panel. Was he dreaming? Then his protector and a team of militia poured through the sliding panel and entered his chambers. They simply stared at one another for a few moments before everyone began speaking at once.
The Dargons had COMd that they had left a calling card in the wind. The Gattonians were all but finished as a race and must evacuate or face more of the same.
As leader of his people, he had heard of the environmental expungers but they existed two galaxies away. How had they come to be near their planet of Ganz?
His visions revealed a kaleidoscope of horror that

1

no one could have anticipated or prepared for. The Dargons had laid in a virus which targeted their females. Many writhed in agony, spewing their insides, ejecting their female organs where they lay. Many died and many more were hopelessly deformed in both body and spirit. And almost all were rendered infertile.

Their finest Med-techs could not find a way to treat the afflicted, merely alleviate their pain and watch them suffer an agony so horrid that suicide was becoming a problem among the males.

He could only watch as the female population of Gattonia withered...while he and the other males suffered no side effects. What kind of evil could conceive something so diabolical? A helpless tidal wave of rage, hate...and fear swelled within him until he choked with it. He was their leader and their guardian. He was responsible for their safety. He had failed them and failed himself.

Now the monsters were coming again. He could feel it. Silently, lethally and this time...

"Nooo!" he screamed as he tumbled off his mat covered in sweat and disoriented.

He sucked in a deep calming breath and rose. It was the nightmare again, replaying images that he lived with day and night. The horror, rage, and fear that would not recede but resided inside him like a malignant growth. He sank back onto his mat and raked his hands through his mane. Zazu, who was he kidding. He was not having a nightmare; his life was a nightmare.

Chapter One

Earth 2027

Zorroc of the House of Ra, Province of Gattonia, had not planned to take her this soon, but time had run out. He had spent the last day and a half studying her and conferring with those assigned to watch her, planning how to spring his trap. He did not want to make it harder on her than need be or frighten her unduly, but capturing her attention completely and laying his first snare in this game she could not win had been tricky. The right tone had to be set. If he simply transhifted her to his ship, she could become disoriented and be of no use to them when they required her cooperation. To steal her in her sleep could end in a similar result.

He had no use for hysterical, unstable females. Therefore, he would appeal to her romantic nature, a prominent force in her make-up, so he had been informed; then take her. She was a scattered little thing who thought she believed in destiny and all manner of metaphysical phenomenon. Well, destiny was about to make an appearance and destroy the course of her world forever. He smiled grimly. He enjoyed his role as predator far more than his role as leader, but his own destiny had interfered with his enjoyment all too often of late.

He came from an ancient race of predators and the compulsion to hunt, capture, and tease ran strong in their lines. Though, as civilized beings, they did not often give in to that part of their nature; in this case he looked forward to acting the exception. Females of other races reacted with barely constrained sexual fervor to what they perceived as a dangerous edge to their species. They enjoyed being dominated and controlled. Surely, this female would prove no exception.

On several occasions, he'd materialized at the foot of her bed in deep night to observe her sleeping peacefully, her comforter barely registering a ripple to expose her slight form. Others times he watched her from a distance interacting with friends and co-workers. He did not understand the streak of molten anticipation that grew within him with each sighting of her. Or why her unremarkable presence, when compared to her friends, filled him with unaccustomed warmth.

He and his protector were seated at a small round table in the shadowed corner of Grumpy's, a bar and eating establishment attached to the shopping mall. Apparently, a favorite meeting place for Catarina and her two friends. Arriving scant moments later, packages in hand from shopping, she settled on a bar stool, legs crossed and swinging in time to an internal melody only she could hear, then commenced conversing and laughing with the bartender.

"Is she never still?" Prolinc muttered in churlish exasperation. "We have watched her for more than a quarter hour and she has not stopped squirming for an instant. If it is not her leg then her hands flit in tandem with her mouth, as well as her other three thousand movable parts. Are you sure she possesses even a drop of our blood? It does not seem possible," he concluded, slouched in his chair.

Zorroc turned his head slightly in contemplation, all the while fighting a grin. It represented a primary Gattonian trait, their stillness of form and spirit. "Yes, I am sure of her bloodline, though she is rather...animated. After studying her these last days, I am becoming accustomed to it." He shrugged. "Even her hair flows around her in perpetual motion much like the clouds over Gattonia," he softly murmured.

His gaze returned to Cat. She was small for an Earth female and slight of build. Her dark, undisciplined auburn hair curled around her delicate features and half way down her back. Her large, almond shaped eyes, a stunning asset, shone like emeralds, revealing the essence of her being.

Zorroc suddenly stilled, riveting his attention on the bartender whose eyes appeared glued to Cat's unbound breasts as they gently swayed, nipples hardening slightly from the constant brush of her midnight blue sweater. "The bartender behaves over-solicitous toward Catarina, does he not?" Zorroc growled, wanting to take her that very second, to Hell with planning and finesse.

"Over-solicitous of her breasts, perhaps," his friend replied merrily. A hiss escaped Prolinc as his gaze lit on and followed a blonde female proceeding across the room heading toward the bar. Sleek wheat colored hair piled atop her head accentuated the graceful curve of her neck. His gaze traced over large lush breasts to a tiny waist and grazed over legs that went on forever, exposed by a tight fitting short skirt. She approached Cat and the two greeted one another like long lost friends. "Who is she?" Prolinc demanded.

Zorroc shrugged, "One of Catarina's companions. Dee is her name; she is a law-upholder, I am told. And if you can take your eyes from her for a moment you will see Angel winding her way toward them."

Prolinc studied the three unabashedly, missing nothing. Physically, the females shared none of the same attributes. Oh, all were attractive, but in diverse ways. Angel, tall, willowy, and black as night had an exotic beauty rarely seen in an Earth woman.

Dee was as light as Angel was dark and as lush as Angel was slight. Catarina, dwarfed by the other two, brimmed with motion and mischief setting her apart from her friends' more sedate demeanors. And while her curly hair billowed around her, putting him in mind of a wood nymph, the other two had smooth long silken hair, Angel's worn loose and Dee's braided and intricately coiled, exposing the creamy expanse he would love to nip...or bite.

Cat suddenly straightened in her chair and scanned the room.

"Does she sense us?" asked Prolinc, breaking the silence.

"No, she is an untrained Earth-bounder and not aware of her innate capabilities, if in fact, she possesses them," grunting his last words with disgust at her ignorance and poor handling by her parents. "All her thoughts remain centered on her friends."

"You read her with ease, and though I am the stronger telepath, I cannot."

"It is a puzzle," Zorroc admitted softly to his life-bonded friend.

Actually, the three of them were a puzzle, Zorroc acknowledged as he watched them interact. They embodied the phrase "polar opposites" and he wondered what they found to talk about; but whenever he observed them, the three spilled words on each other more drenching than the monsoons of Kadeer. His sources had researched Cat's background for over a year and gathered a very comprehensive portfolio of her past. She had been enrolled at the local ed-center at six years of age and met Angel and Dee almost immediately. The three had boarded together year-round until graduation and forged a bond stronger than family. Though Cat's parents still lived, their work with Earth's space program took precedence over their only child.

When Zorroc learned that her parents had visited a mere handful of times since childhood, he found himself outraged on her behalf.

She now lived with two aunts who had shown up on her doorstep close to a year ago. They were purported to be her mother's older sisters and quite a surprise for Cat, because growing up she had not been aware of their existence. Now they took care of her, or she of them, depending on the circumstance.

Cat began filling her friends in on her latest booking, a Sci-fi Convention set to commence in a little more than a week.

"So I decided to change it to the downtown convention center. With William Shatner and over fifteen-hundred attendees expected, I didn't think Lindsey Hall would be large enough," Cat continued, while taking a sip of her drink. "So that will be two weekends in a row for other-worldly pursuits with the Tarot Assembly scheduled for this weekend. Do you think you can attend both?" she asked in a rush, eyes flashing back and forth between her friends.

Dee and Angel slid a knowing glance at each other in silent communication. "We'll show for both weekends if you spill about your date with dreamy Dennis last Saturday night. Dating is quite the monumental leap for you and we demand the juiciest details," Angel asserted in her soft southern accent.

"Uh, it didn't go all that well actually," Cat confessed, studying the intricate designs that the salt made close to the rim of her glass. "What is it with guys these days? They take you out for dinner and a movie and think it entitles them to get lucky by the end of the evening! Well, he didn't get lucky and I doubt dippy Dennis will be back for more." She shrugged. "He was a centipede. I guess you have to kiss a lot of centipedes before one turns into a man, huh?"

"You kissed him?" the surprised duo gasped.

"Ick, barf! No, I didn't kiss him, who'd want to kiss an octopus with the body of a centipede? *He kissed me* and let me tell you there couldn't exist a slimier set of non-lips on the planet. He started out as an average type guy, but as the night and the margaritas wore on, I began to see his true form take shape. He began to drool, his eyes drooped, sweat broke out on his face and hands, and that's when he started inching toward me. Before I could escape, he had me pinned and prone on the cushioned bench and splat—" she emphasized by slapping her open hand flat against the bar top making both Dee and Angel jump. "His drooling fish lips hit mine."

"What did you do?" they asked, horrified.

"The only thing appropriate; I kneed his shortest and hardest appendage. He seized up into a ball and rolled away like the slug he was," Cat ended with a satisfied feline smirk, taking another sip of her Margarita. What she wouldn't give for a bona-fide Prince Charming that wouldn't pull a shape change on her at the slightest provocation.

"How's the Habi-Cat going?" Dee asked Cat, deciding on a change of subject.

"As a matter of fact, we're celebrating tonight. In closing both the Sci-fi and Tarot conferences in one month, a sizeable bonus will be added to my paycheck. It will keep the cats in food and medicine for several months!" Finishing off her margarita, Cat ordered a 'Death By Chocolate' dessert for the three to share.

With the help of her aunts, Cat had opened the Habi-Cat eight months earlier, depleting her savings, plus a hefty donation from the aunts, to set up the safe haven for every breed of feline. The need for this facility could be summed up in one word. *Uitti.*

The year 2022 had brought with it the self-

8

proclaimed religious prophet Dr. Cecil Uitti (better known to his enemies as Dim-Witty) whose mission espoused the elimination of world hunger and disease. Of course, his aspirations went deeper than that. His closest minions knew his final goal included world domination—power and wealth beyond imagination and control over its people. And the first step toward his goal was chilling in its simplicity.

The utilization or annihilation of Household Pets! Animals that served no purpose save companionship, yet consumed an alarming amount of sustenance, depriving humanity of their one possible contribution—the sacrifice of their bodies for the betterment of science, and the nutriment and longevity of the human race.

In the beginning, the public had laughingly scoffed at the ridiculous notion of using their pets in such a sinister manner, but three years later they'd stopped laughing. Somehow Dr. Uitti had persuaded the government to outlaw most pets and mandating the confiscation of existing pets from their owners. These included hamsters, guinea pigs, rabbits, birds, ferrets, monkeys, rodents, amphibians, and reptiles of all kinds. Selected breeds of dogs and cats remained exempt. Dogs, for their contribution to society as helpmates and work animals, and cats, for the present, because there arose such a swell of outrage against it. Stray, wild, or unclaimed felines, however, stood fair game and thus the reason behind and creation of Habi-Cat.

"What's the cat count for the week?" asked Angel. She had conflicting feelings about the changes set in place by Dr. Uitti. While confiscating existing pets from their homes made her distinctly uncomfortable, the scientist in her acknowledged the need for animals in laboratory testing. Many people's lives had been saved because of them, to say nothing of the improved quality of life. However, the doctor's idea of processing one half of household pets for food to feed the masses caused a knee jerk reaction of abhorrence. Who in his right mind would want to eat his own or someone else's beloved pet? She shivered at the image and tuned into the tail end of Cat's latest tally. One of her workers had rescued a litter of kittens from a citizen trying to capture them for the fee he would collect from the humane shelter. Shelters remained clearinghouses for animals, only now sold their charges to meat processing plants and research labs. In trading their non-profit status gladly, the shelters rolled in money, rapidly growing to become a top member of the New York Stock Exchange. The selling of pets had become highly lucrative.

"It's fortunate one of your assistants happened along when he did," Angel commented. "You know I support your efforts where pets are concerned, but you have to admit that animal testing and additional food are essential for the quality and prolonging of human life."

Cat released a long-suffering sigh. "And what exactly makes human life more important than other life forms?" she asked. "Remember that Star Trek movie where beings from another planet thought whales the supreme life form on Earth, and after believing humans had exterminated them, proceeded to try and eradicate our species like some sort of parasite?"

Dee and Angel looked at one another with underlying commiseration before Dee spoke up as the voice of reason. "I think you should get therapy for your addiction to fantasy and sci-fi movies. One day you're going to fall into one and not be able to get out. And you have to admit that in real life, humans are the superior and most intelligent life form on Earth."

Dee, who dealt in solid facts and logic to locate and transport bail jumpers and Angel, who as a scientist, believed in nothing that couldn't be proven by two or more methods, often found themselves at a loss as how to react to Cat's occasional jumps into never, never land. Cat knew her two friends sometimes found her two Twinkies short of a box, but she held firm to her ideas, convinced they were every bit as logical as her friends.

Cat snorted, "Oh, please. The arrogance of humans never ceases to amaze me." Especially when she found it in her own friends. "What makes you think we are the most intelligent species on Earth?"

"It's a scientific fact proven conclusively by every renowned scientist and academic on the planet," Angel concluded.

"A scientific fact proven by human scientists and human academicians who made up the criteria of what intelligence is, then proclaimed their own species the most intelligent. Prejudicial data built to support flawed theories. Maybe if our intelligence enabled us to communicate with other species, we would find that they viewed things in a wholly different light. We know that ants communicate telepathically, therefore, probably impart knowledge a whole lot more effectively than humans; aren't those attributes the mark of superior intelligence? Maybe cats are really the most intelligent species on the planet and should be worshiped by us, like the ancient Egyptians did, instead of systematically slaughtered for food." Cat always felt particularly philosophical when sipping margaritas.

Angel and Dee studied Cat with twin expressions of bemusement, confusion, and frustration before Angel summarized. "Cat, sometimes I think you're from another planet."

Chapter Two

"Sometimes that girl worries me," Dee mused, her gaze following Cat's retreating form as she made her way to the exit. "She insists on cat-sitting every evening until early morning even though she has competent staff to handle any difficulties. Her energy and dedication boggles my mind. Maybe all that sleep deprivation is catching up with her and affecting her judgment," she proposed, meeting Angel's amused glance.

The two burst into fits of giggles, delivering twin declarations of, "Nahhh. She's just different than we are," Angel said, pausing to gather her thoughts, "fanciful, almost fey with one part of her rooted to reality while another, I don't know, exists in a realm we can't reach. And yeah, sometimes that concerns me a little."

"When she watches one of her Sci-fi classics, she gets so engrossed I think she half believes them. And if I have to listen to another lecture on the pyramids..." Dee added.

"The Egyptian civilization was not advanced enough in engineering to design or construct such masterpieces of architecture which supports the theory of 'beings' from another planet," Angel mused, starting the two giggling all over again. "I guess it's that combination of imagination, naiveté, and intelligence that makes her so precious."

"You're probably right and we two pragmatists will always be here to protect those qualities."

****

Heading to her car, positively buzzing from a

sugar high, with packages and purse making her progress awkward, Cat contemplated the unsolvable equation of what makes a friendship solidify into a bond stronger than family.

Considering this latest puzzle, she began chewing on her lower lip; a habit she employed to help her ruminate on inconsistencies, whether involving people or situations. Caught up in her thinking, she didn't register what had materialized directly in front of her and when she did, still could not believe it. She froze. He stood clearly illuminated by the powerful parking lot lights but she refused to grasp what her sugar-soaked brain communicated. Obviously hallucinating, she stared grappling for an answer. What other explanation could there be? Okay, it could be a costume, some hair dye and weird cat contact lenses—or this could be Candid Camera; she scanned the area for potential tricksters—or it could be…a *pooka*?

Oh, this was too much. A pooka in the form of a cat. That entire drivel about cats being the most intelligent species mixed with the Margaritas and chocolate must have pickled her brain.

Think, think…he was the right size, around six four, the right shape, obviously human but…different. His skin gleamed a deep golden bronze, which beneath the powerful lights looked as smooth and shiny as polished marble. He had cat-like-eyes that settled on her in a very direct feline manner and had yet to blink. Add to that his Sean Connery eyebrows, and it equaled an absolutely, drop-dead gorgeous *cat man*.

So, what should she do? Walk up and say hello? Ignore him? Run like hell and hope that he disappeared when the Margaritas wore off? He stood utterly still and silent and more to the point, he blocked her car as if he had the right. Time to brazen it out; a hallucination couldn't hurt anyone, could it?

She approached slowly and cautiously, blinking rapidly in an effort to clear him from her vision. He exemplified male perfection beyond anything her overly vivid imagination could conjure. She studied him slowly from his head down to his toes, pausing briefly at the bulge between his legs and felt tell tale color flood her cheeks. Boy, what an imagination she had! His hair, mostly sable in color, possessed two defining streaks of gold on either side of his temples; his cat-eyes matched the golden streaks. His muscular shoulders and body looked sleek and hard, exuding a leashed power that should have been intimidating, but instead acted as a lure. He wore fitted black jeans with a short sleeved, V-necked black T-shirt. Moreover, he emanated a hypnotic magnetism that proved impossible to resist.

"Hello," she croaked, then cleared her throat to try again. "My name is Catarina Achilles, are you, uh, real? Silly me, of course you're not real, ha."

She forged on, determined to make an even bigger fool of herself. "Are you lost or possibly an escapee from a costume party?" She inched a little closer and whispered, "Are you an alien cat species worried about your relatives here on Earth and decided to pop in for a little look-see? I promise I'm doing the best I can."

She faltered at his continued silence then put her hands on her hips, frustrated with both herself and him. "Look, I know this is some sort of pooka mirage gone awry, but I'm going to touch you just to make sure, okay? If you have a problem with this and prefer I keep my hands to myself, now would be the time to speak, got it? Or better yet—disappear." She waited for something to happen. A poof of smoke, a waning mirage, did she detect an amused glint in his amber depths?

He'd not moved a hair though she now stood close enough to breathe in his clean musky scent.

His eyes, however, pulsed, vibrantly alive as they speared her very soul...Otherwise, she could have made a good case for an unknown party dropping a statue in the middle of the parking lot, blocking her car. Gingerly, she put out her hand, gently brushing the center of his chest, and then snapped it back as if she'd been burned. He felt every bit as smooth and hard as he looked but warm to her touch—hot, in fact. She had not counted on the heat. Yep, he was real all right, and if she told anyone about this, they would commit her and throw away the key chip. Cat believed that a certain truth surrounded every folklore and legend. She'd spent hours, in fact, researching everything she could get her hands on concerning the subject, but still...could this really be a mythical spirit come to life?

"Why is she not running? She appears nervous, but unafraid. Is she mind-blasted?" Prolinc mindspoke to Zorroc.

"No, she is not crazy; she believes I am her pooka." Zorroc thought back; clearly amused.

"What is a pooka?"

"I knew you never paid sufficient attention to our history studies. It is one of many ancient names for our species before Earthlings could accept the reality of another race not of their planet. They believed us to be mythical creatures, only seen by mind-blasts or addicts. You cannot read this for yourself?" questioned Zorroc. *"She is projecting her thoughts blatantly and loudly."*

"No, I can read nothing. Why is she touching you?"

"She touches me to see if I am solid. She does not believe her eyes."

"You can see me?" he asked, and then mindspoke to Prolinc, *"This will be easier than we anticipated."*

"Duh. Yes, I can see you; we wouldn't be having

this conversation if I couldn't see you. Of course, I've done all of the talking. I thought maybe pookas couldn't speak. Uh, you are a pooka, aren't you?" Cat asked, nervously glancing around for anyone who might be able to confirm her sighting. Twin amber-lit pools drilled into her center. Such beautiful exotic eyes...

"And the others; can you see them, as well?"

"Huh? Others?" Cat took a couple of steps back finally grasping the precariousness of her situation. She swung her head in all directions trying to determine the best route for escape. *A fine time for my flight or fight instinct to kick in.*

"We will take her, prepare to transhift," he telepathed to the others and began to move toward her. She threw her packages at him and turned to run, but got no more than a step before he was upon her. As he jerked her to his chest, Zorroc experienced a disorienting haze of oneness with her. He told himself it was just the effect from transporting together in the same stream, but part of him doubted it. It almost seemed as though his body recognized hers—and then cursed himself for his delusions. *"Bring her bundles, Bandoff; we want no evidence of a forced taking."*

Cat awoke face down in a spacious cabin, lying on a huge soft bed, covered with a thick comforter. All unfamiliar to her. She felt groggy, almost drugged. "Of course," she mumbled, "the Margaritas topped off with enough chocolate to buzz a small hippo." Which failed to explain how she'd gotten here and by the way, where was here? A pooka, she suddenly remembered, a pack of pookas materializing out of nowhere and the pooka she touched grabbing her...but that had to have been a dream. Pookas didn't exist. That must be it, she was still dreaming. She pinched herself. "Ouch!" Would she feel pain in a dream? Sometimes her dreams were so real she actually believed they occurred. At least for a while. Once she'd even asked Dee if a certain something had happened, only to receive a reply in the astonished expression on her friend's face. She sighed and pushed her hair out of her eyes taking note of the tangled auburn mass and crumpled sweater and skirt. "Whew, still dressed anyway, thank the fairies. Well, except for my shoes, eek, and thigh-highs." She rooted around on the bed under the comforter and on top, and came up empty then concentrated on her surroundings looking for a dresser, closet, or bathroom—not necessarily in that order. Her stomach felt queasy and her mouth cotton-coated.

She eased off the high bed and beelined toward a large panel. The room was spacious and immaculate with what looked to be steel walls, until she slid her hand over the surface to discover that they were warm and gave slightly when pressed. Padded walls! Had she landed in a loony bin? Would someone report her location to her aunts? Geez Louise, they'd worry when she didn't come home. Her pulse leapt as she battled the onslaught of heart-wrenching fear. He'd seemed so real. The heat pouring off him. The conversation. She even remembered wondering if she could make him purr.

A built-in desk with a console containing a computer and several rectangular openings took up one side of the room. And something that looked suspiciously like a surveillance cameras occupied opposite corners. Were they monitoring her? She had to use the facilities but whether she'd be emptying her stomach or her bladder first became the question foremost in her mind. She approached the exit and began pushing the buttons on a pad next to it. The lighting blinked to pitch-blackness. "No," she whispered. She imagined herself sucked into an inky black vortex devoid of oxygen, and began to hyperventilate just as a soft glow appeared near the platform bed enabling her to see and press the lights back on. She took a deep, cleansing breath that ended in a sigh. She approached the other panel to the right and it slid open noiselessly. A bathroom with a door that she could lock for privacy, she hoped.

As Cat entered, the lighting came on. The roomy compartment had a clean, woodsy scent. A sunken tub that looked more like a small pool dominated the area, a circular disc on the floor beside it resembled a trap she would not traverse, and two large chair type things rose up from the floor along the back wall. One must surely be the toilet, but which? On examination, one looked like some sort of bidet or foot washer, which made the other the most likely choice of toilet. All this extravagance; had she landed in a loony bin of the stars, possibly mistaken for some famous, crazy country singer?

She leaned over and lost the contents of her stomach.

After taking advantage of the well stocked bathroom, she made her way unsteadily back into the main quarters. Her name reverberated throughout the room drawing a startled yelp and making her veer off toward a clothes alcove with the insane thought of hiding from the voice.

"Apologies, Catarina, it was not my intention to startle you," the all too familiar voice remarked from the speaker on the wall. "My people are on their way, please make easy. You will not be harmed."

Suddenly, more infuriated than frightened, and furious at her own cowardice, she screamed, "Where, the hell am I?"

There was no reply except for the terrifying certainty blasting through her consciousness. It was no dream.

He didn't keep her waiting. There were four of

them. The same pack of pookas she'd glimpsed, briefly, before being nabbed. They appeared exotic in the extreme and no two looked alike. Though tall and muscular, their similarity ended there. One was all black, his skin and hair so dense they absorbed the light. Even his eyes appeared black as they bored into hers. Another had rust colored hair with golden stripes, matching rust skin and vivid green eyes. The third had a brown mane and chocolate skin with golden eyes similar to her cat man and the fourth was solid cream with blue eyes. She peered at them closely, looking for any sign of make-up, contacts or hair dye. There weren't any. They looked real, and though clearly feline, there was no doubt they were also human. She felt sick and disoriented before a bizarre thought struck, making her want to giggle and groan at the same time. It would no doubt be politically incorrect to pet them.

"You will come with us," the rust colored one stated.

She could tell he was used to being obeyed. Feeling distinctly perverse, she decided to toy with them as she had been toyed with. Surprised that her legs supported her, she rose. "Harvey would never order Elwood P. Dowd around; he always asked what Elwood felt like doing and then complied...politely." She waited expectantly.

They looked around the room and at each other like a group of confused Cyborgs. Satisfied to see the universal look of bewilderment staining their faces, Cat relented. "Who are you?" They stilled as one then glanced at one another, clearly not expecting this turn of events. Maybe it was a Rumpulstiltskin thing; she smiled inwardly, beginning to enjoy herself.

The rust-colored one stepped forward, tilted his head, and said, "I am called Prolinc, and I am in charge of security. This is Carpov, our head Med-tech, and these are Sycor and Bandoff, who both report to me."

Okay, Cat repeated to herself; the black one was Carpov, the brown one, Sycor, which left Bandoff, the creamy one.

"I appreciate the introduction, gentlemen, I am Catarina Achilles at your disposal." Silently praying they wouldn't take the comment literally.

"I still believe she is mind-blasted," Prolinc concluded, while propelling her in front of them to take her to the meeting room.

"She is like a crazy little flame. Never have I seen hair with more of a mind of its own. I wonder if it is indicative of its owner," Carpov posed to the group, not really expecting a reply. It was unnecessary to have four males escort her, but Zorroc had insisted. Something about intimidation. She did not look intimidated to Prolinc.

Cat's mind spun as she realized she was on some kind of a vessel; probably a yacht. And what a yacht! The floors, walls and ceiling gleamed with the same look of the silver material that lined her cabin. The passageway, though well lit, had no discernable light source, and no hum of engines sounded in the background. Were they docked? Could she escape? She needed to be aware of exits and get her bearings in order to find her way out to freedom. First however, she needed to gain the sense of direction which, through some cosmic misunderstanding, had been bequeathed to someone else.

The hallways dissected and catacombed; winding, dipping, climbing and shooting up as they entered some sort of an elevator. Could it be a deluxe submarine instead of a yacht? It reminded her of an ant farm—zapping her back to the last conversation she'd had with Angel and Dee about telepathic ants. She felt her control slipping toward hysteria, as if at any moment, her meanderings would get the better of her, and she'd start laughing at nothing, unable to stop. Honestly, who else on the planet could get kidnapped by a tribe of pookas?

They came to a wall that silently opened before them, the message, all too clear. When she stepped over the threshold, her gaze froze; caught by twin amber flames that flashed heatedly, drawing her to him. They belonged to her cat man.

"Where am I?" she demanded breathlessly, refusing to budge.

"You are aboard my ship, the Stellar," he answered softly, unwavering in his scrutiny.

Had she fallen into a sort of altered reality or was he just some rich tycoon with a massive boat and a cat fetish?

She faltered, mesmerized. Some force pushed at her mind to approach him but if she gave into temptation, would she be forever trapped? Everything in her screamed silently in the affirmative. The image of a butterfly cocooned alive in a spider's web, waiting to be devoured, materialized inexorably.

She felt disoriented, dizzy, and overwhelmingly warm. What was that feeling?

Sexual promise rolled off him in heady waves, drenching her senses. Lounging in a massive chair, he dwarfed it. A carafe, cup, and bowl of fruit resided on the table beside him. He sipped languidly on a twin cup held in his long elegantly formed hand. He hadn't taken his hooded gaze from hers for a moment, studying her like his next meal. He looked utterly relaxed, and as lazy as a sated tiger. He also looked positively sinful, good enough to eat and she was suddenly ravenous. In fact, he looked downright hungry, too. It would be the ultimate karmic justice, Cat decided. An alien race of people-eating-cats invading a planet on the brink of harvesting cats for people food. Cat looked closer and thought it might be pleasant to be devoured by this particular predator. She felt close to melt down and consequently confused by her reaction to the big jungle cat. Could she be experiencing passion and physical attraction; the chemically induced reaction to pheromones that Angel and Dee had tried to explain? If so, what they described more resembled a twenty-watt bulb compared to this overpowering current of 2000. Her heart pumped uncontrollably and she feared he could hear it, though she remained across the room.

Zorroc blinked lazily at the heady revelations. Though impolite to read another without invitation or knowledge, this qualified as a special circumstance requiring special measures that overrode edict. Anyway, she belonged to him, and she seemed to sense it, at least on a physical level. It had taken almost an Earth year to free himself of his obligations and make the journey to claim his future mate. Now that the time had arrived, he grew impatient to uncover her varying facets.

"Come to me Catarina, and share some Gattonian spirit; I will not bite you," *yet*, he silently amended. He smiled artlessly. "What is a pooka, I am not familiar with this Earth term, and who are Harvey and Elwood P. Dowd? I fear you have us at a loss," Zorroc added silkily, filling the waiting cup then extending it to her. She slowly made her way to him. Her hand trembling when she took it from him. "I believe you will find the fruit to your liking as well; I had it provided especially for you."

"Thank you, that was very kind," she murmured; her inbred manners kicking in while her mind took a vacation. She sat gingerly and took an experimental sip of the liquid; it tasted sweet and tangy and surprisingly easy on her stomach. Cat squirmed, had he been monitoring her the entire time? How else would he have heard about Elwood

P. Dowd and Harvey? How did one go about explaining them, and in particular—pookas— without divulging her vulnerability? This autocratic, oversized feline would most likely find a way to use it against her. Okay, okay, so she'd secretly longed for her own pooka, a confidante and companion to help her through the unsteady realities of existence. He, however, did not qualify so how could she extricate herself gracefully? What would Angel do in a situation like this? Prevaricate. She took another pull on her drink and tried to look preoccupied by her surroundings.

The large room reminded her of a space-aged boardroom. The ceiling, though high, softly glowed, making the walls and entire room shimmer comfortably. A large oval table that would seat at least twenty dominated; while electronic equipment lining the entire wall behind it blinked and softly hummed. The cozy sitting area they occupied completed the massive space.

"It really is not important. I drew the wrong conclusion, obviously. Who *are* you, if I may ask?" Cat interposed, trying for a combination of guilelessness and curiosity, the later unfeigned.

He smiled knowingly but answered. "I am Zorroc, of the House of Ra, from the Province of Gattonia, on the planet Ganz," he stated. His body held perfectly still as if waiting for her reaction.

"Oh," she barely croaked. Her mind derailed, conjecture-overload seizing her every brain cell. She gulped. She'd always believed in intelligent life on other planets but being faced with the reality seated across a very small table from her, proved daunting to say the least. Quite a mind-set shift from boat to space ship. "So, umm, you are from another planet," she began haltingly, "one that I have never heard of unless we have inadvertently misnamed yours. Where exactly is Ganz?" Surely he lied. God, it had to be a lie...if not...

"I have answered your question, Catarina, and now you will answer mine. About the pooka?" He tilted his head, pinning her to the chair with a glance.

Well, he had answered her question; but what did it mean? For though she had never heard of a planet called Ganz, she knew one thing. It was not on any American Airlines flight schedules.

She took a deep breath. "Pookas are mythological creatures from Celtic folklore that appear only to some people, usually those who have had too much to drink, like me tonight. There was an old movie called Harvey. He was a pooka and Elwood P. Dowd, his companion. I was only kidding around with them and didn't really believe that you were..." The lie caught in her throat. "I apologize for approaching you the way I did." *And touching you,* she silently added, remembering the feel of him. "I have no excuse but I really must be running along. Could someone show me the way?"

He ignored the question and asked one of his own. "Do you want me as your companion, little one?" He gently ran his finger down the side of her throat and the outside of her right breast, causing her nipple to bud tightly.

"No!" Cat yelped, as if she had been prodded. "No," she repeated more gently and quivered. "Of course not. I just, ah, really need to go home now. Ah, I have all the friends I need and, ah, need to be getting back to them."

"No," stated Zorroc softly and then smiled, stretching his legs out in front of him and crossing his ankles.

She blinked, "No?" Just no with no excuse, no reason, no threat, and no justification?

"No," Zorroc confirmed, still studying her carefully, anxious for her next move.

This human held a fascination for him that he could not pinpoint. Maybe it lay in the role she would play. Her mind shared opposing facets of directed and scattered; stubborn intelligence and whimsical fancy. He would enjoy taming her. Her body hummed to him, responding to his touch and he wanted badly to accommodate her. Her heart spoke to him and he knew that if he could win her to his side she would be loyal beyond measure. He and his people could not accomplish their quest unaided, as much as it chaffed him to admit. He would like to avoid a confrontation so soon in their union but how to bring her around? And then he smiled, confident he had a way.

"You see, Catarina, you may not need a friend, but like Harvey, I am in great need of one."

"It was the other way around," Cat corrected.

He read her determination to escape him. And her amusement at his obvious ploy.

"Leave us now," Zorroc commanded the four guards still stationed at the exit.

Prolinc shrugged, murmuring to his team, "What could one small Earth female do anyway?"

Zorroc regarded her in silence; she had read him exactly right. He would be more careful in the future not to underestimate her. The unvarnished truth rankled; he greatly disliked enlisting the help of a female he barely knew but would take to mate. "Our civilization is dying," he finally confessed. "We need women."

Cat snorted, suspecting another ploy. "Mars Needs Women? Excuse me but that has been done before, you realize," recalling the old science fiction classic.

His mood snapped and he shot from his chair; he should not have to beggar himself, especially to an Earth female. His frustration and helplessness at their situation pounded at him and when he

25

answered, he did not recognize his own voice as he towered over her. "We are from Ganz, not Mars! And while you find this amusing, it means the death of our people and civilization. Is this clear to you, or are you too stupid and shallow to understand the obvious?"

Cat closed her eyes, unable to watch the pain and accusation crawling across he features. They beat at her both from within and without; his anguish becoming her own. Could he really be telling the truth and if he was, what could she possibly do to aide him?

"But how could I help?" she found herself asking, looking straight into his tortured, ruthless, feline gaze. "At least, I assume you want my help. Else I wouldn't be here."

Zorroc sighed and ran a hand through his mane. He looked beaten and road-weary as he once again focused on her. "We need help finding willing women. Our two races have mated successfully in the past. Many times throughout the centuries, in fact, so we know this is possible. We are looking for females willing to come with us to our home planet and provide us with offspring."

"What's wrong with your own women, don't you produce them any more?" Cat probed, trying to understand exactly where she fit in. Not liking any of the answers. Lord, if he was asking her for help, he must really be desperate.

Zorroc gazed at her surreptitiously and took a sip from his drink but she knew he was fighting to remain civil. "The women of our world have been infected with...a virus of sorts which makes them infertile." Or worse, his expression implied.

"Well, how are they going to feel about a bunch of alien women invading their territory and procreating with their men?" she asked, trying to hold onto her last remnants of tact. And sanity.

"They know it is necessary," he growled warningly, "there will be no trouble."

"Uh huh." The guy was clueless when it came to the opposite sex. 'Never give in, never surrender', recalling the line from Galaxy Quest—this mission was doomed from the get-go. How could she eject herself out of this Sci-fi soon-to-be-female-fury-detonation?

As she observed his shuttered countenance, she wondered if she *could* help them in some way. She'd always believed that humans create their own limitations through lack of imagination and that all you need is a spot of ingenuity to break free.

An idea worked its way into her already clogged brain. Oh well, no guts, no glory. "I will try to help you. Let me sleep on it tonight and come up with some ideas and we can meet tomorrow morning at my home. When you take me to my car, you can follow me so you'll have the direction. My aunts live with me and I know they'll be very worried now, so..." Maybe things would work out after all.

"No," he refused softly, pinning her with his now familiar implacable stare.

"No?" she repeated, frustrated that he held all the power and could keep her against her will as long as he chose. Even when she'd agreed to help him and lead him to her home. Maybe endangering them. What did she know about him anyway? "Look, I won't say anything to my aunts or anyone else. For one, who would believe me? I don't know if I believe it myself. It's too bazaar; but I do give you my solemn promise to keep your secrets and do all in my power to assist you. But you have to let me go or my aunts could panic and call the police and I don't think you want ques..."

"No," he cut her off more forcefully this time.

"No, just no. Is yes in your vocabulary?" Ignoring his affirmative reply she forged on. "You are no longer in the terrible twos. You can't just say no! You have to follow it with a reason like I don't think that would be a good idea because why ever or it will not be possible this evening because whatever or I am not totally losing my mind!" Her voice escalated to match her mounting panic. Facing him nose to nose, she no doubt resembled a ferocious mouse to his saber-tooth tiger.

"No, I do not think that would be a good idea and it will not be possible, and I am not totally out of my mind yet, but given a few more days with you it may come to pass. Satisfied?" he responded.

"Immensely, so what happens now?"

"You are going to make this difficult."

"I'm going to make it hard as Hell."

"You already have, my cream." He shifted trying to find a more accommodating position for his alter id. "You will stay with me tonight and we will have our meeting tomorrow in the afternoon. You may contact your aunts to let them know you are well, but give no details." He crossed to a video screen and punched in a number. Her number.

She wondered how he knew it but decided it could wait until she spoke with the aunts. The question was, what to tell them. *'Hi Aunt Helen and Aunt Marie, I'll be a little late; I've been kidnapped by a rogue group of alien pookas who slightly resemble cats'*—Hmm; probably too direct.

Marie picked up the phone and Cat flooded with relief at the normal greeting from her quirky aunt.

"I'm running a little late, Aunt M. It's difficult to explain, but I got carried away and lost track of the time. Actually I may just spend the night."

"Since we didn't expect you until now it's no problem, cupcake. Helen and I ate an entire large Pepperoni pizza with extra cheese. I feel like a snake that swallowed a rabbit whole." There was a pause, then Marie asked tentatively. "Is everything all right, dear?"

Cat fought back a sob. "Just fine, M. Love to you and Aunt Helen."

"Goodbye, dear. Give our love to Angel and Dee and we'll look for you tomorrow."

Of course, they'd assume she was with her friends. She usually was. At least she didn't have to lie outright. She was dismal at it. Would that be the last conversation she had with them? Not a comforting thought. Her life had been changed immeasurably with the coming of the aunts. They had swept into her life like two befuddled semi-rumpled fairy godmothers and not only encased Cat in the first secure family situation she'd known but had informally adopted Angel and Dee, as well. They were eccentric to the extreme, yet their optimism was catching, and they filled her world with a cock-eyed sense of wonder. She did not want to lose them. Heck, she did not want them to lose her.

"So, how did you know my number?" she asked as she terminated her call. Zorroc merely smiled as Prolinc appeared at the door and propelled her from the room.

"She is secure?" Zorroc asked when Prolinc returned.

"She is crazy," Prolinc retorted with the hint of a smile. "I believe she thought I would leave her quarters unsecured if I thought her unable to find her way off the ship. She made a point of explaining this on the way back to your cabin. That and inquiring if I had a wife."

The last comment caught Zorroc's attention. "Why would she ask that?" he questioned as he studied the COM in front of him.

"Who can say? I told you she is mind-blasted." His eyes, twinkling with amusement, observed the storm swirling around his friend. He did not have long to wait to catch its direction.

"She is mine, Prolinc, I have plans for her. Is this clear?" he demanded.

"Clear as uncut crystal! What do you intend to do with her now that she is yours. Do you plan on informing her as to her new status?"

"She will know when I am ready," he grumbled, snatching up his Jive and taking a long satisfying drink.

"Now that you have spoken to her, how much do you intend to reveal about our mission. And will she agree to her part? The aunts seem to think she can be trusted to help but only if you are forthcoming about the situation."

"Never be forthcoming with a female, Prolinc, next I will think you mind-blasted. I will tell her only what I have to, in order to ensure her acquiescence."

"You think she will be easily led? She seems quite stubborn in her way, more cat than lamb," Prolinc concluded, then promptly dropped the subject noting Zorroc's deadly expression. One could only press so far with their Leader if he wished to survive with head intact. He turned and left, leaving Zorroc to his own company.

Zorroc stared broodingly at the closed panel. He had received yet another COM from Gattonia on his return to the ship. He must hurry, and he must be successful. Massive changes would occur with the arrival of the Earth females and there was no guarantee they would be unaffected by the virus. He could be responsible for killing many innocent women by bringing them to his home planet; and it was not their fight.

Viral warfare loomed worse, crueler than any weapon to date devised by any world. Zazu, what a mess! There had been talk of testing the Earth females on the way to Ganz, but the risks probably outweighed the benefits. Extensive tests on Earth's air and atmosphere determined that it had been so slowly infused with pollutants; the effect on females, where child bearing and birth defects were concerned, seemed minimal. There was a better than average chance that the virus would have little effect on their immune systems.

The Gattonians had lost ten percent of their own female population, so far, with countless more sterile. The progressive virus attacked the reproductive organs and, in some cases, spread from there. The males had been spared; they had no reproductive organs to engage the virus, no entrance for the organism to take hold. He wondered if the Dargons had intended just that. The Gattonian males watched those die who they had sworn to protect.

Making war on babies and females, it made him sick to his very core. Hell, maybe the males had been infected in their own way, after all; their spirits were being crushed every moment in a slow, painful death of the soul. He had to find a way out of this and destroy the Dargons who had loosed this nightmare on his people.

And what of Catarina? How would the planet affect her bright light; he did not think he could bear to see it dim and extinguish. Mentally, he shook himself. He could not continue along that path. He had a mission, and he would see it through. His people must come first. He'd remain emotionally apart from his impending mate and concentrate on important matters. Not that he did not intend to enjoy her sweet body. *"All right, little Cat, it is time to begin your training. "* He exited and made his way to his living quarters, shedding his morbid thoughts for predatory ones.

Chapter Three

Cat felt rested, calm, warm and protected. She didn't want to open her eyes, didn't want to lose this secure euphoria. What a detailed nightmare! Pookas, cat people from outer space, kidnapping, Mars Needs Women, maybe she did need to lay off the sci-fi and fantasy movies for a while, she giggled at herself and yawned, snuggling closer to the heat. She had an arm and leg draped across the firm body pillow bringing her up prone against the impossibly hard...and...breathing... She eased open her eyes to find a pair of golden cat-eyes studying her curiously. *His eyes!*

"*Aiaay!*" she screamed, bounding off the bed with the dexterity of an Olympic gymnast.

"Eek!" Noticing her lack of clothing.

Zorroc winced and then yawned, Zazu, the female had lungs. She was quick; too. Had she never woken up on a male's mat, as his aunts had intimated? The panel of his quarters opened and three guards charged in, weapons drawn and pointed at Cat.

Cat screamed again, diving back onto the mat, and under the covers, clinging to Zorroc.

"She is quick," Prolinc commented, "and loud." And perfectly formed he noted, drawing a growl from Zorroc.

Prolinc smirked. "My apologies, Leader, they have not yet learned of your affect on the gentler species. I will leave you to your privacy." He turned, moving stealthily through the exit, the panel sliding shut behind him.

Cat groaned in mortification, slowly peeling herself off him. "Where're my, uh, clothes?" In commandeering the comforter to cover everything below her chin, she had exposed Zorroc to below his navel. He smiled. She gulped. They had slept together naked.

Striving mightily for a level of sophistication she didn't possess, she remained facing him rather than cowering back under the covers. Doing so brought her eye level with his chest. He was smoothly chiseled with powerful muscles and...no body hair. Carefully avoiding his nether regions, her gaze skimmed his torso, arms, and face; equal parts perplexed and intrigued. She longed to touch him and feel his marble-satin skin beneath her hands.

"Many humans lack an over abundance of hair on certain areas of their bodies, your American Indian a good example of such. We are not so different," he pointed out softly, taking her hand and running it slowly over his chest and abdomen then groaning his appreciation.

Giving her access to his sculpted perfection, she wondered how deep a shade of red her face had become; judging by the heat it radiated, she'd bet it exceeded beacon proportion.

"What are you doing in my room?" she squeaked.

He smiled intimately. "These are my quarters, I live here."

"Then what am I doing here?"

"You live here too," he replied logically.

She blinked, licked her lips, and ventured forth like she hadn't fallen down some alien rabbit hole. "Zorroc," she began carefully, "we have known each other for less than twenty-four hours. I have family, friends, and a career, which I will not forfeit to leave with you. You don't know me and I don't know you, add to that our differing cultures, not to mention diverse planets and well...we're different. We're too far apart to successfully build a life together and too dissimilar for any kind of a relationship besides friendship. I appreciate your problem and sympathize, and will help you in any way I can, but you must realize that my life is on Earth. Surely you can't expect more from me than that."

"And you must realize, my little Cat," he returned with equal gentleness, brushing a wisp of hair from her cheek and then slowly rolling until he had her body trapped beneath his, "that your body reaches for and clings to mine in the night. Your eyes follow me whenever I am in seeing distance, and your mind is consumed by thoughts of me and what it will be like to be touched by me, as a male touches a female. All of you are mine for the taking.

"You will help me do what needs to be done for the good of my people and all else I require."

"That is utter nonsense!" Was she that transparent? OK, she did find him mesmerizing; who wouldn't? But he merely aroused her curiosity. No—not aroused, there would be no arousing going on. He merely peaked her curiosity in a cultural sort of way. Kind of like hands across the water but without the hands. Well, obviously with the hands because his hands and body were playing havoc with her libido at the moment. Whew. "I am an American and proud to be one. I have no intention of flying off to another planet for a visit and you can't keep me prisoner if I am to help you recruit women. I have an idea, but it will take planning and my freedom," she countered, pleased her voice actually worked.

"We will discuss your ideas at a meeting scheduled for later this afternoon, but now it is time to begin your lessons." He moved to cover her mouth with his.

Lessons? Echoed her last coherent thought as he began to tutor her in the finer points of intimate explorations.

****

Zorroc still could not read her. They were on their way to the meeting to discuss how to secure women for Gattonia, but Zorroc's mind focused solely on Catarina. Her mind suffused a murky sea of confusion. Desire battled with shame; confusion with determination; trepidation with temptation. He had quite short-circuited his little Cat. Unacquainted with desire and sensual pleasure, inherent to all Gattonians, she defined innocence, infinitely more naïve and unaware than Zorroc realized. He blamed himself for his own naiveté where she was concerned. Determined to make her acknowledge his physical claim on her, he completely discounted her inner welfare. He could barely accept what his mind transmitted with persistence and certainty. She was a virgin. Unable to stand her inner turmoil a moment longer, he pulled her into the first chamber they came to and secured the panel. Cat looked around, confused, but before she could pose a question, Zorroc leaned on the table and pulled her between his legs, enveloping her in his warmth and his scent. Cat stiffened, unaccustomed to the physical contact, but soon relaxed, letting his heat seep into her and finally turned her face into his chest putting her arms around his waist. She sighed.

He had unwrapped her the night before and been awestruck by her perfection. Her almond eyes, already bewitching with their combination of siren promise and childlike innocence, left him unprepared for her body...she was a miniature goddess. His very own fairy sprite.

"Everything will be fine, my own, you have my vow on it," Zorroc whispered, gently stroking her lower back, neck and gently smoothed her rebellious locks. As benign as he intended his ministrations, she began the journey toward sensual overload, yet again. She will be fire in my bed, he perceived with a satisfied feline smirk; she will incinerate us both.

"We should go; we will be late for our meeting," she mumbled into his now pebble hard nipple.

"They will not proceed without us," he defended, pleased he could read her once again.

As he stepped forward to release the panel, he snagged Cat's waist, not wanting to relinquish his connection with her for even a moment.

"Good afternoon gentlemen." Cat slid onto the soft bench like seat Zorroc indicated. He crowded in beside her, leaving her surrounded but untouched, with their thighs connected only by body heat and his arm draped on the bench back behind her. She'd rehearsed her presentation countless times that day in between bouts of sensory overload brought on by recollections of her first lesson. Now, if she could just get her mind focused on the meeting and off the feel and taste of him, she might actually make sense; he moved slightly closer. Focus! Think of something else!

She observed the Gattonians present and identified them as the same four who'd escorted her the day before. She reviewed her strategy one last time. Employ a business-like attitude, take charge, show that she won't be intimidated or controlled but will remain sensitive to their problems and ready with solutions. She'll be charming and endearing, someone they can trust, she'll take a deep calming breath... Bad mistake that last bit of advice, her senses filled with his scent. She groaned inwardly. "I work in public relations and sales for a company called Gemstone Media Solutions; we book motivational and metaphysical conventions. In one week we'll be sponsoring a Science Fiction Convention that will run through the weekend and are expecting over fifteen hundred attendees. Many will be in costume and all will be particularly interested in extraterrestrials.

"I can book two of you as speakers on the possibility of life on other planets or some such and your appearance, even as you are, won't draw the attention of any wannabe E. T. Exterminators. You haven't by chance seen Galaxy Quest, have you?" At their stunned silence and universal blank looks, Cat concluded they had not. "Well uh, the point is you'll fit right in. You can have the rest of your people circulate and pinpoint those you think would consider being mail-order brides for another planet and enlist eligible women from there. Mail-order brides are a time-honored tradition on my planet. Well, not off-world mail-order brides that I know of, but the old west was a big believer in them. So, what do you think?" No one moved. She had obviously rendered them speechless with her creative approach and innovative solution; all except for Zorroc who'd had some kind of coughing fit and dashed from the room.

Prolinc, though the first to recover, looked like a bug under a light. Definitely the right approach, Cat confirmed.

"What kind of presentation would be required?" Prolinc choked out.

"Well, you are the head of security; why not talk about how to thwart bad guys in the future? Maybe discuss where weapons research is headed and how it will protect and defend us good guys."

"An excellent suggestion, Catarina," Zorroc affirmed behind her. He'd returned, she sighed thankfully; the room lacked warmth without his presence beside her. Where had that thought sprung from? He probably just represented the most familiar figure in her current altered reality.

"I believe Cat has come up with a workable plan, quite ingenious, Catarina," he complimented in a purr. "You can speak on futuristic weaponry, Prolinc, and you, Carpov, will speak on future advances in medicine, hypothetically, of course. Maybe you will catch the eye of an Earth female of your own," he commented merrily, "who would like to be your mail-order bride."

Prolinc and Carpov looked sucker-punched while Sycor and Bandoff began to cough.

****

"You must let me go," Cat persisted. "If I don't show up there will be questions asked and plans jeopardized—mainly yours. The future of your people could be contingent on my showing up for work and setting everything into motion."

They had been arguing since arriving back to his quarters an hour before. He did not want to let her out of his sight and though she could not escape him, he did not want their connection weakened by the familiarity of her former life. Something might happen to her without him there to protect her. Completely trusting and guileless, she represented an irresistible target for any desperate, unscrupulous male, like himself. Not that she lacked intelligence; she had a quick wit and flexible mind with an imagination to match. The plan she had come up with to locate women was brilliant in its simplicity. Clearly, though, the sprite needed a keeper, and he disliked his orders being questioned. "I will think on what you have said and come to a decision within your Earth hour."

Cat sat on the bed which she had been informed was called a platmat and tried to evaluate her emotions. It wasn't easy. She obviously had never been truly kissed before. His had zapped her to life in a most dramatic demonstration of possession and control, making everything previously familiar suddenly disorienting and strange. And all from one touch of his lips on hers. A touch that possessed and bombarded her with conflicting inner missiles of passion, fear, desire, logic, love, wariness, need and most of all confusion. She needed some space, some time alone to recover her equilibrium, some time away from him to get her crazy infatuation under control.

What did she find so alluring anyway? Sure, okay he was beautiful, sexy, had a voice like hot chocolate syrup and a lazy predatory heat that poured off him in rivulets, only to settle unerringly in her lower belly. Gentle, when he wasn't demanding obedience, and sometimes even when he was; smart, yet attuned to what she had to say. Other than that, he was nothing special except for the fact that he slightly resembled a cat...

She was doomed.

Even cultural differences aside they would never be on an equal plane. Comfortable with his sexuality, she defined the princess of prudes. Big, brawny, and beautiful, she exemplified scrawny and average. It would never work. Why would he stay with her? Certainly not because of her overpowering allure, didn't the man have eyes? Men did not notice her with Dee and Angel around. That was the problem with having drop-dead gorgeous friends; men's eyes popped out at the sight of them at which point a general stampede ensued. Sometimes it was all she could do to duck out of the way before being trampled. It probably accounted for the reason she was so quick on her feet. Whoever said life was fair? Her panel slid open. Sycor and Bandoff had arrived to escort her to Earth.

They went to a chamber that looked a lot like a Star Trek transporter. They would not allow her to go unescorted, and waited until Zorroc showed up who insisted on holding her throughout transhift. "I can do this by myself, you know," she insisted, "it hardly requires a sense of direction."

"No," he taunted, just before she lost consciousness.

Cat awoke in her own bed to the sound of her Aunt Helen opening the blinds then deftly explaining, "I called Gemstone yesterday and told them you were feeling a little under the weather but would arrive as chipper as usual for the Tarot Assembly Conference today. Breakfast will be ready when you are, sweetheart, but I think it would be wise to start moving." Cat gazed at her aunt and then around her room; neither had changed. No way could the last twenty-four hours plus have been a dream...or nightmare, she conceded. "Aunt Helen, where have I been for the past twenty-four hours?"

'It must have been a very good party, indeed, or I'm sure you would remember. You were with Dee and Angel, I assume, and got in some time late last night, else why would you be here?" she responded logically while glancing at her niece a little awkwardly.

She was hiding something. Cat knew it. "So, you didn't see me arrive."

"No dear, we didn't wait up for you."

She wouldn't meet her eyes this time. Well, that mystery would have to wait; she had a conference to put on. As she jumped out of bed and headed for the shower, she wondered how her aunt had known to call her in sick the day before.

"I have never seen so many weirdoes gathered together in one place. The freak police are probably going to invade and cart us off mistaking us for one of 'em." Angel nodded toward a couple of particularly colorful tarot queens of a "certain age". The gathering flaunted the most colorful array of fruitcakes, genuine talents, and costume aficionados that Angel had observed in some time and she could tell that Dee shared similar thoughts.

"I doubt it, we stick out like two black and white characters in a color movie, do you think these fortune-tellers will recognize us for the frauds we are and attack us with Technicolor," Dee asked.

"Don't worry, I'll protect you," Angel returned comically in a rare role reversal soliloquy. Dee lived and breathed self-defense and protection, to the point of forcing martial arts lessons on both her friends until they could beat Jean-Claude if they had to. She made them train with weapons, as well. The three were formidable.

"I never pegged you as a comedian, Angel, have you spotted Cat yet?"

"Behind you." Cat surprised both of them. "I don't have time to talk, meet me at Grumpy's in an hour. This is serious. No is not an option," she reiterated and disappeared.

Sitting at Grumpy's, Cat had no idea how much, or even what, to tell her friends and, furthermore, didn't know when her cat man would come to reclaim her. A surprised Todd swiftly concocted a frozen Margarita as he greeted her. He made it a double, surmising correctly that she needed it. He engineered two more when the remaining threesome entered.

"Don't say a word, just let me talk." She scanned the room, as if looking for someone she wasn't sure she wanted to see. "Thursday evening on my way to the car, I met this cat person I mistook for a pooka. He was beautiful and blocking my car, and well, he kidnapped me. As it turns out, he wasn't a pooka at all, but a Gattonian from a planet called Ganz, outside our solar system, somewhere, and they asked for my help in finding women to return with them to their planet to make babies. Their women are sterile because of some sort of virus." She scanned the room again. "Anyway, we're going to use the Sci-fi Convention as our hunting ground for prospects, so I don't think it would be wise for you guys to be in the vicinity...just in case. I plan to slip away during the function. Got all that?"

Even knowing her for over eighteen years, Dee struggled to grasp what her friend relayed. Angel recovered first. Cat had a disorienting effect on people, at times, and dull moments proved amply rare. "Slow down and make sense," Angel directed, looking around for some kind of boogey man to appear. "I know we've watched Harvey at least two dozen times, but surely you know there are no such things as pookas."

"Well, I know that *now* but tell the truth; which makes more sense: Pookas in the form of cats or cat people from outer space? I mean, if you saw a cat guy, what would you conclude? He's standing there in front of you, a foot from your rear bumper and doing an outstanding impression of an inert object, you go up and touch him...to verify he's real, of course, then you look around for Candid Camera and well, what would you think?"

Over the years, Catarina had rendered them speechless with maddening consistency; now provided no exception.

Dee took a turn. "Are you sure that's who they are; what proof do you have?"

"Uh, gee Dee, they take me to their space ship via beam-me-up-Scotty technology, then tell me about their problem and ask for my help. I've counted at least twenty-five of them, I just don't see how much clearer it could get," Cat burst out, unable to contain her agitation.

Dee and Angel looked at each other then back at Cat. As impossible as it seemed, it had to be the truth. They'd known each other too long and been through too much not to trust each other implicitly. Dee shook her head to clear it before stating, "You can't go alone, that is out. We stick together and for God's sake, *do not* agree to go with them. I know you, if you agree you'll follow through. They haven't asked, have they," Dee demanded.

"Uh, it's been mentioned but I don't think it'll come to that." She fidgeted slightly. "I mean I can't see them actually forcing someone against their will. Besides, when they see the other women they have to choose from, I'm sure he'll forget all about me."

"Who is he and what's wrong with the way you look?" Angel asked.

"Uh, he's nobody important."

Dee snorted. "Look, sweetie, there's nothing wrong with you," Dee insisted. "Except your trusting nature and overactive imagination. Anyway, we'd better put our heads together and come up with a plan before we're interrupted. Later we'll discuss this sudden inferiority complex you developed overnight."

"What do you read from her, is she committed to the path you have set for her?" asked Prolinc, reaching for another double taco with extra cheese, sour cream, hot salsa and jalapeños. "If they talk much longer, we will need another platter of tacos." The unusual food proved better than catnip to the Gattonians. Zorroc along with Prolinc, Sycor and Carpov lounged companionably at the mall taco stand across from Grumpy's, garbed in appropriate Earth attire and sunglasses—and inhaling, none too fastidiously, platter after platter of extra large tacos.

Zorroc shrugged, not willing to discuss Cat's failure to comply with his wishes. "She will co-operate, but she does not plan to make the voyage with us. Her friends intend to help her avoid us when departure approaches. Dee is doubtful we intend to recruit the females, she believes we may just take them."

"Not so mind-blasted as your mate...what is their plan?" Carpov asked, reaching for his sixth helping.

"They intend to walk away," he responded dryly. "Just disappear in the midst of hundreds of humans.

They believe they all look alike to us. They will travel to Angel's cottage, or actually her mother's cottage, that she never inhabits. They believe, in that way, to avoid discovery. I see no reason to disillusion them until departure time. Everything is well in place. We are ready. And now if you will excuse me, I will go retrieve my mate." Sycor and Prolinc looked crestfallen at the empty plate in front of them before exuding a last belch and requesting the check.

He showed himself to all three; they had bought into his existence, after all, why not confirm it. "These are your friends are they not, my Cat," Zorroc suggested most charmingly. "I am Zorroc, Cat's future mate, she has spoken of you."

"I have not!" she sputtered, jumping up to face him.

"Did he say 'mate'?" Angel whispered to Dee.

"No?" Zorroc replied with a lethal gleam in his eyes. "Then maybe I read your mind," he challenged, facing her down. She had pushed him too far. *We will take all three, Prolinc, transhift,*" Zorroc messaged, and they vanished.

Cat awoke in their quarters lying beside Zorroc, who was settled on his side with a hand resting possessively on her stomach. She studied him for a minute wondering what would happen next. "Did you take Dee and Angel too?" she asked tentatively, wondering at his remoteness. His eyes appeared shuttered and an eerie stillness surrounded him.

"Yes," he replied simply, and continued to observe her.

The one time she would have preferred hearing a "no". She blinked and licked her lips. His eyes focused on her mouth and followed the movement of her tongue. The blame for the entire situation lay directly with her; she should have never spoken with her friends, never gotten them involved. Now she had to extricate them somehow, although at present she hadn't a clue as to how to go about it. She wondered where they'd been taken. Had they been separated or allowed to remain together, were they scared or even worse—had they tried to employ self-defense tactics after their disorienting experience? Would the Gattonians hurt them? She'd only known them for a couple of days and had no way of knowing what they might be capable of, if provoked. Would she see her friends again? "You don't intend to keep them here, do you?" she croaked softly, fighting back a sob.

"That will depend solely on you, for the present."

She began to unravel. Her cat man had disappeared and been replaced by a stranger with all the warmth of a frigid mannequin. Even when she'd first seen him in the parking lot he'd been approachable, touchable and solicitous toward her and had made her feel linked to him in a way that no one had before. Polar opposites from this current remote-controlled Prolinc clone. He had effectively locked himself away from her and his abandonment left her feeling lost and exposed. Deserted. Again. How could she explain and make things right? He'd obviously overheard the conversation at Grumpy's. How had things snowballed so quickly into this avalanche of longing? What spell had he cast that suddenly made her loath a life without him? She shivered; no doubt because of all that snow. His gaze grew warm and softened, almost as if he had read her thoughts and took pity on her. Her eyes filled with tears and her floodgates burst. He eased onto his back, placing her on top of him as his hands moved up and down her body in a slow hypnotic rhythm. He began to whisper into her hair that all would be well, to trust him to take care of everything. Slowly, she regained control of her emotions and relaxed.

His Catarina had had a rough few days, he mused with a slight smile. He must not forget all that had been thrust on her in such a short time. He would need to make allowances for her occasional rebellious spurts. She had panicked at his withdrawal. He found that decidedly promising. He would use her insecurities and need for affection to bind her to him, and control her through sexual play. Finally, he would break her gently but thoroughly to his will.

Satisfied he had the situation well in hand he began to issue his encompassing ultimatums.

Chapter Four

"Your friends will be released after I have some
assurances from you. I want your word you will come
with me to Ganz and no longer plot against me." And
then, lowering his voice to a honey seductive whisper
added, "You will admit to me, sweet one, that you
are mine and will remain mine."

He'd returned to the overbearing male now
familiar to her; she squirmed, cornered. Out of the
frying pan and into the inferno. Now what? Silently
she reviewed her options; lie and run if necessary to
her sanity; go quietly, relax and enjoy the sex
education classes; or go kicking and screaming all
the way. She wondered if she could get him to
compromise on some of the finer points of his wishes
but one look told her he expected that tact. The
birdcage had been sealed, barricaded, and the key
chip incinerated. Yep, she'd been plucked, cooked
and readied for feasting; and he looked as though
he'd devoured a flock of canaries with a chaser of
cream. She hoped he had indigestion for a month
and lowered her lashes, pleased with the image.
When she shot him a sideways glance, he looked a
little less satisfied. Fine, let him wonder what went
on in her active little imagination.

His Cat had a mean streak; he blinked,
surprised to discover the thought did not displease
him. A little spunk he deemed accountably desirable.
After all, he wanted to tame her, not curb her
natural exuberance. He smiled ruefully, hoping her
spunk did not surface to bite him in the ass.

"Okay."

Immersed in his thoughts, it took a moment to register her answer. Then he experienced such an uncharacteristic surge of satisfaction and relief, it rendered him temporarily speechless. He shook his head to clear it. "Okay what, Catarina, be specific, I want to be sure of what you are agreeing to," he grated softly, wanting to hear the words.

Somehow, she had just known he wouldn't accept victory gracefully and drop the subject. Oh, no, he wanted her to grovel and reveal every vulnerable bone in her body. It already hurt. She decided to stall. Maybe she could get him to emit a bead of sweat to signify the teensiest bit of insecurity before her final defeat. Why did he have to lord over everything and everyone, and why did he have to win all the time, didn't he know it was impolite? "What do you want from me, Zorroc, my blood, my body, my soul? I said okay, you get your way," *again*; she silently amended. "I'll go with you, just let my friends go." Angel and Dee would kill her.

"Sorry, not good enough, Cat. Continue." Obviously relishing his latest win.

She groaned, here it came. "I will accompany you willingly; you don't need to be concerned that I'll try to avoid you. If you want me, Zorroc, then I am yours," she ended on a subdued note, and then ruined the effect by snapping, "Satisfied?"

"Immensely," he confirmed. Cat rolled her eyes. He gave her an electric smile that lit her insides and charged the air around them. Small consolation, but she guessed it might be worth it. She discovered she enjoyed making him smile. His eyes took on a predatory gleam that threatened to ensnare her. She bolted off the mat, trying for a clean getaway. She had two friends to save. She paused at the foot of the mat to straighten her new one-piece suit-dress, purchased for the Tarot assembly. The emerald green shade exactly matched her eyes, and it hugged her small frame to perfection. It revealed a slight amount of cleavage while showing a lot of leg; emerald spiked heels completed the ensemble. Cat looked up after smoothing down her suit and could tell she was on the menu.

Zorroc decided the time had arrived for her next lesson.

"Uh, Zorroc?"

"*Shh*, everything is how it should be, we will begin slowly," he slurred softly as if too transfixed to annunciate properly.

He put his fingers through her hair and tilted her head to a more accessible angle. She swayed toward him, mesmerized by his husky voice and the determined glint shining through his slumberous eyes. Her women's liquid seeped languidly, dampening her panties. She colored slightly. Zorroc gave her a half smile like he understood, then took, and took her mouth. Invading her moist cavity his tongue began a dominant rhythm in tandem with the rocking of his hips against her stomach. His hands first caressed her fragile ribcage, thumbs barely grazing her breasts then moved down to cup her buttocks still grinding into her. Her legs gave way. Cat, beyond stunned, felt as if she rode atop a huge tiger, striving for purchase. She began panting heavily, but so did Zorroc. Keeping one hand under her rear, he let the other roam to sweep her waist, firmly cup her breast, then pinch, and squeeze her nipple. She reached overload and collapsed. She would have landed in a heap at her cat man's feet if he had not caught her at the last moment, swept her up into his arms, and gently laid her on the platmat. After a moment or two, she eased her eyes open and looked dazedly at him. "I don't understand, Dee and Angel never said anything about swooning while in the process of a kiss. Does it happen often?"

She had short-circuited again, and Zorroc found

himself unaccountably pleased that he could affect her so. How could he explain desire and chemistry to her, but even more perplexing, how did he explain it to himself? He had lost control. It had not happened before and with his vast years of sexual expertise, would not have believed he could become so aroused; let alone, by a female virgin who barely knew how to kiss. Waiting silently for his answer, she looked uncertain and vulnerable. He needed to reassure them both.

He shrugged nonchalantly and tilted his head in his usual manner. "It happens sometimes when chemistry between two people is...strong, as it is with us, sweet one. It is just further proof that you belong to me. It will go very well between us when I put myself inside you and make you mine," he finished matter-of-factly.

"Can we send Dee and Angel home now, I can be ready in just a few minutes, no time at all really." Escaping toward the bathroom.

He started and she realized that she'd caught him completely off guard by her verbal change of direction. She surprised other people all the time, why was it not the same with him? Rarely did he stare in that particularly confused manner. One more puzzle, she sighed, and concentrated on her rumpled appearance. Her eyes were dilated, her lips, red and slightly swollen and her hair looked like it barely survived a close encounter with a wind tunnel. Her cheeks flushed a rosy pink. Everyone would take one look and know what she and her cat man had been up. What a plain Jane to his Adonis, she thought with a sigh. Exiting the bathroom, she noticed Zorroc regarding her carefully as if she'd become a complicated matrix he couldn't fathom. Could it be he wasn't as confident as he pretended? Suddenly she felt better. Smiling brightly, she grabbed his arm; propelled him toward the panel and proceeded to babble all the way to the transhift pad.

Angel and Dee had obviously arrived well before they had because while Angel stared fixedly at Carpov, locked in suspended animation, Dee was advancing on Prolinc, screeching like a banshee. "How dare you malign me you over-grown, over-bearing, over-egoed, autocratic, furry fathead." Accompanying each adjective with a firm poke of her finger to his chest. Prolinc stood frozen in statue mode with no expression at all showing on his chiseled features.

Time to act. "Well, hi everyone, I see we're all getting to know one another. Communicating with new friends is always so invigorating, don't you agree, Angel? And being polite and respectful are important, as well, when you are a guest in someone else's space ship and about to be transported home, isn't that right Dee," she annunciated loudly toward her friend. Dee blinked twice then looked down at her finger, still planted solidly in Prolinc's chest, and paled. She slowly raised her head to look into his eyes and gingerly lowered her hand, never breaking eye contact.

What did she think he was going to do, bite her? Hiss at her? Cat glanced at Zorroc to see what he made of the situation and found him block still, as well. Could it be a common Gattonian trait, this popsicle impersonation? She couldn't figure out if the point involved calming their prey into complacency by not making any sudden moves or a fear that they'd explode into action if they moved one tiny muscle. Then she peered into Zorroc's eyes to discover that it was taking all his considerable control to keep from laughing. Dee stepped back carefully, and asked if everyone was ready to leave, still not taking her gaze from Prolinc's.

"Well, I'm ready, that's for sure." Cat replied,

ready to get her friends to safety. Zorroc fastened his eyes on her and she recognized his intentions before he opened his mouth. When he did, she cut him off exclaiming, "Oh, look at the time, I can't come with you guys, after all, Zorroc and I have a hot date this evening, don't we, sweetums." She beamed in a fake manner managing to both hug and push her friends toward the trans-pad.

"We will accompany you down." Prolinc told them; the first words out of his mouth since Cat arrived five minutes before. She waved as Angel in Carpov's arms and a subdued Dee in Prolinc's, disappeared.

"I've known that woman for more than eighteen years and I have never seen her lose control in such a personal, in your face manner. I wonder what he did to her." She tilted her head up and looked quizzically at Zorroc.

"Prolinc can be overbearing from time to time," Zorroc admitted, eyes dancing. "Over bearing, furry fathead," he quoted, "I thought he would split in two. None of our people would address him so; he is much feared and respected. I have not witnessed anything so amusing in a great while." He began to chuckle. "And I have rarely seen him at such a loss, I think Earth females will be very good for Prolinc, you can be very entertaining creatures. Now come, little Cat, I must feed you. When I touched you this afternoon, I noticed you need more weight. You have not been caring for yourself as you should." Cat groaned; talk about overbearing, furry, fathead.

****

The week passed quickly for Cat. She transported down to her job in the mornings to make final arrangements for the Sci-fi Convention then spent a few hours at Habi-Cat doing paperwork and playing with her charges. After that she visited her aunts and scooped up more clothes, then met Zorroc.

The aunts concerned her. They'd always been somewhat on the nosy side, interested in her movements and lack of love life. Now she spent each night away from home, clothes for the next day in hand, never returning them, and what was their reaction? Not a peep, not a squeak, not a question. They babbled on just like normal, glad to see her when she came home, and waved goodbye merrily when she left. Maybe her alien friends had some sort of mind-muddle capability; maybe her aunts didn't even realize she wasn't there at night. If Zorroc had done something further to confuse their already less than crisp minds she'd...she'd...well she'd think of something.

She'd specify her family and friends off limits to the Gattonians or all agreements were off. Thinking of agreements made her think of the nights. She sighed. He held her each night, wrapping her in a cocoon of languid sensuality that stayed with her through the day. He touched her everywhere, controlling her every response, playing her and making her aware of her body, and then drifting off to sleep leaving her restless and unfulfilled. She happened to know lovemaking entailed more than that. This was the twenty-first century and Angel had done a graphic job of explaining things to her. So, why did he stop? Had he changed his mind about her now that she was no longer a challenge? Maybe, she'd become no more than a toy, and like all cats, they played hard, devoting all their attention to it, then walked away, bored, knowing it would be there when they decided to play again. How could he extricate himself from a situation that he, himself, had instigated? Zorroc probably feared she'd make a scene and cry all over his uniform again. Men hated it when women cried. Maybe that's what changed his mind after he'd had a chance to think about it. She exhaled a frustrated breath; when it came to the man woman thing, hopeless didn't even begin to cover her ineptitude. Well, she'd see Angel and Dee at Grumpy's the following evening; maybe they could shed some light on the incomprehensible male psyche.

She was mind-blasting him, he snarled verbally, leaning against a wall a half a block away, waiting for her to notice him. Who could follow her female logic? He knew she had some, he could read it at times, but then her reasoning would take a hard right and lose reality faster than a rodent fleeing a tornika, leaving in its wake the most convoluted scatterbrained muddle he never wanted to mind read. He had discovered she had never been held or touched, even as a child. What could her parents, Rowan and Nancia, have been thinking to leave their child abandoned and needy; every animal needed nurturing, no matter the species. When he saw them next, they would not be at all pleased to see him.

She obviously had misunderstood his motives for not yet taking her. She needed to learn that to fully appreciate lovemaking she had to be more attuned to her body, and attuned to his as well. Lovemaking required two equal partners, each responsible for the other's pleasure. He could not have her swooning whenever she approached climax; she would never experience the best part. He had taught her how to be touched; tonight he would show her how to touch him. He had exhausted his self control almost beyond endurance in the last few days, and it would only become worse from here on out. He grunted; she did not even appreciate his sacrifice. Someday he would torture her beyond endurance and then she would understand and be grateful for his selflessness. Imagining how he would accomplish this made his already too tight jeans even tighter. He groaned again and went to claim his disordered little flame.

Zorroc looked very uncomfortable as he gingerly moved toward her. He'd been injured, she realized, rushing up to support him. "What's happened, where are you hurt, where is a good bodyguard when you need one? Don't worry, I can protect you, I'm very handy at martial arts." Cat whipped her head around in all directions looking for danger or assistance. She would be prepared for both.

"It is nothing, sweet one, but let us go quickly, I must shed these Earth torture vessels," he extruded through clenched teeth. "*We are prepared, Prolinc, transhift quickly.*" A soft chuckle sounded in his head.

She awoke on their platmat feeling rested and relaxed but noting Zorroc's absence like a tangible thing. She now sensed whenever he was near, though she didn't know exactly when it had started. She supposed their lessons had sensitized her to his presence, somehow. Then she recalled with a heart-thud, he'd been hurt earlier that evening, where would he be? The Med-center, she decided, as she shot off the mat, bee-lined to the clothes cove, rushed to the bathroom to freshen up, and then barreled toward the exit panel.

"What is she doing?" Prolinc asked, as they lounged in the COM room watching in fascination as Cat bounded off the platmat and started charging around the room bouncing off surfaces as fast as any pinball. The two had been conferring on the days ahead after Zorroc had placed Cat on their mat following transhift.

"I cannot tell," Zorroc replied lazily, "she has short-circuited again; I cannot read her when that happens."

"Does she always dart around so quickly, how do you keep her still long enough to have her?"

"Let me out of here this instant!" the COM

shrieked, startling both males from their seats. "I still say she is mind-blasted, we had better let her out before she hurts herself," Prolinc muttered as he opened her panel.

"I will retrieve her," Zorroc announced unnecessarily, already moving down the hall. She collided with him almost immediately and started spouting a barrage of unintelligible sounds at the sight of him, burrowing into him and hugging him so tight it felt like she was trying to crawl inside him. He figured out why in the next instant. Since he could not mind-read her, he had to rely on her garbled cacophony. Ah, he had it; she woke up worried about him, she thought he had been injured and panicked when she found him missing. He decided he liked this side of his little pinball and began crooning that he had not been hurt; his pants had merely become snug; she had misunderstood. He lifted her and carried her back to their quarters, looking forward to what was to come; he just hoped his rod did not get so hard it snapped off.

She still felt disembodied and disoriented when she arrived at Grumpy's the usual time. Her lesson with Zorroc the night before had aligned things into much better perspective and she could barely wait for the next one. She glanced up and saw Dee and Angel, both early, with drinks in hand, staring at her with undisguised concern. What now? Time to crash back to reality, but it had been heaven while it lasted. "This is unprecedented, ladies, what gives..." Her voice trailed off, as she got closer. Something dreadful had occurred, had she just stumbled onto her own demise?

Angel addressed the bartender. "A round of doubles Todd, but bring them to the corner table over there," motioning to a table in the back, "we need privacy. Move." This last directed at Cat.

"We have several issues to discuss so let's get to it," Dee began. "Why you?" Two pair of eyes pinned her with grim purpose.

Cat looked back, puzzled, who had kidnapped her best friends and replaced them with the interrogation team from The Matrix, and what were they talking about? Cat glanced around uneasily.

"Why you?" Dee repeated. "Out of all the people on this vast planet, why choose you? We love you and think you're special, but what do the Gattonians want with you?" she probed taking a large pull of her Margarita.

Suddenly, Cat felt sick to her stomach; they had an undeniable point. Why hadn't she been asking herself that same question? She'd already had numerous talks with herself wondering at Zorroc's interest. Why hadn't she taken it one step further and questioned the Gattonian motive, as well; sucker punched, by her naiveté and lack of awareness. What an unqualified twit. Angel and Dee looked at her with love-laced pity and a pinch of wariness but those wouldn't help her now. "Okay, I'll bite, why me?" *she returned and waited.*

"Let's logic it out, but before we can do that we need more information; explain the circumstances precipitating your initial contact with Zorroc, " Angel proposed coolly perusing the area for stray cat men.

Cat thought back and tried to organize her thoughts, not an easy thing to do when her entire reality had exploded in her face, once again. "H-he was standing about two feet from the rear bumper of my car, as still as a statue, I remember because I thought not even a hair on his head moved. I realize now that he was totally focused on me.

"Remember how Prolinc remained absolutely still while you poked away at his chest?" she glanced at Dee and took a sip of her Margarita that had just arrived. Dee nodded and motioned her to continue.

"Well, when I saw Prolinc, it reminded me of Zorroc that first night and I recalled thinking it must be a Gattonian thing inherent in their nature; something they do, either not to lose control of themselves or because they don't want to startle their prey." The three looked at each other uncomfortably.

"But you have an excellent point, why me? I am an unwanted child with no real place in the world; I'm not rich, not famous, not beautiful, not a scientist or doctor, not much of anything. So, maybe it was just a fluke and I happened to be in the right place at the right time—or maybe the wrong place come to think of it." Angel and Dee both shook their heads.

"Could they be after your parents, and thought kidnapping you would be a good way to secure them?" Angel prodded, continuing to scan the room. Cat shook her head. "That makes no sense. If they were interested in getting to my parents through me, why not lock me in a room and send a COM? These guys are totally focused on this mission. I believe them about their women. I've overheard them numerous times planning for the conference tomorrow down to the finest detail. Trust me, they are serious. Maybe Zorroc's just hot for my body," she quipped in an effort to lighten the mood. They merely stared at her. "All right the part about the body is a stretch."

Dee's head snapped up, her gaze boring into Cat's. "When have you been around them? You've been at work everyday, I know because we've talked to your aunts and they assured us you were just working hard and would call when you got a moment or connect with us."

Oh, spit.

"Well, I've been going to work then home to visit with the aunts, and after picking up some things, reporting back to the ship. In the mornings, they simply transport me back to work. It's worked pretty smoothly, actually." Surveying the room, she noticed how quiet it had become. She glanced nonchalantly at her friends, and then jerked her head back for a closer look. They were absolutely still, damn if they didn't look just like cat men.

Dee blinked. "You've been spending the night up there every night; why would you want to do that? He's not forcing you is he, has he threatened you in any way?" She fired a look at Angel and finished. "We are going to neuter that 'tom' if he's laid a hand on you; tell us you're not sleeping with him."

This definitely called for a strong come back if she wanted to save Zorroc's private parts, she smiled secretly, and they certainly deserved saving. "Back off. I'm a twenty-six year old woman, perfectly capable of choosing whom I sleep with, but as it happens, we haven't done *that*; he's just giving me lessons."

"What's he teaching you, the violin?" Angel mused, this was getting interesting, she'd been doing a lot of day dreaming about Carpov; maybe she could get him to give her lessons, surely she had something left to learn.

"What have you told the aunts, certainly they would want to know where you disappear to every evening? Do they know you're popping off to a space ship to do the dirty with an Egyptian Cat God every night?" Dee spurted, getting more worried, scared, and confused by the moment. Her intuition wailed like a siren for her to grab her friends and run as far as they could get, but an opposing force told her time had all ready expired; they were doomed. A thick blanket of dread settled around Dee and she knew the truth. Her sixth sense rarely misled her. She also intuited the Gattonians closing in fast. She had to try. "We need to leave here now, if we don't, none of us will have a prayer of escape, you know I'm seldom wrong when I get one of these feelings, now move."

Cat jumped up like she'd been whoopee-cushioned, "You two go ahead; he'll find me no matter where I go. It will be much safer for you if we don't see each other again. I'm not sure he'd let you go a second time. I just wanted a chance to say goodbye and that I love you and will miss you, now go while you can. And stay away from the conference this weekend." She shoved her friends toward the back exit like the hounds of hell pursued them.

The Gattonians came in the front entrance as she reentered from the back. She walked calmly to her table, acting as if she had visited the restroom. Todd eyed the five suspiciously. When she sat down, they flanked her on all sides; Zorroc spoke first, of course. "Where are your friends, Catarina, we came to join you for a drink."

How could he purr and talk at the same time?

"They had a pressing engagement and had to run. You'll see them at the conference tomorrow." He gave her a knowing look that said *you're lying.* How did he do that, she sighed, "I knew you'd arrive soon and want to collect me."

"And what do you want, Catarina?" he purred again, beginning to make her very nervous.

"I want some very specific answers to some interesting questions, so I suggest we blow this Margarita Ville, big guys." With that, she stood up, grabbed her purse, and moved toward the exit. Todd called her name, willing to intervene if she asked. She just waved.

God save testosterone.

Chapter Five

She awoke with the scent and heat of him surrounding her and, once again, knew a deep subliminal connection. It felt undeniably right; could she be so far off in her feelings? Was he actually a diabolical body snatcher with a plot to kidnap women then use them for food on the way back to his home planet? No! No way could she love someone like that. She froze; connection and love were not the same. You had to trust someone before you could love them, and no way did she trust him. Well, she may not love him but she sure loved touching him.

The convention began that afternoon. She was glad she'd be too busy to think for the next few days. Her gaze rested on her sleeping Tiger, and ran her hand softly over him grazing his hard planes, ridges and bulges. A glorious, magnificent beast. What could he possibly want with her...and did she really want to know? Instead of the truth setting her free it might destroy the tentative hope and other unnamed feelings blooming inside her. Her unsettled gaze noted the way his inky lashes trapped a few of his long amber strands. Why kidnap an unremarkable marketing rep from a mall parking lot outside a small bar on the edge of Nashville? How could someone from outer space even find Nashville and why would they want to? You'd think they'd pick a large city on either coast. New York or San Francisco. So many questions with no answers. She was riding on pure instinct in trusting him as far as she did when he, no doubt, had the power to annihilate her and probably her planet.

She wasn't concerned he'd hurt her physically but she was beginning to fear for her heart. He possessed a complex mind, an aura that exuded great inner turmoil revealing a man who took his responsibilities seriously, and steadfast heart—a heart that could be trusted and depended upon. She needed to grill him on his motives for choosing her but checking her watch, knew the moment would have to wait.

Cat eased from his from his side and watched the slow rise and fall of his chest and his relaxed almost boyish expression. She'd give anything to be able to scan his thoughts for a glimpse into the inner workings of his being.

"*Maybe next life,*" a voice echoed in her head.

****

"What a crush, you've done it again, Cat, congratulations. I guess this means another bonus." Her boss, Greg, sent her a broad smile, clearly pleased. He moved on, shmoozing the crowd and shaking hands. It's what he seemed to do best, and he should be pleased; they'd turn a very substantial profit. Zorroc, due to arrive at any moment, would be pleased, as well, she thought. Many young attractive women prowled the area looking for their very own alien.

"*Purr*" sounded softly behind her ear as arms reached around to draw her to him. She snuggled into him comfortably, becoming more accustomed to his touch with each day. What started out foreign and awkward, only the week before, now made her feel safe and connected. She turned to face him, putting her small hand in his.

"Have your people arrived?" she asked quietly.

"They will start mingling with the crowd in your next half hour. All is ready." He faltered. "I have not thanked you for all you have done for us. We would have prevailed eventually, but you have made an immeasurable difference in timing and the quality of women. I am in your debt." He nodded his head in cat fashion. He'd never thanked her before; she was touched.

"I require no debt, I would always help you if within my power to do so," she responded, trying to emulate his more formal speech pattern. He must have noticed because his eyes emitted a strong Amber pulse. Yep, he was a happy space-hopper. He left her staring after him, not quite knowing what had hit her.

Seven hours later her face hurt from smiling, her head and feet pounded with staccato precision, and her back throbbed. The day had produced record-breaking crowds and two remaining days of endless torture loomed ahead. She longed for a quiet corner in which to hide. With waning patience and growing malaise she'd looked on as Zorroc left the main auditorium with one beautiful woman after another—probably sampling them personally for suitability purposes. He couldn't have had many interactions with Earth females previously; maybe he'd meet someone he preferred over her. She'd probably just been an appetizer to prepare him for the main course. Maybe his thank you was really goodbye. Then she considered the bright side; did she really want to go to another planet and used as a baby-making machine?

****

"How much of the operation is she familiar with? It will be difficult to hide what we are doing from her, especially you, my friend," Prolinc said, trying to read behind Zorroc's still countenance.

They had planned to approach willing females, first to determine marital and family status, then measure their willingness and controllability. They targeted females who lived alone with no close family members and were sexually active. Ones whose absence would not be noted for some time. Females accustomed to disappearing for days at a time, enjoying a new partner.

They tested their plan that morning and it had succeeded beyond their wildest hope. Easier than shooting fish in a barrel. Gattonians subliminally shouted 'wet dream' to Earth females. Like lures in a crowded sea of starving fish, they could not wait to be caught. It had taken no effort. They had more trouble fighting them off than catching them. Prolinc had not initially planned to collect females on the first day, but several insisted on accompanying them as they took their leave. A total of twenty-three, now slumbered peacefully in their ship's hold, not to be awakened until they left Earth's atmosphere and their final plans solidified. Zorroc checked the time and smiled, they still had more than an hour before closing.

"Cat believes what I have told her." Zorroc shrugged. "We will meet willing females and invite them to a private assembly that researches UFO sightings. We, supposedly, have information all but proving their existence and will share our findings at the meeting. She believes we will then make our needs known, and enlist those who are willing. Cat scheduled it for Sunday at the conclusion of the convention. The center will be available for our use."

"What will she believe when you keep disappearing with one beautiful Earth female after another for the next two days. I have been watching her watch you and her usual sparkle is fading," Prolinc stated. Could Zorroc's understanding of females be so lacking, or was he simply accustomed to controlling everyone around him and did not expect to be challenged? Prolinc wondered just how long it would take Cat to become angry enough to separate his ego from his head. He found himself looking forward to the coming days.

Though half Gattonian, Catarina's emotions overruled her logic, as her loyalty swayed her common sense. She would never question or betray him; her heart and mind shined clear as crystal. This, however, made him question his own actions and what could be perceived as betrayals against her. If she attempted to do the same to him, he would never forgive her; never relent. He might even damage her given further provocation. He shook his head not liking where his mind-shift led. She would understand and accept the choices he made, she must; she belonged to him. He would bind her to him so tightly that nothing he could do would rent her from his side. He had no doubt of her weakness for him. It would conquer her misgivings and allay any rebellious thoughts or actions. Satisfied with his logic, he growled warningly at Prolinc and went to collect his mate. Only to be interrupted once again.

"Hi, stranger. Where did you find the costume, it's positively, divinely sinful," the woman purred, stroking Zorroc's chest and arms. Though the day had proved gruelingly long, he gave her a very male, knowing smirk, signaling his willingness to follow her tail.

"I am part of the Gattonian Assembly; some of our people are speaking at the convention this weekend. You should attend; it will be quite...fascinating. Are you here alone, it does not seem possible a man would let you run loose."

"Umm, I prefer to play the field, and enjoy what life delivers. How about you, are you unencumbered?" She began, rubbing her private parts against his. Zorroc smiled wider; letting her draw her own conclusions when suddenly the atmosphere changed.

"Excuse me," Cat challenged.

Zorroc's eyes pinned hers and demanded, "What do you want?"

"A word," she fired back, lightning shooting from her emerald depths.

After observing him pickup one woman after another for the last ten hours, "tom cat" had taken on a whole new meaning, mainly illustrating that her 'tom' couldn't wait to get laid by any slightly in-heat-female available. He obviously cared more about assembling his harem than securing women for his planet; ready, and willing to repopulate it single dickedly. Her patience snapped. The time had come to state her position and ascertain his.

His hand brushed the cheek of his latest find, as he whispered to the witch. "Do not move from this spot, I will not be long." His eyes promised hot things to come; then he turned to Cat with murder in them. He followed her to an empty meeting room.

"What are you doing, beginning a new career as a male prostitute available to any halfway attractive sleezette?" Cat accused, her eyes shooting enough fire to supply Hell for a year. Every part of her vibrated with rage and betrayal.

His glare, boring into hers, was colder than she would've believed possible; derision and disgust fought each other for supremacy. She felt like her soul had frozen. Her time with him had clearly come to an end. "Do not question me! I will save my race by whatever means required and no small, inconsequential, sexually suppressed Earth female will get in my way."

That about summed it up. She was out of there. With her commitment to the Gattonians fulfilled, she was taking her shattered heart; no, her shattered ego; and disappearing like so much used trash.

Zorroc wondered if he had perhaps overdone her latest lesson, he could have used more tact, she had, after all, worked hard on their behalf. However, she should never have questioned him; what had she been thinking? Perhaps she was just tired, he conceded. Hell, they were all tired. He would fix it later when he finished with this overly eager female. Confident everything would be fine with his out-of-joint mate, he once again assumed the role of available male. "What is your name sweet one?" he inquired, as he approached, noticing she had not moved from the spot he had left her. Zorroc smiled, pleased, that she had followed his direction without question, unlike his own Catarina.

"My name is Sandra," she responded. "Can we go somewhere more private?" she wheedled with a practiced insipid pout. She would do very well, Zorroc observed, and led her out of the building.

Cat went home to collect the rest of her belongings in preparation to leave town; she'd tell the aunts, only, that she'd be in touch and not to worry. Everything appeared quiet as she let herself into the house. Everything had disappeared—her aunts, her kittens, the furniture, everything. She ran up to her room and checked her closet and found it empty, as well. What could have happened? When she visited yesterday, all seemed normal.

She sped to Dees; the three would leave for Angel's cabin immediately. She pounded on the door for three minutes before realizing no one was home and proceeded to Angels convinced the two were together. But as before, everything was still. She fetched the extra key kept under the porch and let herself in. The place stood empty, deserted. Good God, she thought with dawning horror, the Gattonians had stolen them. All of them. Everyone she held dear in this world. Cat sank to the floor unable to control her grief, her guilt, and the crowning devastation. *She'd trusted him and he'd betrayed her with a ruthlessness she could barely conceive.*

Zorroc found her huddled in the middle of

Angel's front room holding a key. He and his crew had searched for hours, going first to Grumpy's, then the aunt's, the roadways, hospitals and everywhere he could think to look all the while castigating himself for bungling their last confrontation. He'd let fatigue, frustration and male pride rule his words to her.

"Prolinc," he mind-thought, *"I have located her; have Carpov ready to assist."* He gently lifted her boneless form and they melted away.

Things moved quickly as Zorroc arrived on the trans-pad. Med staff transported Cat straight to the Med-center for treatment, while Zorroc resided in a self-imposed hell; he would never forget how she looked when he found her. She had shrunken into herself looking profoundly shaken. He knew her upbringing had made her vulnerable. For all her resilient outer shell, she remained fragile and he had shattered her with his lack of sensitivity and careless arrogance. What must she have thought when she discovered everyone she loved had been taken from her, along with his own commitment and regard?

Cat sensed Zorroc's presence at Angel's but lacked the strength for another battle; content to retreat into the depths of her consciousness. When they arrived on the ship, she could have told them she was fine but decided against expending the effort, not when she'd been expending so much just to keep herself from flying apart. She wondered idly what caused him to visit Angel.

"Catarina is in shock. I have given her something to make her sleep, after which she will be fine," Carpov informed Zorroc softly. "Angel and Dee are on their way to her so there is plenty of time for you to rest because to be honest, you look worse than she." Zorroc's state of mind concerned him more than Cat's for the moment. He had not moved for hours, would not speak to anyone; would not say what had occurred to put his pinball in her current stagnant state.

Zorroc, determined to repair some of the damage his careless words had set into motion, grimly proceeded to the Med-center. As the panel slid open, two sets of accusing eyes glared at him with suppressed rage. He came in and touched his beautiful, still Catarina, gently smoothing her hair from her face. She looked peaceful, sweet, and innocent. What had he been thinking to treat her so carelessly? He had told her he would take care of her, protect her, and he had failed—just as he had failed to protect his people. What kind of a leader did that make him?

Just then, she looked up and smiled sleepily at him. "You look so stern, come to bed and hold me, I'm cold."

Everyone in the room froze; Carpov had just entered and stood staring purposely at Angel. Cat sensed the undercurrents in the room and looked around, her eyes widened as she took in the occupants. She couldn't fathom why everyone in their chamber stared at her. Had she grown a few inches overnight, had her hair gone straight? She glanced beseechingly at Zorroc, begging for an answer.

"Leave us, I will take care of her." Angel and Dee gave him identical looks of skepticism but did not challenge him. Carpov shrugged uncertainly, glancing first at his patient then at Zorroc and strode after Angel.

"What do you remember, flame?" he asked while softly kissing her brow and eyelids. He wanted to assess the damage in an unobtrusive manner. As her gaze drifted up to meet his, he held it in an effort to divine the truth. He still could not read her; her mind remained static.

"Why did you call me that and what are my friends doing here on the ship, did I get sick?" she inquired with detached curiosity.

"Flame is what my crew named you when you first came aboard because of the color of your hair and the way you move. They have been very concerned; you have slept for some time. What is the last thing you remember?" Slowly her eyes focused on his and became hard. Obviously, she had remembered a great deal.

"What do you want with my friends and family; you have your harem, you don't need us. I will not be one in a long line of willing sleezettes, Zorroc; the only way you'll have me is by rape, and I'd think that you're huge, arrogant ego would keep you from that course." She sat up and leaned forward. "You have countless others at your disposal, why bother with one small, inconsequential, repressed virgin?" she hissed, throwing his words back at him. "You can and have done better, as I witnessed first hand."

He flinched as his words hit their mark. He had not enjoyed luring unsuspecting females into a situation they may not survive and had taken his frustration out on Catarina without realizing what exactly he had said or how she would interpret it. She looked around for the first time to discover she was in the Med-center and bounced off the mat, determined to leave his company. Zorroc, however, had different plans.

"I know how it must have appeared. We do what we deem necessary in order to ensure the continuance of our race." His full considerable concentration centered on her. "Our people, when they lifemate, are monogamous; that is what I plan for us though the ceremony has yet to take place. The women I lured from the conference; nothing happened. I was not with them sexually." He pushed his hair straight back gripping the back of his head with both hands, his face a study of hard shadows and plains as his eyes continued to bore into hers, "I think you must know this in your heart and maybe are just afraid of the inevitable." He stared at her with purpose and began advancing on her. Cat began subtly backing away, not wanting it to look like a retreat.

"I am not afraid of you, because there is no inevitable for us. Let my friends and my aunts go; they are not a part of this. I have said I'll go with you and I will; but if you don't release the others, you will never have my trust again and I'll strike at you in any way I can," she threatened, hands on her hips, her eyes riveted to his.

"Carpov wants Angel, and Prolinc, Dee, when he is not considering throttling her," he admitted haltingly, "and your aunts are not your aunts, but my aunts. Female Gattonians sent to evaluate your suitability as my mate and to look after you until I could claim you."

"They can't be your aunts; they look like your regular, run of the mill, eccentric humanoid aunts; my parents *told* me they're my aunts, do you expect me to believe my parents lied to me in order to deliver me to you?"

"Marie and Helen are both citizens of Gattonia, they are a mix of our races. I told you our races had frequently mated and they are a result. Their job has been to monitor the progress of your planet and execute certain assignments, such as yours. Your parents are both half Gattonian and gave their permission to collect you. It was not easy for them, but you have Gattonian blood on both sides. It was imperative for our race to have you." He watched, warily.

She'd been betrayed. Who would have thought that her parents would sacrifice her and not even COM to let her know? She'd had two strangers living in her house for almost a year, how could she have been so stupid. And Angel and Dee—their capture rested directly on her shoulders. How could they forgive her? She'd ruined their lives. She felt like a bowling ball that had just made the mother of all strikes. Her glazed eyes began to clear and settle on Zorroc, his expression showed concern and pity. He ought to pity himself, she decided, he was as stuck with her as she with him. The perfect way to incinerate an already doomed relationship.

"Well, at least I'm good for something. So, should I lay spread eagle and make the rape easy or are you going to wait until I'm asleep to attack?"

"Do not push me Catarina, we both know I can take what I want from you and make you like it, and if you continue to push me I will do exactly that. I want to make love to you, my cream; it is the only way to push through your barriers until you admit that you are more afraid of your feelings for me than in the situation you now find yourself. I will take you as many times as necessary until you face the truth about us. We are bound." He moved in.

Cat knew exactly which way her cat man was blowing by the smoldering in his cat-eyes and the pole jutting prominently from his uniform. Unlike jeans, every male reaction could be seen clearly because of the flexibility of Gattonian clothing. The amber in his eyes had caught fire, burning her from the inside out. The final lesson had arrived. It would be an inferno and she would not be the same at its conclusion. Well she'd see if she couldn't give her proposed mate a little return fire. She relaxed her stance to let him know she accepted what was to occur. He read the change in body language and gave her a sexy, knowing smile.

"You will not regret this, my one," he purred. "I will teach you well and satisfy us both beyond bearing." He closed the distance between them and reached for her; she in turn took his hand, stepped up, and kneed him in the groin before whipping around and throwing him to the ground. Score one for the Earth girls; she knew those self-defense lessons Dee had forced on her would come in handy some day.

She exited the Med-center in search of her friends, leaving Zorroc doubled over on the floor.

Chapter Six

Cat had no problem locating Dee; she just followed the verbal hurricane centered on Prolinc. She entered without knocking, feeling particularly pleased with herself for getting a little of her own back from Zorroc. She sighed; it looked like an exact replay of the first time she came upon them, sans Angel. She looked around for a moment, realizing they were in a sleeping chamber. Though not quite as elaborate as Zorroc's, it still provided spaciousness and comfort. They didn't notice she'd entered so she waited for a break in the action to make herself known.

"I see communication between you continues to spark, Dee, but you're going have to learn to keep your finger off Prolinc; he could get the wrong idea and think you're trying to have your way with him. This is a different culture after all, and Prolinc, I've noticed, tends to take things very literally."

Silence finally. "Prolinc, I'm sure you'll excuse Dee, we need to round up Angel and disappear. Please meet us in five minutes at the trans-pad and your chest will be finger free forever."

He looked at her oddly, trying to change gears from Dee's assault to her Miss Congeniality act, no doubt. She smiled sweetly, grabbed Dee's arm, and propelled her to the exit panel, looking back to make sure Prolinc didn't intend to stop them. Nope, he still looked as befuddled as the first time she'd seen him. They almost made it through the exit but as she turned, she hit a solid wall vibrating with suppressed energy; make that wrath.

"Dee will stay with Prolinc, you will come with me. Now." Zorroc ducked down, scooped her over his shoulder, and proceeded toward their quarters.

"Zorroc, be reasonable, it won't work between us, so you may as well let us go home. You have an entire harem to choose from; what's a little Gattonian blood, when all is said and done? Think of this as ensuring the continuance of your family line because if you don't let us go my knee will constantly be planted exactly where you don't want it, which could cause serious repercussions long term.

"Zorroc—will—you—hear—me!" she shrieked, punctuating each word with her small fist pounding his back. To hell with a finger.

"It will not work between us? I will prove to you exactly how wrong you are, little cat." The hand on the back of her thigh moved slowly upward until his fingers were tucked against her sex where he began to caress back and forth. Cat bit back a groan. "I know you feel the hot-wired connection between us. You want me every bit as much as I want you. Why do you continue to defy me? Besides, your protestations come too late, we left Earth's atmosphere while you were under sedation. Your friends, the aunts and seventy-three additional Earth women are bound for Gattonia, and you, my obstinate mate, are bound for my mat."

Cat was stunned. Seventy-three? How had they found seventy-three willing women in one day? The answer was perversely clear. They'd stolen them. He hadn't even had to lie about it; she'd gone along willingly and condemned all of them to an uncertain future at best. He'd manipulated her as easily as a parent bribing a child with a puppy. Only she wasn't a child. She wanted her old life back and her friends safe from these dictatorial feline space pirates.

"This is cave man strategy, let's discuss it, you're about to do something you'll be sorry for later," she pleaded, knowing it to be fruitless or fruitful depending on how things progressed.

"It will be my strategy with you from now on, accept it," he said as the panel slid silently open then shut with finality.

He dumped her on the platmat and began to strip with slow purpose. She had seen him naked before, of course, but the unleashed raw sexual energy oozing off his powerful frame held her spellbound. She stared helplessly; he personified the most awesome force of nature as sensuality surrounded him...and engulfed her senses. The top of his uniform seemed to separate on its own as he slowly drew it down his shoulders and torso; she'd have to be dead not to be affected.

She squirmed at the dampness between her legs.

He smiled.

God, he was breath-taking. Her very own living, breathing, burnished gold statue. His massive shoulders and arms rippled with power; his stomach muscles, clearly delineated, clenched as her gaze fastened on them.

She couldn't catch her breath.

He continued to reveal himself, drawing his garment past his abdomen to his manhood. He hung huge and hard and she grew nervous, wondering how it would fit inside her. Angel had assured her they did, but then she'd been talking about men, not Gattonians. Were they larger down there? Would he rip her to shreds? She began to have second thoughts about the whole process, and the more she stared, the larger it bulged and jerked. He discarded his uniform in a rectangular panel that opened and sucked it in then turned and headed toward the console. Hard and firm, his buttocks flexed in time to his strides, and his legs, long and solid, corded and gleamed as he leaned over to issue orders of privacy.

He would take no chances of being disturbed this night. She inched closer to panic mode. Her destiny had arrived too soon.

Zorroc read her unease and prepared himself for yet another futile round of negotiations. He would have his way in the end and nothing she could say or do would alter the outcome. He had a lot to teach her and he wanted to give it his full, considerable attention.

His Cat looked in danger of bolting. A little fear was a good thing he decided; just look what she had done to him earlier. She could have crippled his male root for life. Luckily, it seemed to have recovered nicely. She had many weapons at her disposal, as he continued to learn first hand.

"I will have you naked, Catarina," he began calmly as he sauntered toward his female. "I will help you undress and then we will begin the petting," he whispered, all the while mindspeaking that all would be well, they would fit as a hand in glove; her pleasure would be his foremost desire. "Now, my present, we will unwrap you."

Her disquieting scrutiny pooled into his unfaltering one for a moment and then she relaxed, equal parts wary and expectant. He went to the front of her slacks and released them expertly. She wondered at his expertise as he stripped her of her slacks and panties in one deft motion. He was pleased with the possessive thought.

"Don't get too confident, cat man, I still have more weapons."

He looked at her, incredulous for an instant; would she continue to fight him? He studied her, reading the bravado behind her words. Though uncertain, she would trust him in this. Would she again trust him in anything else?

"I have unwrapped the best part first," he crooned softly. "The part that will take me inside you and make you mine beyond challenge." He gently brushed her hips, thighs, and abdomen with the back of his talented fingers. "You are perfectly formed; your legs are long and lithe, you thighs creamy but firm and I can circle your waist with my hands. Your belly is soft as a cloud and slightly rounded to remind me of how our babies will be cradled there; your hips, so small and compact that..." He grew silent and stared as if seeing her for the first time; the width of his one spread hand spanned her hips completely. With their many lessons on touching, why had he never considered her size?

Gattonians, as a race, were larger than Earth humans though not so much so that mating constituted a problem; but she was tiny even by Earth standards. What had her parents been thinking, and Helen and Marie as well. Would she be capable of carrying their children or, after everything...perish birthing his offspring. He had vowed protection and care, is this how he would repay her?

"I have recalled an obligation that can not be postponed; I must leave, no matter how much I wish to remain," he declared, hurriedly donning a clean uniform and spouting, simultaneously, a non-stop stream of platitudes. "You are exquisite Catarina, I will return as soon as I am able. In the interim your friends will keep you company." And with a last haunted glance toward nothing in particular, Zorroc jettisoned through the retreating panel.

****

"What'd you do to your poor Gattonian, Cat?" Angel asked. "Earlier, Carpov told me Zorroc had issued orders regulating our time together. He didn't want the two of us getting between the two of you. And he didn't trust the three of us not to get into mischief." Not that Angel minded overly much. That meant more time with Carpov. He had a serious nature like her own and their specialties in the fields of Biochemistry and Medicine blended surprisingly well. He'd filled her in on what had occurred on Ganz and she had promised to assist him in finding a vaccine to help his people.

Dee snorted, "What'd he think we were gonna do; blow up their ship and float home? Zorroc must be one autocratic alien, but hey, aren't they all," she complained, testing out a hand co-ordination game she had found in Prolinc's quarters.

Dee and Angel had been delivered to her fifteen minutes before and Dee hadn't stopped pacing and protesting. "I have been quarantined in Prolinc's quarters for hours; locked in, held prisoner—as in 'Most Wanted'," she charged, continuing to circle the room mumbling a constant stream of expletives.

Angel and Cat studied one another. Both were acting quieter than usual, each wondering about the other; then as one, shifted their attention to Dee. She acted like a top spinning out of control; neither had seen such erratic behavior from their friend before, but since butting chest with finger on Prolinc, she hadn't been the same.

"And you," directing the telltale finger at Angel, "he told me you were staying with Carpov but had the run of the ship." She took a breath and began winding down to normal Dee mode as she concluded, "and did you know that there are seventy-three women sleeping somewhere on this vessel?"

"Seventy-five not including us," murmured Cat, effectively silencing the room, "the aunts are here too." Before she could explain, Angel interrupted.

"That makes no sense, Cat. Surely, they wouldn't have kidnapped your aunts. What possible use could they be; their reproductive organs probably dried up before any of us were born."

"I think I should be awarded first place for *most*

clueless in the history of gullible dolts. Not only did he use me to kidnap seventy-three innocent women along with the two of you; Zorroc also informed me that Helen and Marie are not my aunts, but citizens of Gattonian. It appears I have Gattonian blood on both sides of my family and they were sent to discern my suitability as a receptacle for Zorroc's sperm." Putting it into that context further flattened Cat's already squished ego. Her two friends resembled twin snapshots of dawning speculation. No one moved for a few moments, taking in the import of the information.

Dee whistled softly. "And you passed."

"Well, that answers the provocative question of why you," Angel summarized.

"Yeah, my model parents set me up. Hell, I don't think they even sold me, they just delivered me to the Gattonians and said "boink yourselves out". I don't care about me, so much, but condemning the two of you on top of it all is beyond forgivable. I've ruined your futures and possibly cost you your lives." She pressed her hands over her eyes to keep the tears from falling.

"It was a plot, Cat, well laid out, and cannily executed. If there is one person blameless in all this, it's you. The fact that they took advantage of your guileless nature is the part I find reprehensible. The lying sneaks," Angel hissed. Just wait until she got Carpov alone, she would hit him where it hurt most both verbally and physically. When her thoughts proceeded to Zorroc, her lips twitched menacingly.

"But that's just it, he didn't lie; I just didn't ask the right questions. If I hadn't been so starry-eyed over his exotic appearance and caught up in his touching lessons this whole thing could probably have been avoided."

"The king of creeps would still have taken you, questions or no and I would've shot them out of the sky if they'd left us behind. Actually, they've fallen right into our trap; they might have been able to defeat one of us but not all three together." Dee's light humor in the face of their current disastrous situation made Cat hurt even worse. "Ah, come on Cat lighten up," she coaxed. "It's always been all for one and one for all, what makes you think we'd let you off the hook now. One thing for sure; I doubt this will be a boring adventure. And look on the bright side, you're starring in you own science fiction movie. Think of the money you'll save on DVDs."

"Humph, if this *were* a movie, it'd carry a rating of B- on content and an X for adult situations," Cat grumbled morosely.

****

"How do we proceed from here?" Carpov moaned as the three studied the COM in Zorroc's quarters. He had been working hard to gain Angel's trust, but how could he compete with her friends? The three represented a vexatious force. He glanced at his friends and thought of ways to accomplish the divide and conquer strategy. He would take her tonight and make her acknowledge the bond between them; it was the only way to secure her against her friends' erratic behavior and then he would keep her very, very busy. Carpov grew hard at the prospect.

"She is impossibly tiny, why did I not notice it before? Even her friends dwarf her," Zorroc commented to no one in particular. He would confer with the aunts to get some explanations. Someone should have told him she would be unsuitable because of her size. He wanted *in* her and the High Council depended on him to impregnate her with all haste. A deed that could not be faked.

"Do you comprehend the hell I will face with my fireball when she is returned to my quarters? I will be up the entire night with her finger in my chest," Prolinc finished, resigned to his fate.

The three Gattonians commiserated while their women plotted. Focused on the COM, they realized the truth; they would be plagued for eternity by these three Earth females.

****

"Zorroc has handled this poorly, if he'd been honest with Cat, she would have understood. Instead she's feeling betrayed, threatened, used, and little more than a pawn in someone else's game." Angel had returned to Carpov's quarters clearly shaken. "I told them nothing per our agreement, but I feel like I'm deceiving them, as well as myself, by keeping silent."

Carpov, after his first glimpse of Angel, had known she belonged with him. As a result, he had revealed their entire dilemma and asked for her assistance. With her intelligence and expertise in germ warfare and biochemistry, he hoped to pool their knowledge and come up with an antidote or even a cure for the virus that had been blanketed over Gattonia twenty-some months previously.

"Angel, I want to mate with you," he blurted, unexpectedly. "It would be a lifemating, I warn you. Afterward there would be no other female for me and no other male for you. I could take you and make it so, but I would prefer honesty and trust between us." Carpov studied her trying to divine the palatable wariness behind her eyes. He sensed something amiss; he read panic in her suddenly haunted countenance. He had been sure that the feelings he had for her were mutually shared.

Angel thought furiously about how to respond. She used sex as a tool for manipulation and gratification in that order. It sounded as if Carpov offered the equivalent to marriage in her culture. How could she tell him that she was soiled goods; not worth his time or attention; let alone his name and protection, and perhaps love?

Angel had fallen hard him from the moment he appeared, looking fierce yet not frightening. She'd felt an invisible force field of protection envelop her the moment his gaze settled on her. She'd been a victim of sexual harassment by the president of her company recently, and had felt threatened and isolated—a feeling very similar to the one she'd experienced at the ed-center. The job that had begun as a challenge and refuge had become a nightmare. Being kidnapped by the Gattonians, in truth, had felt more like a rescue. She and Carpov had spent hour's together working on a solution for the virus plaguing his planet, and conversing on all manner of subjects. He had not tried to approach her in a sexual manner even though his every move sparked sexual awareness. She felt flushed and breathless whenever they shared the same work space and wanted to explore the chemistry between them to discern the truth behind the pull she encountered whenever he drew near. The chances of that, however, emerged slight. He deserved someone better...cleaner.

She closed her eyes and took a breath. "I can't lifemate with you, Carpov; it wouldn't be fair to you. I've been used by men and used them in return. I'm ruined and certainly not good enough for you." There that should do it; for once she'd done the right thing.

Carpov smiled gently. "Angel, in my culture we become sexually active at a very young age. Until we choose a mate, we are free with our bodies to whoever is handy. I seriously doubt you could have more experience than I, and I would expect fidelity only after our mating. Anything before means nothing to us now. Do you desire me Angel, do you want me inside you hard and pulsing until you know you belong to me? Do you want me to make love to you until neither of us can stand?" He started toward her. "Answer me now or it will be too late."

"Carpov, a man at the school I attended, raped me repeatedly from the age of thirteen until I was seventeen. I don't make love, I have sex; and I never enjoy it, not like a normal person. Is that what you want in a mate?" she proposed, horrified by her own admission. She'd never told anyone of her ordeal and now that she had, her life sounded even more sordid. She couldn't meet his eyes to see the disgust and pity she knew would be there. She turned to leave with her head high and quiet pride intact.

"Who is the bug-dropping that did this to you?" he thundered, stalking over to her and touching her shoulder. "You have to know it was not of your making. The shame lies with him, Angel, never with you. I cannot believe your friends would let you feel this way," he hissed, gently bending down to lift and carry her to his platmat then follow her down, holding her as one would a wounded child.

Angel cried. She cried with all the shame, anguish, hopelessness, and fury that she'd kept bottled in her soul for more than ten years and Carpov cried, as well, feeling every emotion along with her. His Angel had been misused and he would die before anyone but him touched her again. He could not change the past but he could do something about her future and vowed that her future would also be his.

He began gently, by kissing her tears away, then moved to her forehead, earlobe, and pulse-point on her neck that increased in rhythm with each lave of his tongue. He worked her clothes off her, first her shirt and bra, next her leggings and panties. He paused to look his fill. She surpassed everything lovely. Her breasts, while not large, distended firm and high, her waist proved small enough to eclipse with his hands, and her hips flared proportionately to the most beautiful legs he'd ever seen on a female. He rose quickly to shed his uniform and returned to her side. She, in turn, perused him. Her eyes, which only moments before had looked defeated and desperate, had begun to smolder with hot anticipation.

He was bigger, better and more potent than any space pirate or bandit in one of Cat's old DVDs. He was black all over; his hair, skin, eyes, and even his shaft, as it jutted larger and thicker than any she had known, and she had known a lot. Angel looked up to realize she'd been caught licking her lips.

"Does it meet with your approval?" he drawled with mixed expressions of arousal and amusement clear in his onyx eyes.

"I think I could get used to it, but you need to show me how it works." She flashed him a wry grin.

It proved all the invitation he needed. His kiss was open, moist, and hot and it seared her to her toes. He started running his tongue along her neck and shoulders, working his way down. Almost as if he were cleaning her, freeing her of her past nightmares. He suckled her nipples until they budded tightly then moved on to her rib cage and stomach; he discovered every erogenous zone she possessed leaving not one square inch ignored. He moved between her legs and holding her buttocks in his hands, spread her legs wide and began to feast. She had become so sensitized with his ministrations; she almost came straight off the mat as he then proceeded to purr into the soft folds of her womanhood. Never had she felt anything so intoxicating. She climaxed almost immediately and when he moved up her body to meet her eyes, her expression shouted disbelief and amazement. She had just experienced her first orgasm with a man.

"What are you people, some new sort of pleasure weapon?" She pulled him to her and launched her own counter assault. She rolled him over and attacked his manhood with her mouth licking and sucking him while kneading his inner thighs, abdomen, and chest with her adept touch.

"Enough!" he croaked finally, and grabbed her upper arms, rolling until he covered her from shoulder to thigh. He buried himself inside her with one hard deep thrust. He did not try to control the tempo of their mating; he just gloried in the sensation of finally getting her right where he wanted. He pumped with sure hard strokes until she begged; then he lowered his hand between them and placed his thumb on the swollen nub nestled there. She shot off, crying his name repeatedly as he followed with equal enthusiasm. He bit into the place between her neck and shoulder hard enough to draw blood. The sensation of pain and pleasure caused her to climax yet again forcing a satisfied grunt from Carpov.

It was done; she was his mate. Zorroc had but to witness the bite and it would be official. He left her sleeping peacefully and headed toward the late night meeting with Zorroc and Prolinc.

****

Zorroc paced like a tiger in a cage. Back and forth, back and forth, he made the aunts positively dizzy. It was most Un-Gattonian of him. Usually, when one of their race became agitated they stilled to immobility; Zorroc flew in the face of this behavior, clearly off the charts with frustration. His aunts remained perfectly still, observing him. What an incredible relief to be with their own people once again; it had been difficult to maintain a human demeanor for so long and at such close range, while residing with Cat. They had grown to love her as a daughter and knew her adjustment to this new situation would prove a difficult one; they only hoped she would choose to forgive their deception and let them assist her in navigating the coming changes. Spock and Scotty observed Zorroc with equal interest, both sets of button eyes following his every movement as he fumed. The kittens had been near death when dropped at the Habi-Cat several weeks before. Cat had taken them home to be cared for and they had simply remained as a part of the family.

"Why did you not tell me this mating would be impossible," Zorroc accused. "Your entire purpose was to evaluate her suitability; what were you thinking to let this taking go forward?" he demanded ferociously.

The aunts were not intimidated; they had helped raise Zorroc since birth. "Whatever do you mean? You have received our reports; she is entirely suitable. She is intelligent, warm, kind, loyal, attractive, maybe a little fluff-headed from time to time but you can't expect everything, my dear," Helen explained. "Personally, I think it gives her a certain charm, don't...

"She is too small!" he exploded with impotent rage. "If I don't tear her apart in her taking; my offspring surely will. I want her but cannot have her and she is a temptation I am not sure I can resist. How do you propose I get around this? I trusted you and you have placed me in an untenable position."

"She is a carbon copy of her mother, Zorroc, you knew exactly what you would be getting when we planned this," Marie snapped, having heard enough of her nephew's ravings. "She will take you and your offspring just fine. She is small but sturdy with a strong spirit. She is beyond suitable, if you would just do the deed as Zazu intended," she finished.

Zorroc stilled. It took him a few moments to grasp the gist of her declaration. They were right of course; Rowan was every bit his size and Nancia could not be much larger than Cat. She must be muddling his brain, it was the only explanation; he would take her when he saw her next and that would set his mind and body to rights.

"I have a meeting to attend, thank you for your time," he muttered politely, slightly chagrined as he bent to kiss his aunts on their cheeks. Maybe everything would be all right after all; he would take Catarina tonight and proceed from there. Zorroc headed to the meeting room feeling lighter with each step.

Chapter Seven

Prolinc and Carpov were waiting when Zorroc arrived. Prolinc looked churlish while Carpov looked pleased and relaxed. Ridiculously pleased, he realized, on closer inspection. "We will make this meeting a quick one. I am sure we all have places we would rather be; Carpov what do you propose," Zorroc asked, wanting to make this uncomfortable decision as quickly as possible.

"The women are still asleep; we could choose several, inject the virus and await possible symptoms. If they begin to have problems, at least they would be unaware of the changes taking place in their bodies and we could keep the ones we experiment on well away from the others, as a precaution. We have another month in space before we reach Ganz giving us plenty of time to evaluate possible side effects. The real problem remains dosage. It will be impossible to match because of the method of administration—injecting the women with the virus versus airborne exposure. The remaining option, of course, is not to inject them. The extensive testing we conducted on Earth's atmosphere indicate a better than average chance the Earth females will suffer minimal side effects from the virus. Plus it will have dissipated even further with time. Maybe we should do nothing and let nature take its course." Carpov, uncomfortable with the choices in front of them, took a sip of jive.

Dee had collected Cat moments before, telling her she'd seen their Gattonians slip away for a meeting. They weren't hard to locate, they normally assembled in the conference room and this night, hadn't even bothered to secure the panel, obviously confident that everyone would be safely tucked into their platmats. Because of the miscalculation, Dee and Cat heard enough of the conversation to freeze their blood. Bad enough, they had taken innocent women, put them into suspended animation, and were speeding toward their home planet with them. Now they discussed the possibility of experimenting on them like laboratory rats. Cat reeled sickeningly. How could she have been so wrong about their motives? The conversation proceeded.

"What if the females have a severe reaction to the serum," Prolinc posed. "How would this affect our females?"

"We would jettison them while asleep; it would be the kindest and safest thing to do all around." Zorroc stated thinking of Cat. If he had his way, he would jettison the serum. Discussing the possibility of testing the females before they procured them, proved daunting enough, but now, with identifiable faces and distinct personalities to take into account, combined with the strong instinct to protect those under their care; made the situation they contemplated more than he could stomach.

Sirens began to sound all around them as the ship jerked sharply to the left then jarred and shuttered. "We are under attack!" Zorroc shouted incredulously. "Carpov, get those women out of suspended animation and assign crew members to care for them. They are helpless in their current state. They will be confused, disoriented, and frightened with all this noise and their current situation; instruct the crewmembers to turn on the charm.

"Prolinc, secure our females, I will get to the main deck and determine our situation. Do not be long, Prolinc, meet me on deck as soon as you can; I will silence those damned alarms." He strode purposefully from the room tripping over Cat and Dee, in the process of scrambling to gain their footing; they had been knocked off their feet with the ships unexpected jarring. He realized they must have listened in on the meeting and cursed his carelessness but could not waste time worrying about his oversight. He grabbed Cat by her upper arm, secured Dee with his other hand, and barked at Prolinc to grab Angel from Carpov's quarters; he had the other two.

He marched them quickly toward his destination. "What in the hell is going on," Cat screamed, dragged at a run beside Zorroc. Dee had a slightly easier time of it graced with longer legs, however she still maintained a trot in order to keep up. A sudden decent occurred that would have knocked Cat and Dee to the ground again if not for Zorroc's firm grip.

Dee's mind worked on the ramifications of this latest crisis. They were under attack and Prolinc was head of security and guardian to Zorroc, she needed a quick weapons lesson in order to back him up. He his own people, of course, but she had more of a vested interest in him. And after the conversation she and Cat just overheard, she had not even begun to make him as miserable as she now intended. Zorroc threw them into the jet-quik and propelled them to the main control level. The deck proved a study in chaos. Flames loomed directly in front of them. Zorroc grabbed a flask from the wall and extinguished the growing fire like it happened regularly.

"The situation Sycor, now," Zorroc demanded, as he fairly stormed into the main control room depositing Cat and Dee into two seats away from the action. He proceeded to the main board and punched in the numbered sequence required to silence the warning sirens. He checked the console to confirm that the shields remained up and holding then checked an adjoining screen to assess the damage to the ship. It had to have been a well-planned trap to catch them so off guard, which meant only one thing. Dargons—the ruthless warrior race with no discernable ethics, morals, or rules except to destroy all in their path.

A sudden explosion bounced Dee and Cat to the floor again, while the main COM began smoking, setting off another series of alarms. Zorroc had a bad feeling about the survival of his ship; it lurched at an odd angle that did not bode well for it or them. How had the Dargons located them? Had they known of their mission to Earth? That sounded impossible.

Sycor met his gaze with somber clarity. "The news is bad, it was an ambush, and I think it is clear by whom. The ship will not survive. I have scouted available planets reachable by trans-pad and Pod and there are three. My recommendation is to transport to all three, spreading out as much as possible. We will be harder to track and if one group does get hit the others will have a better chance for survival. I think they are too far out to have us on visual, but if they do; our tails are cooked. Our beacons are untraceable to anyone but our own people and I have sent a COM to Gattonia apprising them of our situation and location; we have food and survival equipment for three weeks, which should leave adequate time for rescue," he summarized gravely.

"Make preparations to abandon ship as soon as possible; we cannot take a chance with our female cargo." Zorroc turned and spoke into the COM. "Carpov, I need an update, we have to prepare to abandon ship with all speed; how are the females faring?"

"They are awake, some are adjusting better than others, we will begin herding them toward the Pods with all speed, where is Angel?"

Zorroc whipped his head around to search for their females; Prolinc emerged with Angel and his gaze met and locked with Zorroc's. A message passed between them before Prolinc left again to implement evacuation plans. "She is safe, Carpov, and anxious to see you from the look of her. Which Pod will you head for; one of the crew can deliver her to you." Zorroc noticed the mating tattoo visible on her neck and knew the reason for Carpov's earlier mood and present concern. "And Carpov, your mating has been witnessed."

Angel, Dee, and Cat huddled together trying to stay out of everyone's way. "We need weapons," whispered Dee, "and someone to instruct us quickly. If we get separated, swear to me you will be armed." Cat gauged the seriousness of their situation from Dee's level of focus, which had streaked past the next reality somewhere.

"We swear," promised Cat and Angel in unison. "But let's solve that little problem by not getting separated to begin with," Angel proposed.

"We may not have a choice considering the circumstances," Cat replied. She couldn't have been more correct. A member of the crew took Angel to be evacuated; then someone came for Dee leaving Cat alone with Zorroc, feeling frightened and unsure. Gattonians poured out of the control room like cats escaping a monsoon. Zorroc, cool under fire, calmly issued orders and tracked the progress of the evacuation teams, memorizing each location of the evacuees. Sycor entered and motioned that it was time for their departure, the ship was losing ground quickly. The three descended to the trans-pad where about ten women waited. She recognized Bandoff, as he attempted to calm the confused and frightened

93

women. Sycor pushed a sequence of buttons on his wristband and they exited the failing vessel.

The planet, red, barren, and hot, had breathable air but no breeze, and no movement of any kind, not a bird, a tree, a cloud, nothing. She felt like she had just fallen into a surreal photograph. Sycor and Bandoff along with three other crewmembers completed their party; the women looked disoriented and worse for wear. She recognized one in particular, the one who had crawled all over Zorroc at the conference, the one they'd had the argument over. Terrific! She'd already begun devouring him with her eyes, smoothing her hair and licking her lips. Out of seventy-three women, why her?

She stood about the same height as Dee, Cat observed objectively, but while Dee's curves were courtesy of Mother Nature, Sandra's looked implanted. She dyed her hair a garish platinum blond and wore too much make-up, which had smeared, in proportion to her ordeal. Couldn't have happened to a nicer sleezette.

Had Zorroc chosen Sandra to accompany their party? He'd seemed very interested at the conference and had clearly changed his mind about joining with her. He'd fled their chamber with lightning quick finality. Maybe he'd chosen the loose shrew instead. Gee, newly awakened Sleeping Beauty stranded on a strange planet with her very own combination of Hans Solo and Chewbacca; what a perfect set up, and with the way she drooled over him, she wouldn't be hard to get either. Fine, she told herself, Sycor would suit her purposes just as well. He was cute, a bodyguard, and someone who could secure a weapon for her and teach her how to use it. Screw Zorroc, she sure wouldn't get the opportunity. She walked away and ignored him while they set up camp.

She spent the following hours worrying about Dee and Angel and where they had landed; she hoped it turned out better than this place because aside from the oxygen, it resembled hell, literally. With thoughts of her promise to Dee ricocheting through her brain, she approached Sycor. "Can I help you with anything, Sycor? I'm sure I could be useful." She never *had* learned how to flirt. Sycor looked unsure but not opposed to her advance.

"Everything is under control, Catarina, you should try to rest. The shelter over there is for your use, it will offer some relief from this heat."

She really did like him.

Zorroc wondered at his intended's mood as he worked to set up camp and appease the females. Sandra clung to him like a barnacle while he focused on Cat and Sycor with the same intensity that Sandra had fastened herself onto him.

"Sycor, I know you're busy just now but I have a favor to ask." She lowered her voice to a honey cream texture, Sycor's eyes widened. She moved closer and touched his arm. "I made a solemn vow to Dee that if we got separated, I'd be armed with a weapon and instructed on its usage. I've had extensive training with hand guns and lasers, so I'm sure I'd be a quick study."

The Gattonians seemed the type to be into vows. Certain she'd hit upon the right tact, she continued...only he looked slightly hunted. She took a step closer. "I'd hoped you could provide me with a weapon and instruct me." Looking straight into his horrified gaze. At the same time she registered his expression, she also noticed the air behind her had begun to churn. Sycor backed away mumbling about work and survival.

"May I be of assistance, Catarina," Zorroc challenged from behind her. He telepathed Sycor's demise if he came within four feet of his mate again. Sycor had received the message. Zorroc further messaged to get that she tornika, Sandra, off his back, permanently, by whatever means necessary. Sycor scrambled to intercept the problem before it could approach the couple.

"Excuse me, I think your witch went that-a-way, I'm busy just now." Cat took two steps before Zorroc threw her over his shoulder and escorted her to their shelter. She parked her bony elbow in his back while the palm of her hand cradled her chin; she didn't bother to comment or struggle.

The shelters had taken on the colors of the landscape making them almost impossible to detect by an enemy. He lowered her to the ground mat and secured the shelter opening. Cat looked around and noticed it was really quite spacious. Tall enough so Zorroc could stand up straight and move around; it resembled a large teepee. It was also noticeably cooler within. How did they manage that, Cat wondered idly while watching her cat man...put on another strip show? She couldn't take her eyes off him. His gaze bore into hers with concentrated thoroughness. Cat began to get nervous. "What are you doing Zorroc, practicing your technique for the wicked witch of the east?"

He stilled and tilted his head in the feline gesture native to his race then smiled and began to close in on her. "You are jealous, little Cat, it is unnecessary. The only interests I have are getting us safely to Gattonia and feasting on you. The feast will come first; you have run out of time to prepare. My aunts have assured me it is safe to take you and take you I will."

She realized with dawning clarity how perfectly his chiseled features matched his uncompromising manner, and with those twin axioms directed unflinchingly in her direction, she felt her will crumble under the force of his. He wanted her, he'd said; well, he could have what he wanted, but first she needed answers and assurance.

"We have issues to resolve Zorroc; for instance, how are you going to conduct your Dr. Jeckel/Mr. Hyde experiments now that your female rats are awake, or will it matter?" It proved almost impossible to concentrate with his scent and form sending her into sensory paradise. However, responsibility for the women rested solely with her and she wouldn't let them be further jeopardized—hell, they might not survive their current situation, come to think of it. Who attacked them, anyway? She just had too many questions and concerns with no definitive answers.

He read her guilt and distress concerning the women. Cat took too much responsibility for things completely beyond her control; he would ease her mind first and then her body. "There will be no experiments on the females; the serum perished with the ship. I doubt we would have tried it in any case; we were uncomfortable with that option. We will, therefore, implement our second plan. I will answer the remaining questions in your mind later, Catarina; right now I intend to address the ones your body has been asking of mine." Naked and hard, he advanced on her placing one hand on her upper thigh with fingers splayed; his thumb grazed the place between her legs. The other worked her hair free of the pins that had been unsuccessfully securing her unruly mane and massaged her scalp.

Cat gulped, striving to concentrate. "You tried to answer those questions once before but got cold feet and ran away. Why do you think this time will be different?" He began to undress her moving faster this time. He couldn't wait to enter her. She thought he would be too large to fit, even while she stared blatantly at his erection. Zazu, he hoped he didn't burst before he got in her.

"Your body will be well prepared, my cream, you can be certain of that. You can and will take all of me."

"Were you reading my mind or was the question in my eyes?"

He peeled her boots, socks, and jeans from her. "Yes," he smirked, easing her panties down, devouring her with a look. When he lifted her top over her head, her hair flew in all directions. She looked like a miniature Valkyrie, fierce and feminine...and she wore no bra. He had been focused on her breasts the entire day, wondering at the natural flow of their movement and their occasional budded peaks. When he laid her down, her hair flared around her in disarray, her skin glistened, creamy and warm to his touch, and her emerald eyes glowed with curiosity and anticipation—she wanted him. He spoke softly to her as he explained what would occur and what he would do to her. "In our previous lessons I touched you with my hands and you touched me with yours; now I will follow my hands with my mouth. You will be pleased."

He proceeded to demonstrate. His hands gently stroked her neck while his mouth seduced hers demanding entrance. How could a kiss be overpowering and entreating at the same time? Cat felt weightless and defenseless, willing to let him do anything to relieve the pressure building inside her. When she opened for him his tongue began to plunge into her mouth showing her his internal rhythm. His hands moved to her breasts that were large in proportion to rest of her body.

He massaged her globes then worked her nipples until they drew up into hard rosy buds he could not wait to taste. She groaned deep in her throat as he replaced a hand with his mouth, suckling and licking until she writhed helplessly. He told himself to proceed slowly; he wanted to make sure she stayed with him for every step of this dance. Leaving his hands on her breasts he began kissing and nipping her ribs and stomach slowly working toward her abdomen giving special attention to her belly button. Cat headed toward sensual overload; Zorroc read in her fevered mind.

"Not this time, Catarina, you will stay with me, do you understand?" When he mindspoke to her, she stilled. That cooled her off a little, Zorroc smiled to himself; let her concentrate on that for a while as he prepared her body for the taking. He moved slowly down her body while issuing instructions. "Bend your knees and spread your legs far apart, I am going to taste you, my cream." He put a pillow under her hips and spread her legs even further.

"Zorroc, please, I don't know what to do," she panted, wetting her lips in an unconscious gesture of pure sin.

She had a sheen of sweat coating every part of her. He nudged her nether lips apart exposing the nub nestled there and looked his fill, then his eyes raised and locked with hers. "Do not worry, it will come to you. Now I will pleasure us both." He put his mouth onto the entrance of her. His tongue licked her inside and out, feasting and sucking. She tasted like ambrosia and he was instantly addicted. Cat began to hitch and shake uncontrollably, grabbing onto the mat for stability. Then he began to purr into her, his tongue plunging rhythmically until she bucked straight up and emitted a long keening moan. Zorroc didn't halt his assault as she climaxed into his mouth. He lapped and drank as she continued to convulse.

It was too much; he had lost her again. It was better this way, he decided as he rose up and prepared to enter her, maybe she would not feel the pain of her hymen being perforated on his claiming. Above all things, he wanted her to never know pain from him. He plunged into her with one sure thrust; his mind reading hers to discern her level of discomfort but it continued in its foggy state. Waiting for her to come back to him before proceeding approached torture but he willed himself still. Filling and stretching her until he imagined his cock butting her womb, she cradled him in hot, wet euphoria. Sweat broke out on his brow; with all of his training and experience in the ways of pleasure; she made him feel like an untried youth. He nestled the pulse point on the side of her neck and she sighed. She reached to entwine her fingers with the hair on the back of his scalp and then closed her small hand into a tight fist trapping him for her kiss. Her other hand began a slow exploration of his shoulders, arm and back, reveling in the power of his body, compounded by his powerful reaction to her touch. She took the lead and began kissing, licking, and nipping him first on his lips then his cheeks, neck, and earlobe. Inwardly he groaned. He needed to take control or the deed would be finished before it had begun. He began to move.

"Is this uncomfortable for you?" he growled roughly, his control waning dangerously.

"Umm, more." Her reply unleashed the last bonds of his restraint. He began pumping faster and harder until he roared with the rightness of it. His self-control in shreds, he pummeled into her until her moans cascaded to a scream. He felt her convulsions milking him firmly and he followed her, putting his mouth onto the sensitive cord at the base of her neck and biting hard then licking the area to begin the healing process. She did not utter a peep; clearly out again. They would have to practice long and hard to keep her with him after her climax; he smiled and enfolded her firmly in anticipation. She belonged to him.

He rolled onto his back then drew her on top of him; a common Gattonian gesture of possession meant to provide comfort and warmth to their mate;

they slept. Later that night he took her again impaling her thoroughly, branding her, once again, as his—afterward falling into a deep contented sleep.

Cat remained awake and restless after their last bout of lovemaking. Her neck, while tender, proved nothing compared to the confusion she felt. She still hadn't gotten any answers on the fate planned for the women, or even her own for that matter. She had many issues to address with Zorroc, but every time she got within four feet of him, everything whizzed out of her head like ants fleeing insecticide.

She slid into her environ suit and exited their tent to take a quiet walk into the red desert. The horizon glowed like a built in night-light and it had cooled down to a comfortable tepidity. Cat far preferred this planet after dark she decided. She found a boulder and climbed onto it tracking the swirling sky...and finally relaxed. Zorroc had promised to answer her questions; she'd just have to keep her hands off him long enough to ask. She glanced down catching a movement out of the corner of her eye and froze. She didn't think anything alive existed here, what were they? They looked like a combination of a slug and a snake. Fat, slimy, and over ten feet long, they quickly multiplied, surrounding her—trapping her. Oh God, she was slug meat. No one was awake to help her and if she screamed it might be over before she could shout 'Slime me'.

She became more frightened by the second, and silently told Zorroc she loved him and apologized for leaving him this way. Everything crystallized in that moment; she loved him and wanted to have a real marriage complete with love, trust, lust, friendship, and even children. The giant slugs were closing in for the kill. She closed her eyes.

"Sycor, Bandoff! Weapons now, Cat is in

trouble." Zorroc had never known greater fear. Cat's abject terror had become his own; she would die if they could not reach her in time. Her horror fueled his own as he charged out of the tent and ran into the night. He located her almost immediately; she had not wandered far, but syphors surrounded her. Reliably, the deadliest scavengers in the universe; they ate anything alive. Varying atmospheres did not affect them so they could survive anywhere. All ships now had Syphor detectors to prevent infestation to other planets when it was discovered that was how they spread.

"Never have I seen so many Syphors, Zorroc, what do you propose, whatever it is it had best be fast, they are ready to attack," Sycor mind-thought to Zorroc. *"One would be enough to kill her,"* he added unnecessarily; they all knew the situation. The giant parasites had not sensed the Gattonians; too focused on their prey and unintelligent to sense danger.

"We will form a triangle around her and create a force field of protection then eliminate the slugs; watch your backs for more of them."

Before Zorroc had completed his orders, they moved into position and mind-merged a force field around Cat. Zorroc mind-thought to her that she was protected and safe but not to make any sudden moves, they were preparing to kill the Syphors and did not want her in the way. Cat focused on him as if it would be her last glimpse and silently nodded. The Syphors attacked en masse but could not break through the barrier. It did not take long to zap the slugs and when they finished, Bandoff messaged to the other two that this would keep them in fresh meat for weeks. Sycor yipped aloud when Zorroc mind-zapped him then moved in to snatch Cat from the boulder and sprint toward their tent.

Chapter Eight

"There he goes again, prowling the perimeter of the camp. Probably an excuse to get away from me," Dee uttered to herself, as she watched another couple enter a tent to copulate.

They should've been called bunnies instead of Gattonians. They'd been stranded for two days and that dwelling never seemed vacant. Their camp resembled a high tech Indian village. Most of the women had been delivered here along with the Gattonian crew. They camped by a large lake surrounded by mountains. It was quite beautiful, abounding with lush vegetation, fresh water, and clean air. She felt like a transplant into the Garden of Eden.

Teepees littered the entire area including a cooking station, med-facility and a group of five tents that acted as small procreation palaces for anyone who wanted to partake. Anyone except for her, of course. The women were acclimating extremely well to their situation; the Gattonians, tall, muscular, and hypnotically sexual, were very hard to resist. Some partnered with a particular male while others seemed to want to sample them all, and what a selection to choose from, not that she had been invited. The males all treated her like the plague. She shared quarters with Prolinc; their mats separated by at least six feet. He hadn't come near her and she questioned her desirability and non-existent appeal. To top it all, her highly arousing dreams blossomed steadily out of control until the line between fantasy and reality bled into one. Every night he came to her in her sleep with his deep rusty mane and mossy green gaze feasting on her with fervent abandon. Every morning she woke up soaked between her legs, alone.

Dee wondered why they even shared a tent; he obviously had zero interest in her. He'd probably been ordered to watch over her by Zorroc or more likely, Cat. The poor, hunky protector could have had any woman in the camp, but instead, ended up stuck with her. She hadn't seen him near the palaces yet, but supposed it was only a matter of time before he joined the legions of his fellow males.

She wandered down to the lake, to the cordoned off section reserved for the women. A cold bath was just what she needed most. She grabbed her soap, a change of clothes, and what passed for a towel. Although tiny, the five-inch square cloth dried her completely. She found the area deserted, for once, and looked forward to a long, cool soak. The women had each been provided with two garments. Each was one piece and resembled a cat suit that opened from the top; the Gattonians called them Environ-suits. The special material adjusted to varying temperatures and conditions similar to the tents and took on the colors of the immediate area; blending in with chameleon like precision. Matching Environ-boots completed the ensemble. Their culture did not approve of the physical restrictions caused by underwear. Every tent had what Dee thought of as a private dry cleaner—they really knew how to rough it.

She concentrated on the beauty of her surroundings as she stripped and sank into the soft cool water. Long reeds framed this section of the lake with occasional white fairy blossoms that dotted the waters edge. The lake sparkled a delightful golden shade clear to the bottom, showcasing a myriad of plants and sea life. At first, she just swam and then floated, enjoying the flow of motion over her body. After about ten minutes, she made her way to the shore, retrieved her soap, and began to loosen her braids. They fell in sunlit-ribbons down to her waist. It made up her one true vanity. Though much more practical in a shorter style, she couldn't make herself lop it off, so she kept it up and out of the way. It made her think of Cat and Angel, they had made a pact as children to keep their hair long like their favorite fairytale heroine, Rapunzel, and, so far, they all had. She hoped they would be together again soon, she felt stranded in this sea of strangers.

Prolinc had never seen her hair down, and the sight of her naked body with all of that hair caressing it proved impossibly erotic and, as a Gattonian, he was an expert on erotic. He smirked, watching her touch herself as she washed her hair, neck, breasts, and between her legs to which she gave special attention. He had been mesmerizing her for the past two nights and making love to her in every way imaginable until the early morning. In trance, she had been incredibly responsive but he wanted more from her, he wanted her to be alert when he next made love to her. He wanted her to know that it had all been real and that her body craved his just as his returned the favor. He made himself turn and leave so she could enjoy the remainder of her bath in privacy. His crew knew to avoid her; he had made his intentions very clear. She was his property.

One of the females glided toward him with purpose; Ava, he recalled vaguely. Though small in stature, she had a cap of raven black hair, blue eyes, and pert breasts. Her eyes held unmistakable humor as if she laughed at the world as well as herself most of the time.

"Hey big boy, you ready to try me out?" She was

one who preferred to pleasure many and not ashamed of her sexuality. He liked her but she did not hold his desire.

"I would move on to more fertile ground," Prolinc responded with a rare grin. "I see Zanan by the mating tents looking for someone to spend his break with, he is a good male, Ava, and worthy of your time and attention." Still grinning, he headed toward the edge of the camp to check with the on-duty crew concerning disturbances signaling a possible attack from the Dargons or others.

Dee witnessed the exchange and the Cheshire grin Prolinc wore as they parted company—Ava toward the palaces to instigate a come-on to the Gattonian waiting there and Prolinc toward the perimeter of camp. Had they planned to meet later?

She'd made Angel and Cat promise to be armed; the time had come to follow her own orders. Maybe it would take her mind off sex for a while. She approached Sark, a high-ranking guard, and excellent marksman. "Sark, I need your help, if you have a moment." She smiled and moved closer. "I need a weapons lesson. I'm a former police officer and a detective and could be valuable if we run into trouble." *And so far trouble followed these guys around like a friendly puppy.* "I hoped you could demonstrate the use of your side arm and find one for me."

Sark looked astounded for a moment and then lost all expression. "Prolinc will instruct you should he deem it necessary." Then turned and stalked away.

Dee cursed a blue streak; incensed and confused. What was wrong with her? They treated her like day old vermin. She turned and bumped smack into Prolinc. "Why did you approach Sark?" His grin conspicuously absent.

"I need a weapons lesson and since you refuse to

get within six feet of me, I thought Sark would instruct me. Obviously, I miscalculated. What is it, have I contracted some dreaded disease? No one will have anything to do with me, including you." She stormed to their tent and collapsed onto her mat. What was happening, she hadn't cried since she turned eight.

"I will instruct you, Dee, you had but to ask." Having followed close on her heals, he now observed her curiously, tilting his head in a Gattonian way. What did she expect of him, he wondered fixedly. He had been working hard to develop a less volatile atmosphere between them. He needed to secure her trust and from there, her surrender but whenever he approached she threw up her shields. One moment she cast a wall of fire against him and the next a frigid gorge longer than the ice province of Arctica. He had yet to find a way around her barriers to her trust-center.

He had strategized that a combination of acquainting her body with his at night through trancing, coupled with a non-threatening distance between them during the day would draw her to him. Could he have miscalculated? As a supreme tactician, that did not seem likely. Her compliance to lay with him was essential to his plan of making her his chosen one. He wanted her to crave him like a drug, for the role of chosen one would be difficult for her to swallow with her overabundance of pride.

"Get a grip," Dee moaned as she rose wiping her eyes subtly and told him she would like a lesson at that time, if convenient for him. He gently took her hand and led her beyond the perimeter they had set up for camp and explained the use and inner workings of their firearms.

They worked from energy similar to Earth's solar power. They never ran out of juice or charges as Prolinc explained. Light, smooth and exacting,

Dee had no problem figuring distance and accuracy. Prolinc was amazed at her proficiency but did not tell her what a rare skill she had mastered in such a short time. She would put many of his crew to shame with her precision and reflexes. He had not realized what an aphrodisiac her skill and ease with his weapon would prove. He wanted to take her right there, in the meadow, well away from the camp. He began to advance. Dee noticed a decided change in the atmosphere and looked into Prolinc's eyes. His usually shuttered, unreadable gaze had changed to one of piercing hunger, directed unflinchingly at her; she licked her suddenly dry lips.

"Time to get back to camp, I suppose, we'll be missed before too long," she suggested uncertainly.

Since the very first, Dee had wanted nothing more than to wrap her small hands around his huge, corded neck and strangle the living daylights out of him, never had she felt such an overwhelming reaction to another human being. Now she saw her reaction for what it was; she wanted him worse than a starving man craved a Whopper. Maybe she could lure him to their tent, if the message in his flaming cat-eyes signaled what she hoped.

He smiled and shook his head slowly. He reached up and began dislodging her braids. After her hair hung completely free, he started on her pantsuit unfastening the top and slowly drawing it down over her body. He watched for signs of reluctance from her but all he saw was his own blatant hunger reflected back at him in her stormy sky gray eyes.

He smiled; she wanted him.

He had taken her repeatedly every night since they set up camp but it had been pitch dark in their tent; therefore, he had not seen her naked body until earlier at the lake. To see his dark hands cover her soft, flesh and watch her body respond to his touch, boiled his blood to flashpoint. Every lush curve, mysterious hollow and graceful line proclaimed her a masterpiece; her scent made him harden instantly as his nostrils flared to take more of her essence. He stared markedly at her deep golden complexion, an ideal compliment to her cascading wheat colored hair...as she flushed a rosy hue from her chest up; he froze, mesmerized. He had embarrassed her with his bold appraisal. He leered and continued devouring her in frank appreciation while he finished stripping her of her suit.

When she stood naked in front of him, he began to shed his own clothing. She swatted his hands away and took over. Her hands flowed over him in a smooth cadence of desire and need. The light caught her hair, setting it ablaze. *His blaze.* Her hands proceeded down his body, followed by her eyes until they found his erection. He bulged formatively; she knelt down so her mouth was parallel with his tool and took an experimental lick. He jerked at the contact and she moved in for more, moaning her pleasure. She couldn't get her mouth around all of him so she licked, sucked and kissed, stroking him with one hand, holding him in place with the other at the base of one buttock. Prolinc, equal parts enraptured and horrified, stood on the precipice of spewing right into her mouth; he tried halfheartedly to disengage her and then held her to him as he erupted violently into the strongest orgasm he could recall.

Prolinc, who had always prided himself on his control, had used his intended chosen one like a common whore. He sunk to his knees in front of her, not sure of how to apologize for his disrespect and lack of reserve, but when he saw her licking her lips and caught the wicked gleam in her eyes, he attacked instead. She gave a surprised yelp as he knocked her back onto the soft fragrant ground and proceeded to torture her with his body, hands, lips, and teeth. He rubbed against her like a cat in heat while his hands fondled her breasts and mound, his talented fingers separating her and then playing on her nub and swollen labia before teasing one finger and then two inside her. His mouth fused with hers and his tongue massaged hers in the tempo to come. Hard as granite once again, this time he would explode into a different orifice.

She grabbed his mane on either side of his head and feasted on him as eagerly as he covered her. She was more than ready, he gloated; it was time.

So focused on their love play, he at first thought the ringing in his ears signaled intense desire, but when the siren increased in volume, he jumped to his feet in one motion and grabbed his uniform. "We are under attack," he rasped, "hurry, and dress."

Dee stared at him, dumbfounded for a couple of seconds until her brain ignited; then she scrambled into her clothes and boots. "Trouble again," she swore to the breeze. "I want a weapon, Prolinc," she shouted after his retreating form.

She arrived at the camp greeted with barely constrained chaos. Scattering like mice, some ran toward the reeds by the lake while others headed toward the hills. The remainder ran hell bent for a group of boulders about a hundred yards to the left of base camp. She felt like a deserted rat that had missed the last life raft and when she glanced up, she knew she'd pegged it right. Some sort of monster had her in its sights, barreling toward her too fast for her to react. At the last possible moment, it exploded, coating her with debris and liquid that smelled worse than anything in her experience. Next, she was tackled and thrown up over someone's shoulder that moved like lightning toward the boulders, when they reached cover; he placed her carefully on the ground. She landed flat on her back only to look up and focus on Prolinc's ferocious molten green orbs. She smiled wickedly. "Got a gun?"

****

Back in their mutely lit environ tent, Zorroc gently eased Cat onto his lap as he sunk into the long seat. He did not know who emerged more horrified of the two of them. She had come so close to dying his mind could not caption it. The Syphors first bite their prey injecting an agent to paralyze their muscles and nervous system; it works instantly but not immediately-lethal. They preferred warm living organisms to dead meat allowing them plenty of time to suck and devour their quarry. Zorroc, locked within the terror of his imagination, did not hear Cat's query.

"Zorroc, you spoke to me inside my head, didn't you?" she repeated tentatively, trying to fight down her panic.

"Yes," he replied hoarsely, striving to couch an answer in a manner that would not further traumatize her. "We call it mindspeaking, messaging or telepathing; our race has had the capability for centuries though some of our people are much stronger than others." He focused on her, knowing what her next question would be.

"If you can send me messages, can you also read the answer?" She scrutinized him closely as if seeing him for the first time. Had he read her mind from the very first? The thought dawned too demoralizing to contemplate. Shit and shinola, where was a good hole when you needed one?

"I can't read you all the time, my one. You sent me a message while crouched on that rock and I received it; I knew you would die if I could not reach you. I mindspoke Sycor and Bandoff to assist me."

"We mind-melded a force field around you so the Syphors could not hurt you while we dealt with

111

them. It is a fairly rare skill even for our race and those so gifted usually become protectors or bodyguards."

If he expected that to take her mind off his ability to read her mind he had another thing coming. She slid off his lap to face him. She smoldered, definitely on a precipice, and knew what lurked beyond. "Can the others read us too?"

The question caught him off guard and he started, "No, it is a Gattonian trait, we can only read and mindspeak to other Gattonians and none of my crew has the ability to read you, you have only exposed yourself to me." He winced slightly at his clumsy wording.

She began to pace around the room her hands either clasped to her head or fisted at her sides. He had stilled. This made no sense Cat thought frantically. He could read her mind and send messages to her telepathically, the Gattonians could communicate with each other but not with the women and not with her. Zorroc could read her but not the other women—she was losing it. Was he lying? Could the Gattonians mind read everyone but didn't want to tell her for fear she'd be even more humiliated and incensed and possibly spread the word? She didn't think Zorroc had lied to her before, left pertinent information out, sure, but an outright lie? She didn't think so. So what did that leave? He could communicate with her telepathically and could read her mind sometimes; how much had he read, how much did he know about her? The air around her began to crackle. Could that be the reason he stayed two steps ahead of her and knew what she planned even before she did?

"You say it's strictly a Gattonian trait, but I'm only part Gattonian."

"More than half," he corrected.

She waved her hand through the air as if to

brush away his distinction. "If everything you've told me is true; how is it you can read me? And why can't I do the same with you?" Trying to divine the truth or lie behind his words.

"That is a question I have no answer for. I am a strong telepath but not so strong as Prolinc, and yet he cannot read you at all. There is a bond between us, my Cat, a truth you can no longer dispute."

She glared at him and demanded, "What am I thinking now!" *You snoopy, officious, bossy, conceited, oaf*—she faced him head-on.

He smiled at her and shrugged. "I do not have a clue. You are too upset for anything to come through."

He knew exactly what she was thinking and he sure did not have to mind-probe her to know it.

She pounded her dainty foot on the ground and presented him with her most effective drop-dead, cut him off at the knees, scowl. "I'm going to bed," she growled. "Alone!" The staccato screech loud enough to make him jump.

Cat marched to her mat, climbed in, and gave him one last dirty look that dared him to approach her, before rolling over and playing dead. He thought that, in general, their talk had gone rather well; she would cool off and forgive him; he would leave her no alternative.

He turned to his mat thinking it had been a very long night. Sycor had reported that afternoon that a mother ship was in transit to their location and would COM them when they reached a good pivot point to the three planets. It could not be too soon for him, he would be better able to protect his mate on Ganz than on some red devil planet. There existed no end to the dangers Cat could find when left to her own devices. Maybe he would tether her to him while they slept to keep her from wandering into disaster, not that he would be sleeping any time soon. Zazu, she had scared fifteen years from his life when he had read her fear.

****

They entered the tent and surrounded her. She felt the first sting just below her ankle and felt it go numb, spreading up her leg to her stomach and beyond. They advanced, crawling on her, sliming her with their sticky coating as they commenced chewing on her legs and shoulder. They gnawed and sucked, eating her alive and she couldn't move, couldn't scream; couldn't even close her eyes. The one eating at her shoulder moved up to her face and after giving her what looked to be a malevolent smirk, closed in to start feeding on her face. Oh God, she could see the constantly moving suckers lining its mouth, moving onto her eye and—

"Stop it Catarina, you are having a nightmare, wake up, wake up now," Zorroc shouted both aloud and into her mind.

She gasped for air and threw herself into Zorroc panting and drenched with sweat. She'd been so sure it was really happening. She looked around tentatively to reassure herself they were not there, frightened that maybe this was the dream and they were still devouring her.

"No, my one, you are with me and safe; be calm, when you become more alert you will see it was just a terrible dream. I would not let them have you, Cat. I came for you the first time and I will always come." He began stroking and kissing her as one would a frightened child. He lay with her on top of him and petted her back to sleep. For the flash of an instant, he thought they really had her. He closed his eyes trying to block the vision.

They remained entwined until late the next morning when word arrived of the attack on Zeba II, the planet that sheltered most of his crew and the women. Sycor stood over Zorroc with a frustrated, hopelessly vexed look on his face. He had been trying to shake him awake. Zorroc opened his eyes and mindspoke that he could have just messaged him; his physical presence was not required nor appreciated. Sycor messaged back that he had been doing just that the moment they received the message with no response. Zorroc grunted, eased off the mat naked and commenced dressing. Sycor noticed the bite on Cat's neck and smirked, all was going according to plan.

Reading his thoughts Zorroc growled, *"Take your eyes off of her, Sycor."*

Sycor's head shot up briefly meeting Zorroc's deadly stare then exited mumbling that he would await him outside.

Sycor and Bandoff conversed together quietly as Zorroc approached. "What is the situation," he asked gruffly.

"The message was brief; the Dargons are attacking by air, using exploders so they can target specific people. It seems they are trying to pick off the crew, leaving the women unharmed. Kidnapping seems the likely motive."

"Do we have enough power to trans over, Sycor? The women will not last thirty minutes under Dargon care." Zorroc began reviewing options in his head. They could not leave the women on Zeba II unprotected but the Dargons may have pinpointed the location of their party, as well, which could leave Catarina and the others at risk; bringing them into the battle, however, seemed equally as repugnant. Cat had to be protected at all costs; she could be carrying the next leader of Gattonia.

"We have enough if we leave the supplies behind, it is our only option, Zorroc, no matter the risks; the women must be kept safe," Sycor stated, glancing past him as Cat emerged from the tent, watching the three curiously.

"We may be the difference between their safety and their death, we are among the strongest telepaths and marksmen on this mission, barring Prolinc. It is our only choice," Bandoff proffered, dipping his head in the Gattonian gesture indicating deference. Though unaccustomed to voicing his thoughts, the COM he intercepted minutes before, sufficiently prodded him into speaking his opinion. They had to save the women at all costs. He glanced at Zorroc and knew he saw the truth of it. Zorroc turned and focused hard on Cat, told the other two to prepare the women, and headed toward those emerald eyes darting questions at him.

"Our enemies, the Dargons, have found our party on Zeba II, Prolinc and Dee are among them. We are preparing to trans everyone over as soon as possible; they need assistance." He put his hands on her shoulders and began to massage her gently, messaging that everything would work out to their favor. Gattonians were excellent warriors. Suddenly, Cat stiffened to her full 5'3", grabbed him by his uniform, and started issuing demands.

"I'm not going anywhere without a weapons lesson. If I show up not knowing how to use one, these Dargon creatures will never get a shot at me; Dee will kill me first; and who are these erasers and what do they want with us. This is not some random little happening; these guys are rabid for your hides. What have you gotten us into? You can start explaining while you take me for a little target practice; this is not open to negotiation, Zorroc, so get that determined look off your face right now." She stared him down, daring him to ignore her wishes this time. If the situation were not so serious, her fierceness would have amused him.

He sighed. "The weapons are difficult to master, Catarina, I could not teach you in time." He actually looked sorry he could not comply with her request.

"The Dargons are our enemies. They are destroyers of worlds; it is their sole purpose, so far as we can determine. They want Gattonia and eventually all of Ganz. We have been the recipient of their tactics for two of your Earth years." He closed his eyes in tired anguish and concluded. *"The virus that attacked our females was infused into our atmosphere by the Dargons; their latest contribution to viral warfare. It attacks a female's reproductive organs...sterilization, its most far reaching though not worst side-effect."* He could not bear the growing confusion and denial clearly reflected in her wide, innocent eyes yet he continued, deciding to deliver the blow in one Herculean implosion.

"We have mated with your species for centuries as you know and have produced many offspring with you. Your planet, in addition, has been polluted with many varying viral strains over time and the impact on child bearing and birth defects seem to have had a minimal effect on your species. Your immune systems are able to handle these poisons much more efficiently than our own since Ganz has been free of pollutants and sickness for many centuries. The tests we have conducted on your environment, though not conclusive, suggest that your bodies could successfully fight off the virus. These two factors of compatibility and evolutionary adjustments to disease make the women of Earth ideal for our purposes. And that, my little Cat, is the short version of what has brought us to this juncture." He gave her a half smile of self-loathing and messaged his understanding that he had most likely damaged any chance of her future regard.

Several moments passed while Cat studied Zorroc and then one side of her mouth kicked up into a rueful grin. "So much for clean air."

Zorroc drew his hand down his face. He would never understand the female mind.

"A weapons lesson, Zorroc, it's the least you owe me." He gave her a measured, defeated look, drew his weapon, and instructed her for the next ten minutes.

Chapter Nine

They arrived into an area surrounded by boulders, the women gathered in the center, in prone position, while the Gattonians lined the perimeter, guarding the females and shooting at the enemy. Dee, of course, had weapon in hand, causing a good bit of damage from what Cat could observe until she saw her and jumped up to grip her friend in a fierce hug. "Thank God you're safe. I was worried despite Prolinc's assurances. Did you get a weapons lesson, we could use the help."

"Damn Dee, you stink, what did you do, soak in a pool of dung?"

"I got coated with Dargon innards, it's a long story but right now we need to destroy these giant dragon flies. Grab a weapon and let's get to it, you *do* know how to use one of these don't you?"

"I've got it covered, sort of," the last uttered under her breath, as she spotted a small cache of unused blazers protected by a clump of rocks. Cat dove for one, positioned herself next to Dee, and proceeded to practice what Zorroc had demonstrated only a few moments before. It took a little time to master the intricacies of aim, weight, and balance but eventually she succeeded in hitting her targets more often than not.

"Wow, these guys look like flying Gorns from that Star Trek episode, don't they? Remember the one where Kirk gets stranded on a strange planet with this large, ugly, scaly creature and they have to fight it out only Kirk won't kill him?"

"You truly are certifiable Cat, shut-up, aim, and

fire," Dee stated with suppressed humor. Cat never failed to lighten the worst situation; they'd been under attack for close to two hours and things had been looking pretty bleak, but with the added firepower and her friend beside her, her energy returned.

"So, how's the explosive duo making-out, has he bludgeoned down your door and crawled into the honey pot yet?" Cat teased as she squeezed off another charge. Cat watched Dee blush and scowl while Prolinc glanced over and leered his best cat smile to let her know he had overheard and understood.

Dee decided to get a little of her own back and inquired sweetly, "Who's been chewing on your neck, Cat, is your kitty really a wolf in cat's clothing?"

"As you can see, my cat man has been doing some bludgeoning of his own," she tossed back, inordinately pleased with herself as she popped another Dargon out of the sky.

The revelations leveled by Zorroc answered many of Cat's questions concerning his position and responsibility and how they had landed in their current predicament. He obviously had been charged with the task of saving his race, an awesome and nearly impossible feat. It reassured, rather than discouraged her that Zorroc had been the one chosen with the duty of balancing the women's safety and welfare against his obligation to his people. The two must seem diametrically opposed, at times. No wonder he emanated both unrelenting control and weary resignation. What an overwhelming challenge for one so relatively young. It probably explained why, sometimes, he looked the picture of autocratic superiority, and at others, more like an angry panther, trapped in a cage.

Zorroc witnessed Cat's talent at weaponry and cursed himself for being an arrogant fool. He should have known her declaration of arms use would prove no idle boast. His woman was no ordinary female; he would have to acclimate himself to her way of expressing herself and take nothing at face value. She looked totally at ease with their situation as if she had been a part of his world, and life forever. She was an odd mixture of vulnerability and resiliency and his heart squeezed with unfamiliar tenderness and another emotion he could not name. She did not look defeated by his confession; in truth, she acted relieved. Would he ever understand this female?

One heated gaze followed Zorroc's every move. So far, Sandra had been totally thwarted in her efforts to seduce Zorroc. The other cat men had been easy enough to control, giving her their full attention again and again; why not him? How could she steal his attention from that little bitch? They appeared glued at the hip but there had to be some way to separate them. She'd overheard a conversation between two of the crewmembers and learned that Zorroc wielded a lot of power among his people; if she had to be permanently stuck on some God forsaken planet, she intended to do it first class.

Her mother had dragged her to every charm school and beauty pageant to groom her little girl for the life of leisure they both craved. Sandra counted herself an expert at reclining her way to the top, using any means at her disposal to fulfill her appetence. The Gattonians served as interchangeable widgets to use for her pleasure or to do her bidding. Her mother couldn't help her here, but she'd have no difficulty arranging things to her satisfaction. Obviously, these flying monsters had no interest in harming the women; they steered unerringly clear of them and instead concentrated on the Gattonians. Having Zorroc rescue a damsel in distress would suit her purposes very well.

Sandra knew what it took to dominate men; their larger brain resided below their waist and it fell to her to lead them by it.

Timing was everything, she told herself as she scanned Zorroc's location and her surroundings, looking for the right time to act. She waited until the last possible moment then ran screaming from the protective circle, catching Zorroc's eye in the process. She wanted it to look as if she'd panicked, and she got the exact result she had counted on. He surged after her, tackling her some ten feet from the boulders protecting her body with his.

The Dargons reacted quickly trying to pick Zorroc off and grab the female. Suddenly Cat appeared, standing over them guarding their backs.

As one came straight for them, she braced herself for a precise hit when another surprised her, snatching her from behind. Cat and the Dargon rose quickly heading away from the melee. She looked down to see Zorroc neutralize the other Dargon.

She aimed her weapon at her captor's head. "Land now and get your dinky little arms off me or I'll blow your snout off, buster," she bluffed. He snorted and knocked the blazer out of her hand. If she'd taken him out, the fall would almost certainly have killed her and he knew it. She'd have to bide her time. An absurd thought struck her; the scene below looked a lot like the flying monster monkeys that grabbed Dorothy in the Wizard of Oz.

"Catarina, look around and get your bearings, you have to tell me where they are taking you; stay calm and think clearly," Zorroc broke into her thoughts. He gnashed his teeth in frustration. He had to let her go; it was too dangerous to fire. What had the little fool been thinking; could she not stay out of trouble for one moment? Every time he let her out of his sight, she charged hell bent into another disaster. Why could she not just stay where he put

her? When he got her back, he would give her an obedience lesson in...well, obedience; he would train her to never endanger herself or disobey his wishes in the future.

She had risked her life to protect him; she truly was mind-blasted. He had kidnapped her, practically forced her compliance, set her up to enable him to kidnap her two best friends along with seventy some other females, put her life in jeopardy on more than one occasion; and how did she repay him? She would die for him.

Zorroc grabbed Sandra and sprinted back to the group shouting orders for Prolinc and Sycor to follow him. He dumped Sandra unceremoniously on the ground, barely sparing her a look of unveiled disgust.

"What weapons do we have on the Pods that may be of use to end this quickly?" Zorroc asked, his fear for Cat growing with each second.

"We should have known that she-devil would pull something like this, you should have let her go, Zorroc, she would have caused more damage to the Dargons than any weapon in our arsenal," Sycor spat caustically. The woman had acid for blood; Sycor had seen through her from the first and felt dirty that he had lain with her, directive or no directive.

Prolinc had always admired Sycor for his easy, relaxed manner with everyone, especially females, so it surprised him greatly to hear Sycor's scathing vehemence toward Sandra. "She just panicked, Sycor, it happens. I'm sure she feels badly that her actions caused this situation."

"All that woman has wanted from the beginning is to get her claws into Zorroc, and the only thing preventing that, to her way of thinking, has been Catarina. I am sure she could not have known Cat would be taken because of her actions but I am equally as sure she does not feel badly about it," Sycor persisted then turned to Zorroc and detailed the munitions available.

"The Launcher is the most effective tool to end this, however, it contains but one charge and once deployed we will be vulnerable should future conflict persist or strengthen," Prolinc stated.

"We will deal with that problem when it occurs. Sycor, get to the Pod and fire at will, I want those Dargons blasted into Hades. Afterwards, we will meet to discuss how to rescue my loco little flame." Zorroc turned and commenced firing with ruthless determination while Sycor ran for the hidden Pod. Prolinc returned to his place beside Dee to fill her in on their plan and assist with Sycor's cover.

It had not gone according to plan, Sandra acknowledged. That stupid little bitch had tagged along after them and gotten herself kidnapped. Cat always managed to get in her way. And then she smiled; believing the chances better than average that after the flying monsters finished playing with her, death would follow. An unforeseen benefit lay inherent in every situation, after all, and she deserved the break. Sandra had tried her best to look contrite and helpless giving Zorroc her best pout but he'd turned away before he could appreciate the full effect.

Dee approached Zorroc and softly asked, "What will they do to her, Zorroc, will they harm her, eat her, use her?" He looked into Dee's worried, almost frantic eyes and wished he could give her a better answer.

"I do not know Dee but we are linked together with our minds and she is tracking where they are taking her so we can rescue her."

"Jesus Zorroc, you're talking about the most directionally challenged female on Earth, she gets lost absolutely everywhere she goes, you'd better come up with a better plan, bud, or she'll be lost to us forever." She shook her head, taking her place next to Prolinc adding her firepower to his in an effort to veil Sycor's coming surprise.

Cat and her stinky captor traversed some mountains, and a sun, or moon, or whatever it was, that appeared to her left. The Dargon had her in a vice like grip leaving her free to glance around at the passing terrain and mindspeak it back to Zorroc.

"You are doing just fine, sweet one, Dee told me your sense of direction is not the best so do not worry about north or south just concentrate on landmarks and distance."

Cat had the urge to laugh at the bizarreness of his statement. North and south remained foreign concepts to her in Nashville, what would make him think she could figure it out on this, three mooned, yellow-skied bewilderness. *"We're coming down on the other side of the mountain and heading toward a clearing surrounded by massive trees on three sides. The trees are tall enough to stand out from the rest of the area; it should make a decent landmark. We have been traveling very fast, Zorroc, I can't tell how far— and tell Dee to stop spreading those vicious tales about me. We've landed, there is a cave built into the side of the mountain and fairly well hidden by the trees and brush. Tell me you got all that,"* she concluded while being escorted, in a rather courtly fashion, to a cavernous room.

A platform built into the side of one wall the size of a queen size bed, took up one side of the room while a ledge that could pass for a table, protruded from the opposite wall. Zorroc mindspoke that he had received her message and would let her know when they were ready to come collect her.

"What is your name, child?" the Dargon inquired politely. These female Earth creatures, Gorn assessed, were puny, weak and odorless beings, not worth their notice under ordinary circumstances, but if this favor would ensure the acquisition of Gattonia for them, it would be a small enough price to pay.

His English sounded guttural and not easy to understand but it surprised her that he spoke it at all. "How do you come to speak English?" Cat wanted to know, decidedly reluctant to identify herself. She needed to assess her situation before co-operating with this ugly, stinky cross between a rhinoceros and dragon. At about ten feet tall, three feet wide and covered with brownish-black large slimy scales, he took up most the room and emitted a nauseating stench. His legs and feet, close to the same circumference, looked like sawed off tree trunks. His wings were large, extending from his shoulders to the ground when he had them closed, as they were now. His arms, skinnier and shorter than Zorroc's, looked out of proportion with the rest of his body. His face, she noted, only a mother could stomach, or another Dargon. He had a snout that took up most of his face and beady little eyes that examined her as closely as she scrutinized him.

"We Dargons are not barbarians, we are familiar with many languages, English being one. Now I would have your name if you please."

Well, he was polite, she'd give him that, but why did he care about her name? Zorroc messaged not to divulge her identity, and told her the other Dargons had started back her way and he would follow shortly with a team to retrieve her.

"Gertrude," Cat stated openly while pretending to observe her environment, "but my friends call me Gerty." She finished with a glowing smile.

"That is unfortunate, we search for another," he responded, giving her a calculated look and a grimace that she assumed was supposed to pass for a smile.

"What's her name, maybe I know her," she

inquired, wondering how they knew the names of any of the women and why they were looking for one of them.

"It is not important for you to know the one we seek," the rhino-roach told her as he shuffled toward the opening.

Gorn snorted in disgust. The female, overly brash and insubstantial, would, no doubt, split apart on his first thrust. There would be short-lived pleasure from her, he snorted. They would find the one they sought, when the others returned with the rest of the females. Gattonians were no match for the powerful Dargons.

"Wait," she called too loudly, "I gave you my name, what's yours?"

He paused, turned, and stared at her with one beady eye. "I am called Gorn."

Cat choked and sputtered hoping to disguise her laughter. "Oh...well...thank you," she ended, positive he would not see the humor his name evoked. He turned back to her a second time and stared, before turning and securing the door behind him.

Alone at last, she wondered how long it'd take for the stench to dissipate. She sat on the platform surface and began, what she assumed, would be a long wait. She hoped they were vegetarians.

Of all the names in the universe, he had to be called Gorn, what were the odds on that, she wondered idly, trying to keep her fear under control. What a bizarre set of weeks it had been; this constituted the first moment she had to reflect on all that had transpired. Her thoughts drifted to Angel and the aunts, wondering how they fared. It still hurt that her parents had set her up to be kidnapped and mated. She touched the side of her neck for the bite mark Zorroc had left; it would be a permanent reminder of the first time she made love. He'd branded her his by more than just the mark though; he'd employed touches and words and deeds as well. He'd infused her being like a drug and it had taken a surprisingly short time for her to become addicted. She wondered if he suffered the same as she. After all, one good addiction certainly deserved another. She wanted nothing so much as to feel him inside her again, penetrating her with his warmth and strength. She hadn't had a prayer from the beginning; snared in this unbreakable net of love and desire. Sometimes he seemed just as smitten but it was difficult for her to gage; he could turn it off so quickly she wondered if it wasn't just a role he played to amuse himself.

She was, after all, just a pawn in the game of 'Can This Race Be Saved'. She couldn't kid herself that he would have even looked at her if not for her Gattonian blood. What a terrible reason to be wanted. Now she knew what it felt like to be in an arranged marriage. It wouldn't matter if he was attracted to her or not, he'd force himself, and her, to tangle as frequently as necessary in order to provide heirs. And as she'd learned, he took his responsibilities very seriously. She just hoped she counted as one of them, surveying the cold darkening den. Would it really matter to him if she didn't survive or would he simply consider it a minor inconvenience and move on to Sandra?

She was doing it again, Zorroc noted with severe frustration—she was thinking! He sat in a meeting to determine the best way to extricate Cat from the Dargons but it proved hard for him to concentrate with her little female brain zinging at lightning speed to all the wrong conclusions. Zazu, they were mated; he could not get more committed than that. He had no understanding of the dianetics of love but certainly had a close acquaintance with its destructive after effects. He only had to point to his father. She had his protection, infinitely better than love and safer for both of them. Of course, if she thought she loved him, she would be easier to control; people in love did all sorts of stupid things they would not normally consider in order to please their mate. Maybe he would encourage this love of hers. He could not, however, acknowledge how her love affected him; that it filled a gaping hole within him and made him warm inside, that he felt whole when he held her closely to him.

"Zorroc, your attention please," Prolinc demanded for the third time.

"He has been doing that a lot lately," Sycor supplied helpfully, "I think he is becoming obsessed with his crazy little flame and his lower region."

Zorroc snarled at Sycor and then gave his full attention to Prolinc. "The safest and surest way to get her out safely would be to pod over and transhift her out once we are sure of her location; did you put a locator on her?"

"Yes, it is in her suit, she should be easy to detect once we get close enough. Will the Dargons be able to identify our presence? It will be dangerous to take her while under attack." Zorroc silently thanked Zazu for his foresight in bugging her environ suit and prayed that she still resided in it when they reached her.

"One of our Pods has cloaking features, we will un-cloak only for the short time it takes to bring her aboard," Prolinc responded. "Can you still read her, we need to be sure that she is prepared and preferably alone. I hope that we can be on our way before they realize she is missing which brings us to the next problem. They know our location and will surely retaliate, but this time they will be very angry to have lost their prey. There is not time to both move the camp and get to Catarina, what are your orders." Prolinc finished looking grim.

"We received a COM while Zorroc was staging his daring rescue of the fair Sandra," Sycor volunteered with a perfectly straight face. Sandra was becoming a tiresome obligation among the men for her blatant availability and tireless pursuit of Zorroc. "They are very close, ETA in two point five hours, they may be able to aid us with Cat's rescue, but in any event the rest of our party will not have long to wait for assistance."

"They will probably be able to pinpoint our location easily with the explosive fire ball you threw at the Dargon party. I have never seen the Launcher in action at such close range; those who were not blown away went flying. It presented a very satisfying sight; you have my compliments, Sycor. Now let us prepare to leave. Prolinc, pick four of your finest; the rest will remain to defend the camp until the ship arrives, which one is due to arrive, Sycor?"

"The Miramid with Commander Rosik in charge." Sycor announced, satisfactorily. Rosik, known for his ruthless tactics in battle, particularly hated Dargons. They wiped out his entire family in their initial attack.

Zorroc grinned openly and stood. "Meet me out front in five minutes." Zorroc headed for his quarters grateful that the time had come to liberate his property and get her safely back where she belonged.

Hold on, Catarina, we are coming, he mindspoke, moving quickly to prepare for departure. Nothing, she was not there, Zazu, they needed to hurry.

Dee cornered Prolinc when he exited the tent, determined to be in on the rescue of her friend as well as back up for Prolinc, but before she could present her case, he grabbed her around her waist and kissed her hard to keep her from speaking. He had noted her determination and resoluteness; he had seen it chiseled plainly in her slate gray eyes. His choice was made; he had been toying with the idea of having her in their party—she was a fierce warrior and an excellent marksman but in a moment of rare introspection, he knew it had more to do with wanting her with him; needing to protect her. He ended the kiss and told her she would be among the team leaving directly to retrieve her friend. Her stormy eyes cleared to crystal silver as they headed toward the Pod. He cared deeply for this impossible Earth female.

Cat knew she had scant moments before losing all semblance of control, caught between hilarity and horror at the scene unfolding before her. Gorn had returned dressed in a cape and a knife and nothing else. God, she thought they defined ugly and smelly before—someone needed to introduce these guys to soap and water, and the way he pounded around spreading his scent wasn't helping either. He looked like an ungainly, upside-down tree trunk flapping his wings and twiggy arms in time to his elephant feet hitting the ground. The whole place shook. This could not be good she realized; in performing the ritual dance, his bobbing appendage had increased to immense proportions. Either he was getting turned-on at the prospect of killing her or he wanted her body for some other purpose. She had a feeling it might involve the later. Finally, he stopped in front of her, as if waiting for some response. Oh, double poop popsicles. What could she do to disarm him and make him go away without killing her or worse? She would not live through either experience; the spike between his legs had grown to the size of her thigh. It was now or never. She jumped to her feet, clapping wildly. "Brilliant, what a performance!" she shouted loudly, making all the noise she could. "Rousing simply rousing." *Dear fairy godmother; now would be an excellent time for a miracle. Zorroc, are you out there?*

If a Dargon could look surprised, this guy looked dumbstruck, clearly at a loss as to how to proceed. And to top it off he looked embarrassed...as well he should with a technique like his. He exited the cave with his cape flying behind him; she would not have believed a being could move that fast on tree trunks.

She prayed he would not be back.

"Zorroc, get me out of here, this guy is getting amorous!" she mind-thought, hoping she wasn't too panicked for him to understand her predicament.

"Catarina, you are almost impossible to read, calm yourself and think clearly, you have been unreadable for some time now, have they hurt you?" he demanded, reverberating in her mind, deafeningly.

"I've got her Prolinc, but she is in trouble, we have to hurry or it will be too late; is her signal on screen, yet?" He glanced over Prolinc's shoulder to get a first hand look at the too quiet tracking instrument. They had taken off minutes before and were traveling toward the mountain range Cat had described. The only Pod with cloaking features happened to be the one with the expended Launcher. Zorroc hoped there would not be more trouble than they could handle. Things could get touchy.

"We will reach her in time, you can read her?" Prolinc asked while fine-tuning to a modified direction.

"Barely, I know she is trying to communicate but she is so frantic; very little is coming through. She must survive, Prolinc, she could be carrying my off-spring."

Cat sat down cross-legged on the floor of the cave, striving to control her mounting panic. In her present state of mind she couldn't even help herself let alone communicate with Zorroc, at least to let him know how much she loved him and that she wasn't sorry he had taken her. She focused on the way he petted her when trying to calm her, the way he'd run his hands over her arms, back and buttocks, soothing her while he spoke softly, assuring her that everything would be all right, she wanted to hear those words again more than life itself.

"Everything will be all right, my cream, I won't let anything happen to you and when I see you again, I will hold you and pet you until you tire of the attention," he whispered into her mind like a gentle breeze, reassuring her as nothing else could.

"I love you, Zorroc," she admitted softly.

"I know, Catarina."

"We have her on screen," Prolinc advised. "She is eight nids due east from our position. Tell her to get ready for a fast transhift, Zorroc. Sycor, prepare to trans on my signal," he ordered, calculating quickly.

"On your signal, commander," Sycor replied.

"Zorroc, they've come for me," Cat messaged, calm now that the end grew near. Her time had definitely arrived, one way or the other.

"Stall them." His short, ordered response.

"Thank you for coming at last, I need to use the facilities; with all this excitement, my bladder is positively bursting. I'm sure that, as a guest, you wouldn't want me to be uncomfortable. Could someone please show me the way to the lavatory?" she asked in her most blatant southern drawl, all the while batting her lashes, climbing to her feet and brushing herself off. The Dargons started shuffling their feet in confusion; then one stepped forward and motioned her to follow. It had worked. He showed her outside and grunted toward a bush. So much for the facilities but maybe she would be easier to transhift this way. The Dargons began to trickle out of an adjacent cave and move slowly toward her, obviously prepared to watch while she did her business.

"Guys, I appreciate your position, but I can't relieve myself with an audience. I cross my heart and hope to die, I will not run away, please give me some privacy," she pleaded sweetly.

They started snorting, panting and drooling as they advanced slowly toward her and began closing in. *"Zorroc, they are surrounding me; please hurry."*

She hoped he'd heard her. She began backing away with her hands out in front of her in a manner to placate as well as stop them from closing in behind her. A wall of four Gattonians appeared in front her, arms raised to fire on the Dargons at point blank range while she vanished. She arrived on the trans-pad and promptly fell to her knees and then on to her butt in a muddled, uncoordinated heap. She liked it much better when Zorroc held her, she decided, looking around as she gained her footing. Sycor stood alone behind the console; she started toward him just as the Gattonian party returned looking victorious and reeking of Dargon guts.

Recognizing Zorroc instantly, she charged him like a torpedo. He caught her mid-flight in a fierce hug that told her more about her narrow escape than she wanted to know. He swung her up and started toward the panel before stopping and turning to humbly thank the crew for their support and Cat's life. Four mouths dropped open as Zorroc proceeded out of the trans-pad room.

He began speaking non-stop, unable to help himself. He had her. "We were unable to simply transhift you up, as we had planned, the Dargons were closing in on you too swiftly. We needed a wall of sorts to separate you.

"Ugh, the stench is almost unbearable, we both need to get clean and then I will lie down with you and hold you until you drift off to sleep." Although at that moment, he feared he would never let her go again. She remained quiet, too quiet. He glanced down to find her fast asleep. He smiled. His mate had had another very busy day.

Chapter Ten

"Where are we?" Cat wanted to know. Dee sat perched on the side of the platmat looking concerned but unflappable and of course voluptuous, gorgeous, and fresh as a morning breeze. Cat figured her own appearance would be an exact antithesis of her friend's. Ugh. Then she remembered what had happened which set off a barrage of questions that began firing from her lips. The first being, "Where is Zorroc? I know he was with me, right? And, how can you be here? Aren't you supposed to be on Zeba II? How long have I been asleep? Am I on Zeba II? Did they drug me, or something? Sheesh, I'm confused," she admitted, finally out of charges.

Dee thought she had good reason to be confused and commenced explanations. "We're on the small ship that came to your rescue, they call it a Pod. We're approaching the mother ship that was sent to intercept us." Dee had watched her friend sleep for the last half hour, not wanting to wake her from mind healing rest. Zorroc had assured her that Cat had not been harmed but Dee wanted confirmation from Cat's own lips. "Zorroc is assisting with the landing arrangements and sent me to wake you so you could dress and be ready to meet the crew of the Miramid."

Cat looked under the covers and colored noticeably while Dee tried to hide her grin. She wrapped herself in the blanket, hopped off the mat, and proceeded to the clothes cove asking Dee to keep talking while she dressed. Dee had to admit that she seemed absolutely 'Cat normal'.

"I was one of the crew members chosen to extricate you from the Dargons but at the time you only had eyes for your cat man," Dee told her with a grin. "You probably wouldn't have recognized me anyway. Damn, covered with Dargon guts twice in one day, I stayed in the clean-room for forty minutes.

"But we sustained no injuries, Cat; it was a clean operation, unless you count the innards of the Dargons, that is. I'm sure they're not too happy right about now."

Cat emerged from dressing with emerald eyes flashing and moist, "Thank you for coming for me, I couldn't ask for better friend but what were those Gattonians thinking to allow you to participate in something so dangerous? The Dargons seemed excessively fond of females but whether for food or sport remains unknown, and thanks to you and the others I'll never find out. Jesus Dee, if I'd been there any longer I don't think I'd be here any longer," she shuddered at the admission. Then Cat filled Dee in on the surreal particulars.

"You clapped, you actually clapped?" Dee groaned; she didn't know whether to laugh or pull out her hair at Cat's blatant audacity. She had a habit of recklessly charging in when she should be standing back and weighing her options. "Did it ever occur to you that he might have taken offense? What if clapping constituted some form of scathing insult, requiring death? Sweetheart, we're not in Kansas anymore," she concluded in her best Dorothy impersonation.

"I'm not sure it would have made any difference." Cat shivered. "If you had arrived one minute later, I would have either been dead or wishing I were." Then her demeanor changed completely. "Guess what his name was Dee, just guess," Cat squealed in obvious delight. At Dee's blank look, she couldn't contain herself. "Gorn, he called himself, *Gorn,* can you believe it? I thought he was kidding and almost laughed but caught myself in time. These guys take themselves even more seriously than Gattonians."

Dee groaned again at how that might have been interpreted by her captures. Cat had been very lucky.

In one of their rare relaxed conversations, Prolinc had confided to Dee that one of the nicknames he had for Cat was Pinball. Dee had gotten so used to Cat's modus operandi that she hadn't understood the significance of the name. Now however, seeing Cat transform in typical Cat fashion from traumatized to amused, she understood how she must come across to the very deliberate, controlled Gattonians. Cat shone like an inextinguishable light in the night, she couldn't be beaten and she invariably found something humorous or positive in every situation. Her latest near death experience obviously proved no different. Like a ping-pong ball on an ocean, she may become temporarily submerged by a wave but inevitably would pop back up to the surface.

Dee wondered, once again if Zorroc had any idea of the precious gift that was Cat...holy cow patties, what would Zorroc make of Cat's episode with the Dargons when he learned the details? Well, she wasn't going to be the one to tell him. She might tell Prolinc; maybe she could get him to crack a smile. Felines were supposed to be curious, playful and impulsive like Spock and Scottie, but just thinking of Prolinc and the kittens in the same admixture constituted an oxymoron. Gattonians had deliberate, controlled, somber, almost brooding temperaments except they didn't show that much emotion—Prolinc being the worst of the pack. The closest he'd come to a smile occurred when they'd had their almost interlude in the meadow. Dee had spotted a telling grin of fierce satisfaction and a definite gleam in his vivid, green eyes for a brief moment before the attack.

Since arriving back on the Pod, however, he hadn't given her a glance either in interest or with his usual scowl. He had no doubt come to his senses and wouldn't bother to pursue her now that the mother ship prepared to intercept them. His obligation toward her had been fulfilled. At least they hadn't consummated their disunion. Then she'd be feeling even stupider than she did now. Oh well, nothing like a new man to help you get over the old one, maybe she'd check out Rosik. The crew quietly bandied about tales of his prowess in battle and in bed. He was said to be charismatic and sinfully sensual even for a Gattonian; and irresistible to any female he wanted. Maybe he'd help her forget her very un-charismatic cat man. When Cat inquired about the Miramid, Dee launched into all she had heard, enthusiastically.

"Rosik, the first in command, is supposedly impossible for any female to resist. He lost his family in the first clash with the Dargons and since then, has been cutting a very wide swath through the female population on several galaxies.

"With Angel mated to Carpov and you with Zorroc; maybe I'll stand a chance with him." Dee hadn't yet broached the subject of the mate mark she'd detected on Cat's neck but when she'd had a conversation with Angel through COM relay, she'd told her all about the mating ritual and irreversible ramifications. Divorce did not exist for Gattonians. Like everything else, they took their vows seriously. Angel had explained that lifemating consisted of three parts. 'The Granting' in which the male asked the female to mate and she accepts. 'The Claiming' where the male enters the female after preparing her; and 'The Taking' where the union is consummated by a mating bite or tattoo to show possession and a bound union. If Cat, by far the most forthcoming of the three; had lifemated with Zorroc voluntarily it would have shot out of her mouth with the speed of light. Dee looked briefly uncomfortable, focusing on Cat's neck, before finishing her dissertation on Rosik.

Cat wondered exactly how much she had missed with her two-hour nap. She'd thought Dee and Prolinc had bonded together like two active atoms reacting explosively until smashed together to form an inseparable element. The sparks that the two had been shooting last time she'd seen them together burned hotter and much friendlier than the former encounters she had witnessed. What happened to change that? Dee acted every bit as unreadable as Angel; why couldn't Cat do that? You'd think that growing up with two enigmatic glacier geishas would have given her similar traits. Why did her every thought have to be plastered on her features like yesterday's news? And even worse; now Zorroc could pluck it out of her head if any doubt existed.

The panel whooshed open and Cat noticed Prolinc's countenance seemed even more inscrutable than normal, as if his body had shown up without his mind. He ignored Dee like she wasn't in the room and addressed her.

"We have landed and are ready to disembark; you will follow me." Prolinc ordered distractedly. How had the Dargons found them, he wondered yet again, and why had they seemed intent on capturing the females? Cat had told Zorroc they looked for one female in particular, what could that mean? From the corner of his eye he noted Dee's slightly mutinous, confused expression. She did not understand, that, although he had interest and plans for her, his primary allegiance remained to Zorroc, Gattonia...and eventually to Nadia, his betrothed. He sighed; life seldom proved convenient.

As Dee and Cat moved as one toward the exit Cat straightened to her full height and showered him with a factious glower. She decided she wasn't happy with these Gattonians. Why did he ignore Dee? Where was Zorroc? "Where is Zorroc, he owes me a long soft rub and a lot of holding."

Prolinc shot a look at Dee as if to ascertain whether this passed for common Earth banter for women, but Dee just looked at him guilelessly, like inquiring minds want to know. He got the feeling they were laughing at him but could not determine the jest. He had yet to understand the female of this species and Earth humor, in general.

"Zorroc has duties and obligations to attend to now that we have arrived. I will be your escort off the Pod and to your new quarters." His attention eerily unreadable, he faced Cat. "Zorroc sent this, he wishes you to wear it."

She leaned down to inspect the band with interest. Four inches wide and made of three intertwined metals each with its own texture and color; it looked as exotic and complex as Zorroc, himself. She recognized the crest; it matched the ring that he wore on the middle finger of his left hand.

When Cat reached to take it from Prolinc he grabbed her hand, slid it above her elbow, and tightened it flush with her skin. It gave with the movement of her bicep but remained fastened securely.

"How does it come off?" she asked uneasily. She began to examine it more carefully to determine its purpose and workings. Was it some sort of slave I.D. band or maybe a concubine shackle designating ownership? Dark feelings clouded her mind and blotted her vision. If it was some sort of marriage band, Zorroc would have presented it himself and asked her to marry him. Wouldn't he?

Her fears were confirmed as Prolinc announced, "It is permanently fastened. Now you will follow me, if you please." It was not a request and Dee seemed to dislike the implication of the band as much as Cat. She stepped in front of Cat and took up a relaxed fighting stance that Prolinc didn't seem to recognize.

"Come on, Lincky, don't I get one too?" An irresistible compunction assailed Dee to strip Prolinc of his thick veneer of control and unveil the beast within.

Prolinc looked thoroughly non-pulsed as he informed her that hers would be along later and reiterated that they were expected at the exit momentarily.

"Sorry sour-puss," Dee corrected, "but the only place we're going is home, I know how the Pod operates and how you Gattonians operate and frankly we choose the Pod, so go on to your wonderful mother ship and let us fly away home." Cat understood exactly what was about to happen. Did Prolinc believe he could dismiss Dee as if she were a part of the air? Cat hid a grin.

Did Dee actually expect it to be that easy, Cat watched the expression on her face that told her she was begging for a fight and confident she'd get one. Cat thought it would prove an educational experience for both of them and stepped back to prepare for the show. Cat knew the Gattonians wouldn't lift a hand toward a weaker female species because of their superior size, strength so she wasn't nervous about who would best the other. She smirked; let the games begin. As if Dee had read her mind, she stepped forward and told Prolinc to move aside. He froze in Gattonian control awaiting her finger in his chest; instead, he got a knee to the groin, a karate chop to either side of his neck and a double fisted blow between his shoulders on his way down.

It ended in less than five seconds. Dee turned with a satisfied smile and said, "Um, just pussycats. Let's see how much mischief we can incite. Most of the crew will have already exited the ship and no one will know our plans, so act natural and let's head toward the navigation center." Dee sauntered out the exit and headed down the hall. Cat followed, wondering just how far they'd get before being reeled back in. Even though she knew what Dee proposed would ultimately prove futile; Cat thought that they'd scored a small victory. Sometimes minor battles proved the most satisfying. They reached the navigation center to discover it deserted. Jesus, Cat thought, were they really going to try this? What would happen if they succeeded?

Just as the entrance panel slid shut, it opened up again. Zorroc appeared with three of his crew; Sycor looked as if laughter was about to burst from his eyes while the other two projected abject wariness, as if ready to protect their private parts at all cost. Zorroc looked furious. Oops, Cat thought. The three flanked Zorroc and circled Cat and Dee.

"What are your intentions," Zorroc grated roughly, laziering them both with an amber fired glare.

"What does it look like," Cat responded, "we're going home. Dee's a pilot and has been observing the flight procedures needed to navigate us out of here and we're out of here," she dared. It was childish but she wanted to strike back at Zorroc for not coming for her himself—that and his imperious self-control and cold-hearted dedication to duty, of which she was one. Apparently a minor one.

"Take her," Zorroc pointed at Dee, "put her in retention, and secure her. Leave us."

Cat jumped in front of Dee and confronted

Zorroc. "Just what do you intend to do with us, because where Dee goes, I go; and I will tell you right now that no one lays a hand on either one of us. I am sick unto death of being ordered about, manhandled and in general treated like a cat toy you can pull out and play with when it suits you then ignored out of paw. And just what is the significance of this band?" She held out her arm for his inspection.

Zorroc, Sycor, and the other two crewmembers froze like inert objects. Prolinc, arriving behind them, had no such movement problems; he stormed around the inert objects, skirted Cat, who knew better than to get between the two of them and watched as Prolinc advanced on Dee. Dee looked like a ferocious kitten. "You will accompany me now," he ordered softly. Cat noted that, for once, his feelings were clear; he was livid. She had second thoughts about interfering, would he hurt Dee, after all? If Dee had wanted a reaction, she had certainly hit the jackpot.

Dee beamed a drop dead, radiant smile at Prolinc, sauntered up to him, patted his cheek and said, "What took you so long, sweetie, lead the way." She turned to Cat, winked, and then glided sensually out of the room. All male eyes riveted to Dee's behind as she left. Cat thought them pathetically easy to read. Things were definitely looking up until she noticed Zorroc's gaze had focused unerringly on her.

"Prepare to disembark immediately," he spat at the remaining crew, his gaze still locked with hers. The males shot through the exit and secured the panel behind them while Zorroc studied Cat. Her heart began a staccato beat as she tried to discern his next move. She didn't have long to wait. He moved closer and gently touched the back of his fingers to her cheek, captured a wayward curl and

144

fondled it slowly before tucking it behind her ear. His behavior confounded her, she'd expected anger, demands, explanations; almost anything except what he now allowed her to see. He looked defeated. How had that happened, didn't he know she'd never had serious intentions of leaving him? She had simply been supporting Dee's momentary "Star Wars" fantasy; she knew they'd never let them depart with one of their Pods. Was this some new way to manipulate her? If so it was working like a charm. What did he expect of her?

He lifted one side of his mouth a fraction and thought it a very good question. Word of her attempted escape would spread like wild fire to the crew of the Miramid. It would probably be viewed with varying negative pre-conceptions, which he began to tick off to himself. His mate intended escape; if he could not control his female, what did that say of him as a leader; he had made a faulty determination in bringing the Earth women here and then lifemating with one; his decisions had led them into another confrontation with their enemies...the list could go on and on. It had been difficult to persuade many of his people that this was an essential course of action. Many just wanted to try to find a cure for the virus and restore fertility to their females. They actively pursued that option, of course; indeed, Carpov and Angel worked around the clock on the planet Jasper, the only inhabited planet of the three available for their survival. The Jasperi, though not particularly advanced technically, and all but defenseless militarily, had given up their main laboratory and three of their top scientists to assist in a cure and antidote for what they had labeled FIS, Female Infertility Syndrome. Even if they came up with a cure, it may not save him now from political ruin. He would lose face. His enemies would rejoice. And what of Cat? Would she stay with him in disgrace or choose to go back to her home planet and her former way of life. And what if her friends decided to follow? How would Carpov and Prolinc react...and what of his sister, Nadia? What an unholy mess he had made of things.

Cat waited for him to speak but how to explain? Maybe he would go with her and live on Earth for the remainder of their lives. He was weary of the responsibility and pain of watching his people suffer. Walking away seemed suddenly an irresistible temptation...however, one he would never take voluntarily. His commitment to his people ran far too deep to let him give up his responsibilities. He would stand and fight his enemies in whatever form they took and Catarina would remain by his side to assist him.

"How are you feeling, Catarina? Are you rested?" he whispered with a self-deprecatory smirk. He knew he had confused her with his reaction; he himself was confused at his behavior. He should be railing at her, punishing her for her actions but he could not bring himself to do so. He was the one at fault. He had not told her of his status as leader to his people, had not spoken to her of the sensitive political situation created by the Dargon virus, had not even brought home the significance of the mating mark on her neck. If he had explained these things, the current situation, most likely, would not have arisen. He had miscalculated once again.

"I am feeling decidedly confused. Why did Prolinc force this on my arm; he told me it was permanent, that it couldn't be removed. What is it for?" She knew her actions had caused problems, she just couldn't figure out how. She played a very small pawn in a very large game. How could anything she did hurt him in any way? And she wanted to be held and reassured. If he could read her mind, how could he not know that, and if he knew but didn't want to hold her, what did that mean? She peered up at him looking for answers.

He gave her one of his rare smiles and encircled her with his arms, his warmth, and his scent. She hugged him back fiercely, pressing her face into his hard chest. He whisper-purred her name and when she looked up to meet his gaze, he cradled her head with one large hand and lowered his lips to hers in a mind shattering, open-mouthed kiss. He kissed her as he had never kissed her before, with warmth, intense passion, tenderness. The tenderness was new. She reveled in it. When he broke the kiss, she groaned in protest and then heard a small choir of chuckles coming from behind him. They had company. She peeked around him to see a group of unfamiliar faces. She knew without being told which one was Rosik; the rumors about him had not been exaggerated, he looked sinful. Zorroc growled. She smiled.

"What is it Rosik, I am occupied," he grated in a voice filled with frustration and chagrin.

"We heard that an attempted escape, by two of your Earth women, had taken place and decided to investigate, but as with most rumors, it proved a great exaggeration—unless you intend to send this one to Nirvana with your attentions. I think perhaps, she already has traveled part of the way.

"Is she yours Zorroc, or can she be shared, I would be delighted to escort her the remaining distance to completion," Rosik offered as he proceeded into the room and stood too closely in front of Cat. The commander exuded such raw, potent sex appeal that Cat grabbed on to Zorroc to keep from being sucked into his vortex. As quickly as the feeling had begun, it vanished. What had happened? Rosik had stilled, in statue mode, in front of her then abruptly moved back three paces.

"My apologies, Mi Divitta, I meant no

disrespect," he murmured as he turned toward Zorroc. "Obviously, our assistance is not required but since we are here we will escort you onto our ship in formal procession."

As they proceeded toward the exit Cat mindspoke to Zorroc, asking what had happened back there. He replied that Rosik had tried to trance her and then went on to explain that it was a form of hypnotism used by the Gattonians to control others. *"He should not have employed it to attract you; in fact it should not be used for sexual attraction or gratification at all; unfortunately not everyone adheres to our strictures. Rosik remains an unrepentant rogue and proud of it. If not such a valued warrior, he would no doubt be reprimanded, and for his conduct toward you, he may very well be."* He placed a proprietary hand at the base of her spine. Obviously, Zorroc did not share his toys, Cat concluded; she heard a responding rumble.

Zorroc read the fear and confusion infusing Cat's mind. They had exited the Pod to a formal Gattonian greeting of respect for their leader. Every male and female knelt on bended knee, right fist over heart, left arm extended toward him. He had not expected the show of support they bestowed upon him; he was touched...and embarrassed by their loyalty. He bowed his head; the sign for them to rise; and thanked them for coming to their aide in such a timely manner. He told them that he owed them his life and the life of his mate and that he was more grateful than he could express.

The crew cheered. Gattonians cheering? Cat felt like she had swallowed a golf ball as she stared at the exhibition before her. She stared open-mouthed at Zorroc. Who was he? They treated him like some sort of king or something. Hell, Americans didn't treat their President with that kind of reverence. *What had she gotten herself into?* A litany that continued to grow with maddening consistency, since first setting eyes on Zorroc. She located Dee and Angel in the crowd to find them almost as stunned as she, herself.

Angel looked positively luminous. Happiness seemed to envelop her like the silvery long flowing gown she wore. She resembled a dark, ethereal angel, which she certainly epitomized. Carpov definitely agreed with her.

The crowd parted for Zorroc and Cat like the red-sea, in order to let them pass. A contingent of guards flanked them. Cat became uncharacteristically subdued as they made their way on to the Jet-quik that would take them to their quarters. She felt them drop rapidly leaving her stomach behind, similar to the times she'd ridden a particularly steep roller coaster. The interior of the ship, though larger and more opulent, reminded her of the Star-ship Enterprise. She began to think that there was no such thing as science fiction...just future science. With all the people she had observed above, she realized the ship must be massive of size, similar to the huge vessel in Close Encounters of the Third Kind...or a medium city the size of Nashville.

Their quarters, beautifully lush and detailed, overflowed with thick, richly colored carpets and intricately designed works of art. Easily twice as large as the quarters they had shared on the Stellar, her gaze swept by and then riveted on to a now familiar crest of massive proportions that hung above the huge platmat, the same crest worn by Zorroc and now her. Who, in heaven's name was this guy?

Zorroc eyed her uncomfortably.

Chapter Eleven

"There are things I should have told you, things you need to know. I will talk and you will listen until I am through, do you understand and agree?" He looked impossibly harsh and serious. How many shoes did this cat man have, because she felt another one about to drop? She nodded.

"I belong to the House of Ra. It is a powerful house, a ruling house. I am ruler of my province and Supreme Leader of my people, as my father before me, but I am also young. There are those who seek to use this as an opportunity to take my power and strip me of my station. The opposition grew stronger when the Dargons attacked; I sometimes wonder if...but that does not signify right now. As I stated, I have political enemies that question my strength of command. That is why, when you and Dee staged your escape, it could have been interpreted as a sign of my ineptitude. After all, how can I rule my people when incapable of commanding the respect and support of my mate?

"I ask that you show me that respect in the same way you support your friends, I need this from you, and only you can grant it. Will you, Catarina? Your support or lack of it will not change the fact that we are bound. That is permanent."

As speeches went, it scored a direct hit but the questions he had answered only spawned new ones and the time for answers lay at hand because this time she knew what questions to ask.

"First, answer some of my questions; what does this armband signify?"

"You are very tenacious for one so scattered, my curious Cat. It serves multiple purposes. The emblem encases a very strong tracking device so I will always be able to find you. It designates you as a member of the House of Ra; and it identifies you as mine. The band cannot be removed; it is imbedded into your skin and muscle tissue and permanent for all time." His eyes glowed at this last revelation.

"Uh...yours...um...mated. Is it some kind of mistress thing or is it more of a wife thing? I never heard you *ask* whether I would agree to either or anything to you, for that matter," she pointed. She wondered why she wasn't more nervous at the prospect of being tied to him; she knew what he meant to her but what did she mean to him; aside from her heritage that is. He knew all of her secrets and she knew so few of his, would he ever confide in her? Well, she would just keep pressing until he did.

He colored, he actually looked ashamed for an instant, but then focused on her and gave her the unvarnished truth. "You know you were chosen because of your Gattonian blood, your mother is from a High House and it became important to choose a mate with strong blood lines and a fertile womb. It further became essential for political reasons; my son will someday rule Gattonia and I want no one to be able to dispute his right to rule because of impure blood. I have advised you that Gattonians, when they mate, mate for life. It is a *monogamous* binding. There will be no other females for me, and no males for you. We are as husband and wife only more binding. It is called lifemating and that is the term of our joining."

"You said you belong to the House of Ra; are we talking Egyptian Ra?"

"Ours is the first House of Ra that we know of. Your Egyptians represent a fairly new civilization, similar to your own."

"Okay, then have you ever been to Egypt?" Before he could answer, Cat held up her hands and said, "No, no wait. Have your ancestors ever visited Egypt?"

"Yes."

"Congratulations, Zorroc, you learned a new word today," flashing him a teasing grin before continuing with her interrogation. "There has been speculation for centuries about the pyramids and artworks of Egypt and whether a race from that era could possibly have had the engineering technology, imagination or skill required to build such massive and complex masterpieces." She paused to gage how her ensuing hypothesis affected Zorroc; he watched her like a newly discovered life form, his attention, fully engaged. "And there has been further speculation as to whether the placement of the pyramids could have been some sort of landing signal for incoming spaceships and the pyramids, themselves, landing platforms."

"You have an awe inspiring imagination, my one," he pointed out softly. "It is one of the many things about you that fascinate me." What fascinated him more, however, pertained to her blatant disinterest in wealth and power. Anyone else in her position would be questioning him about his assets—his monetary assets. Catarina's focus ran more toward people and all living creatures, not monetary trappings. But what truly captivated and delighted him entailed her dedicated one-mindedness and determination toward solving the mysteries between both her cultures, for in truth; she had one foot clearly rooted in each. A fact he did not believe had yet sunken into her incredibly absorbent mind. Unfortunately he could not allow her to continue on her present course. Her compliance outweighed all else.

Cat's mind whirled at the possible implications.

He hadn't discouraged her theory and where it led. The realities overlapped staggering. "Tell me, I'm on the wrong track."

"Tell me I have your loyalty and support, and that you give yourself freely to me."

"You are exasperating."

"And you could have written the book on it. Tell me, Catarina, say the words," he commanded softly.

She exhaled loudly. "What will my duties be and will there be some sort of a formal ceremony commemorating this romantic and loving union?"

He winced, "I have feelings for you; you must know this. Things between us will be very good once we reach Gattonia and settle in to our new life. There will be a formal mating ceremony when we arrive home. You will have many beautiful gowns to wear and be much admired by all. I am considered quite a catch." He smiled uncertainly at his last comment. He had not been able to read her for the last few minutes. Was she learning to block him or simply pre-occupied or upset? "Do I have your support?"

"Will you answer my questions about your people?"

"Do not withhold this from me, Catarina."

"Do I honestly have a choice?"

"No."

She sighed and relented. "Well—then I guess you have my loyalty and support."

"And you have mine and more," he whispered, somewhat defeated. He bowed and left her.

When had his way with females vanished? She was fragile, almost defenseless, an Earth female in an unfamiliar world, depending on him to protect, provide and care for her in the way she cared for him and he had made it sound as if she had no options, no value and little chance for his devotion. He had never had this problem with females before. He had always taken his incredible success with them for granted; it came naturally to him. He considered himself a female magnet of sorts and not simply because of his powerful position amongst his people. He had been described as polished, attractive, charming, and pleasing to females sexually. His joinings had always ended well; each satisfied and ready to go on to the next partner.

The problem with his mate, he realized, lay in the fact that apart from their cultural differences, he did not know how to be a lifemate. Providing for the emotional needs of a female eclipsed his experience, let alone an Earth female. She had said she loved him and he knew she believed herself sincere but what she had overlooked in her naiveté was that love, her brand of love, lingered as an unessential even undesired ingredient to a successful union. As far as he could tell love proved little more myth, made up by males to get their females underneath them voluntarily. He could assure Catarina of hot joinings, mutual regard, and affection for one another. It would please her well, once she became accustomed to it, but anything more he could not provide. How to make her understand that the Gattonian nature espoused sexuality without the pointless corresponding emotions of love, adoration or jealousy?

True, they could be affectionate, playful at times and territorial but it did not emulate the ideal of romantic love. Still, he needed to bridge this gap between them before it could grow much deeper. Her disillusionment and disappointment buffeted him like waves on a shoreline, eroding his resolve.

He escaped to the botanical solarium, his favorite sanctuary, and sat on the floor toward the back of the facility. Zorroc fought against the merciless undertow, slowly pulling at his confidence and determination—bonds of responsibility, navigation of political waters, and the emotional quick sand that formed Cat. He had made Catarina suffer for it all. He had lifemated with an Earth woman he barely knew, battling a species that embodied the very definition of genocide, and about to embark on a social challenge never before attempted by his people. And he could not control any of it.

He lost all sense of time as he sat there weathering the bombardments of duty and obligation but finally, noting his lack of progress toward any resolution, forced himself to rise and take up the battle that shaped his existence.

Hours later Zorroc headed to the COM room so he could observe his mate and better judge her state of mind. Whoever said Earth women were easy, obviously, had never met one.

Prolinc lounged before the multiple screens, monitoring the ship through Internal COM Link or ICL when he arrived. "Your luck with your Earth female remains consistent, Zorroc, what did you do to her this time to put her into her present state?"

"I...she...does not understand our ways; it has made her out of sorts."

Prolinc crooked an eyebrow but otherwise remained unmoved. "Normally, I would advise sending her friends to her but if they see her like this, your private parts may be in jeopardy; ask a Gattonian who knows." He would never underestimate his little warrior again.

Dee emerged every bit as capable as his other officers' only much nicer, rounder, and delectable to look at. She drew him mentally, as well as physically, and had no intimidation problems with him as most others of his province. They were well matched. Lifemating with Dee, however, would be out of the question. Both he and Zorroc were betrothed to Gattonian females—normally a commitment of honor impossible to break. The alliance for Prolinc was essential to his family and their future, whereas Zorroc, being the leader of their people, could sever his alliance of honor for the greater good. The mating of a concubine could be challenged for the rule but a true legitimate son could not. The fact that Zorroc's betrothed had been infected by the virus and rendered infertile had left him no alternative but to choose another more able to give him offspring.

Prolinc's family had served the House of Ra for centuries. He and Zorroc had been raised together, trained together, educated together and caroused together; and in three short years, he would lifemate with Zorroc's sister, Nadia. This would elevate his families' status to one of the top three families of Gattonia and in his mating with Nadia; he would be in line for the rule, as well.

His family could barely restrain their elation at this opportunity, for indeed they saw it as their opportunity, not because of any particular talent or worth Prolinc held. His brother, mother, and father all preened in anticipation of their upcoming triumph over their peers; it manifested as one of the few times Prolinc could recall sharing familial approval. Ordinarily his family tended to view him as some undesirable barnacle that had grown on them. Prolinc did not care about status. His job was to protect Zorroc with his life and he had determined that if anything happened to his friend, Prolinc would most likely perish beside him.

In addition, he harbored no illusions about the coming union; Nadia's heart did not beat for his nor his for her; still they liked one another well enough and would rub along. In the meantime, he would inject Dee with as many babies as possible. She would be his concubine or Chosen One and he would provide for her and theirs, long after he lifemated with Nadia. Forever, if she would let him. She would be content for he would let her raise their children. Maybe motherhood would blunt her sharp edges. He would love to see a softened Dee with his offspring. He would love to see her expand with his babies. He needed to formalize their union quickly; she needed to know how she would fit into his life. It would have to be enough for her...It would have to be enough for him, as well.

"I too have had a demonstration of their defense skills." Zorroc quirked his head toward Prolinc with a bemused half smirk. "They are very effective for ones so small and delicate. Cat told me of the special training she and Angel endured from your female. The three are a formidable threat to unsuspecting males; maybe we should outlaw the training of other Earth females under our protection. We would no doubt be safer for it," he added only half jokingly.

He fastened on Zorroc's last statement with dawning, nauseating clarity. Self defense not a good idea for the Earth females? A concubine counted as fair game for male attention; Dee's defense skills may be essential from time to time when he was not there to protect her. His reputation would be enough to keep most males at a distance but not all, and not his equals in rank after they reached Gattonia. Dee was beautiful and alluring. It would be a challenge to keep her from lifemating with another peer. It was what she deserved; he just could not give it to her.

Suddenly, he knew that self-defense skills were exactly what each Earth female required. Lifemated women would have less trouble but those who serviced many or chosen ones would need extra protection from not only overly aggressive males but also assorted Gattonian females. The decision to bring a contingent of Earth females into the Gattonian society for the express purpose of mating with their males had not been a popular one, especially among the females. The monogamy strictures that had been in place before documented history, faced deletion; which meant their civilization faced massive disruption in the very near future. The Dargons constituted no more than a temporary glitch compared to the social storm currently hurtling toward Ganz.

"I disagree," Prolinc asserted in a deadly tone.

Zorroc, surprised and caught off guard by Prolinc's sudden change of mood, waited for him to expound. His council had helped Zorroc avert disaster on more than a few occasions and Prolinc saw it as an important facet of his duties.

"The Earth females are small and vulnerable to the more domineering will of some of our males; our females too are larger, stronger and for the most part unhappy at the prospect of bringing in foreign females to produce what they are no longer capable of producing. I believe it imperative that they be trained in self-defense tactics. I have a feeling they will need all the protection they can get. We have less than a month to equip them with what they will need to survive in our world. Education in protocol, customs and comportment will also be necessary." Prolinc glanced up to his silent friend to see him directing all of his focus into what he had proposed. For once in the last month he paid full attention to their situation instead of his mate.

"I see the truth in all you have said; I think you have saved us from a potentially internecine situation. Our three women will instruct the rest in self-defense while Bandoff can instruct them in our ways. He is mild, non-threatening and can be trusted not to become overly enthusiastic in his regard for the women." Then he added. "And keep Rosik away from them at all costs!"

Zorroc put his head in his hands and grumbled, "How could we have foreseen the complications we would face when we began this venture to save our race? I thought Earth females would be simple, uncomplicated and eager to please in whatever capacity we chose for them; instead they are as complex as our own females, some more so. They expect, even require love. Love! How can they expect that kind of regard after only a group of days?"

While Prolinc left to set everything into motion, Zorroc directed his gaze toward the monitor focused on his now sleeping Cat. Her tearstained cheeks yielded no answers. He would visit the aunts...again...

"You numb sculled, dweeb-headed, clueless, clumsy boy! Did you desert your finesse in Gattonia?" The aunts had picked up their share of Earth slang while monitoring the progress of their American cousins, and now Marie demonstrated her verbal aptitude. "Why does it matter whether you credence the idea of love; the point is that Catarina does. Just tell her that you love her and make her happy. You are, after all, mated and therefore celibate; what is a little terminology between mates?

"You call it desire and she calls it love; it still is what binds you, if not the mating ritual itself. You implied that her only value lay in her bloodline. I have watched you handle all your other females with the perfection of a master manipulator, what is so different about this one?" Marie *humphed*, frustrated at her nephew's inability to improvise. "First you complain that she is unsuitable for joining, which obviously you have overcome, and now you complain that she requires an emotional bond that you cannot reciprocate. All you have to do is say the words and she will be putty in your hands. The word love is powerful and important to her because of the way her parents raised her—or failed to raise her. She needs security and the surety of a permanent union and you are giving her mixed

159

signals of reluctance, duty to your race and vague assurances of protection. It will not due for her. You have to be there—all there for her or you are courting disaster for you both."

Helen took over. "Have you no feelings for the girl, no care for her physical or emotional well-being?" She paused and riveted her nephew with knowing purpose. "Tell me Rocky, do you withhold the words she needs for lack of love or because of your depth of it?" She then picked up the remote control and began surfing channels on the console, seemingly ready to drop the subject, until she muttered. "Not that it matters in the long run; she is your responsibility now. I have often thought that we all laid too much responsibility on you at too early an age. Seventeen cycles is impossibly young to run such a large province as Gattonia but with both your parents lost, well, there remained no one else of choice."

Helen sighed and seemed to deflate a little but then resumed her plea. "Talk to her. Confide in her and she may surprise you with her council, she is bright. I think she could be of great value if you would but give her the opportunity. It would also give her a definitive place in your life. She would feel needed for herself instead of her bloodline. In truth, that has worried me the most in this genetic gamble for survival—the fallout of how she would translate this union. How it would affect her self-esteem and her already strained relationship with her parents. She is a beautiful young woman. Nancia and Rowan don't deserve her and they never have; but that can't be helped at this late date, we can only go forward. Think of the loving union your parents shared and take a page from them." She fixed him with a look that told him he would be held accountable for mending Cat's world.

He suffocated under their advice and his many

other obligations. He could not do it, any of it. He may be a ruler but he was not a God. Why did they have to bring up his parents? They were dead and no longer of importance in any way that mattered. He made his way toward the main level to confer with Rosik.

Zorroc had adored his mother and worshiped his father but in the end, neither emotion had been enough to save them. He had not been enough. He flew back into the gyre of his youth. His upbringing had been practically idyllic. He was the treasured son of the ruling family in the powerful House of Ra. His aunts and the staff doted on him and looked after his every need. His parents loved him, though were primarily attuned to one another. In the end, the devotion and love they shared caused his father's demise and in a way his own. Alternatively, maybe the end marked the beginning of the male he would become. His father had always preached about the balance of life. His balance had been his mate on one side and his leadership responsibilities on the other. When at the age of thirteen, Zorroc's mother died, their family axis skewed irreparably. His father, who had always been an indomitable force, became a weak and ineffectual leader with the loss of his wife. He watched his father go slowly down hill; not caring that his people suffered, not caring that his son grieved along with him, not caring about anything, ever again. He slowly faded away and died when Zorroc reached the age seventeen.

By that time, he had been running the empire for over two years. He had to grow up very quickly, too quickly some said, but he had no regrets; it had made him strong. Love emerged the weakness and he would be damned before he succumbed to its ravages. It had ruined his father more completely than any drug or sickness.

Love had destroyed his father and almost

toppled an empire.

He had to make Cat understand that the fantasy of love posed a dangerous threat better left to fools who could delude themselves; neither of them could afford the cost. Already it had begun tearing them apart.

****

After Prolinc completed his instructions to Bandoff, he headed toward the X-center where Dee was toning both her defense skills and her delectable body. He knew she would be pleased with his directive to train the women. He just hoped she would be equally amenable to his other proposal. Somehow, he did not think it would be that easy. Nothing came easy when it involved his woman. He would take her first and talk later. He pressed his wristband and issued orders for COM blackout of the X-center until further notice. Satisfied, he almost grinned.

When he entered, he observed Dee throwing one of his junior officers around. She did not understand that they would not lay a combative hand on her for fear of her safety—and theirs—if Prolinc found her injured in any way. "I see Abzu is assisting you with your workout today, banshee, why not let me take over and give him a chance to live and train another day."

Dee lit up at the sound of his voice and decided it would be as good an excuse as any to touch him.

"I would love to train with you, Prolinc," she replied, giving him a somewhat confused look. What had he called her, it had sounded suspiciously like banshee, but surely, she must have just misheard and had addressed her with his usual 'my Dee'.

Prolinc dismissed a very grateful Abzu and secured the panel into the lock position before turning to face his blond goddess. Sweat glistened and glowing, he would soon stake his right of possession on her. Prolinc opted for no protective gear and approached.

She moved very quickly with an agility and deliberation that almost challenged him. She was magnificent. His warrior took herself very seriously, he had come to realize, and when her loyalty was given it would endure unshakable. But how to gain it? She had many barriers to her heart—trust, only one of them.

So caught up in his musings, he was flabbergasted when one moment his feet were planted firmly on the ground and the next found him flying through the air. The wind was knocked out of him several seconds later when he hit the floor with loud resounding boom. He studied the ceiling and waited.

Chapter Twelve

Dee rushed to his side, horrified. He had yet to move, oh, what had she done? She'd surprised him somehow, and with his size and momentum, he'd flown nearly ten feet before colliding with the floor flat on his back. These Gattonians were not nearly as tough as they appeared. Size wasn't everything, after all. She straddled him with her legs on either side of his hips then placed a hand on one side of his head while her other gently brushed back his hair to get a better look at any damage she may have caused. He groaned. "Linc, sweetheart, tell me you're all right, that I haven't hurt you, please Linc, do I need to go for help?"

Nothing from her lips could have motivated him more to assure her of his recuperative powers. She would not get away from him this time. She let out a strangled whoop as he flipped her onto her back and pinned her with his body. He looked deep into her eyes, debating his plan of attack. Better to join first and talk later as she lie sated and yielding by his side. She had barriers that needed to be loved away before imparting his plans for them. He would love her slowly, with deliberation. He would make her blaze for him. Dee's eyes had gotten huge in her perfectly heart shaped face. She comprised the sexiest, most physically appealing, most mentally exasperating, female he had ever encountered and he would make her his, really his, no more trancing, he wanted her soul.

The Hell with going slow, they would go slow later.

He attacked all of her senses at once, giving her no quarter, no opportunity to think or question his sudden turn toward passion. How could he be stone one moment and molten lava the next?

Only she was the one melting.

He assaulted her body with hands grazing every inch of her, his tongue plunging deeply into her mouth, his lips ravishing her lips with sucks and nips and grinding pressure. He parted her legs with a strong muscular thigh and kneaded it into her mound. As she erupted into flames, Dee realized they were still fully clothed. Deciding to rectify the situation, she put her hands on each of his huge shoulders and pulled his suit fastenings apart with an efficiency born of desperation.

Prolinc tore his mouth from her swollen lips, his eyes drilling into her heavy-lidded, glazed gaze. "There will be no going back," he warned, rasping out a threat he had every intention of enforcing.

She only nodded and continued on her quest to get them both naked. He thrust himself off her and stripped, then grabbed her uniform and shed it off her in one movement. He looked down on her, eating her slowly with his eyes. Enough foreplay, he wanted in. He dropped down and covered her, spread her legs wide with both of his, and entered her in one fluid hard motion with his hands tilting her buttocks for deeper penetration. She stretched fully to accommodate him, causing his dick to swell even further. Prolinc felt her withdrawal and stilled. "Have I hurt you, banshee, I fear it is too late for me to stop no matter the answer."

"You're so big, I can feel you butting against my womb," she admitted self-consciously. Prolinc propped himself up on his elbows and stared at her for what seemed like a full minute before responding. Then he flashed her a most sensual, confident, mind bending smile. It lit his eyes to an

almost iridescent mossy glow and gifted her with the
first glimmer into his soul; he was letting her see
him, truly see him. She gazed back in dazed wonder;
he was inviting her in.

She relaxed and found that the too full sensation
no longer proved unpleasant. She moved her hips
slightly to confirm the feeling. She began to throb,
she wanted him deeper, wanted him to move.
Looking up at him once again, she silently pleaded
for more. The response was instantaneous.

"I will find my way to your center, Dee. You will
take all of me, I promise; now relax and let me work
you."

This last, a spoken purr, before then she began
to feel it; his whole body seemed to vibrate, as his
purring grew louder and stronger. She hummed and
vibrated everywhere, her breasts, her stomach, her
buttocks, and deep inside of her. He began to move
within her as well. He pumped into her slowly but
firmly, at first, then harder and faster with an
unrelenting rhythm that quickly took her to that
marvelous precipice. He moved like a jackhammer
and she flew apart like so much concrete. She burst
into a million pieces, each piece echoing his name.
He let out a long keening answering snarl of
triumph.

He cradled her to his heart, rolling onto his back
to cushion her from the semi-hard surface of the
floor. She engulfed his senses both physically and
emotionally. How had this Earth woman captured
him so neatly? It would require extensive research;
exploring all of this creatures peaks and valleys and
soft plains. He had had many females of various
races and had pleasured them, as well as being
pleasured himself, but pleasure did not touch the
way this female made him feel.

He had always been number two. Number two
son, number two in rank, number two in life's

offerings, but Dee took him beyond numbers to a magical private world designed just for them. Could he bind her into the role of Chosen One by sex alone? He did not think so but he would do anything for her compliance, anything.

When Dee roused from her groggy and sated stupor, she focused on him with wonder and awe, doused with a sizable dollop of apprehension. She swallowed hard, at a loss as to how to proceed. She had a few questions as to his technique and wanted to know if this would happen every time, or if it had happened at all; because, if so, she didn't think she'd survive much past the coming week. Talk about a mind flyer, his lovemaking reined the most exhilarating, fulfilling, frightening experience of her life. It felt like the dreams she had on Zeba II. She feared she had just become a Prolinc addict with a zero possible cure-rate. He probably believed his special talent alone intoxicated and enthralled her and she'd probably let him believe that for a time, but the truth of the matter proved much more alarming. Prolinc himself formed the secret ingredient that ignited her fire. Anyone else would just be a hot body, gentle hands and a very large vibrator. Ordinarily a hot prospect in itself but Prolinc eclipsed every preconceived notion Dee had ever envisioned of intimacy, chemistry, and fantasy. He'd become her found key that unlocked her soul and freed her to the possibility of love. Still peaked on emotional overload she glanced to Prolinc for guidance. He seemed to understand because he gently brought them to their feet and proceeded to carefully dress her like a treasured doll. When they both were clothed, he led her down the hall to their quarters. She liked his mindset. They weren't done yet.

****

Something busily chewed on her toe while

another something had entangled itself in her hair, gnawing on her ear. Syphors...no kittens. Spock and Scotty greeted Cat in their usual manner and there droned a consistent beep on her COM signaling a message that must have awakened her. The kitten's antics had become so familiar they no longer roused her. The aunts had managed this surprise, no doubt, in an effort to make her feel more at home. The mini-terrorists looked like two matching black spooks with perfectly round moss-green orbs. Spock had a tiny white tuft on his chest while Scotty looked pure black, even though she knew black cats were in actuality a deep, deep mahogany. They had grown in the short time she'd been away but remained as open and playful as always. If she hadn't known better, she would have believed they had actually missed her. She had certainly missed them. Finally, she acknowledged the persistent beckoning of the COM and rose to approach her incoming.

As Zorroc proceeded toward his quarters, he could hear a gaggle of female voices chattering and giggling like schoolgirls and he knew the three friends had connected with each other again. Somewhat surprised it had taken that long; he surmised Carpov and Prolinc must have been keeping their women very occupied. He had intended to confront Cat to see if he could make things better between them and delve further into her Dargon confrontation. Something there was amiss. He had a niggling in the back of his neck that told him Cat would have been horribly used had they had deduced her identity. He would like to question her immediately but maybe gossiping with her friends would provide what she needed most, for the moment. Zazu knew what she would have to say about him but decided not to intrude anyway.

Dee and Cat finished their accounts of the past week and now it became Angel's turn. She almost didn't know where to begin. How could someone's entire being change within another's heartbeat. Most of what she had to impart surpassed glorious but there loomed one thing she dreaded to share. It would hurt them. She decided to start with it and then bombard them with the good stuff afterward.

"Remember Octapaws at the ed-center?" Angel broached, while focusing on the way Spock jumped and swatted at the proffered length of ebony hair she swished for his enjoyment.

Dee and Cat exchanged matching blank looks. Of course, they all remembered that lowlife; he constantly laid in wait for a quick feel from a passing girl, and rumors had persisted of worse. They had tried, on more than one occasion, to get him fired but his brother, a trustee of the board, dismissed their complaints. Octapaws, however, being informed of the grievances, would retaliate by cornering the accuser and making her life a living hell. It proved a compelling reason for the three to stay glued to one another as much as possible. They found safety in numbers. Had Angel met someone like that on board the ship, where had Carpov been?

"We remember, Angel, his clone is not lurking in the hallways, is he? I'd say the three of us could take him out easily these days." Cat tried for a little levity but at the somber expression on Angel's face, decided on the direct approach. "What brought him up?"

"He caught me alone in the lab a few times. He raped me," she whispered, unable to meet theirs eyes.

"I knew we should have killed him when we had the chance. Why didn't you say something, Angel, we would have stopped him," Dee fumed while trying to grasp the import of what Angel had just reveled.

Angel lowered her lashes, her lips forming the half smile of a seraph, and then gazed at her friends with all the love in her heart. "I feared you'd succeed in killing him for me and spend the rest of your lives in jail. Then where would I be?" She sighed, working up to the real reason. "He said if I told, that you two would be next. I couldn't let what he did to me, happen to you."

"Typical Angel, trying to take the lead sister role again. We could have dealt with him and kept each other safe, if only we had known. Never again, Angel, never again hold back on us," Cat threatened as she and Dee exchanged twin glances of guilt.

Cat should have picked up on the situation by the changes in Angel, beginning about the time she turned thirteen; the cloudiness seeping steadily, over time, into her fathomless dark eyes. How could she and Dee have missed it?

Because Angel kept them innocent and naïve.

"Gods, I fell like such an idiot," Dee lamented.

Cat patted Dee's back in commiseration. "She shielded us and kept us safe with her own body. Jesus, sweetheart, why didn't you let us help you?" Then another thought occurred to Cat. "Why are you telling us this now, after hiding it for so many years?"

With a wider smile Angel admitted, "Carpy made me do it; he told me you'd be pissed but would most likely let me live."

Angel's eyes, finally free of darkness, glowed like shiny black halos. At times, she embodied such ethereal goodness Cat and Dee wanted to weep. "Carpy...and you call him this because he carps at you worse than Cat and me?"

"Uh-huh." She proceeded to fill them in on her life and love with 'Carpy', their progress relating to the FIS vaccine and her very full play of passions.

"You know the aunts stayed with us on Jasper, don't you Cat?" Cat nodded and began rubbing Scotty's tummy; he was the more laid-back and affectionate of the two. "They want to see you and explain. They feel like they've become your real aunts and they love you. Promise me you'll listen to them and give them a break for the deception, okay?"

Cat frowned and looked away. "They COMd me earlier but I was saved from answering when you two busybodies showed up. I guess I could visit them one of these days to hear what they have to say." Cat deflated like a balloon only to re-inflate like a blowfish and pin both of them with her best no-nonsense glare. "You do realize that the reason we are all here is because Marie and Helen set me up, don't you, and as a result entangled both of you in the snare," Cat cast back, determined to score one last point in this already lost battle. "We emulated a small school of minnows swimming merrily into the net, not realizing it would end the world as we knew it and our freedom to boot," she ended with the flair of a splashy triggerfish.

"Yes," Angel sighed, "and I don't know how I will ever return the kindness."

"At least they feed us well," Dee added.

"Probably just fattening us up for the kill," Cat concluded.

Everyone believed Angel to be the 'brainy, aloof one', 'The Ice Princess'. If they only knew the truth. In actuality, she was as shy as Dee was brassy and kindhearted to a fault. Like now. Not the shy part of course, the shy part disappeared when she got to know you and morphed into the bossy part. Bossy and kindhearted, who could win an argument with someone like that? *Only a sycophant, whose main enjoyment in life involved drowning little kittens,* Cat grumbled silently to herself.

Dee and Angel exchanged a conspiratorial nod; the aunts would be jumping out of their tennies. They all needed the aunts, they represented the only family the three of them had known in a very long time and had become an integral part of their lives.

****

The aunts were euphoric and ecstatic to see Cat; and nervous, apprehensive, agitated, flustered, and all together ruffled.

Cat felt better already.

They launched into a soliloquy of how they'd transported the kittens and kept them safe; how they gave notice to Cat's employer so they wouldn't worry about her; then added that they hadn't given Angel's company notice on purpose. Let them wonder what had happened to her. They would probably conclude that she quit and left the state, which is exactly what she should have done when that mess began with one of the owners of the company. After everything she'd already endured with men, well, they deserved to worry and wonder whether she intended to speak with an attorney about a sexual harassment suit.

It took them about another fifteen minutes to finally wind down to a blessedly silent, pregnant pause. Clearly, at a loss as how to proceed, the two went Gattonian still and fixed twin gazes on Cat. That's when she noticed it. They had matching tawny cat-eyes.

She couldn't help herself. "What happened to your eyes, they used to be brown."

"Well, dear," Helen cast an anxious look at her sister, "these are the real color of our eyes; when we are on Earth we wear contacts to blend in."

"That must have been extremely uncomfortable for you, considering the length of time we lived under the same roof together," she observed politely.

"You're damn straight it was," mumbled Marie.

"Oh my, this isn't going very well at all," Helen messaged to her sister. Catarina was a fey little creature with too much openness, enthusiasm, and

naïve generosity. The three friends had raised each other and done a fine job of it but there remained missing pieces in each of them. They needed an anchor to firmly bind them together as a family and she and Marie had, long ago, determined that they would be that anchor.

They had decided to fix the three girls' lives as best they could and had been working diligently toward that end. They hoped Cat would let them stay in her life long enough to finish the job. She was a member of their family now, as were Angel and Dee, being extended sisters to Cat.

Cat observed 'her aunts' sitting too still as if waiting for some invisible axe to fall. They looked like two peas in a pod, literally. They reached no higher than five feet...and were plump. Well, maybe a little plumper than plump. They currently looked like two overfed, colorful Prairie pups propped together on the sofa that lined their quarters in an L shape. She had to let them off the hook.

"Zorroc told me he sent you to evaluate my suitability as a mate for him. I understand that you had no choice but to carry out his plans. I also know that my parents, if not the instigators, certainly facilitated the plan," she improvised, determined to clarify her parent's exact role in this dilemma.

"All the people of Gattonia were contacted for potential fertile females, darling girl. You belong to a High House with noble blood and therefore were considered the strongest possibility. Your parents knew this and, indeed, put your name into the hat, so to speak. They will be very proud that you mated with our leader," Marie explained logically.

"So, given a choice between duty and daughter, they chose duty. Is that the gist of it?"

"They thought you would be pleased once you got used to the idea, dear, they didn't mean to hurt you with their decision," Helen suggested, in an effort to comfort their charge. Cat had a distressed, pinched expression with too large eyes. Not for the first time, the aunts wished that Rowan and Nancia had just *once* put their daughter before a mission.

Cat had a tinkling concern hovering behind all else that had occurred. What would happen to Habi-Cat and its occupants now that they had departed? Who would be there to fight for, feed and protect them and keep them safe from needles, electrodes, deadly injections, and meat-grinders? She needed to know. Uitti could not be allowed to succeed. "What of Habi-Cat?" she finally voiced.

The aunts, at first startled at the change of subject, smiled brightly. "Oh well, dear, I think you could say we wet Cecil's wick and soon it will be as rotten as the rest of him—with the world looking on. It turns out that Dr. C. Uitti has another use for animals besides dietary. He apparently enjoys having conjunctional relations with them, or so the photos will depict. The un-retouched photos."

Cat stared, stupefied, viewing her aunts in a completely new light. "How?" she croaked.

"Where there's a will, sweetheart, there's a way," Helen beamed. "I just wish we could have stayed for the show," she sighed. "I guess the reports will have to suffice. This will not guarantee the safety of pets, by any means, but at least the movement will have been discredited for a time. One of our people has taken over the Habi-Cat to make certain your charges are protected and an influx of funds accompanied the new director. Have no fear, Cat, we have taken care of your feline orphans."

Cat loved these two incredible women. They may not be her true aunts, but they certainly were the aunts of her heart.

Marie decided that the time had come to change the subject. "What of you and Zorroc, is he making you happy?" Cat realized by the way they both tensed that they knew the answer already.

Cat squirmed under the aunt's avid attention. Well, it had been the primary reason she decided to visit sooner rather than later. "He's fulfilling his obligations to his people and to me but he doesn't...I'm merely another responsibility heaped on to his many others; I feel like yet another millstone around his neck. I had hoped you could tell me if this is Gattonian normal for mates or whether I am doing something wrong."

"Catarina Achilles, you will stop that this instant. You are much more than a responsibility to Rocky. We raised him from an infant and know more about him than any other living soul and he cares for you deeply, he just doesn't know what to do about it...or you," Marie *humphed* looking an awful lot like an older Merryweather in Sleeping Beauty.

"He's made it clear that I am nothing more than an obligation, baby making machine to preserve his family's holdings and status and populate future generations. Where do you get that he cares anything at all for me, beside my bloodline and reproductive capabilities," Cat demanded, dry-eyed and hands clasped together.

"Maybe he doth protest too much," Helen suggested while giving her a moment for her comment to sink in. "Has he told you anything about his family; about how his parents died, dearling?" Helen ventured not sure how to present the trauma that Zorroc had undergone at too young an age, but then, any age was too young to loose a parent, let alone both before you gained maturity.

"I know that you are his aunts, he mentioned a sister briefly but he hasn't spoken of his parents. I assume his father is dead or he wouldn't hold the rule; but aside from that, he hasn't shared his life with me. We're like sexually mated strangers and frankly, I am at a loss as to how to proceed." She blew a wayward curl away from her right eye before jumping out of her seat to dart from one end of the room to the other, pausing briefly to collect her thoughts and proceed. "One moment he's impossibly gentle, and attentive; like he truly does care for me, but in the next he's spouting bloodlines and procreation with no emotional attachment in evidence. He turns himself off completely. Can you tell me what I have obviously missed?"

"Child, we will do all we can for both you and Zorroc; we love you both. His mother died when he was thirteen in childbirth, you know, but she successfully delivered a girl child named Nadia. It was over quickly and it devastated both son and father. Shortly afterwards, Zion, Zorroc's father seemed to succumb to a wasting illness and lost the will to live. We believe that Zorroc blames the love that his parents shared to be the cause of his father's eventual demise four years later.

"During his father's illness Zorroc came to sexual awareness. In all of his relationships he never became personally involved. They consisted of unions based on uncomplicated sex. We kept waiting for him to progress into more rounded relationships, incorporating friendship and respect but that never materialized. We believe that he sees love as a great weakness to be avoided at all costs instead of the strength it provides to make one stronger. The more drawn he is toward you the more he retreats. We know this will prove to be quite a challenge for you but one you will meet successfully. A little patience will go a long way in this particular situation and even though we know patience is not one of your stronger points, we are depending on you to win him over with perseverance and love. You do love him do you not? Otherwise, why would you care about his changeable moods." Marie looked inordinately pleased with herself after this latest observation but

Cat was grateful for the confirmation of what she'd begun to ascertain herself. She and Zorroc actually had a great deal in common. She had never experienced emotional ties with anyone of the opposite sex and neither, for all his sexual prowess; had he.

"I love him," she admitted, "...and you!" She launched herself on the aunts for a long overdue hug.

Cat returned to her quarters with renewed determination and purpose. The time had come to take her tiger by the tail and yank, then hold on for dear life. She prepared for one hell of a ride. She COMd Angel to learn about acquiring tactical armor. A formal dinner, held to honor the Earth females, had been set for that evening and Cat wanted a dress to stun some sense into her Gattonian. Angel COMd the simple instructions back to her and Cat proceeded to procure a dress to die for.

Amethyst and demure in front with a high neckline, long sleeves, and covering everything down to her toes; the gown in the back, presented a different picture entirely. The material clung lovingly to her shoulders but was backless, exposing her shoulder blades, the delineation of her firm contours almost to the crack of her behind and showing off the dimples dotting either side of the base of her spine. It shimmered and flowed down to her strapless three-inch heels, which completed the outfit. She let her hair flow freely to play peek-a-boo with her back and took extra care with her make-up. As she clasped on the final addition of dangly earrings, the panel of their quarters slid open and she turned to face her heart-stopping male.

Zorroc's heart skidded at the sight before him. She appeared more confection than human and she was his. Her hair billowed around her like a live entity. The color of her dress set off her emerald eyes to perfection. He had never seen her dressed thus and it took all of his considerable control to keep from pealing it off and skipping dinner in favor of a more enjoyable meal. Gods, it clung lovingly to the landscape of her body...right down to her pebbled nipples. How could he be expected to keep his hands off her? And from the look in her eyes, he did not think she would object. Then a nasty thought interjected. Whom had she dressed for? It would not be him; he had destroyed her blossoming affection with his last barrage of careless banter.

"You look..." he croaked, and cleared his throat. "You look like a treasure." Feeling every bit the untried youth.

She smiled gratefully and replied, "Thank you. You look good enough to plunder me at will." Then she turned around and faced the mirror for a last check on her appearance.

He blinked, not believing what so blatantly appeared before him. Her well-toned back spoke of the hours spent honing her defense and yoga skills, the dimples on either side of her spine hinted at the firm buttocks just below; she comprised sheer perfection and he grew instantly hard. "You will not leave our quarters undressed as you are, the other males will be all over you." Then realizing the harshness of his tone, softened it to add, "Your body is for my eyes alone." With deceptive calmness and hooded eyes he then inquired, "For whom do you dress, my one, he will not touch you. You are my mate now."

Jealousy became him she decided; the dress had done its job. She smiled seductively noticing the considerable bulge between his thighs and purred, "I dressed for you, of course. I have no interest in anyone else. As you stated so succinctly, we are mated. I only want to please you."

"If you pleased me any more we would be

discovered naked and starved six days from now while I took my fill of you." He looked suddenly unsure, befuddled actually, Cat noted. Good! She smiled sweetly and sauntered toward him. He looked even more unsettled. Perfect!

"What's the matter, sweetheart, Cat got your tongue?"

"You will pay for this later...*sweetheart*," he responded, hooking her waist then swooping her into a hot, wet, deeply pulsing kiss. It answered every single one of her insecurities and she gave herself up to his raw dominance. He backed her into the wall as his hands found their way into the back of her dress then groped the silky skin of her back, buttocks and under. He lifted her slightly and supported her with one hand while the other traced down her spine past her crack and found her wet center; with two fingers he entered her spiking and massaging until they became coated in her cream.

She made up the most potent drug he had tasted and he wanted her more than breath. What game did she play? She acted like their last confrontation had never taken place. She was making him crazy with her irrefutable optimism. "You minx, it was not supposed to be this way."

"And what way is that, my very own?" Cat groaned, riding him hard. He altered the position of his fingers and massaged a spot deep inside her then slowly withdrew leaving her on the verge of orgasm.

He devoured her with a kiss promising further attention then shook his head and grumbled something about being late. He lowered her slowly to the ground and then slowly and thoroughly sucked the fingers that had been inside her, never losing eye contact. Heat blossomed on her cheeks and radiated to her lower abdomen. She doubted her legs would carry her. It also hit her that 'cream' had just taken on new meaning.

Chapter Thirteen

The dinner proved festive, lively and extravagant and all eyes followed the striking couple's progress to the main table. Cat did not appreciate that kind of attention; she didn't know what might be expected of her and was not accustomed to such lavish accoutrements. She felt as if she'd just stumbled into the Cinderella role at the ball while her seximometer scaled higher than five Margaritas. She thrummed uncontrollably and did not relish an audience to witness it. All she wanted to do was jump Zorroc and force him to finish what he started. *Get a grip,* she ordered herself and then remembered the grip Zorroc had on her not scant minutes before. She blushed as a drop of fluid wended its way down her inner thigh. Zorroc's mind collided with hers at that moment and his eyes caught fire scorching her with the knowledge of her own thoughts. Her blush grew in proportion to her discomfort. Zorroc groaned inwardly seating first her and then himself. His discomfort bulged before him and Prolinc, for one, had noticed, and tried, without success, to maintain his usual inscrutable expression.

Catarina strove to focus on her surroundings. Floor to ceiling murals lined the walls depicting exotic structures, landscapes and people. Many of the structures were pyramid in nature, while others resembled obelisks rising high into a red-orange sky as if to hold it up. Could this be her first glimpse of Gattonia? She wanted to go over and take a closer look at the wall art but knew it would have to wait until the dinner ordeal concluded. The massive assembly hall held the off-duty crew as well as the women with ease. She hadn't realized that close to half of the crew were females. Like the males, they were attractive to a fault; tall and lithe with varying complexions and hair colors. Next to the Earth women, they seemed exotic and rare. She wondered what the Gattonian males could see in the Earth women, and what Zorroc could see in her. She felt like a wren in a flock of peacocks. She sneaked a peek at Zorroc and caught him regarding her intently.

"You out shine every female here, my own," he whispered.

Spit, she thought, was he reading her again? "Thank you," she muttered politely, not believing him for a moment. She became distracted from further ruminations with the arrival of her friends— Carpov in tow holding firmly and possessively to Angel. The gowns worn by Angel and Dee were of a similar fabric looking like soft lush velvet but where Angel's was stark white, Dee's was jet black. They reminded her of ornate chess pieces belonging in a very exclusive brothel. Then it hit her—wasn't that where they were? On the other hand, maybe it was more like a community harem with multiple sheiks. Yikes! What a mind-boggling thought.

Would they be forever shut away in luxurious gilded pens? What really awaited them on Ganz? Horrified by her meandering; she yipped when Zorroc grabbed the back of her neck and pulled her toward him growling softly in her ear.

"You are mis-thinking again, Catarina, and will stop immediately." Turning her to him, he gave her a deep open-mouthed kiss in front the entire crowd. Well, if anyone wondered about the state of their carnal relations it was now tattooed onto every brain cell of each attendee. She felt stuck in that nightmare where you're in a group of hundreds of people and looked down to realize you don't have a stitch of clothing on and that all eyes are centered on you. She felt like a harem girl being claimed by the head Pooh-Bah.

Zorroc broke off the kiss, chuckling helplessly, as moisture gathered in his eyes. The times she had seen him smile she could count on two hands; the times she had heard him laugh she could count on a single finger. The Gattonian tablemates froze in head-tilted unity while Dee and Angel smiled in appreciation. There remained hope for these serious-minded, overly-autocratic-cat-people yet.

"You were reading me again, you cretin." She socked him in the arm. "I thought you told me it was impolite to do that without permission and that you could only do it at certain times."

"It is becoming easier and harder with time." As he spoke, he enfolded his large hand in hers and guided it to his male-part for a demonstration. "That fertile imagination of yours sprouts fantasies faster than pollen in spring. You are playing hell with my composure and you must stop before my reputation as a solemn, dignified leader is forever besmirched."

"Well, geez, then don't listen or read or whatever it is you do." She decided to focus on something mundane like...her drink. The aunts had done a fine job with the Margarita recipe. Maybe too fine. She, Dee and Angel had each tried one and found it definitely high test.

The meal was lavish and delicious. Five courses were served over two hours, one course more mouthwatering than the last. She just wished that one of them looked remotely familiar. She opted not to ask the ingredients; ignorance definitely equaled bliss in this case. Cat felt like she would burst if she put one more crumb into her mouth. Both Angel and Dee looked sated and relaxed, as well; their eyes slightly glazed and unfocused. They sure weren't feeling any pain. She would have felt the same way but her nipples had become sensitized and her breasts swollen, as they jutted into the front of her gown. She was also becoming sensitized down there, and having a hard time not squirming in discomfort. Next time she'd pick an outfit she could wear underwear with. She'd have to have another lesson in clothes conjuring; that much was apparent unless...what ingredients had they used in this supposed Margarita? The aunts had told her that they had ordered the recipe special but did they actually stock Tequila, limejuice, and triple sec on board? She took a closer look at her now squirming friends and then focused on Zorroc with a definite question in her eyes.

Before she could voice her thoughts, he whisked her drink off the table, taking a substantial taste.

Then things seemed to take on light speed proportions for the three friends trying to hone in on reality while their hormones honed in on their males.

Zorroc spat an expletive that Cat was not familiar with and then spat out "Assyllis". The three males popped up like jack-in-the-boxes and proceeded to launch their three tipsy females to their feet and escort them quickly from the hall. Cat turned back, explaining to Zorroc that she'd wanted to study the murals for a while, but he scooped her up over his shoulder and kept moving toward the jet-quik. Why did he always do that to her? Sticking her palm under her chin and elbow into his back, after the third try, she concentrated on the landscape of his hard flexing buns as he propelled them toward their quarters. She'd wanted time to formulate the perfect strategy toward seduction but maybe a little spontaneity would work just as well.

****

It was an aphrodisiac consisting of fascinating properties, actually; some of which Angel had never heard of but that Carpov described to her in graphic detail. Science had never sounded more orgasmic. He'd been riding her for three hours and both of them were drenched in sweat and cum. Carpov had kept up extremely well considering he was not the one afflicted.

He'd explained that Assyllis, a local Gattonian flower, when mixed with a number of synthetic ingredients and processed in a specific manner, increased the natural aphrodisiac existing in the flower, ten-fold. Available in liquid or tablet, the couple usually ingested it at the same time. Most of the time, it was administered medicinally to couples involved in an arranged alliance where love and natural attraction did not exist. It was harmless and non-addictive except for the sexual high it produced and usually took only a couple of hours to pass through the system. It was against the laws of his people to slip it to someone without their knowledge and Carpov seemed sure that Zorroc would be on the warpath to track down the person or persons responsible for spiking the Margaritas. It could be considered rape because of the mindless sexual craving it induced, and therefore had the status of a controlled substance on Gattonia.

He silently grew concerned that Angel, after three hours of non-stop sex, still suffered from the effects of the drug; not because it could harm her but because she had worn him out and did not know how much longer he could hold up. Every drop of sperm had been sucked out of him this night.

The drug had worn off an hour or so before, but Angel hadn't wanted to stop her love play with Carpov. Never before had she felt so light, so free, and so completely captivated. He must truly adore her to have put forth such a Herculean effort to keep her sated. She supposed it was time to let him off the hook...

****

"Oh God, Linc, what's happening?" Dee groaned while writhing on the platmat.

"A powerful aphrodisiac was added to your drink this evening and you are beginning to suffer the effects. It will get worse but I plan to join you." Prolinc opened the drawer beside his mat and retrieved his stash. He uncorked the small vile and downed the bitter liquid then focused on Dee.

"What did you do?"

"I took a dose of the same mixture in your drink. We will be together in this for as long as it lasts. I will please you as many times as you need and you will please me as well."

"Did you do this? Did you lace my drink so you could force me into submission? Because I'd rather die than become the hidden woman in your life, what's more I turned down your gracious offer of free sex earlier this evening, in case you have forgotten, so go away and leave me in peace."

"I did not drug you, banshee, nor would I ever stoop to such a despicable prank to gain your compliance as my Chosen One. You will need me tonight, love, and here I will stay. What you are feeling now will only become more intense until it will not matter who the male is, you will take anyone. I will not let that happen because shortly I will be in the same shape as you. The decision not to be mine, I will accept tomorrow but for tonight I will be the male to satisfy your needs." Prolinc swayed slightly while his eyes took on an un-Earthly glow. "The drug has taken effect, I need you," he rasped and collapsed onto the mat capturing her mouth in a raw feral kiss. She moaned and tore his clothes off before stripping, and impaling herself on his rock hard sex.

185

****

"How do you feel, my cream," Zorroc asked while efficiently slipping the sinful Amethyst concoction down Cat's body.

"Like I have a million tiny fire ants running around under my skin descending on and attacking my most private parts. What was in those drinks?" she ground out, beginning to feel the pain out-way the pleasure.

"Assyllis, it is an ancient flower that grows wildly in Gattonia. It is found on no other planet that we know of and is harvested in mass quantities by our people for export to other lands. It is normally ingested by two people together, to enhance sexual relations. Since our chemistry is potent to begin with, I am afraid the discomfort you feel will be increased," he finished this last with a half smile and shed his uniform. She grew almost mindless with the effects of the drug; he hoped he could bring her down to a tolerable level. The drug approximated torture if sexual relief remained unavailable.

"How do you stand it? How many times have you taken this stuff?"

"I have never taken it, as you can see it is mind-altering and I would be unable to perform my duties as ruler under its influence. The time has come to help you, all will be well." He sank onto the mat and began touching her firmly on her breasts, belly, and inside her vulva. She was soaking. This would not be a subtle joining; finesse would not be required or even appreciated for some time. He took her roughly and fast and that seemed to take the edge off for a few minutes. It would be a long night.

After the effects of the drug wore off, Cat fell into an unconscious slumber and they slept for hours. Zorroc stirred first and proclaimed it a day for breakfast on their mat, though the hour had long since passed. She would be hungry and most of all thirsty, a side effect of the drug. He himself felt like he could eat a dozen swirls. He had lost count of how many times he had taken her, or she him, after the sixth. He went to the COM and ordered enough food and liquid for four people, then proceeded to the clean room. He looked forward to the day.

When he was clean but still in the buff, he stood over his mate and inspected her. She was a mess. Her compact body had sprawled taking up more than half the mat. Her hair had spiked out in all directions except the strands glued to her cheeks, shoulders, and chest by perspiration. Her cheeks were rosy below the thick half moons of her lashes and her lips had swelled to a plump berry red.

He noticed several bruises and love bites on her neck, thighs, arms, and breasts and recalled the feel of her skin, like satin against his mouth but he had not intended to mark her as he had. Still, she formed the most breathtaking vision he had ever seen or could imagine and decided that lifemating could be a very enjoyable state. Never had he felt so replete, or experienced such an intense marathon of gratification. In that moment, he wanted to shower her with joy and spoil her to distraction. He turned and headed back to the clean room. He would fill the massage pool and let her wake in his arms while letting the healing water flow over their bodies. She would be sore and the pool would give him an excuse to hold her again. He had wanted to try the accessory since coming aboard the Miramid; most ships did not provide such opulence.

She barely stirred as he lifted her into his arms and sank with her into the pool. He washed her hair and body gently, taking great pleasure in administering to her. She surfaced slowly into reality to register Zorroc cradling her to his chest and surrounding her with his muscular legs, and the sensation of gently swirling warm currents moving around them. "Z, where are we?" she slurred.

"Hello, sleepy one, we are in the massage pool. I thought you would be sore after so much sex sport last night; how do you feel?" He began to lick and kiss her left shoulder and she sighed tilting her head to give him better access. He had lost control at one point during the night and given her another mating mark lost in the throws of a particularly violent orgasm.

"I feel like my muscles have turned to honey and I'm floating in a babbling brook of warm scented water. How are you, did I hurt you last night?"

"No, you did not harm me," he gazed her bemusedly, "but you were very enthusiastic." He smiled widely, reached over for a glass, and placed it in her small, slightly trembling hand. "Drink this, you must be thirsty from the drug; it is a juice similar to your Tangerine, I think." She drank deeply and sighed.

Breakfast surpassed delight with an array of fruits, pastries, cold meats and other delicacies that the two inhaled like two starving refugees. They were still without clothing and Cat felt decadent and a little self-conscious, but very pleased. Things seemed to be going very well in her quest to catch her cat man's heart. She'd never seen him more relaxed and playful with his barriers lowered and she reveled in this new side of him. At the end of their meal, he chased her around the room catching her on the mat where he entered her and began reciting all the names he could think of for the act they engaged in, punctuating each term with another thrust.

"There is tupping, tossing, toppling, twitching, and tooling," he began. "Then we have swiving, screwing, shafting, rutting and fucking. And we cannot forget rolling in the hay, raiding the honey pot and sucking the pump dry, which is what you did to me just last night." His eyes danced merrily until tears ran down her flushed cheeks.

"Wait a minute, what about boffing, rocking and riding?" she asked in mock inquiry.

"You, my pet, are a very quick study. And speaking of studying, do you feel you mastered your lessons last night?"

"Umm, yes, I believe I am now qualified to write the fiftieth book of the Kama Sutra."

"In that case, I think a test is in order."

Chapter Fourteen

She felt lazy, sated and deliciously sore as she headed toward the large dining hall with all the murals. They transcended art and seemed to tell stories about the history of the Gattonians. Engrossed in her examination, she didn't notice Rosik until he stood beside her. "These are simply lovely, do they depict the history of your people, or are they just beautiful pictures?"

Rosik answered thoughtfully, "They tell stories of our ancestors. It is an ancient craft handed down generation to generation. We have artisans that do nothing but study art form and history from the time they are toddlers. It is a much-respected pastime and they are well compensated.

"This grouping depicts Gattonia with our skies and buildings, while these over here tell a story of our early encounters with the Egyptians and the constructing of the pyramids."

"You used to wear space-suits. There are similar drawings in the tomes of the pyramids, but where theirs are primitive, yours are lush and detailed," she spoke reverently as she examined each scene in detail.

"We wore pressurized suits to protect existing life forms from our contaminants, not for self protection. After the Egyptians and other species we encountered had been sufficiently inoculated, we shed the protective attire. But this precaution is already familiar to you because of your own history with the Native American Indian." He spoke matter-of-factly. Her head positively spun from his revelations and what it all meant. She felt like he'd just opened the door to *OZ*.

"I asked Zorroc about the pyramids," Cat commented absently as her gaze lit on another grouping. "This group of murals seems to illustrate Gattonians and Egyptians working together to design and build several pyramids complete with larger than life sculptures of varying shapes."

"Ours was one of many species to visit your planet. Egypt was designated the universal landing point onto your world, and the pyramids, the result of the combined effort of many off-worlders, all of whom were treated as gods. Egypt nourished a simple and superstitious people. Not only were off-worlders treated as gods but many of there own creatures, native to the land, were too. And if an alien species remotely resembled one of their native creatures, as ours did, they became even more revered."

"What do these represent?" The section of wall showcased a group of four murals. The first depicted a beautiful, young Egyptian woman and an equally handsome man talking to a group of Gattonians. The next mural portrayed a journey by boat to lands far away with battles fought along the way. The third conveyed a land of green rolling glens with simply clad people, fairies, goblins, leprechauns and pookas in various shapes and forms dotting the hills and trees. And the final mural showed a space ship lifting off into the sky leaving the bustling hillsides below.

"This tells the story of Scota and her husband Mil Espaine and their service to our people when we were in need of assistance. One of our ships crash-landed north and west of Egypt, stranded in a foreign and unexplored land.

"Scota, the daughter of a powerful pharaoh called Nectanebus, and her husband, Mil Espaine, a commander in her father's army, were preparing a journey to Mil's homeland. It happened to be close to the location of our downed ship. Though Mil perished in a battle along the way, Scota continued on and led us to our crew. She became so revered by Mil's people that eventually they named that particular piece of land after her. In ancient times it was known as Scotia. Now it is called Scotland. The Celtic people, initially confused and unsure of us because of our appearance, later gave us the name of an already established spirit called "pooka" because of our feline eyes and humanoid body."

Fly specs! She'd been wallowing in fly specs while miracles surrounded her at every turn. It made so much sense. So they really were pookas, she'd been right all along. She was married to a pooka. She yipped and flung her arms around Rosik to thank him for the history lesson but was immediately hurled away by the force of a frosty gale wind named Zorroc. Her cat man had arrived at an awkward moment. He had the look of a glacier but was panting too hard to be totally still.

Rosik looked amused. "You have a very curious mate, Zorroc," he intoned calmly.

"How much have you revealed to her?"

"Pretty much everything. She is a very enthusiastic pupil," he added while lewdly arching his eyebrows.

Zorroc leveled a censorious look at his mate and commented softly, "Curiosity, killed the Cat."

"Yes, but satisfaction brought her back," she returned playfully. "I think I'll write a book titled 'I married a Pooka', what do you think, best seller material?"

Zorroc gave her a mock look of ferociousness before turning an amused eye toward Rosik. "There is a meeting to debrief Catarina on her abduction, to try and make sense of how the Dargons found us to begin with. You will both accompany me." He snagged Cat's waist in a possessive gridlock and led them to a large conference area where Sycor, Bandoff, and Prolinc waited.

"Tell us all you can remember, Catarina, take your time for this will probably take the remainder of the afternoon," stated Prolinc in pure security mode.

She licked her lips and began her tale trying to leave nothing out.

They determined it had been no random finding. Their party had been set up and it almost had to have come from one of their own crewmembers or a high-ranking official apprised of their location. That being the case, it followed that they remained at risk. Which woman had they been after; because it was clear, they searched for a specific name. Was it Cat? Zorroc had a sick feeling that was exactly who they had targeted. For what purpose, blackmail, ransom, murder? None of the options were palatable. Could there be an assassin among the crew that would eventually go after Cat?

"It is impossible to believe one of my crew could be capable of such perfidy," Zorroc stated as the full measure of betrayal began to take shape.

"Maybe they are not. Maybe they just think they are reporting routinely to a friend or higher source—who in turn relays the information to the Dargons?" Rosik proposed. "You are the Leader of our people, Zorroc, surely you have political enemies who would kill in order to fulfill their own political aspirations. I am sure our viper will be found in that nest."

Zorroc considered the Commander thoughtfully. Rosik had never before served directly with Zorroc, therefore the two did not know each other well; but with each passing day he began to trust Rosik as one of his own command. His mind was razor sharp and if Rosik had a less than stellar attitude, well, Zorroc supposed he had earned that much. His loyalty toward Zorroc had been unflinching and was greatly appreciated.

"There is something else," Rosik continued. "The Miramid had been ordered to another galaxy three days before the attack on your ship. If not for crucial repairs necessary for galaxy jump, your distress beacon would not have reached us. Your rescue would have been postponed for days at least, maybe even a month. It was sheer luck we remained to assist you."

"The muck gets deeper the more we probe. Catarina," Zorroc directed, "there was a time that you were blocked from me and I could not read you; what was happening?" All eyes turned to Cat; the question eliciting surprise from Rosik. He had not known they were mind-linked.

"One of the Dargons came to me stark naked except for a stupid cape and a large knife. His name was Gorn. I guess you guys don't know about Star Trek either, huh?" Her hunch was confirmed by their blank stares. "Well, he started pounding around in some sort of Aboriginal type dance and his appendage grew to massive proportions.

"What! Use your imagination. Anyway, he smelled terrible and the entire cave reverberated and then he stopped right in front of me, waiting for me to do something," she finished, reliving the picture of the sweating, stinking, panting monster with a dick the size of her leg and shuttered.

"What happened then," Prolinc asked almost against his will.

"I clapped," she answered.

Surely he could not have heard right, Zorroc stared fixedly at Cat; he thought she said clapped. "Clapped? You mean clapped your hands?" he asked.

"Well, yeah, what would you have done?"

The room went silent for several seconds. That is when it began...a slow rusty vibrating rumble from inside Zorroc that escalated into a roar of laughter so loud no one could move for the astonishment it produced to the others in the room.

He should be furious, she could have been killed, but instead he could not stop laughing, the image of a naked, embarrassed Dargon was too clearly etched in his consciousness.

****

Cat's days took on a pleasant routine. She spent her early mornings with Zorroc, eating, loving, and bathing followed by intensive training with the women at the X-center teaching self-defense tactics. Both Gattonian males and females showed up from time to time to observe and even participate in the classes. There were three instructors; Dee, Cat and a Gattonian female named China. The entire group was getting to know one another and she'd met a number of both women and Gattonians that she particularly enjoyed. Angel, closeted with Carpov, worked around the clock on a vaccine for the female crewmembers and women.

The afternoons represented free time and her evenings were spent in the great hall having dinner and socializing. Sandra continued to take every opportunity to sidle up to Zorroc. The male crewmembers had taken to calling her 'Sandra the Syphor'. A nickname started by Sycor.

China observed Sandra's latest foray before focusing on Cat. "Does it not distress you that she constantly dogs your male? If she were after my mate I would cut out her clitoris and feed it to her."

"China, just the mental picture alone is enough to make me nauseous. Besides, not even Sandra would be stupid enough to get between you and Westel. Where is he tonight?"

"He is on skeleton duty for the next five days. It happens to both of us once a month. Usually we try to time it together but this time it did not work out.

195

Look, Prolinc is headed toward Zorroc; I think he has decided our leader has suffered enough."

"Prolinc looks like a dark thunderous cloud since Dee moved in with the aunts. I think we have a great deal to learn about your culture. Just how demeaning is the role of Chosen One?" Cat asked, relieved to see Sandra saunter from the room.

China studied her for a moment before answering. "Many middle houses agglu-mate to create an alliance with a higher house. These alliances are business arrangements and rarely form a love match. Although the match is required to produce heirs, tender feelings are not normally involved. A Chosen One is the love match for a male or female in this situation to make the alliance palatable. The female is restricted from taking a lover until two offspring have been produced then she too is free to take a Chosen One. These are normally life-binding joinings and except for the producing of heirs with the agglu-mate, monogamous. There is no shame in being a Chosen One and the relationship is less binding than agglu-mating or lifemating, for the Chosen One may lifemate elsewhere if she or he so chooses," China finished knowing that Dee remained much over-rent by Prolinc's coming alliance to another female.

"Do you know Prolinc's intended?" Cat inquired while studying Zorroc in a board game with Prolinc.

China started uneasily. "You do not?"

A bad feeling clogged Cat's throat making it difficult to answer. "No."

China hissed and seemed to deflate. "Well, you did not hear this from me, agreed?"

Cat nodded hoping she could block the knowledge from Zorroc.

"Nadia is Prolinc's intended; Zorroc's only sister."

"Spit Snap!" She glanced again at Zorroc to

confirm his attention on the game. "Come on let's walk, I don't think I can sit still to hear this."

"The solarium is down this way, it will give us privacy." The two moved silently down the corridor. "You know that Zorroc's mother died in childbirth and there was a child?" With Cat's affirmative nod China continued. "Nadia's father had little to do with the babe so the responsibility rested with the aunts and house staff along with Zorroc and Prolinc to raise her. She followed them everywhere like a small puppy and they tolerated her well and spoiled her in the bargain. With the death of his father, Zorroc became legal guardian of Nadia and that is when Prolinc's family began to make their move.

Prolinc had been sent to live with Zorroc when the two were small children and were inseparable growing up. Prolinc's family used this bond to forge an alliance with the House of Ra thereby elevating them to a level that should have been impossible to attain."

"Wait a minute," Cat whispered and shook her head as if trying to fit all the pieces together. "If their houses stood so far apart, how did the two boys get together in the first place?"

"Even as a small child, Prolinc had very strong telepathic and guardian abilities. The two were raised together in order to form an unbreakable bond of friendship and mind-link. Prolinc is charged with guarding Zorroc with his life for the rest of their time in this realm. He was chosen for his talent and his family fastened onto his tail for the upward rise in status."

"I take it Prolinc's family is not on you're A list of favorites."

"They are users. They used Prolinc as a boy, use him still as a male, and make him feel less than he is in the process. They treat him as an unnatural anomaly and they would bind him to a female he thinks of as a little sister, just for their own selfish gain," she ended, with a disgusted hand gesture.

"How do you know all this? Either Gattonia is a very small place or it must have one hell of a grapevine. Is all this stuff chronicled somewhere for curious cat people?"

China saw the humor evident in Cat's sparkling eyes and realized the jest for what it was. "Either Earth women have very skewed humor centers or this defect resides solely with you," she volleyed back. The two grinned in growing affection and camaraderie.

"Spill, China, how do you know so much about the situation?"

China shrugged. "From my parents mainly; I am cousin to Prolinc. Our families, for better or worse, mainly worse except for Prolinc, are joined and as an adult watching this farce of an alliance is frustrating. She is sixteen years and innocent as a babe while Prolinc is a male grown. Theirs will be an unnatural union."

"Why doesn't someone call it off? Surely the aunts and Zorroc want something better for Nadia, to say nothing of Prolinc."

"Zorroc sees it as a way to help his friend and protect his sister and Prolinc sees it as a way to please his family, I believe. He remained ambivalent about the union before the coming of Dee; she has definitely put a monzu in his suit."

"What's a..."

"There you are, my Cat, I thought I had lost you. I trust you have been entertaining my mate well, China," At the sound of Zorroc's voice, the two jumped in startled synchrony.

China excused herself and beat a hasty exit while Zorroc and Cat followed at a more leisurely pace. He kept a light hold on the back of her neck and played with the soft hair at her nape. She calmed him, she challenged him, she loved him, and she made him laugh. He was beginning to treasure her, Zorroc realized uncomfortably.

****

Equal parts exhilarated, befuddled, anxious, and frightened, Cat contemplated her changed world. The tapestry of her reality had unwoven. Reality. Perception. Truth. Fact. Ontology. All of these had splintered into a million gleaming shards. She truly felt like Sleeping Beauty awakening after a lifetime of dreams. She recalled a poem by Edgar Allan Poe that she'd memorized at the ed-center.

'You are not wrong, who deem that my days have been a dream.
Yet, if hope has flown away in a day, in a night, in a vision or in none—is it therefore the less gone?
All that we see or seem is but a dream within a dream.'

What dwelled in our make-up that allowed us to create our own reality when truth stared us in the face? We blithely deny what we don't want to acknowledge, perfectly at ease in our ignorance, in the very small box we have encased ourselves. Her box had been comfortable but confining, she now could admit.

Why hadn't she seen that Marie and Helen were different? Well, actually you'd have to be blind not to see they were different. But from a different planet? She snorted, they were not even related; shouldn't she have intuited that on some level? She'd just accepted everything at face value and what aligned compatibly with her limited frame of reference. Had she ever really believed in the existence of extraterrestrials or unexplained metaphysical phenomenon or Santa Clause? Okay, okay! She was pretty sure about the Santa Clause thing...wasn't she?

And what of Zorroc? He'd stood directly in front of her and yet it had taken several confrontations before she'd begun to accept the reality of his existence.

When had her species lost the ability to detect the miracles swirling and cascading around them? A true reality. And, was she changed as a person after discovering the truth of her background? In many ways, the past weeks had flown by with the surreal reality of a chimera—make that cyclone. She'd had scant time to ponder the mysteries of her ancestry or how it affected her as a person. Angel and Dee treated her the same and she, herself, felt no different. To think she belonged to this ancient, exotic civilization eclipsed overwhelming. Yet, she still embodied the sum total of all her experiences plus her core being. Something no one could change or steal.

Instead of feeling overwhelmed, she felt freed. Never again would she accept anything at face value. She'd look beyond or within and try to determine the truth or her truth, and not what outside influences conveniently fed to her. The sleeper had awoken, as Paul Atredies had declared in Dune.

****

When Bandoff entered COM Central, he recognized the now familiar uneasiness. The feeling that had grown steadily since Dyfainius had approached him at the onset of their mission. As senior member of the High Council, he ranked number two behind Zorroc and wielded unparalleled political leverage. At first, Bandoff had been flattered beyond measure to be singled out by this great and powerful leader. His directive had been simple and seemingly harmless. Just report in every week to let him know, personally, how their ship fared.

Dyfainius had been relaxed, genial, and complimentary of Bandoff's efforts to date and Bandoff could go far as one of Dyfainius's minions. His parents and Milli, his intended, would be so proud. Why then did he sense something amiss? His suspicions had grown with the attack on their ship but surely if anyone could be trusted with unimportant and non-confidential information, it would be the members of the High Council. Maybe he could broach the subject with Sycor, he seemed comfortable and at home in political waters. Zanan was on COM duty. After the two greeted each other, Bandoff said he needed to COM the home planet.

Zanan started uncomfortably. All COM personnel had been given explicit orders. Under no circumstances were there to be any outgoing COMs and all who tried were to be reported to Prolinc immediately. "Everything all right at home Bandoff?" he inquired casually.

"Oh, yes. Uh, everything is fine, thank you for asking. I just wanted to send a short message, nothing more."

"Well, I am glad all is well because our outside COM is out; a disturbance of some sort. Should I let you know when it passes?" Zanan offered.

"Thank you but it really was of no importance."

Zanan contacted Prolinc.

A summons arrived for Bandoff five minutes later ordering him to report to the planning room at once. His uneasiness grew. Prolinc, Zorroc, Rosik and Sycor waited in telling silence as Bandoff entered and took a seat. Prolinc seemed to study the writing utensil rotating from his fingers for a full two minutes before he asked the first question. "Who were you going to COM Bandoff?"

At that moment, he knew his growing uneasiness had been justified. "Before we departed

201

from Gattonia I was contacted by the High Council and asked to report on the status of our journey and confirm that all progressed smoothly. It seemed a small enough request," he answered.

Zorroc swore under his breath.

"What kinds of information did the High Council request," Prolinc asked.

"At first just general inquiries. Were we on schedule and the ship malfunction free? After we arrived they asked about Earth, my impressions of the women, and how our plans proceeded in procuring them." He paused to evaluate the change of pattern that had occurred once they departed for Ganz. Why had he not questioned it before? He thought he might be sick.

"And once we had accomplished our purpose and began the journey home?" Sycor asked, not unkindly. He felt sorry for his friend; he knew Bandoff incapable of subterfuge; and attracting attention of any kind, whether positive or negative, made him distinctly uncomfortable. This situation must be tearing him apart. Sycor had often thought Bandoff would be much better suited in a low profile clerk's position but with his phenomenal abilities and trueness of heart he had been given no alternative but the very high profile position of Guardian to their Leader.

Bandoff sat up and leaned forward. "The requests grew detailed. They wanted to know how many women we had aboard, how they were being stored, and if all crewmembers were accounted for and unharmed. They were also curious if there were any females of particular interest to Zorroc and if so what were their names and backgrounds? In addition, of course, they wanted to know our location, but unlike our journey to Earth, they wanted specific co-ordinates. Is that how the Dargons located us?"

"We think so, yes," Zorroc spoke for the first time.

"I do not understand; could there have been a COM leak in our transmissions? It does not seem possible that anyone on the council..."

Ignoring Bandoff's queries, Zorroc once again took over. "Were you reporting to all members of the High Council or ones in particular?"

"There has been but one contact. Dyfainius. Surely you cannot suspect him; he was your father's trusted advisor, the head of the High Council, the father of your future..." Bandoff reframed from saying what all knew. His daughter had been chosen to lifemate with Zorroc until the virus struck. There would be no lifemating between him and Zana now. Was that a reason to turn traitor? If Zorroc had lifemated with Zana and something had happened to him; rule would have fallen to Zana who in turn would have ceded to her father. Zazu, that had to be it. Bandoff winced but did what he considered appropriate under the circumstances. "I resign my commission effective immediately unless you would like to employ a more fitting punishment."

Chapter Fifteen

"There will be no resignation Bandoff. You have compromised no one; you are the one compromised. However, we can use this to our advantage by feeding Dyfainius false information as to our whereabouts and situation," Zorroc stated.

"How much does he know of our flight plans and progress," Prolinc asked.

"I have not COMd him since our rescue so he knows little. My time has been spent guiding the women in protocol and Gattonian customs...and to be honest, I grew uncomfortable relaying information to Dyfainius and therefore, had put off reporting to him until today. Thank Zazu."

"I believe we have found your viper, Zorroc, but why would he side with the Dargons when there are many other species that would like what Gattonia has to offer and all much safer to deal with. Are there others on the High Council or citizens that would support him?" Rosik inquired.

Zorroc thought for a moment and shrugged. "The answer to that question will come in time. For now, Bandoff, you will COM Dyfainius and begin our subterfuge. Sycor will assist with false co-ordinates. Begin to hint that I am interested in another woman and have lost interest in Catarina," Zorroc paused then smiled grimly. "Tell him that a ravishing goddess by the name of...Sandra...has caught my eye and I am having second thoughts about continuing my alliance with a daughter of Gattonia. Does he know that Cat is my mate?"

"My last COM transmitted almost four weeks

ago. I did not discover you were lifemated until we had seen a week on the Miramid. He cannot know unless others have COMd him."

"There have been no COMs since the report of your rescue," Rosik explained. "It is standard procedure for COM blackout until we are well away from possible detection by the enemy and have evaluated our situation. He cannot know unless we have a traitor among our COM personnel and the chances of that are miniscule. I think your plan is a solid one," he finished still clearly calculating any holes in his logic.

"Several directives must be adhered to in order to make this work," Prolinc directed softly. "One: What we have learned does not leave this room, either to our women or any other essential party. We cannot take the chance of a careless word. Two: Bandoff's COMs will be limited to two minutes so our position cannot be traced. Three: We meet tomorrow to begin formulating a plan to determine how we'll proceed after landing at Gattonia. So far, we have no absolute proof of Dyfainius's guilt or how many may be involved. Is this understood and agreed upon?" After affirmative nods, they adjourned.

The conclusion of the strategy meeting the following day left Zorroc feeling beaten, depressed and with an overwhelming sense of impending doom. Not because of Gattonia politically, or Dyfainius and any co-conspirators but because of his mate. Almost certainly, she would see this as an unforgivable betrayal; indeed, a large part of the plan depended on it. Above all things he had to keep her safe, temper tantrums or no. Even now, she might be carrying the future leader of Gattonia.

The plan was simple. Keep Cat safe by feigning disinterest, conceal the mate-mark confirming the union, and divine the Gattonians involved in traitorous acts against the empire. The crewmembers would be sworn to secrecy. They would be arriving on Ganz in two days having sped up to full power on the off chance they were being tracked. He would love his Catarina fiercely for the next two nights in preparation of harder times to come. Maybe that way, she would know in her heart that he bided with her, even if they could not be together for a short while. Zazu, he hoped it would be over soon and all revealed. He told himself that a small separation would provide the exact solution he needed to gain perspective on their union.

He had been growing addicted to her delectable body, her quirky mind, and her irradiant, precious soul. He was very much afraid that he had too much of his father in him. He must not let her conquer his heart as his mother had his father's. When his mother had died and her soul floated to nirvana, she had taken his father's with her, leaving behind an ineffectual shell of a male. Maybe with the separation, Zorroc would learn that she was not so important to him after all.

****

"I'm telling you Dee, being a Chosen One is not the insult we assumed. I had a long talk with China and got the slim-skinnies on mating customs and Prolinc's intended. Are you interested or are you just going to hide behind the aunts for the next twenty years," Cat taunted, trying to elicit some kind of response. Dee had been holed up in the aunt's quarters for the last two and a half weeks only surfacing to teach defense classes. She'd never known Dee to run from anything and wondered if she hid from Prolinc or herself and the strong pull she felt toward him.

Dee looked close to exploding before expelling an anguished whoosh, resting her head against the back of the seat and closing her eyes. "I'll listen, just don't leave anything out, and don't expect me to change my mind."

Half an hour later Dee began pacing. "Well, why couldn't he have just explained that? I've been going through hell these last weeks!"

"I'd venture, because you didn't give him a chance," Cat replied before pausing to gather her thoughts. "Prolinc is a proud male with semi-battered self-esteem. I don't think he'd beg or try to explain for fear you'd use it against him and possibly still turn him down."

"Why would I want to do a hurtful thing like that? I mean aside from the fact that he hurt me first. God Cat, I think I might be in love with him. He only told me he'd been promised to another and couldn't mate with me and would I become his Chosen One. What was I to conclude?"

"This is a different world with its own unique rules and rituals. I think it will take time to understand how everything works and we're going to have to learn to ask questions first and assume never. Not a skill that either of us excel at. I sure could use an 'Angel fix' right about now, have you heard from her?"

"She left a message on my COM yesterday while I was in class to saying she's fine, happy and close to a vaccine for the virus. I've never her heard this relaxed and content. Carpov fits her perfectly." Then she groaned. "I'm going to have to seek out Prolinc, there's no way he'll approach me at this late date."

"I'm afraid you're right about that. Look, there's an officers dinner tonight, why don't you come with us? Come by at six and we can design some killer dresses first."

"Oh, Cat, do you think it will work?

"Positive, Dee, I just know it."

With Gattonia less than forty-eight hours away, morale among the crew surged to an all time high.

For the first time in over two years it looked as if the female crewmembers would be allowed to step foot on their homeland. The buzz and energy in the air proved contagious, even for the Earth women. Some had acclimated very well but others were having emotional problems, now that the reality of their situation had sunk in. Initially, it had seemed like a grand adventure, however now that they approached their final destination, probably never to see Earth again, some exhibited symptoms of shell shock.

The Med-team distributed relaxers to those with the most severe symptoms and, so far, no one had totally lost it. They were all being handled with kid gloves. Keeping them busy with comportment and defense classes had been a stroke of genius, as it turned out. It provided a non-threatening and, for the most part, non-sexual medium for the Gattonians and women to get to know one another—evolving into a productive lesson for everyone. The women posed no threat to the female crew, because they had been off planet at the time of attack. In fact, many of the females on board, including China, had halted previously encouraged birth control measures and were currently pregnant. They looked forward to having their offspring born in Gattonia. The unattached males, of course, had been overjoyed to have such free access to the women and many planned to continue their alliances once home.

Excitement overflowed as Dee, Cat and Angel arrived at the dining hall. Angel had surprised them by showing up at six-thirty looking her breathtaking self. While Dee and Cat got ready, she filled them in on her last few weeks and imparted the news of her pregnancy. The three were ecstatic.

Dee had never looked more beautiful when she approached Prolinc and asked if she could sit next to him. He almost knocked over his chair in his haste to stand and pull out the chair.

Cat hadn't seen Zorroc since early morning and wondered at his absence. He'd sent word late that afternoon that he would meet her at dinner, because he'd gotten tied up in meetings. Normally, she saw him at least three to four times a day and she missed his presence. Angel was pregnant and Cat wondered if she would be right behind her, she'd missed her period the week before and usually she could set her clock by it. Nausea crept up on her at the strangest times, as well. She'd broach the subject with Angel later, in private, to see if she had an extra pregnancy test.

Her eyes lit on Zorroc as he made his way across the room and her heart leapt at the sight of him. Before making his way to her, he stopped at another table to converse. Sandra was seated in the group and he actually initiated a conversation with her. What was happening? As if he could hear her question, he looked up and met her eyes briefly before returning his attention to Sandra. He smiled charmingly and touched her on the shoulder before turning to join Cat. Her heart sank into her shoes and she had difficulty catching her breath. Zorroc engaged Dee and Prolinc in conversation as if nothing was amiss and seemed pleased to see the two together once again. The mood grew light and carefree. Everyone seemed to be having a wonderful time except Cat. Zorroc politely ignored her and as the dinner wore on a black mood settled on her shoulders like a two-ton weight.

By the end of the evening Cat was numb. What had gone wrong, what could she have done to cause his alienation?

Cat had become impossible to read but her agitation surrounded her like a shroud. Zorroc hated himself for what he had to do but if he told her everything, her reactions would not be genuine and that could put her in further danger.

He loved Cat's body desperately, long into the early hours, but the darkness refused to lift, and by the time she awakened, he'd gone. Instead of going to her defense class, she spent the day playing and cuddling with Spock and Scotty. She'd grown exceedingly weary of this love thing. She stayed constantly off balance and her mood seemed to mirror Zorroc's attention toward her. It was simply pathetic now that she acknowledged it. She needed some distance to get things in perspective. She always thought that women who based their world around a man were weak, spineless parasites waiting to be squished. But what of her mate-mark, she pondered; well she'd just cover it up and go her own way. These were Gattonian rules, not hers and she'd never given her word not to dissolve their union that she could recall—especially when he'd engaged himself elsewhere first. Zorroc could get bent, she swore, and then dissolved in a puddle of tears.

Cat visited Angel later that afternoon and got the news she now dreaded...she was pregnant. Angel was thrilled. Cat was determined. She'd make love to him and show him how deeply her love for him ran...and if she couldn't make him love her back, she'd simply walk away.

Maybe she'd been just a temporary diversion to ease the boredom of a long voyage. She had to admit she'd been entertaining, at least. She'd learned her lessons well and he'd succeeded in getting her pregnant. All of his plans for her, obviously stamped accomplished. She wondered if he knew about the baby, and had simply moved on to unplowed territory. Perhaps he'd already confirmed it by reaching out to his little mind. That had to be it; he had teased, charmed, indulged, and loved her until certain of her condition and then turned it off like a spigot. Well he may have achieved his goals but she wasn't giving up on her own just yet.

She washed their room in candlelight, took a long leisurely bath laced with Wisteria oil and finally slipped into the naughty negligee she'd ordered. And then waited for her cat man/pooka to arrive...and waited...and waited...and waited.

He entered their room and froze. Candles illuminated every surface bathing the room in muted golden warmth. He watched the slow rise and fall of his mate's breasts, her hair framing her delicate features in an auburn wreath. She wore a see through concoction of black, filmy, intricate webbing that looked as if it would tear at the first gentle tug. She had wanted to seduce him. Did she not know he had no need of candlelight or sinfully tempting gowns to attract his attention? His miniature goddess had issued an invitation he had no intention of ignoring. In all likelihood it would be the last for some time.

She dreamt of him once again, touching her everywhere, loving her intently while she melted right into the mat. She wanted it to go on and on. He purred suckling and nuzzling first one breast and then the other while his hands roved over every inch of her. And then nothing. With the absence of his touch, she awoke. The glow from the candlelight illuminated his powerful frame working furiously to shed his suit. No words could describe his untamed beauty. Her hand moved over her abdomen—and she now held part of him inside of her.

"I love you," slipped from her mouth before she could stop it. He stilled and stared then eased down next to her.

"Remember that Catarina, promise that you will not forget in the days to come. I will be busy with the High Council and state responsibilities and you will not see me. In light of that, the last thing I want to do tonight is talk."

Their lovemaking throbbed like a wild, live entity. He smashed the barriers that she'd tried to erect for self-preservation until she was left with nothing but his murmurs, his touch, his scent, his sex. There existed no Zorroc and no Cat but one powerful force that neither could deny. He invaded her with his mind and his body, and she invaded his. He took her fast and hard then slow and thoroughly and then began all over again. He spoke directly to her soul, saying things that could not be expressed in words. His lovemaking carried an edge, nevertheless, that had not been present before—an almost panicked attempt to memorize her, as if never to have the chance again. So in turn, she gave him everything inside her to reassure him that she would always be there with him. They made deep, abiding love and Cat thought she had never experienced anything as shattering or as healing. He loved her, it was clear to her now and she would not doubt him again. He may not say the words but it was there, entwining them both.

Zorroc was flummoxed. She had assaulted him with her whole heart, her whole soul, her passion, her woman's scent, her entire being. She had seared him from the inside out; branding him, burning him in a way he did not think existed. He had fallen into the same trap as his father. Was he doomed to the same fate? Thank Zazu, he had slipped the collar on before he touched her or she would have yet another mating mark. He studied her carefully but could not fathom the why of it. Why her?

He had had sex of every kind from the time of adolescence enjoying fully the bedroom gymnastics he engaged in, but love with her the night before held no similarities to his previous encounters. She had taken everything from him, and given him back everything she embodied in return. She had proved more potent than any aphrodisiac; he would never get enough of her. Moreover, if something happened to her, he could not even imagine of the consequences to his empire, his people, or his duty. Would he disintegrate as his father had and become a myopic, morbid fool? When had she stolen his heart? He smiled slightly as she shifted on the mat revealing a plump luscious breast. Her hair looked like a riotous declaration of independence.

Her body, hopelessly small and compact overflowed...with dynamite. Zazu, what was he to do about her?

They would be disembarking soon; he would have responsibilities, obligations that would demand his attention *and* the plan to avoid her at all costs, to be set into motion. It would give him time to get his perspective back and his mind off her. The enforced close quarters, most likely, accounted for the reason she held him in such thrall. Things would no doubt right themselves once he resumed his role as leader to his people...he postulated, like a drowning man grabbing for a twig to keep him afloat.

Cat stretched languidly, looking for Zorroc. She'd missed him. He probably had a million things to do to prepare for their arrival to Gattonia but she'd really wanted to tell him about the baby. He had wanted no words last night so she'd decided to wait until morning to tell him what she knew he'd consider fantastic news, unless he already knew.

As she finished dressing, her panel buzzed, signaling company. Had someone come to escort her off the ship? She answered to find Dee decked out in all her glory and looking magnificent. The reconciliation must have gone well.

"You about ready? A team will come later to collect our belongings; here, I brought this to put Scotty and Spock in." She handed her a carrier large enough to house the kittens.

"You think of everything, what are we supposed

to do, just wait for a summons?" Cat asked while rounding up the darting fur balls and depositing them into their temporary home.

"We're supposed to stop off at the Med-center and get inoculated for FIS. Angel and Carpov think they've got it licked," Dee shared, knowing what this meant to all of them.

"Does that mean the Gattonian females will be allowed off the ship? China told me they've been sequestered here since the initial attack," Cat commented.

"I assume so, where'd you get the collar?" Dee wanted to know, carefully examining it. It resembled a fine chain mail of silvery material that looked Egyptian in style with a one inch band surrounding her neck and then another three inches fanning out over her collarbone and shoulders, back and front. "Geez, is this another one of those 'it doesn't come off' things? I'm beginning to think Zorroc has some major control issues."

"I didn't get a chance to ask him. I woke up with it on last night and he wanted to make love not conversation. I'll catch up with him later for an explanation; I also need to tell him about the baby."

Dee's eyes bugged out before she realized she must be talking about Angels coming bundle but she queried, "Are we talking Angel's little angel or yours?"

"Angel gave me a pregnancy test yesterday afternoon that confirmed my own suspicions. I haven't decided how I really feel about it but at least I know I'm in love with the father," she concluded as her stomach lurched.

"I wonder how many of us are in the same way. These Gattonians seem abundantly potent," Dee mused while calculating how this would affect the existing game plan that Linc had outlined in between bouts of lovemaking. "Look Cat, we need to let Zorroc know about this as soon as possible. They assigned me to guard your body until further notice, they think you might be in some kind of danger because of your relationship with Zorroc and because the Dargons hunted a specific woman. Zorroc and Prolinc don't want it to seem like you are being protected, though, so they chose me to stick to you like glue. We'll be sharing quarters, as well. Any questions? Because when we leave this room, they said not to mention it again."

"Spit, I guess I should've seen this coming but I thought I'd be with Zorroc. He'll be too busy, though, huh," she murmured almost to herself as she sat down to absorb this latest bulletin.

They exited onto an impossibly huge docking grid that had to be at least one hundred feet off the ground. The building they occupied looked to be the size of an entire town and reached well into the red clouds as seen by the massive clear dome over head. They were escorted onto connecting trams and transported for miles on a track several stories high toward a dot on the horizon; their new home.

It embodied everything depicted in the murals and so much more. Small flying vehicles whizzed around at dizzying speeds. All of the buildings had holes through them where the vehicles appeared and disappeared. "Holy Jetsons," Cat whispered aloud. "So, what do you think Dee, mega radical isn't it?" Dee, too stunned to respond, nodded. An orgy of color greeted them everywhere they turned. The red glowing sky and buildings, cast in a myriad of purples, reds, yellows, and fuchsias, presented an overpowering picture. The foliage bloomed every bit as colorful as the buildings, and gold speckled roadways out-lined the roller-coaster hills and mountains surrounding them. Talk about psychedelic. She headed toward sensory spinout in an effort to take it all in and reached out to Zorroc with her thoughts but found no response. Obviously, he was otherwise occupied.

They arrived at a holding pen of sorts where their names and personal information were taken and toiletries dispensed before being assigned quarters. They tried to separate Cat and Dee but when Dee mentioned Prolinc's request, the matter was dropped. His name worked like a magic key that would unlock any door. He visibly intimidated them.

A ceremony and an informal welcome awaited them at the grand hall after everyone settled into their new quarters.

The women filed into a large hall where half as many Gattonians presided, along with a panel of very official looking males, most of whom looked ancient. The air crackled with conflicting energies that almost made Cat dizzy. Something appeared off kilter. She looked over at Dee to see if she'd noticed anything and she obviously had. Dee carefully scanned the room trying to detect areas of unrest. When all had quieted, a tall gaunt and knurly looking dignitary rose to speak. His silver gray hair flowed half way down his back and he looked like a poor imitation of Merlin. An air of forced joviality and suppressed antagonism shrouded him as he introduced himself as Dyfainius.

"Welcome, we are thankful that you have arrived safely and wish to thank the crew of the Miramid for your timely rescue." A smattering of applause ensued before he continued. "In addition, the people of Gattonia would like to extend our gratitude for your co-operation and assistance in a most difficult time in our history." He then drew himself up with considerable effort before explaining. "We estimated your arrival to be several days hence so not all is prepared for your comfort. Please be patient with us. A formal welcome will be forthcoming and know that we look forward to enfolding you into our community. Those of you lifemated or chosen will be transferred to chambers more private as soon as it can be arranged. Now a dinner to honor your arrival will be served in the dining hall just down the hallway and to your right. Please enjoy your first meal in Gattonia."

When Cat turned, she spotted Zorroc focused on her. She tugged Dee's sleeve and they started in his direction. When they got within four feet of him, a sparkly motion caught her eye and she watched as a truly ravishing creature threw herself onto Zorroc and proceeded to kiss him long and hard, rubbing herself on him in a blatantly sexual manner. He seemed to enjoy her ministrations.

"Remember what we did to Octapaws that time we spotted him waiting to ambush a young girl in the hall?" Dee asked casually.

Cat's vision cleared and she nodded and grinned. Together they moved directly behind Zorroc, positioned themselves with a leg directly behind each of his, and bent their knees before stepping aside. Zorroc and his clinging female toppled to the ground in an undignified muddle. Zorroc groaned while his companion sputtered and spat obviously displeased with her less than graceful descent.

"Who is that horrible midget." Cat heard her hiss, as they retreated, and then heard Zorroc's chagrined reply. "No one to concern yourself with, lovely one." Cat didn't turn around but did flip him the bird as she and Dee proceeded toward the dining hall.

Chapter Sixteen

Cat's and Dee's quarters were a little close but comfortable enough. A bedroom sat on either side of the common area that included a sitting room and a dining console. They could choose from a full menu or order one of several dishes featured each day. The Gattonians had no specific foods for breakfast, lunch and dinner; just one fare, and you chose whatever you wanted. In the following days, Dee and Cat sampled their way through the options to discover which dishes pleased and which did not but most proved definitely above average. Their hosts provided reading materials, mostly on the history of Gattonia, or they could watch a wide array of programs on a flat monitor screen the size of one complete wall called an IVVS or Interactive Virtual Video System. If they wanted to listen to music, they simply flipped a switch on the COM unit and music filtered throughout the living area. Since all the women, except the aunts and Angel, remained housed in the dorm, for the time being, groups would get together for slumber parties and exchange life stories. Gattonian females from the Miramid, and their friends, also participated and it appeared as if all was working better than anticipated.

Cat and Dee spent time with Ava, who sparkled like a pixie and took nothing seriously, Drew, who took everything seriously, and Faith, the cosmic philosopher of the group. If she hadn't been missing Zorroc, she'd be having a fine time. When they weren't grouping at Dee and Cat's, Cat made herself scarce to allow Prolinc and Dee their privacy, and made an effort not to be jealous of it. Cat had sworn Dee to secrecy about her pregnancy wanting to impart the news to Zorroc herself, if she ever saw him again up close. When she caught glimpses of him at scheduled functions he always arrived in the company of Sandra or the Gattonian female she'd seen glued to him the first day of their arrival. She'd discovered her name was Zana and had been betrothed to Zorroc before the Dargon attack. Cat didn't want to think about what kept him occupied every night and away from her. As her memories of their last night on the Miramid continued to fade, she wondered if she had misread the entire situation. Maybe he'd simply been trying to find a nice way to say goodbye. She refused to dwell on it; however, she had a baby to grow. At least she would always have a piece of him.

The following week China showed up looking uncharacteristically serious, though she attempted to hide it. She'd been dropping by with more and more frequency hinting around at Cat's unhealthy color and obvious weight loss. Her growing baby had a voracious appetite—unfortunately Cat's continued to wane.

"Hello, Cat, I think we need to get you out more, you are always here when I drop by. Is everything all right?" China, at five months pregnant had begun to show and she looked absolutely precious.

"I'm fine. The only thing really occupying my mind these days is whether anyone aboard the Miramid did not get pregnant; aside from the guys that is."

"Is that a less than subtle way of telling me you are carrying, too?" China probed softly.

"Yeah, but you, Dee and Angel are the only ones I've told. I've tried to contact Zorroc to impart the happy news but so far he's been too busy to answer my COM or mind messages."

"That is one of the reasons I came by today; I am to tutor you on thought blocking. As far as we know, Zorroc is the only one able to read you, but here in Gattonia at least seventy-five percent of the population have telepathic abilities in varying manifestations. All of our talents differ and are considered as individual as a fingerprint. What I am trying to say is, we cannot guarantee Zorroc is the only one who can read you, so we need to teach you to focus and cloak your thoughts." Cat's lessons commenced that day until a few weeks later, when she mastered the technique.

During this time, Cat asked endless questions about the goings on politically, socially, and with Zorroc specifically. It did not sound encouraging. Motions surfaced, to rescind the lifematings that had occurred onboard the Miramid, or at least grant the Gattonian males, one Gattonian lifemate, and one Earth lifemate. The High Council had further proposed that the Gattonian lifemate be granted custody of any offspring, assigning duties of procreation to the women and childrearing to the female. All motions to date had been voted down, with Zorroc, supposedly, the staunchest supporter for keeping the matings in place and monogamous.

As weeks turned to months, time became Cat's greatest enemy. She rarely left the dorm and protected areas because of the possible safety factor; and while the other women slowly integrated into the tapestry of Gattonian society, she remained locked away like Rapunzel in her tower. A reoccurring theme in her life. The women made outside friends and used previous skills or learned new ones, in an effort to become productive and valued for more than their female parts. All proceeded much more smoothly than anyone had foreseen, mostly due to the bonds forged between the women and the crew of the Miramid. They acted as intermediaries between the land bounders and the newcomers and finessed understanding and acceptance between the two factions. One by one, the women found independent lodgings or mated with their very own cat man, forging their own life. If she could've been with Zorroc her happiness would have been complete, but that remained the crux of her dilemma, she'd had no contact with him. He'd become her limbo factor.

She couldn't move forward or go back...she was trapped.

A festival had been announced to celebrate the coming of their light season when the days would grow longer and the skies would take on a golden-orange glow. It meant gentler winds and many outdoor activities. Rosik COMd, asking if she had plans to attend, and as it happened, she did not. The festivals seemed to be great pairing off occasions and although she'd received numerous invitations to accompany other couples, she grew weary of being the extra person, so turned down all well-meaning offers. So when Rosik arrived at her quarters, she launched herself into his arms the second the panel slid back.

"Tell me you've come to release me from my mundane existence of colorless walls and tedious responsibilities and take me to a far away place packed with glorious adventures and mysterious pookas, impossible to resist."

Rosik spun her around laughing and carefree.

He played her entertaining pooka and trusted friend throughout the day, cheering her up and catering to her every whim. However, he was disturbed. He had felt the slight protrusion of her belly; while, overall she had lost weight. She looked bird frail and impossibly fragile. Had Zorroc been notified?

Cat laughed more in that afternoon than she

could ever remember. Rosik made the ideal companion; the reality of him far exceeding his reputation.

A week later, as Dee and Cat enjoyed a lazy afternoon, their panel buzzed. "Are you expecting China or Rosik, Cat?"

"No, could it be Prolinc?" She offered with a shrug. The buzzer sounded again and Cat felt an inkling of trouble. Dee, of course, had already figured that out

"Things have been getting a little dicey recently, so let's not take any chances. Stay behind me when the panel opens and for God sake protect your stomach."

"Enter," Dee voiced to the panel.

Five unfamiliar males, armed and formal, entered. Surely, they wouldn't attempt to arrest them, Cat, at a loss, mindspoke to Zorroc that she and Dee had unwanted visitors in their quarters and needed assistance. Nothing. No response. It was up to them.

"You," the leader stated, pointing at Cat, "will accompany us."

"Why?" Cat demanded. She had no intention of leaving with these yahoos. Dee concurred silently; as one, they relaxed into a fight ready stance.

"You will know when we arrive," he stated as they inched into the room.

"If it's all the same to you, I'll take a pass; I'm expecting an important COM from your Leader." Pandemonium broke out. The males tried to rush them and were unprepared for the reception; one male after another went flying or was felled by a well-placed elbow, knee or kick. Just as the two thought they had everything under control, the leader pulled out his weapon and fired. They collapsed, soundlessly.

Zorroc wondered if Cat's message constituted a

ploy to gain his attention and probed gently into her mind. There was nothing, no static, no thoughts, nothing. She was either unconscious or neutralized. His worst nightmare had materialized. She had called to him for help and he had ignored her. He mindspoke to Prolinc, Sycor, and Bandoff, that Cat had mind-blacked, and to mount a search immediately. He had no doubt that Dee had been taken as well. Bandoff and Sycor headed for the dorm while Prolinc manned the security cameras, scanning the perimeter of the building for a visual. Zorroc activated his band to locate her. *"Prolinc, she is in the building on one of the ground levels. I am on my way."*

Five minutes later, he had them on screen. *"I have located them Zorroc, they are being carried into the Med-center on level B-2. I will meet you there with Bandoff and Sycor."*

"What the devil is going on?" Prolinc swore out-loud as he headed toward the dorm at a dead run.

Prolinc doubted his control should Dee or Catarina be harmed in any way. They had looked still and vulnerable; he had never seen his banshee vulnerable and he longed to hurt those responsible. When he arrived, Bandoff had just ordered the guards to stand down along with a Med-tech who visibly trembled. He and Sycor held them at weapon ready with their settings on terminate. The five guards, some of whom still bled, remained perfectly still, their weapons across the room.

Commander Ryder was confused beyond measure. Why such a fuss over an unattached Earth female taken for a pregnancy scan? Then when the Guardian arrived followed, almost immediately, by the Supreme Leader; he knew a moment of overpowering dread. He glanced uneasily at the females.

Zorroc held himself together by a thin spider's

strand as he approached his mate and felt for a pulse. Though somewhat weak, she would survive, unlike the guards who had harmed her. He stared coldly at the males responsible, and then proceeded to the COM unit. "Carpov, report to the Med-center at the Dorm stat; we have two casualties in need of immediate medical attention. Bring Angel." If he had never earned Angel's approval in the past, this would cook him for all time.

"Sycor," Zorroc commanded softly, "I want a team of ten loyal males down here now to escort these...prisoners to black-out." Then mind-thought to him and Bandoff to put blazers on stun and immobilize them in order to guarantee their inability to communicate with those who sent them if they had not already. The guards sank to the ground before Zorroc had completed the thought.

Carpov and Angel arrived in tandem with the guards. As the unconscious males were carted away, Carpov went straight to Cat to evaluate her condition. Angel had confided her friend's pregnancy on the way so it became their first priority. She had been hit in the shoulder; if they had come close to her stomach, the chances would not have been good for the life growing within. Next, he monitored her vitals; she would be out for some time to come, her body needed to regroup. He heard a groan and knew that Dee had regained consciousness.

Prolinc moved to her side in an instant, taking her hand and gently brushing her hair back off her face. "What happened beautiful one, can you tell me?"

"Five of them buzzed the panel with orders to take Cat. We objected. When they realized we had them beat with hand to hand, the leader pulled out a blazer and shot us. Cowardly wimps," she uttered defiantly. "Did you get them, are they neutralized?"

"The cowardly wimps will never get close to you

224

or Cat again. The blood in your quarters, I assume it did not emanate from you or Cat."

"Like I said, they were wimps. Cat; is she all right, did the baby survive?"

Zorroc snapped his head around, his full attention centered on Dee. Did she speak of Catarina's offspring or her own? He focused on Carpov and softly inquired, "Is my mate carrying my heir?" At Carpov's nod, he sank to a chair and held his palms to his eyes before he rasped. "Will they be all right?"

"To be on the safe side she should rest for the next few days, but there does not appear to be any damage, they shot her in the shoulder, well away from her abdomen," he commented in a matter-of-fact manner. "However she is underweight and overly pale."

"She did not tell me. Why did she hide her condition from me?" he asked himself, as well as the room in general.

"She tried over and over again to contact you through mindspeak and COM but you never answered her; obviously too engrossed with Bimbo and Barbie to spare a moment for your mate," Angel accused turning her back to him to check Cat's pulse. Carpov and Prolinc shuffled uneasily.

A subdued Zorroc asked, "Who are the guards that attacked them, does anyone recognize them?"

"I believe the one in charge is a member of the High Council Guard. I saw him outside the offices of Dyfainius on two separate occasions," stated Bandoff quietly. "The others are unfamiliar to me."

"Everything keeps leading back to the High Council and Dyfainius, could he be acting alone? Could it be that simple?" Prolinc posed, helping Dee sit up. Her color had returned though she remained slightly disoriented.

"Dyfainius is a very ambitious male. He wanted

a match between his daughter and me badly and has been instrumental in new legislative proposals of dual lifemates. However, why go after Cat? What could he hope to gain by harming her? I would still have to produce an heir for Gattonia, if not with Cat then with someone else," Zorroc stated.

Sycor blinked and asked, "What if you lifemated with Zana and then died without producing an heir?"

"Rule would go to Zana initially," Prolinc answered for his friend, "backed by her father, but, as an elder without a male heir, the rule would fall to another house almost immediately. So he would still have gained nothing, and I would venture that his male part no longer functions, so he could not produce one on his own."

"I could not help overhearing your discussion and would add my thoughts," Rosik suggested, sauntering into the room to stand beside Cat's unmoving form. "I was told you had a bit of excitement down here and having a current lack of pressing duties, decided to investigate. How are you feeling Dee?" he asked, never taking his gaze from Cat as he reached out to graze the back his fingers lightly across her abdomen as if to reassure himself of her bundle's safety. At Zorroc's sudden attention, he produced an unrepentant smirk.

"I'm okay, but shouldn't Cat be coming around by now?" she focused on Carpov and Angel.

"I have given her something to relax her, she should sleep for the next few hours," replied Carpov checking Cat's vitals once again.

"How much did you overhear Rosik?" asked Prolinc.

"Enough to have formed my own theory," he retorted, smiling at the grim faces surrounding him. He continued. "What if they eliminated and Zorroc mated with Zana in addition to one of the other women or a female from a Lower House? And what if he produced an heir and then met with an unfortunate accident?"

Comprehension dawned on Zorroc's features and he ventured slowly. "The child, if born to a lower female or woman, could possibly be granted to Zana to raise. This would never happen with a child from Catarina because of her Gattonian blood and her connection to the High House of Tuk. So if custody transferred to Zana and something then happened to me the rule would fall to Zana followed by the child, both guided by the hand of Dyfainius," he finished to absolute silence. "Zazu, and we cannot prove any of it."

Zorroc stared at his sleeping mate and began to formulate a strategy. He stood and approached, smoothing her hair that made her resemble Methuselah more than his flame, in its current state. Zazu, he had missed her. While, initially, he believed that by denying their union, Cat would be better protected, a larger part of his reasoning condensed to his desire to free him from his manic fixation on her. Not only had this path failed to keep her safe, it had become the instrument of unrelenting torture for him. Zorroc dwelled in a self-imposed hell every minute he stayed away and clearly, it had done nothing to bank his raging desire. From now on, he would choose a different tack. If forever doomed to this obsession named Catarina, then he would rejoice in it until another time came. He would take her to his quarters and formalize their union as quickly as possible. He would halt all talk of duel matings and override Dyfainius and all current proposals put forth by him and his followers.

Zorroc would first thwart and then trap him. They would never again have the opportunity to get close to his mate. She belonged to him and he would hold her above all others. The knot that had been squeezing his life force from him for the past weeks began to ease. He would rest peacefully for the first time since the Miramid landed.

"Prolinc," Zorroc barked, startling the group. "Tonight take Rosik and interrogate the prisoners one at a time. We will let them stew for the moment to increase their wariness, as well as the one who sent them.

"You will be the intimidator while Rosik will act the facilitator; you know the information we require. By weeks end I will have handled the High Council one way or another. All proposed legislation will be tabled permanently and my union with Cat announced and formalized. Then we will proceed to trap the viper. The Dargon connection remains a mystery we must solve at all costs. We will meet tomorrow after you have rested to discuss our next move and review what you discovered from the interrogation. It is past time to make my wishes known." With a flick of his wrist he removed Cat's collar to reveal his mark. Fierce satisfaction lit his eyes turning them to iridescent amber. All nodded in formal acknowledgement. Rosik, Sycor, and Bandoff quit the room without a backward glance leaving the others to observe the turn-about in their leader.

"Carpov, I will transport my mate to my quarters and will alert you when she wakes. Prolinc and Dee, you will accompany me to assure no "accidents" occur on the way to my chambers and we will discuss protection for Cat from there." With that, he bent and gently scooped Catarina snugly into his arms and exited the compound.

As Cat rested, the three planned a web of protection around her and made further plans to trap Dyfainius. They agreed that Dee should accompany Prolinc for the 'good cop, bad cop' interrogation since she had been one of the injured parties. When the meeting concluded, Zorroc settled beside his mate drawing her onto him and sank into the first deep sleep he had known in over three months.

Dee was getting her first glimpse of the Prolinc everyone feared and respected. His countenance, though direct and controlled proved frightening for those same reasons. Something savage, fierce and brutal shone in the depths of his being. She almost pitied the guard in front of them who looked equal parts terrified and mutinous. Rosik slouched lazily in a chair off to the side feigning boredom.

After interrogating the team individually, it became clear they had no knowledge of questionable doings or political manipulations concerning the Earth women or Cat specifically. They had followed straightforward orders to deliver selected women for pregnancy scans. They had been appalled when the Commander had pulled his weapon and fired on the women.

The Med-tech was harder to read. He admitted to orders directing him to examine certain females for carrying but remained reluctant to discuss further details pertaining to a detected pregnancy. After being divested of his clothing and placed in refrigeration for an hour, his memory improved and he admitted to a further directive pertaining specifically to the woman, Catarina. In the event she tested positive, she was to be detained and await further instructions from the High Council.

Now the Commander stood before them, the one that had fired on their women. "The others, under your command, have informed us that you were in charge of this mission and the one who fired on the two unarmed women. Your team has been most co-operative and we expect no less from you. Now, now enlighten us as to your precise orders, Commander Ryder," Prolinc requested with deadly calm.

"Nothing unusual, we were ordered to round up

certain women who had not yet been tested for possible contraception in order to evaluate the success of the Leader's program of procreation. The woman, Catarina, appeared the first on our list that morning," he responded nervously, beads of moisture forming on his upper lip and forehead.

"How long have you been in charge of this program?" Rosik inquired, yawning loudly.

"It," he squeaked then cleared his throat and proceeded. "I received orders from the High Council to commence just this morning; the little she witch and that woman," he pointed to Dee, "did not submit, so I proceeded to use what means required to assure compliance. I vow to you we did nothing contrary to the orders of the High Council."

Prolinc measured his words with precision and asked, "Are you aware of the identity of this little she witch?"

The Commander blanched that the words turned back on him held such menace. Why would they bother with one small insignificant whore? She was just an Earth woman of no importance; one that he did not damage permanently nor any offspring she might have been carrying. Add to that the direct orders he had received, what possible problem could there be? Still, he sensed a trap about to be sprung. "She is no one of any possible worth, just an Earth woman come to spread her legs to any and all who would take her."

The facilitator straightened in his chair while the Earth woman growled dangerously, only this time, he had no weapon to protect himself from her. Sweat now seeped into his collar. He waited, frozen into place by this unwarranted display of outrage.

Rosik stood and faced the prisoner, vibrating with the effort to hold himself in check. So much for the good cop, bad cop scenario, Dee surmised, because the good cop looked like the one ready to separate Ryder's head from the rest of him while the bad cop looked to be his only possible salvation. Dee sure wouldn't lift a finger in protest.

"What is the penalty for firing on the Divitta?" Rosik hissed.

"Death without hearing," Ryder rasped, clearly at the end of his tether. "But she cannot be the Divitta, Zana will be Divitta. All affiliated with the High Counsel have been informed of this although no formal announcement is expected until the end of moon tide." He licked his lips and continued, "You have been misinformed; the newcomers are nothing but vessels for our seed. She is but a low birth Earth female."

"*She,*" Prolinc roared both inside and out of the Commander's mind, "is daughter to Princess Nancia, of the House of Tuk and carrier of the next heir to Gattonia. If your fire had endangered the Divitta or the child growing inside her you would already be dead; as it is...do you have any last words for yourself or your unit before you are terminated?"

A puddle formed at Ryder's feet but, other than that, he remained composed and resigned. Dee had seen enough; it was time to step in. "Of course there could be a way to save yourself and your team if you are all willing to swear fealty to the Divitta and Divo, above all others. Don't you agree Linc? Rosik?" It had been the plan all along to use him as a spy to get the proof they needed to snare Dyfainius and any others acting with him, but at the way the vibrations swirled, she thought it prudent to remind them of their intended goal. Dee watched as their two sets of eyes cleared of bloodlust and refocused on the Commander, who obviously retained no loyalty, what-so-ever, toward Dyfainius after being set up for potential termination. Assured of Ryder's co-operation, he departed with new orders.

Chapter Seventeen

"Rocky, what are you doing with a female on top of you," Nadia whispered inquisitively, staring with unblinking amber eyes which closely matched Zorroc's own. "You said you would never bring a female to our private chambers until you had lifemated; and she looks nothing like Zana. She looks more like a midget with broken fire-hair," she concluded decisively.

Zorroc groaned and glanced up at the openly curious entity ogling his mate with relation to his prone form. Zorroc smiled inwardly at her description of Catarina's lengthy, unruly mass of auburn ringlets, which tended to expand and undulate with exposure to humidity or wind. It differed greatly from the straight, weighty manes specific to Gattonians. Their reaction to his mate's hair ranged from delighted wonder to repellant scrutiny. He, himself remained spellbound and fascinated by the vivid color, springy texture and the way it wrapped around his fingers naturally as if wanting to secure and hold him. He enjoyed brushing and playing with the silken, spherical tresses though he would never openly admit it. "Nadia, you will leave my chamber immediately without uttering another sound and meet me in the small salon in five minutes." As his sister moved to comment further, he cut her off with an authoritative growl and then watched as she exited with all speed.

He noted, not for the first time since returning home, that his sister had blossomed into a stunning young female. Her long limbs had grown from gangly awkwardness to reed like agility. She had turned into a beauty before his eyes. He wondered if Prolinc had noticed the changes and how it might further complicate his situation.

He eased Cat off his chest and onto her side before covering her gently with a thick comforter. She looked younger than Nadia, cuddled so peacefully on his mat and his heart expanded when he thought of the precious cargo she housed.

Nadia tracked the movement of the changing Gattonian sky while trying to figure out this latest change in Zorroc. He had been restless, distant, and irascible since returning home; like a beastie finding itself caged for the first time. She had thought it merely a by-product of returning to his daily responsibilities after experiencing the relative freedom afforded him on his voyage that caused his discontent, but now she questioned that theory. She had had ample time to study the two asleep and, as usual, her powers of observation held her in good stead. The soft cloud of hair covering the female's features revealed only a small contented smile. It looked similar to the half smile her tornika, Spooka, donned in the middle of a particularly satisfying dream, no doubt conquering the secret realm of the monzu. Her brother really tipped things, however. He held her possessively, even in slumber like a rare prize he would never relinquish. He, too, looked contented and more relaxed than she had seen him since the Dargon attack. Zana would not be pleased.

In the fourteen months since the departure of her brother and Prolinc, Zana and Nadia had become fast friends. The first weeks after their departure left her feeling utterly bereft without the anchor of her family to fill her days. She had been deserted for the greater good of Gattonia. Zana swept into her life like a burst of swirling energy.

She made everything fun and exciting and for the first time Nadia had a girl friend to share time with. She had grown up almost exclusively in the company of her aunts, tutors and brothers. She had always considered Prolinc in the same light as Zorroc, and they both had coddled and spoiled her as only big brothers could. But Zana treated her as a grown up and a peer, filling her in on all the gossip of the High Council, courtiers, and of course, talking about the time when she and Zorroc would lifemate making Nadia and her real sisters. Zana had confided that her father, in touch with a group of brilliant off-world scientists; were on the very brink of a cure for the Dargon virus and that she and Zorroc would be able to have as many offspring as they wished. Nadia had been sworn to secrecy on this though, because she wanted to surprise Zorroc on his return. Even if the treatment failed, she assured Nadia, her father intended to fix it so Zorroc could have two lifemates and she would not have to be bothered with procreation at all. A female could lose her figure having offspring, she had confided, and Zana wanted to remain beautiful for Zorroc well after she took her rightful place at his side.

All this brought her back to the couple holding onto one another forming what appeared to be one complete entelechy. Was she an *Earth-mate* as they were currently being coined? If so, why would he not choose Zana to be his first and this other one later? At her brother's determined footsteps, she could hear the answers striding her way.

Surely Nadia could not be hearing accurately. Her powers of observation might be keen but there obviously existed a massive blockage between her ears and her brain. Her brother had been lifemated to that woman for months and failed to mention it because her life might be at risk? Moreover, he had not trusted his own sister with this news.

"What of your betrothed, what about Zana," she asked with growing annoyance.

"Zana and I ended our betrothal almost two years ago, the total length of which lasted three moons. It seemed an appropriate match at the time but we never formed a bond or binding commitment past the initial, formal one. Why do you ask these questions, you know even less of her than I do," he pointed out testily, standing before her trying to solve the unsolvable mystery of the female mind.

"She is my friend; my only friend! When you left with Prolinc I endured alone without even my aunts..."

"Your aunts are back," he mumbled while her tirade continued.

"Without my brothers..."

"Prolinc is not your brother," he countered haphazardly.

"And without any company at all; alone, until Zana befriended me. Furthermore, she had everything worked out so she could be with you and become my sister. You should have waited, she loves you; she told me so. She waited for you as you should have waited for her. You have ruined everything!" she concluded dramatically, like a wronged hormonally challenged sixteen-year-old.

"I have ruined nothing because there was nothing to ruin. I have no knowledge of your friendship with Zana but either way it would not matter at this date. My lifemating to Catarina is done and witnessed and in truth, a blessing I probably do not deserve. She will be your sister and no other. I would have you give her a chance. I think you will be well pleased with my choice of mates, if you do."

"Why can she not just be an Earth-mate, then you could still have Zana. She told me this would be acceptable. The Earth newcomers are little more than spreaders for many but she is willing to share and does not care for the mating aspects of it anyway. She would not have her beauty marred by child birthing," she explained helpfully not willing to give up on her friend's cause.

Zazu, Zana had been talking to Nadia about birthing and sex acts, filling her head with proposals, supposedly closeted within the High Council, and poisoning her mind against the Earth women. He would know better next time than to leave his sister unattended while still unmated. How to counter this turn of events?

"Nadia, we need to talk," Zorroc stated with uncharacteristic reticence. "Would you care for Edenwine?"

Nadia blinked, startled at this tactical reversal on the part of her brother. And Edenwine? She had never been offered the potent liquid before. She observed a shifting of emotional atmosphere and squeaked, "Please," as calmly as possible. He had captured her full attention.

Zorroc rose and proceeded to the side bar where he poured a full measure of the liquid for each of them. Another surprise, for she would have thought to be given half of what he poured for himself. She accepted the wine and tested it on her lips. It tingled; she would be respectful of its effect.

Zorroc emitted a half laugh and sighed. "You have grown into a stunning female, Nadia, seemingly in the blink of an eye. I left a fledgling filly and returned to a sleek thoroughbred. I know I have failed to mention this before but it is the truth."

Nadia colored prettily at his words of praise but waited for him to continue.

"I should have told you about Catarina the moment we returned but I had no clear purpose on how to proceed. A force of Dargons attacked us shortly after leaving Earth. They had been waiting for us and caught us in an ambush. If the Miramid had not been within hailing distance there stands a good chance I would not have had the opportunity to see you grow into the beautiful young female you have become."

Zorroc smiled fondly at his sister, enjoying the moment of camaraderie if not the reason for it. "They were looking for a specific woman and we felt certain that the woman was Catarina. The Dargons seized her on the planet Zeba II; I almost lost her."

"How did you get her back?" she asked.

"She mindspoke her location to me and we retrieved her before rendezvousing with the Miramid."

"And this is why you think she is in danger?"

"Because of that and yesterday. A contingent of guards, on orders from the High Council, invaded her quarters, stun-blazed both her and her protector and then took them to a med-tech unit for reasons not confirmed, though it is being seen to.

"In trying to protect her by keeping her presence hidden, I could have caused her irreparable damage. You see; she carries my heir." Zorroc stared intently at his sister to gage the effect of this latest revelation but if he expected her to speak, he was wrong. He could see in her eyes however, a dawning comprehension and wisdom that had been missing minutes before. Maybe this course constituted the right one.

"Are you familiar with the High House of Tuk and the Princess Nancia?" he asked.

Nadia shrugged and wondered at this sudden change of topic. "I know of the House of Tuk, of course, as does everyone but Princess Nancia, I have only heard of for she and her mate reside elsewhere."

"Yes, they assist us off-world. Catarina is their daughter. She is a split citizen who lived on Earth until her arrival here. She could never be an 'Earth-mate', as you named it, for that reason; but she is unfamiliar with many of our ways and that is why I ask for your co-operation in helping her and possibly guarding her."

"Zazu, she is daughter to the Princess of Tuk? Zana has been well and truly trumped and she will not like it. Where do you see the danger to Catarina lying? Surely, it could not be...Zorroc do you suspect Dyfainius? He would go far for his daughter, if all that Zana has revealed is accurate and I am almost certain that it is."

Nadia's mind raced to control the many conflicts and questions flooding into her. The truth suddenly seemed like spirits testing the winds for substance. One truth, however, rang ominously clear; Zana would be furious and was certainly not one to cross when she did not get her way. An evening several moons ago when Zana had come to collect Nadia for a visit to the Strummings of Gillaud, a formal and festive hearing of a popular off-world quartet, Spooka had made herself at home on Zana's cape and infused it with her own snowy white hair. Unfortunately the cape was black, a signature non-color Zana preferred with so much color in Gattonia. Zana would have broken Spooka's neck if Nadia had not been quicker. Now Nadia kept her pet well away from Zana's tempting black outfits. Did her father carry a like temperament?

"Which leads me to the next question. What has Zana revealed of the proposals by the High Council? Is Dyfainius alone behind the duel lifematings and child swapping proposals or could there be others involved? In my meetings with the Council they seem united."

First, he pleaded for her assistance and now he asked her opinion, she felt like checking behind her to make sure he actually addressed her. Her eyes shone with new tempered depth as she mulled his inquiries over. Over the Legions rear, would anyone threaten her brother or his heir, while she was around!

Cat groaned. She felt like someone had taken a hot poker to her shoulder. She eased her eyes open to assess her whereabouts. *Hmm*, incarcerated in the lap of luxury, not at all an uncommon circumstance for her, after all. She sat up slowly and checked her shoulder; it had acquired a reddish purplish hue but otherwise seemed in working condition as she gingerly rotated it. What had happened to Dee? Surely, they'd taken her too. She slid down off the incredibly plush mat and padded toward the panel. Her clothing had been stripped from her and replaced with a sleeping shift, and her shoes had disappeared. Tentatively, she reached out and pressed, it opened silently. Why hadn't they locked her in? She crept down the hallway, taking in her surroundings.

The place looked like a palace. Some prison. It'd be an incentive to commit a crime just to end up here. She'd have to have a talk with Zorroc about it if she ever saw him again. The smooth tiled floor felt cool under her feet and stretched out in a graceful ark extending to her left. The walls, intricately inlaid with cloisonné, depicted exotic vines and flowers that had strange fey creatures playing among them. It shouted serendipity in the extreme. She was delightfully charmed even if they had shot and kidnapped her. She came upon a panel to her left and pressed. It slid open to reveal an elaborate garden completely enclosed with a waterfall and large pool. She stepped under the colonnaded walkway and tried another panel. It led into a large but cozy dining area that had recently been used. Someone had thoughtfully provided fresh rolls and choc-bean tea, still hot in the container. Her stomach and the precious cargo stored there screamed in

239

appreciation. She felt like Goldilocks, the only missing ingredient being the porridge, thankfully. After polishing off three rolls and two cups of choc-bean tea she proceeded to search for Dee and an exit. She wondered at the absence of guards or, for that matter, anyone, as she almost ran head on into a tall, lithe and ravishing female. She had rich, dark golden hair flowing half way down her arms and matching Amber eyes similar to Zorroc's. Cat realized that she herself must look like an escapee from the nearest asylum.

"Hello, you are Catarina and I welcome you to our home. I am your sister," she explained with a shy smile.

Which exceeded miraculous, considering Cat was an only child. She examined her more closely. Any idiot would know the two of them couldn't be related; maybe she *was* in a Looney bin this time. Better to humor her. "Well, it's nice to see you...Sis, but I really must be going. Uh, is there an exit around here that you're aware of? I really have someplace else I need to be."

The exotic creature tilted her head in Gattonian confusion and asked, "Why do you want to leave, do our accommodations displease you?"

Cat began backing slowly down the hallway toward a large, ornate panel she'd spotted at the end of the corridor. "The accommodations have been peachy and don't think I'm not accustomed to going to sleep in one place then waking up in another because it's been happening a lot these last few months. Only usually my mate is with me and so I'll just jot along and find him." *Never.* She added to herself. Halfway down the hall Cat asked, "By the way have you seen a woman with silver blonde hair about five foot seven and built?" The blank look she received provided her answer. She connected with the large panel and with the push of a button, was free.

She didn't think of mindspeaking to Zorroc for assistance, she'd never make that mistake again. Obviously, he thought her no better than the many females he had bragged to her about, beating down his door for attention, but she had learned her lesson. She would take care of herself and their baby and by the time it arrived, he'd probably figure it belonged to someone else. Her run of celibacy had ended. She'd COM Rosik for assistance at her first opportunity. She looked around. Where was this place? Nothing looked familiar. The building she exited looked, from the outside, like a small Coliseum with huge windowed towers interspersed with flat stone panels. Against the panels were a wide variety of flowering trees and topiary. Edward Scissorhands popped into her head just as a voice reverberated loudly in her mind, making her yelp and search for cover.

"Zorroc?" she asked, as the voice dissipated.

"Yes, it is Zorroc, who else would it be?"

"Um, I don't know, it's been so long since I felt you inside my head, I forgot what it was like."

"Stay there and do not move; I am coming for you."

"You know where I am?"

"I am almost there."

The panel slid open behind her and he emerged. She almost cried at the sight of him; she'd missed him that much. He filled her vision as he filled her world, looking better, larger, and more solid than the thousand daydreams she'd had of him in the last few months. She should be furious with him for his treatment toward her these last endless weeks and run far and fast away—but he looked impossibly beautiful and eminently contrite. His eyes began to fill with moisture that would spill at a blink. Were they tears?

He drank in every inch of her, taking in her clouds of hair, her clear, too large emerald eyes in her gaunt face, along with her too thin body. Clearly, the separation had been as telling on her as it had on him. He focused intently on her abdomen picturing his offspring nestled there and was overcome by her beauty, and the essence that made up his lifemate. She just stared, seemingly not able to take her eyes from him.

"Hello, my one," he grated huskily.

"What were you doing in there?" she asked softly.

"I live here."

"Well, what was I doing in there?"

"You live here too," he pointed out logically and then gave her a heart-stopping grin.

He was on her in two strides, scooping her high against his chest and chastising her gently for being outside in her sleeping shift.

Chapter Eighteen

He lowered her onto their mat and slipped her shift off in one determined motion. He examined her shoulder, gently prodding for tenderness and swelling. Her intake of breath told him what he wanted to know as he began to peruse and test the rest of her, now that she had awakened.

"You will lie still and let me attend to you," he murmured softly proceeding to lave, kiss and nuzzle her beginning with her lips, ears, neck now free of the collar, before moving lower. When she began to quiver, lifting her arms to encircle him, he stopped abruptly, silencing her with a finger to her lips and issued his instructions. "I will not have you hurt by responding to my touch, therefore, you will be as motionless as a sitar and let me play on you and in you. I will be your master and you, my instrument that I will make sing. Move at all and I will stop. And if I have to cease again I will trance you to immobility and take all power from you save one; the power to feel, do you understand?"

She nodded imperceptibly and he resumed once more. His focus on her made her more than moderately nervous; her trepidation, alone, keeping her still except for the rapid rise and fall of her chest. It had been months since she'd been touched and her body had changed; would he still find her pleasing? His eyes had taken on an eerie glow, dilating until almost no amber remained visible, as if locked in a hypnotic state or possessed. He positioned her with legs spread wide and straight and her arms spread but bent at the elbows so that her hands rested close to her temples, and commenced his sensuous melody. He touched her only with his mouth, softly trailing his lips and tongue over the underside of her arm before moving to the side of her breast to her waist and then hip. He went very slowly and whisper purred that he wanted her to focus totally on the spot he touched and think of nothing else.

She figured out right away, that would never work, since his warm breath, the soft brush of his mouth and all sensation bee-lined straight into the growing pool located in her lower belly. She could also feel that moisture working its way down into her woman's passage and pushing through her labia like a flower giving up its nectar. She wouldn't tell him this however; her lips, at least the ones on her face, were sealed. She felt like he licked every sensitive place on her body before drawing firmly on one breast and then the other. A sheen of moisture now covered her entire body with the effort it took to keep herself immobile. It escalated into unbearable torture but one she could not give up. Finally he settled between her legs to drink abundantly of all he had wrung from her and when he was through; drove his tongue into her and began to purr inside her to drink even more of her violent climax.

A scream started low in her throat exploding loudly as spasms raked her in rapid succession. Zorroc rose up quickly to cover her mouth with his and then sheathed his engorged shaft inside her until he probed her womb. It felt so good, so right that he could not move for a moment. He shuddered and began to slide into her slowly gathering in force and momentum. He would never stop, never, never, never...and then he was coming, coming, coming...leading her with him into the petit mort.

Their souls irrevocably fused at that moment. He needed to explain and apologize for trying to run away from this...from her. He felt like a fool. Like a moth attempting to out-fly a Pod.

The panel COM sounded and Jaffers relayed that Prolinc had arrived with vital information needing his immediate attention. Zorroc groaned into her throat before responding.

"Enter Jaffers, and meet my Divitta." Cat pounded him soundlessly and tried to burrow further under the comforter while muffling a protest on his poor timing. He smiled wickedly and rolled over exposing her head, shoulders, and gloriously disarrayed hair just in time for Jaffers' dignified entrance. It was Cat's turn to groan.

"Jaffers, may I present my mate, Catarina, originally of the House of Tuk and daughter to Princess Nancia and Rowan, recently arrived from Earth. Catarina this is Jaffers of the House of Ra and main Inner House Facilitator." Then Zorroc leaned back to gloat with misplaced humor at the situation he had set into motion. After shooting Zorroc with dual emerald daggers she turned slowly in Zorroc's arms to face Jaffers, all the while feeling her skin color pass from a rosy glow to an even darker shade, until it radiated enough heat to fry her mate.

Jaffers responded like the professional he was. "She is red."

"Yes, her hair holds the color of our Gattonian sky; it is lovely is it not?" Zorroc responded, pleased.

"But she is all red."

Zorroc turned her head to face him and smiled broadly. "She is blushing."

"She is mortified," Cat snapped testily.

"You are welcomed, Mi Divitta. Do you have instructions for me, Divo?" Jaffers inquired.

"Yes, tell Prolinc I will be with him directly, then order a full feast delivered to the aunt's chambers where you will direct the Divitta when she is ready. You are to further instruct the aunts to feed her until she can hold no more. She is carrying my heir and needs fuel. Her nourishment is now a part of your duties. Thank you Jaffers."

At the panels' closure, Zorroc hopped up and dressed, informing Cat of the location of her clothes and belongings. Before leaving he approached her, kissed her soundly on the lips and confessed, "I adore you."

She froze in place for a full two minutes before scrambling off the mat and heading to the clean room.

****

"We have him on voice and visual communicating with a Dargon called Dung," Prolinc began without preamble. "Dyfainius demanded the antidote for his daughter to restore her reproductive system, stating that he had met his side of the bargain, and more by providing them with the lay-out of secured areas within Gattonia and other sensitive information as to our fire power and size of force readiness. But it revealed much more," he paused with a combination of promised retribution and satisfaction. "Dyfainius went on to accuse the Dargons of failing to terminate the woman after having been practically handed to them. The last bit of conversation I am having transmission-loaded onto your COM so you can review it first hand. They were after Catarina."

Zorroc felt like frozen crystal on the outside and an incinerator within; he would make Dyfainius wish he had never been conceived. "I suggest we discuss our options in dealing with him properly," Zorroc stated with deadly calm. He supposed he owed the Dargons a dept of gratitude in one small measure. It had kept him from mating with the viper's daughter.

The rest of the late morning and early afternoon flowed comfortably for Cat. The aunts delighted in seeing her confirmed as Divitta and pleased as punch they would be residing under the same roof once more. Scotty and Spock acted just as happy; having more hands to pet, feed and coddle them. Nadia joined them with her tornika, which looked like a cross between a ferret and a longhaired cat. Spooka proved mischievous and affectionate and the three animals took to one another right away, their antics going a long way to help Nadia and Cat open the door to friendship.

Later that afternoon Nadia took Cat on a tour of the chambers and grounds, both of which dwarfed vast. Cat knew she could remain lost for weeks in the underground webbing of protective corridors, shelters and computer facilities that regulated everything from grounds maintenance, clothing, food, utilities and upper level appliances. As they headed back to the living chambers, the main entrance panel signaled a waiting guest.

"I will get it Jaffers," Nadia spoke happily into the COM as the panel slid open. Her expression froze as she glanced uneasily from Cat to Zana. Fur was going to fly. Zana, on a mission though, did not notice the changing emotional climate as she bused Nadia on the cheek, greeting her as "sister" and then blithely announced that she and Zorroc had things to discuss. The time had arrived to re-formalize their betrothal and set a date.

Cat didn't know whether to laugh or spy. She would have given anything to be a fly on the wall for this confrontation. When her eyes met Nadia's, she knew they shared a similar thought.

"Come on," Nadia encouraged while propelling her down the corridor. "We need to hide. She will strike you dead if she figures out who you are on her way out. There is a room where we might be able to hear some of the conversation, follow me," she ended, a twinkle visible in her amber depths.

Since her talk with Zorroc, Nadia had figured out that Zana had most likely used her on several levels not the least of which included getting on Zorroc's good side by cozening up to his sister. Nadia realized with new perception that when Zana spoke, Nadia's job entailed listening and being impressed. There had been little interaction the brand Zorroc had demonstrated during their last discussion.

Nadia and Cat needn't have worried about being able to listen in on the conversation when outraged shrieking blasted out of his office and echoed down the length of the corridor. They slipped in to the chamber closest to Zorroc's office and waited silently making out the words 'vile spreader' and 'Earth whore' before all went silent. After several minutes, a light tap sounded on their panel, the two looked briefly at one another before Nadia rose and answered it. It was Jaffers.

"The Divo requests your presence in his main office, Mi Divitta, would you follow me?" Of course, it hardly served as a request; Cat strived for all the dignity she could muster, considering she had been caught eavesdropping, and followed him next door, where she was announced.

"Catarina, my love may I present Zana, daughter to Dyfainius of the House of Tinz. Zana this is your Divitta, Catarina, formerly of the House of Tuk and daughter to Princess Nancia and Rowan." Cat wondered if she would ever get used to the woman that gave her birth, being called a princess. Had Zorroc realized he called her 'his love'?

'Yes' sounded through her consciousness. She inclined her head Gattonian style to Zana and she in turn mumbled a group of words back. Cat had to give her credit, she kept her tone respectful, if quiet, but she looked like a volcano about to erupt.

Zorroc waited until Zana exited silently before grabbing Cat and lifting her onto his massive desk where he proceeded to kiss her Gattonian style, incorporating both his mouth and his mind.

****

She touched Zana languidly while waiting for her to make sense. Zana had arrived at their chambers thirty minutes before and Sandra had yet to hear a coherent sentence. The betrothal was off; she gathered that much, and with it, all the plans they'd devised for Zorroc. Zana and Sandra had been introduced to one another within the first week of ship's landing and recognized a like mind and kindred spirit in each other immediately. They became lovers that night and Sandra moved into Zana's living chambers one week later, as a companion. Zana had told her father that, because he spent so much time away from her, she required company. Her father had jumped at the chance to please his only child and light of his life.

Sandra rose and padded naked across the room for a glass of Jive, a potent liquid guaranteed to relax and intoxicate. The two enjoyed it plain, or laced with just a touch of Assyllis. She brought back a large drought and placed it in her Chosen One's hand, then sighed. Things had been going so well. Lately, Zorroc had gotten into the habit of escorting both of them to official gatherings, signaling to them his intention of taking dual mates. They thought it only a matter of time before the High Council passed the new statutes and Zorroc made formal his commitment. It titillated and tickled them that while he courted them with all propriety, they got down and dirty with each other every night looking forward to the day when he would make them his mates—so they could cuckold him. The vision played deliciously naughty and made them collapse into fits of sniggers when they contemplated it.

Zana did not like the attention of males but had been willing to spread herself for Zorroc, occasionally, for the power and rise in status. Sandra enjoyed the feel of a man inside her and would enjoy riding him to give him the whelps required to seal her place, but Zana made up her other half and for the first time in her life, she knew love instead of the act of sex, alone. She knew Zana loved her in return. Noticing her high-strung beauty had calmed sufficiently, she proceeded to gently pull the facts of the afternoon from her.

"He is lifemated to her and has been for months, we are skirged! She is living with him and he had the audacity to present me to her. I think it is that puny abomination you told me about, the one with hair the ugly shade of a brown-sky flower," she ended in frustrated fury.

"Catarina; was her name Cat or Catarina?" Had that little bitch tripped her up, again? She couldn't, wouldn't believe it.

"Yes, that was it and it is a lifemating, there will be only one for him. All of our plans are ruined."

"Wait Zana, there is still a chance for us. She comes from Earth, if the statutes become law, he can still lifemate with you and then you can bring me in as your companion; it is not ideal I'll grant you but if I'm with you, I can deal with it," she offered sincerely.

"You blind cow, do you understand nothing?" she fumed, looking for an outlet to unleash her fury. Sandra flinched, unused to the lethal vehemence being pointed in her direction. "She is daughter to Princess Nancia and Rowan of the House of Tuk. It is a High House. And, though of split blood, she is Gattonian. It constitutes a bound lifemating; impossible to sever even if he chose to, which he does not from the besotted look on his face at seeing her. No Sandra, all of our plans; they have vanished like wallows mist."

Sandra rose thoughtfully and went to refill Zana's glass with more Jive, only this time with a pinch of Assyllis to put her mind toward her Chosen One and not her enemy. Cat would pay for this, she would see to it.

While Sandra and Zana slept peacefully after hours of sweaty sex, the Guard of the High Council, headed by Commander Ryder, with orders straight from the Divo, quietly entered the private chambers of Dyfainius and arrested him.

At one a.m. they led him into the main interrogation chamber to face the High Council, along with a group of additional personnel including members of the High Council Guard, and Rosik, Prolinc, Carpov, Bandoff, Sycor and of course, Zorroc. Dyfainius showed outrage at being dragged from his mat at such an hour with no excuse given; but mostly he was nervous. They could not know. It was not possible. He had been too careful.

A pre-emptive strike, in his current situation would prove most deflective, he decided, and so Dyfainius faced his peers with political bluster if not confidence. "Though not informed of this impromptu meeting, it happens to serve my purposes well. Fellow Gattonians, we have been patient with this child leader long enough. We have put up with Zorroc's lack of guidance and misdirected actions for many years, and now I, for one, have reached the end of my tolerance and beseech you to join with me in doing what should have been done ten years before. I, Dyfainius, Leader of the High Council, hereby challenge Zorroc for the rule of Gattonia on the grounds of reckless endangerment to the people of Gattonia and contributions to the end of our race. Further, I charge him with the desecration and disruption of the moral fiber of our culture by trying to infuse our society with inferior alien females and then coercing me into proposing indecent statutes. Statutes designed to degrade the females of Gattonia and corrupt the fiber of our males," he accused facing Zorroc, head high, shoulders back, and finger pointed. He was nothing if not a great politician.

Zorroc rose, faced the High Council and delivered his charges against Dyfainius.

"Traitor: Giving confidential and harmful information to the enemy pertaining to male-power, defenses, numbers, and logistics of sensitive and devastating targets.

"Attempted Murder: Pre-meditated plan to murder the daughter of Princess Nancia and Rowan of the House of Tuk.

"Attempted Murder: Pre-meditated attempt to murder the Divitta of Gattonia, Catarina, daughter to Princess Nancia and Rowan formerly of the House of Tuk.

"Suspected Attempted Murder: Suspected pre-meditated murder of the future heir of Gattonia now residing in the Divitta's womb."

Other than his complexion taking on a mottled red pattern, beaded with perspiration, Dyfainius exhibited no visible reaction to the mandatory death charges that had been leveled against him. Shrouded in dignity and indignation, he turned to Zorroc. "You have no proof. What are you trying to accomplish here, son?" he implored, shaking his head sadly. "Your father and I shared a friendship that spanned many decades. You besmirch his reputation by leveling these injustices. My daughter, in turn, ministered to your father when he fell ill after the death of your mother, and nursed him until the day he died. Zazu, our families intended a joining until your incompetent handling of the Dargon attack. Why are you making these implausible and unsubstanciated accusations?"

Zorroc lounged back in his chair never removing

his knowing glare from Dyfainius as he pressed a button on the keypad next to him, and smiled dangerously. The screen came alive showing Dyfainius in thousand-pronged clarity speaking on COM to another party that identified himself as Dung, speaker for Dargons. The High Council listened in mounting horror as the conversation unfolded. The remaining attendees sat motionless, their knowing eyes glued to the unfolding scene. There would be no escape for the accused this night. When the screen went blank, total silence ensued.

"I am not your son, scum of a Syphor," he stated with quiet vehemence, "now what do you have to say to the allegations? The seriousness of the charges negates your right to a hearing but out of respect for my father, I am allowing you to face your peers."

"Well, it is obvious, is it not? The video scan is a counterfeit. Who gave you such an obvious piece of fabrication? It is clear that my lips do not match the poorly faked voice and I demand an explanation! Who gave you this scan?"

"I did." Prolinc stood and spoke for the first time. "Under orders from the Divo, we had your chambers, both private and official, monitored. After the ambush of The Stellar, we realized that the Dargons had been fed the information pertaining to our location and human cargo. While under siege, it became equally clear that they searched for one particular woman and so we monitored all attempted COM relays, not authorized by the Commander of the Miramid. When the male you assigned to report our activities tried to contact you, it confirmed your perfidy but not possible others involved."

Prolinc turned to the High Council and addressed them pointedly. "We remained unsure if Dyfainius worked alone or in conjunction with additional members of the High Council, and equally unsure as to the extent of involvement with the Dargons and movements against the Divitta. When the High Council Guard took her involuntarily, we knew immediate action was vital for the protection of the Divitta and Divo. Thus, the video scan." Prolinc then faced Zorroc with feigned subservience and asked, "With your permission, Divo?" He enjoyed his role in this early morning drama. For years, he had stood by while the High Council underestimated and undermined his friend's authority and abilities but tonight he would see an end to it for all time.

Zorroc had an inkling as to Prolinc's motives and nodded for him to continue. They had long ago dubbed the members of the High Council as the PIPs or Pompous Impotent Politicals. It would be satisfying to see them justify their position for a change. They proceeded to do just that.

Prolinc and Zorroc mindspoke their amusement at the immediate change of attitude in the High Council. In the end, they sang like a choir of castrati admitting to being led by Dyfainius, believing him to be the future guide-by-blood to Zorroc, which would afford him the ability to control the Divo and therefore, hold the greater political power. Although they knew of the existence of Catarina and her presence onboard the returning vessel, they pleaded ignorance to her change in status and her location on Gattonia and, of course, denied knowledge of any contact between Gattonia and the Dargons. Lastly, they had been informed that mandatory pregnancy testing of recalcitrant women had come as a directive from Zorroc.

As for Dyfainius, he collapsed, admitting to all charges, declaring love for his daughter as his main motivating force and of course, had entertained no aspirations toward controlling the Divo. His indiscretions merely reflected the actions of a misguided, overindulgent father. The statutes, he proposed in the event that he proved unsuccessful in obtaining the antidote for his daughter, which had also been his purpose for initially contacting the Dargons. They assured him that an antidote existed and if he would but answer a few simple questions, it would be his. Of course, the questions never ended and eventually followed with threats of blackmail, exposing him as a traitor if he would no longer co-operate.

At this point Carpov told him that there could be no such antidote in existence because an antidote could not execute cell regeneration or eliminate existing scar tissue; it could only halt future degeneration.

"The Dargons used your weakness against the realm of Gattonia and as a result the people of Gattonia and your daughter, specifically, will pay for your treachery. For it is a foregone conclusion that the Dargons will use your information to launch another attack and this time Zana will not be afforded preferential shelter or treatment," Zorroc announced, unaccountably pleased when Dyfainius flinched at his last words. "What made you turn against Catarina in the first place? The plan to bring her here originated from you. Why lure her to her death when she could have remained unmolested on Earth?" he persisted.

"Come, my boy, her existence could not be kept from you for long. You would have been made aware of her in any case. Many others, beside me, knew of her existence; I was even contacted by her own parents. No, much more expedient to control the process and have her secured and neutralized. As the only royal Gattonian female still fertile, she would have to be your first choice, thereby usurping my daughter's rightful place. And what better way to gain your trust than be the one to find her for you?"

He laughed with genuine amusement. "And you never questioned my motives, never believed that I would hold my daughter above your petty wishes for a strong line and your impotent plans to keep Gattonia from the Dargons. They want this planet and they will have it and nothing you can do…"

The chamber let out a collective gasp at the puff of smoke that had been Dyfainius.

"I believe we have heard enough," Zorroc commented quietly, putting his side arm away.

Zorroc, having carried out the mandatory death sentence, stripped Dyfainius and his family of all holdings and decreed the closing and banning of the House of Tinz. His people would be located to other houses and his daughter, provided with a dowry substantial enough to attract an agglu-mating to a Lower House.

With matters settled and the meeting at an end, Zorroc decided on one last piece of business. With the High Council firmly at a disadvantage, none would mutter a word against what he intended to propose, and he had to admit he might never again have them in this weakened state. Ordinarily they would hold endless rounds of debates on the soundness of his proposals and not wanting to appear an autocratic cracker brain; he would listen to all sides. In truth, they had taught him much and tempered his youthful rashness in the years past. Never again, however, would he depend on his father's advisors to be loyal to his rule.

He stood, faced the council, and looked each one in the eye with utter determination before pronouncing. "With Dyfainius no longer holding a seat on the High Council, I hereby appoint Bandoff, of the House of Able, to fill the seat of Lead Member of High Council. Meeting adjourned."

Heartening pandemonium ensued between the crewmembers and guards while members of the

High Council moved their mouths in a gaping parody of suffocating trout. Bandoff sat Gattonian still; positive he had somehow misheard. Zorroc turned and left. Even with a Dargon attack eminent, he felt lighter and happier than he had since assuming the role of Divo to Gattonia.

Chapter Nineteen

Zorroc joined a sleeping Catarina on their mat. If this wave of adoration mirrored his father's feelings for his mother, he could understand the pain he experienced in being cleaved from her, severed in two. It did not explain, however, his emotional and physical abandonment of his children who had been the only remaining part of her. He touched his mate's slightly rounded belly and thought of the life they had created. He imagined that he could almost message his love and anticipation, of being able to see, touch, and nurture his offspring and that even if they could not yet answer, they understood. Cat almost certainly, had three growing inside her but he would not know for sure, or of their genders, for a while, yet. He held this information to his heart wanting to surprise his mate for so little seemed astound her. From the first, she conceded to everything laid before her and even more; embraced it with a calm acceptance, he knew, he could never emulate. She had emerged the bravest most stalwart being he had encountered and knew those qualities would spill into her duties as lifemate, mother and Divitta. He adored her, loved, and worshipped her with his mind, body, and spirit and the time had arrived to reveal those feelings to her.

He began to touch and soothe her, speaking quietly of his adoration and love that filled him as the Gattonian sun filled the sky, with light overflowing onto the lands and into everything living. She was the air that he breathed and the joy of his heart.

A waking dream pulled at her, teasing her psyche, planting the words she yearned to hear him speak. His now familiar touch and unmistakable scent made her aware of his presence the moment he joined her but the rest had to be her wishful imagination imprinting her own feelings that inconceivably flowed from his mouth and mind. What a lovely, perfect fantasy. How many times had she longed to hear the words she had accepted would never come? She needed to open her eyes and face her reality but the dream proved so seductive, so dear. Then he commanded her to open. Open? Open what, her eyes?

"Your eyes, your heart, your mind, your spirit...and your legs, my Divitta," he confirmed to her chagrin. She complied and he invaded her an instant before she read the humor in his eyes. He loved her slowly and fully, all the while whispering his love and devotion and his apology for not doing so sooner. Then they slept a most peaceful, wondrous, and relaxing sleep.

He petted her with a new intimacy as she grilled him on the out come of the meeting, and when he revealed a modified version of the proceedings, he was met with mixed reviews.

"Bandoff must be thrilled and overwhelmed by his new appointment and I think it a most brilliant stroke of genius. He's wanted to lifemate with his Milli for years but her parents opposed because of his Lower House status and commitment to you as Guardian. Now he will lead the High Council, be a leader among his people and you will have someone you can have absolute faith in as your advisor. In addition, he will act as a finger on the pulse of the political climate. You have leveled many hills with one plane, my love," she finished as her eyes danced merrily to his tune. "But I'm a little concerned about the Zana situation. Nadia and she are still friends and I wonder if it is fair to blame her for the sins of her father. Losing her father and her status seems harsh enough, but stripping her of living funds and agglu-mating her to someone, not of her choosing, rides the edge of injustice," she tendered, not wanting to deflate his euphoria in finding the traitor but also concerned about Zana, knowing how she would feel if the same had befallen her.

Zorroc looked incredulous for a moment before articulating his thoughts into words. "If your positions were reversed, do you think she would give a moments thought to you? She would probably insist you be banned to another galaxy with no funds instead of being handed into a secure situation that is her home. She will be taken care of and reasonably content, I promise you, but have you thought past the obvious? How much did she perceive and condone of her father's activities, because I promise you she knew some. She should be very lucky that I do not delve into her involvement in this whole mess. Who is to say she was not the puppeteer behind the puppet; she would be capable of it I assure you."

Zazu, were females never satisfied? He did what he deemed necessary to protect his mate and their offspring and she sat complaining for the protection. Was she so innocent she did not know the dangers of a female scorned?

Fate, in the name of Zana, intervened and halted further discussion. She arrived, begging for an audience and crying to her "only friend" Nadia. He had known this would be her ploy and the confrontation, inevitable. After kissing his mate soundly, he advanced purposefully to his office. He wanted this dealt with and her gone from their lives as soon as possible. He would allow Nadia no further contact with her after this day.

If he had a doubt as to how she would play this,

his vision confirmed it the instant he entered his office. Zana knelt sobbing pitifully on Nadia's lap while Nadia looked helpless and unnerved. He dismissed Nadia and prepared himself for an emotional tidal wave.

"How could you do this to me? Am I not the one who comforted your father and sat with him when he became ill? Have I not loved you for years...years, since just a girl? We were betrothed, almost mated, and now you kill my father who loved yours and throw me away. It is not worthy of the male I know," she stormed heroically, giving a great imitation of her father.

Zorroc decided not to respond and see what else she came up with next and, more to the point, what she had planned.

"My father is lost to me, do not take away my status, I have done nothing. You would sell me to a Lower House as an agglu-mate; that is no better than a drudge, a slave, a spreader. Please Zorroc, if you have any feelings for me at all, let me stay in the great House of Ra as a companion to Nadia until a suitable mate can be found. As it stands, I am to be banished to the Women Dorm where some Earthlings yet remain. Most of the ones there service many; I should not be brought into contact with such filth. Let me stay with Nadia, I have loved her like a sister and would be good company for her, now that you and your mate will be occupied with each other." Her dewy eyes resembled black diamonds.

The serpent of death slid down his spine as he contemplated this, just being in the same chamber with her disoriented him for a moment. There resided an evil in her hidden until this moment. How had she blocked it from him? It made him half believe what he had put to Catarina about puppeteer and puppet. His revulsion mounted so completely, his diplomacy deserted him. "You have other choices open to you that I will explain but keeping company with my sister and residing in my home are not among them." He rose and walked to the window keeping his back to her while he mindspoke to Prolinc and Sycor to report at once to his private chamber office. At their response, he turned back to Zana.

"You actually have three choices. You may submit yourself for interrogation as an accomplice to your fathers' treasonous acts; you may be banned from Gattonia permanently with your personal belongings and dowry; or you may agglu-mate with the male of my choice and never show yourself again to my family or anyone connected with my house. For if you do it will mean your death. Those are your choices; I merely assumed that the third would be the most palatable to you. Please advise me of your wishes, I have many more important obligations to attend to."

Zana's heat turned into a simmer, the simmer to a boil and the boil into an inferno that almost rocked Zorroc off his feet. Prolinc and Sycor entered uninvited at the outraged caterwaul and encountered an unworldly rage swirling around them, catching them off guard. Immediately, a force field formed around Zorroc as he leaned back onto his desk trying to decide how to proceed. She had telekinetic abilities. That came as a surprise. "You will get yourself under control, now, or be stun-blazed," he commanded.

Cat, having seen Prolinc and Sycor race by and hearing the commotion, came charging into the room believing Zorroc to be in danger. She launched herself onto him with all the force her small body could project, only to ricochet off the force field and land three feet away square on her bottom. The impromptu slapstick seemed to hit all of them at once. The kinetic energy subsided, the force field wavered and disappeared and all had their eyes riveted onto the Divitta; legs akimbo in front of her, hands and arms holding her in an upright position and her hair unbound and floating around her head. Zorroc, the first to react, lifted her up like she weighed no more than a rag doll, sat her on top of his desk, and proceeded to gently brush the tumbled mass of hair from her face, all the while murmuring to have a care for their offspring. She wanted to hide her face in his chest and wait for everyone to leave, but knew it would be unbecoming behavior for a Divitta. She cautiously glanced around. She found Sycor and Prolinc frozen into Gattonian statue mode, no doubt trying to maintain their composure; Zana eyeing her with malicious jubilation; and Zorroc studying her like he'd never seen a lovelier sight. He no doubt had *cat*aracts.

Zana, having lost her momentum, sneered her parting shot. "I will go and do as you command but I promise you will regret your treatment of me for the rest of your existence." With the regal bearing of a Divitta, she swept out of the chamber flanked by Prolinc and Sycor.

Later that afternoon China, Dee and Angel paid their first visit to the House of Ra. The aunts and Nadia joined them and it swelled into a festive and lively exchange of laughter, gossip and the latest developments in their respective lives. Dee at first behaved awkwardly and a little resentful toward Nadia. Lovelier than Jasmine in spring, she would one day be lifemated to the one that should have belonged to Dee.

Cat and Angel exchanged knowing looks at Dee's unease but didn't know how to remedy the situation. Nadia, however, with her kindness and newly found perception knew exactly what to do.

"I can see why you and Prolinc have forged such

a strong bond. You are well matched both physically and mentally. You both are straightforward with no wasted movements or superfluous words and are warriors, loyal to the ones you love." Then she laughed good-naturedly. "Prolinc has been a brother to me my entire life and treats me like a butterfly, mindful of my flitting around but gently blowing me away when he has reached his patience quota. We are due to lifemate in a few years but I have a feeling that much can happen in that time. I would like to find a love like all of you have," she ended on a sigh and a self-depreciating giggle.

Who could resist her good-natured chatter?

While conversation flowed around them, Dee studied Nadia. She really had no interest in Prolinc other than as a brother and playmate; anything more and she'd sense it. Furthermore, she found that she truly liked Nadia and she was right; three years was a very long time. The dark cloud that had trapped her suddenly lifted and she felt better than she had since the Miramid.

As the Edenwine flowed and the mood grew even more animated, Nadia stood and made an announcement. "I have a special gift for the new Divitta. It is a very special potion named Ceilia derived from a rare vine found in the northern mountains of Jasper. It is not alcoholic or mind altering and will not harm the baby but it lights you from inside and creates a strong feeling of well-being. I have a small amount that I will add to Cat's wine and then we will toast. One drop is all I have but it is all that is needed." The tiny bottle that contained the potion looked as intricate as a silkworm weaving. It had to be every bit as rare as what it contained. Cat, though skeptical would not ruin Nadia's obvious joy in presenting such a precious gift.

She took a tiny sip as Nadia ended the toast and

she felt an immediate rush of warmth, like a warm, bubbling liquid whooshing through her. It imbued her with a decidedly pleasant sensation.

The filigree bottle passed from person to person for each to inspect until it reached Helen. After admiring it for a moment, she looked puzzled. "Did Zorroc bring this back from his trip? I do not recall any mention of it."

Nadia looked a little sheepish and admitted, "It was a parting gift from Zana; she wanted to give me something special to remember her by. It was the last of her father's stock."

Dee looked horror-stricken and Cat felt a slight queasiness from where the glow emanated. All motion slowed while the churning intensified, but she couldn't form the words to explain, and then the scene faded into darkness as she crumpled to the floor.

"Will she be all right, will our offspring survive undamaged?" Zorroc rasped unable to keep the tears from escaping down his cheeks. She had been poisoned. Did Zana know Nadia would give the bottle to his mate or had Nadia been the target that had missed its mark? Oh Zazu, if he lost her he doubted he could go on. Thoughts of his father hit him with a force that shook his entire being. Would he fall into a black void where nothing could live but his torment?

"Zorroc, the poison was diluted in the wine and she only had a small sip in deference to the toast. We have isolated the poison and are introducing the antidote slowly into her system. I am optimistic she will recover but am concerned for your offspring. The body, in its attempt to rid itself of the lethal toxin, began convulsing internally and all major organs are affected. Normally this would be fine but the contractions could cause Cat to abort your babes," Carpov ended grimly. "We are doing all we can to

265

control her body's reaction to the poison and neutralize it before brain and organ tissues can be permanently damaged. Fortunately, we had a sample for evaluation because, even now, her body does not register any foreign substance that could cause this reaction. Ordinarily, we would have treated it like the flu. We have much to be grateful for. If Nadia had taken it alone in her room she almost certainly would have died."

Zorroc shuddered at the thought and then Zana's parting words came back to him. She had given Nadia the poison even before their interview. She had played her hand superbly...and she would die. Militia combed the area searching for her. She would not escape him except through death.

"Zorroc, I hesitate to mention this now but something about Catarina's symptoms are very familiar," he paused, wondering if now the right time to reveal his growing suspicions. "Her symptoms mirror those of your father's only with greater severity. Zana could have used this drug in smaller quantities to poison your father, with no one able to prove otherwise, or indeed, even aware of it occurring," Carpov concluded grimly, the ramifications almost too staggering to grasp.

"Of course, that would explain so much. Why she visited my father daily; why he began to go steadily down hill; why he died...while I did nothing to stop her."

"Do not begin to think what I know you are already contemplating. You are not responsible for your father's death. If you want to affix blame then blame me for not catching it. The true blame, however, lies with the twisted House of Tinz. The last viper stands exposed, my friend, and Gattonia will be a cleaner and safer place because of it." Carpov sighed tiredly, "The reason I decided to mention this sooner rather than later is because you will no doubt want to include my suspicions in your questioning of Zana."

"May I see her?" Zorroc asked unexpectedly.

After just a moment, Carpov realized he meant Catarina and not Zana. "Yes, that is why I came, I think it would do both of you good to be together right now."

"Will the poison seep into the offspring's' systems?" Zorroc asked with dread while getting to his feet and following his friend down the hall.

"The blood and fluids going to the womb are being screened. The poison did not have time to reach them. The only danger right now is her body's own defense system."

Zorroc nodded listlessly. It seemed a small comfort. Zorroc looked on his mate and could not believe the difference in her. She lay still and waxen, surrounded with monitors, scanners, and tubes running around, in and out of her like so many bustling transways and Pod ports.

He sat down beside her and gently enclosed her small hand in his, gently reaching into her mind, searching for her link. It revealed nothing but a dense gray fog but he kept patiently trying to find a thread that would lead him to her. He stilled; something waited there mewing and distressed, his babies were anxious at the stillness and blankness of their mothers' being. They could not communicate with words or thoughts but reached out to him for reassurance, and he thought he might cry from the joy of it. He reached out with all of his considerable talent and flooded their minds with soothing images of love, comfort and security. He stayed with them until he felt them drift into slumber. He had never experienced anything so miraculous and it kept him sane as the hours melded together.

Friends, Med-techs, the aunts and others seemed to flow in and out like restless waves on a sea. Then on the third day, he realized he had not seen Nadia. He COMd Marie and Helen and asked after her. Helen began to cry while Marie cussed up a storm before blurting out the situation.

"Nadia blames herself for harming Cat and your heir and believes you must hate her now like her father did when your mother died. We have tried to talk some sense into the girl but she will not hear us. We did not want to burden you with another problem so we decided to wait until we knew more about Cat's condition. How is she?" Marie demanded gruffly.

"She is no worse which I am told is a very good sign; the babies are well," he slipped not wanting anyone to know about the triplets until he told his mate. "I am on my way to Nadia now, thank you for telling me."

"Prolinc," Zorroc bellowed into Prolinc's mind.

"Yes?" came his quiet reply.

"Have Dee and Angel stay with Cat, I have something to do that cannot wait."

"They are on their way," Prolinc answered, encouraged by the strength of Zorroc's query. He was coming back to himself. He had not left Catarina's side since her collapse and would not hear of someone sitting with her while he took a much-needed rest. He must be feeling encouraged by her prognosis.

Zorroc did not bother to announce himself; he just strode right into Nadia's room. Curled into a fetal position, she looked asleep. He had sworn to himself he would never fall into the same trap as his father and yet it had happened easily. Well he was not his father, a point he intended to bring home to his precious sister. He sat on the side of her bed, scooped her up and cradled her like a baby, the way he had done countless times through the years. She sobbed and hung onto him while upbraiding herself;

apologizing to him and promising perfect behavior and undying gratitude if he would only forgive her and give her another chance. He wondered if guilt figured prominently in their gene pool and smiled slightly at the thought.

"You promise all that, do you? Well it certainly is a tempting offer. Does this include scrubbing out my clean room when it strikes my fancy and arranging my favorite foods in order of preference? Oh, and do not forget my trans-unit, does this mean you will never borrow it again? Yes, very tempting indeed."

As Zorroc continued to catalog a growing list of requests, she stilled and grew uncharacteristically quiet. When he took a quick glance down, he saw just what he had hoped for. She threw him back on the bed and began tickling him as only she could get away with and the two of them laughed like children enjoying the moment.

"Now," he ordered when the two caught their breath. "You will get into your prettiest clothes, I will get out of this wrinkled attire, and after we have something to eat we will go visit your sister and make her wake up. She has rested long enough, do you not agree?"

"I love you, Rocky."

"And I love you, Dizzy. I will meet you in the dining nook off my chambers." Zorroc left feeling that all would be well; he would accept no other outcome.

After the first full meal either had had in three days, they made their way to the main med-quarters. Three sets of smiles greeted them and Zorroc knew the news was good. "Is she awake, is she better?" he burst out as he moved quickly to Cat's side and grabbed her hand.

"Angel and I believe she is surfacing so I want you to reach her through mindspeak and bring her the rest of the way out, would you like to try?" Carpov grinned at his ridiculous suggestion.

Zorroc eased in and all but staggered at the force of her frustration. *"It took you long enough to get here,"* she messaged with impatience.

"How long have you been awake and why have you not let your friends know, they have been frantic with worry," he scolded.

"I've only been awake for a little while, I think, but I could tell the room needed a boost so I decided to wait for you to stage my wake-up scene. Kiss me," she demanded.

Zorroc turned around and looked at the room full of anxious faces and smiled weakly before turning back to his mate. *"Why do you want me to kiss you, are you sure you are awake?"*

"I'm awake, I'm awake! Kiss me so I can open my eyes, damn it, I'll explain later."

"Okay, my sleeping princess, come awake." He leaned down and gently caressed her lips with his.

"You know this one," she accused as she opened her eyes, smiled mistily at him, and then stretched and whispered hoarsely. "And Sleeping Beauty awakens to true loves first kiss. The beginning."

After three seconds of stunned silence, everyone began laughing, talking, crying and congratulating one another and in general, acting as if she had left the room.

"Water, please," she croaked, completely ignored.

"Water," she asked again even louder. Nothing.

"Zorroc, water now!" she blasted into his mind. He finally rushed to do her bidding.

****

"Where did you find her?" Zorroc demanded. He could not remember the last time he slept and now he had been summoned to direct the interrogation of Zana.

"In the Women Dorm, she had not been expecting us; we found her inflagrante delicto with Sandra," Prolinc commented with a cynical smirk. "I consider you most fortunate for escaping that one."

"Both of them, you mean. Why did it take so long to capture her?" Zorroc asked.

Prolinc shrugged and admitted, "We have held her for three days deciding she could wait, while Catarina could not. Now that she is out of danger and your heir is safe, your judgment and questions will be wiser."

He was right of course. He almost looked forward to his final confrontation with the House of Tinz.

"Ah Divo, I see you are ready to greet your former betrothed. And how is our little Nadia?" Zana sneered expectantly.

"She does not know," Zorroc mindspoke to Prolinc.

"She knows nothing," he confirmed.

"You tried to kill my sister but like the warped quiver you are, you missed your target. As a result you caused no ones demise but my fathers...and your own," he conceded sardonically.

Zana started. She had expected rage, tormented accusations and dementia, anything but his calm façade of relaxed control. She grew enraged but continued to smile. "You should thank me, Zorroc, for making you Divo. Of course, that had not exactly been my plan, my father should have succeeded yours, but I was not quite fast enough with his demise while you, my betrothed, proved too fast. I did not realize the inroads you had made in assuming your father's duties. In truth, I considered you no more than a pampered boy. No one was more surprised than I when you ascended to Divo. I should have finished your father a full year earlier but I did not want the poison detected, a small miscalculation but one that would have been easily remedied with our mating. You see, as soon as I had conceived an heir, you would have met with a fatal accident, leaving my father as temporary Divo until my child could inherit the title." She expelled a sigh, "I guess it is too much to ask that your mouse of a mate was the one who ingested the poison. That would have been truly lovely."

As Zorroc began to lunge, Prolinc telepathed, "*It is just what she wants and, the only stinger she has left. Do you want to swell with her barb?*"

Zorroc immediately drew back, once again grateful for Prolinc's timely intervention. "Do you have any last words before your execution?"

"You may have killed my father but I cannot die," she stated, with insane certainty. Before he could react, a fireball of kinetic energy came hurtling toward him only to disappear inches from his face with Zana's incineration.

Zorroc turned and stared open mouthed at his friend.

Prolinc shrugged and crossed his arms in front of his massive chest. "She was not immortal, after all," he stated smugly, then smiled and added, "I believe your mate is awaiting you and I too am expected elsewhere."

Chapter Twenty

"How far out are they?" Zorroc demanded as he entered the makeshift Strat-room. He had been sleeping soundly with Catarina on his mat, where she belonged, curled into him like a kitten when the alarm sounded.

In the week following her staged awakening, Cat rapidly gained the weight needed to nourish their offspring and with it, the return of her color and energy. She demanded answers about the poison, the health of her offspring and the status of Zana. She guiltily admitted relief upon hearing of her demise and expressed surprise that Nadia had been the target. Who could harm someone so sweet natured and intrinsically kind? Zana had been like a termite infested tree looking fine and healthy on the outside but completely rotted inside. Nadia, he confided, did not seem to garner that she had been the intended target and Zorroc refused to bring the point home to her. In the end it did not matter, the threat to her had disintegrated.

The most profound revelation shimmered to life the night before, as the family gathered for the evening meal. Dressed in a gossamer iridescent gold and silver, floor length gown—slightly resembling a bloated candle flame—Catarina delivered her coup de grace.

"Has it occurred to anyone that your father, in fact, did not die of a broken heart?" She paused to ensure she had his attention. "And that his love for your mother did not cause or even hasten his death but, rather, his love for you both kept him anchored

273

here fighting to remain with the children he adored?" she proposed and took a sip of her soup. "Umm, this soup is heavenly, what's in it?" Before anyone could utter a sound, she amended. "No, scratch that question, it's better that I not know. So what do you think?"

"About the soup or the bomb you just leveled," Zorroc managed.

"I thought it more in the way of a torpedo, you know, the heat seeking kind that follows you around until it finds its mark," Cat volleyed back.

"I would describe it more along the lines of a Sleeper," Nadia added conversationally.

Zorroc indeed felt gutted. Everything about his father's death and his relationship with his mother, their love, his devotion to his children and Zorroc's own conclusions on their relationship instantly came into question. He sighed, "I concede that my father did not die of a broken heart."

"And," Cat prompted.

"And that the love he had for her did not weaken his will to live."

"Therefore," she suggested.

"Therefore, we will leave my sister and our aunts to finish their meal in peace while we explore and analyze your latest juxtaposition."

"Umm, juxtaposition, I don't think you've taught me that one yet," she whispered quietly, only to hear him growl in response.

He smiled at what transpired next...

"*Zorroc,*" Prolinc enunciated for the third time, finally breaking into his friend's thoughts by both mind and voice. "Zorroc," he continued in a more sedate manner, "I assume that the question you asked a moment ago really did expect an answer, so if you are through mind-drifting about your mate, judging by your rapturous expression, then heed me," he finished with exasperated blatancy.

Zorroc flashed him a sheepish grin before assuring Prolinc that he now claimed his undivided attention. "The Dargons are about seventy-two hours out and our screens indicate a massive invasion that will make the last one look like a Choc-bean tea gathering.

"Is everything prepared?" Zorroc asked; thinking of his own plans to keep his family safe.

"Yes, we will be more than ready for them this time and our neighbors on all sides have been contacted and are battle ready to assist us." He shook his head in wonder. "It is strange; we expected their cooperation but not this level of participation. It may be a positive beginning for our planet; working together as a united front. Even the Nefari have condescended to support us. Apparently, some of their females were affected by the virus so they are anxious to retaliate against those responsible."

"Have Carpov and Angel completed preparations for the Dargon virus and are we sure it will be effective against them and not us? Have all of our females and women been vaccinated against FIS in case they decide to spray the agent again and has everyone been informed of probable hot spots for attack and made preparations to stay well clear of those areas?"

"Yes, yes, yes and yes," he drawled. "Sycor, Bandoff, Carpov and Rosik are due here in thirty minutes to go over what we have in place so far, and a meeting with our allies is scheduled for eleven tonight. We expect it to last long into the morning."

"Is there extra serum available for the Nefari females? This is the first I have heard of them being affected."

"A team of our Med-techs were immediately dispatched to Nefar to take care of the inoculations," Prolinc responded. "How is your mate," he ventured, changing the subject. Dee had confided that Cat seemed healthy and very well pleased with her impending motherhood. "Is she back to normal? I mean aside from her considerable paunch that expands daily," Prolinc teased dryly.

"You risk your private parts with your less than flattering phraseology, Prolinc. I would try again if I were you, keeping in mind that Dee would be on my side and revenge could take many, unpleasant forms," Cat advised as she strode into the room.

"You look ravishing, little flame," Prolinc acknowledged with a Gattonian nod.

"Um, better. I assume the Dargons are about to pull a Darth Vader?" she asked matter-of-factly.

"I am not familiar with that maneuver but we have less than seventy-two hours before they enter our air space," Zorroc informed her, vaguely wondering how much she knew of Earth battle stratagems. Had he underestimated her again? "Things will happen very quickly. Have chambers been prepared for our guests? I think it would be best to show them to their rooms before the meeting commences for it will most likely stretch into the middle hours of the early morning."

"Yes, everything is prepared and I've memorized pertinent names and locations. Nefar, the province to the north and closest to us is sending Prince Sherem, the oldest son and next to rule and, from what I am told, a pain in our posterior; Kerr lays to the southeast and are governed by Queen Thanasa who is older than dirt and respected by all. Tena located due west, will be sending the head of their military named Qetu, a friend of Rosik's," Cat recited, a little nervous about entertaining the high level dignitaries in her first official capacity as Divitta.

"Very good, my cream, a clever Darth Vader, to memorize the names and geographical locations of our guests."

A bark of laugh escaped before she could stop it. "Zorroc, Darth Vader isn't a stratagem, he's a bad guy in my favorite science fiction movie called Star Wars. Actually, now that I think about it, the Empire and the Dargons have a lot in common, both exist to conquer and destroy worlds. You could learn a lot from Earth movies. I find your education sorely lacking in a number of crucial areas," she scolded with mock severity.

"I will endeavor to improve," he whispered sexily and then caught himself, cleared his throat and lifted his shoulder in a rueful shrug, aimed at his friend. "Now, have you and Dee familiarized yourselves with the Magic Caverns," Zorroc challenged.

Endless tunnels and catacombs crisscrossed deep into Ganz, with the only known access under the House of Ra. The Magic Caverns, that a much younger Zorroc and Prolinc had dubbed them, contained numerous springs and luminescent minerals imbedded in the walls that provided natural lighting. Cat had been both delighted and horrified at seeing them. Delighted, because it looked like a world fashioned by gnomes and fairies and horrified, because if she wandered down there alone she would be lost for all eternity. Nadia had displayed child like exuberance in showing off the secret hideout that Zorroc and Prolinc had discovered as children, and the three knew every nook and cranny. It, however, remained slightly terrifying for someone who could get hopelessly lost and disoriented in a shopping mall. And frequently did.

"Yes, she showed us. Just tell me the tracking device on my wrist will be strong enough for you to locate me when I disappear in the midst of endless bolt holes and passages," she pleaded tapping down her growing panic as she pictured herself isolated and alone fleeing all those gnomes turned goblins.

"There is nowhere you could go that I would not find you." Zorroc pulled her into the circle of his arms and kissed her lightly on her forehead. "But if you are really apprehensive about the tunnels I will have Nadia take you down every day until you can find your way around blindfolded. Will that help?"

"Yeah, stuck within the pages of the Hobbit for a month; that would help immensely."

He chuckled then looked up and greeted Rosik and Sycor. The meeting would begin in earnest with the arrival of Bandoff and Carpov. "I need to get to work, there is still much to plan and from now on I think it would be wise for all of you to stay within House grounds; no doubt there will be added disquiet and panic when the invasion is announced province wide."

Thus far, the people of Gattonia had taken the news of an impending attack from the Dargons with controlled optimism. They were well prepared, and with the assistance of the other provinces, plus the help of two off-world allies, in addition to the advanced warning not afforded them last time, they were ready to vent the rage that had been building for two years.

Rosik, Bandoff, Carpov and Sycor were briefed on the players set to join them at eleven. "The province of Kerr is sending Thanasa. Although approaching her one-hundred and fiftieth year, she remains the finest negotiator on the planet and has the closest relationship with the other provinces and the Leader of Jasper, Queen Heptshu. We are counting on her to successfully mediate between our off-world allies and the provinces of Ganz. Tena is sending their highest ranking military leader, Qetu, and the Prince of Nefar, Sherem himself, will be gracing us with his guidance," Zorroc had continued speaking over the groans.

Sherem was proud, arrogant and a renowned warrior known for his uncompromising dealings with enemies and allies alike. The relationship between Gattonia and Nefar had always been strained. "Our other off-world ally is Mesper, whose military head is Arisi. Representatives from the three provinces will be here in person while our off-world friends will be linked into the meeting through Video COM."

Sherem dreaded the hours to come. For one, he did not like being under the roof of a leader with little merit who, most likely, had embroiled them all in a confrontation of unnamed proportions. For another, he was not adept at socializing with figureheads unworthy of the thrones they sat on, with the exception of Thanasa. In addition, he chafed at the inevitable wasted hours of bombasting protocol and arse licking when they should be preparing for the inevitable battle. Of course, it might not be that bad, his friend Rosik COMd that he would be in on the planning session. Sherem wondered how he had come to the attention of Zorroc. Rosik and Sherem had met the three years before on Jasper and found immediate rapport. They had similar battle strategies and both liked to celebrate as hard as they fought. In the past year they had formed a strong bond in the midst of shared females, drink and stories. It had been a few months since they last met and he looked forward to fighting by his side.

He pressed the ornate entrance panel announcing his presence to the House of Ra and checked the time. He figured arriving an hour early would allow him ample time to settle in and gather his patience and resolve.

The panel slid soundlessly open to reveal the most exquisite sight his eyes had ever beheld. She had shimmering amber hair clasped back with the ends still visible on either side of her slim waist. She was tall and willowy with golden sheened skin, and high cheekbones above pronounced dimples, as well as large amber eyes that shouted her innocence. Her mouth, however, told a different story; it begged him for his attention with rapt hunger and moist promises. It did not matter who she was or whom she belonged to because from that moment on, she belonged to him. She was obviously a servant of some kind, maybe even a Chosen One to Zorroc. No matter, he would buy her contract, and she would leave with him on the morrow for Nefar.

Never had Nadia seen anything like him and stared in open wonder and curiosity. His hair, a similar shade to her brother's, curled in loose flowing waves past his shoulders. His skin looked dark and weather worn with lines like crows feet accenting his eyes with a scar dissecting his left eyebrow extending into his hairline. He had hair on his face, something she had never seen first hand. It covered his jaw and chin, and circled his mouth, calling attention to sensually masculine lips. A beard, she suddenly remembered; they called it a beard, and she wanted to touch it to see if it felt as coarse as it looked. He was a mountain of a male, taller than Prolinc and broader than Zorroc and he looked dark and foreboding, like a cloud about to storm. His eyes, an unsettling black, had a thin silver ring around his pupils, the only relief from wicked perilous temptation.

Maybe she should run.

Maybe she should call for Jaffers.

Maybe she should touch his beard.

The choice, however, was taken from her when he firmly but gently grasped her shoulders and moved her backward until he had her pinned between himself and the inner entranceway wall.

Both surfaces felt equally hard but where the wall held no warmth, he radiated enough to scorch her. He began to assault her lips with his. His beard, teasing her cheeks and chin, felt soft like thick silken fibers and contrasted with the lush feel of his lips devouring hers. His tongue ran along the seam of her closed lips causing her to sigh...giving him access to her mouth. His tongue plundered its depths, challenging hers to a duel before sucking it right into his mouth. She groaned helplessly, seeking more contact with their bodies, wanting to give him all of her.

She had never been kissed before but took to it like a bird to flight. His hands moved to her rib cage spread so his thumbs could press firmly into her budded nipples. She groaned her arousal. He rasped into her hair, demanding her identity.

"Nadia, I am Nadia," she groaned helplessly.

"You belong to me now, Nadia, who do I see to buy you?" he countered.

Her wings swiftly disappeared and became fins as the freezing waters of Ganz drenched her out of her soaring stupor.

She bit his lower lip and shrieked angrily as her knee came up and greeted his groin. He roared and threw himself away from her. "I am Nadia, sister to Zorroc, of the House of Ra, Leader to Gattonia," she wheezed in confused rage. What had happened? It had been her very first kiss and he mistook her for a whore. Shame warred with fury as she summoned Jaffers and informed him of a visitor and then fled down the hall.

****

Cat undressed wearily and glanced at the time. Two in the morning, boy was she bushed. Greeting the dignitaries, getting them settled and then entertaining them had taken a great deal of her energy. Why had Nadia failed to make an

281

appearance? She could have used her help. She placed her hands on her abdomen silently asking her baby how it fared. *"He is happy and content, my cream. Now go to sleep,"* Zorroc mindspoke, and she did.

The plan was simple, straightforward, and hopefully comprehensive enough to guarantee an end to further visits from their enemy. The meeting lasted through the night and morning and resumed the next afternoon before adjourning that evening. There had been remarkably few squabbles, with all parties wanting to maintain the current face of Ganz and end the virulent practices of the Dargons.

The people of Gattonia, though expecting the invasion, were unprepared for the enormity of the Dargon force. Hundreds of large ships blotted out the sun and hovered over the capital of Ra like a sinister plague, making it appear evening instead of early afternoon. The ships, diamond-shaped and in tight diamond formation had what looked like swarms of locusts buzzing around them. The Dargons had contacted all four provinces twelve hours before with ultimatums. They warned Nefar, Kerr and Tena not to interfere in the taking of Gattonia and they advised Gattonia to surrender, offering safe conduct off the planet. No one acknowledged the communiqués for obvious reasons; the other three provinces recognized they would be next if they allowed Gattonia to fall and Gattonia knew that the chances of being allowed safe conduct off the planet to fight another day amounted to nil. They would no doubt be gassed and slaughtered like sheep. Most importantly, the four provinces wanted to hide their unity from the enemy, an essential element to their plan.

The Dargons would not attack at present, the show of force over the capitol intended only to frighten and intimidate. The attack would follow later.

Gattonia had been productive since the Dargon attack almost two years before. Along with the latest development of the vaccine for FIS, new environ suit materials had been developed and tested for every virus, agent and mist known to them, right down to fire acid. Next, they reinstated headgear and sealed the suits only allowing filtered air to circulate within. Special nourishment pouches attached to tubing could be ingested by mouth. Of course, the suits were only needed when leaving the security of designated shelters throughout Gattonia. The massive undertaking expended indescribable amounts of currency, labor, and time, but the resulting accomplishment meant a safer place for all inhabitants. They had also created a multi-galaxy-knowledge-share in an effort to ensure the safety of other civilizations against viral warfare.

The invasion began in earnest the next morning. Carried out without a sound, the Dargons, flying in flocks without benefit of a ship, dispatched the virus in time-delayed canisters to avoid self-contamination. They would not have been detected except for the atmoscreening and sonic devices that sounded a warning of foreign agents or matter not native to their atmosphere. As the sun rose, an eerie silence pervaded. Civilians were asked to remain in protective quarters and maintain COM silence except for emergencies. Updates and information broadcasted non-stop through the IVVS and everyone stayed glued to them. Cat thought the quiet, low keyed reporting of events and instructions, by the news announcers, sounded like a blow-by-blow account of a golf tournament. Biotechs, Technos, and Engineers were asked to report to the main lab to begin work analyzing the active properties in the new contaminant. Cat, knowing

Angel would be a member of that group, experienced paralyzing fear for her and her unborn child.

****

"They kicked me off my team and sent me here, where I am to remain, until further notice. I was ordered, officially ordered!" Angel fumed, discarding her headpiece and peeling off the environ-suit before continuing.

She had arrived, escorted by two militias, minutes before to the shelter in the House of Ra where an overjoyed melee consisting of the aunts, Cat and Dee fought to bestow hugs and greetings. "I know Carpov was behind this and if he thinks to camouflage his cowardice behind the Science Head I will have *his* head. I didn't even have the opportunity to talk to him about it. I am perfectly healthy and the precautions we take to avoid contamination are rigorous to the extreme. No one in the department has been infected since I've been there; it's perfectly safe."

"But there's always a first time, Angel," Dee advised. "And you'd be the first to acknowledge it under other circumstances. Whether Carpov is behind it or not doesn't change the fact that they want you protected in case something goes wrong. And I for one am happy and relieved about it, now we won't have to constantly worry about you," Dee entreated unflinchingly, enveloping her friend in a warm hug of greeting.

"You would side with him against your best friend?"

"In this case, yes. Now calm down, your hormones are getting the best of you. What's the point in saving Gattonia if it means losing the women with unborn children, of whom you are one?" Cat asked simply.

"We've seen so little of you since our adventure began and if things cascade into disaster we won't

284

have much time left; so can't we use this as a reprieve to catch up with one another and revel in the moment of being together again?" Dee implored.

"Well," she smiled wickedly, "you are my friends so I will forgive your defection to the other side this once, but I won't forgive Carpov! If I stew then he stews, and just because my stew will be a lot more fun than his stew will not play a part in it."

The science teams isolated the properties of the virus within hours. It was not complicated, just lethal. Unprotected people would have fallen sick within twenty-four hours and died within the week. Though quick acting and deadly, it would remain active no longer than forty-eight hours after exposure to the air; then it would lose potency and die out. The Dargons, tired of toying and torturing, decided to go for the jugular and end things quickly. Gattonia would play possum and let them believe their objectives met. It had been risky, allowing the Dargons to lay in the virus, threatening the mass destruction of his people, but Zorroc had great faith in his Scientists and they had assured him that with the proper equipment and preparation, everyone would stay safe. The gamble had paid off. So far, no casualties could be directly attributed to this latest misting. Now the trap they had laid so meticulously could go forward. They would wait for the Dargons to come and inspect their handy work—and fly right into an ambush.

The House of Ra had been designated as battle headquarters. The main level south wing normally used for balls and banquets and to accommodate mass quantities of guests, had been taken over for planning, communication, strategy sessions, and defense. An endless stream of equipment had been installed to make this possible; even the roof above was utilized to ensure the safety and defense of Ra. The lower level had been sealed to protect against outside contaminants. It housed the family, militia, and guards along with food, clothing and supplies. The only two exits located on that floor had two inside guards at each panel twenty-four hours a day with more posted outside.

The household staff occupied one of the two apartments while the family shared the other.

Catarina, Nadia, the aunts, Dee, Angel, and the kittens, which now resembled teen-aged kitty terrorists, crammed into the small space. With the addition of Spooka and occasionally Zorroc and Prolinc, privacy proved impossible.

Their apartment did, however contain the hidden entrance into the caverns.

Therefore, when Zorroc could get away, he and Cat stayed there together in a sizable and well-lit nook that gave them relative privacy. Zorroc had stocked it with mats, comforters and a private reserve of Cat's favorite foods and drink. She also used it to get away and be alone from time to time. Prolinc commandeered a similar spot for him and Dee.

Even with the safety of the environ suits, Cat was forbidden to leave the lower level until the air had cleared. She and Dee, suffering from cabin fever, joined by Angel, often disappeared into the caverns to launch slumber parties, telling stories and giggling long into the night. Forty-eight hours after the misting, Nadia, the aunts, and Angel, while not allowed to leave the complex, could at least ascend to the main level and occupy their chambers. When the all clear sounded some twenty hours later, Dee and Cat raced each other to the main level and relative freedom.

"I was not meant to live the life of a mole," Dee gasped as she reached the entrance panel just before Cat, both bursting into the corridor like two swimmers breaking the surface of a lake after being under water too long.

"It would have been more polite to let me go first, after all there are two of me," Cat panted, holding her stomach.

"Sorry, it's every fetus for himself; he should have kicked you into a faster gear."

"Well, never let it be said that he holds a grudge, we saved you a lovely suite just down from Angel's; let's get cleaned up then go in search of our guys. This is the first time in over three days we'll get to see them in daylight."

They entered the Strat-room feeling clean and refreshed, and spotted Zorroc and Prolinc hunched over a table with a dozen others talking quietly and studying a large screen filled with lines, numbers, icons and a large circle.

Cat fought her tears welling unbidden, blaming raging pregnancy hormones for her lack of control. But she'd missed Zorroc terribly, having seen him for a total of four hours in three days—and they could all be dead soon if things didn't go according to plan.

He turned slowly and crossed to her then led her back to the group crowding the table. "*I have missed you too*," he mindspoke as he placed her in front of him and surrounded her with a hand splayed on her abdomen, an arm circling her above the waist and his chin on her head. Cat tensed, sure there had to be something improper about this public display of intimacy but since no one gave her a second glance she decided to relax.

The viral gas developed by Gattonia would only be used in the heart of the capitol. They did not want to chance contaminating their neighbors and they had a limited supply of the agent. That meant drawing the Dargons into a hundred-nid square to the heart of Ra.

"We have heard from Arisi. The Dargon's Mobil

Space Station remains stationary at fifteen hundred Kromians from Ganz and from the COMs the Mespers have monitored, they intend to stay there through the taking of Gattonia," Sycor reported.

"Did they acquire information as to why the attack has not yet commenced?" asked Zorroc.

"Apparently, they are leery of attacking too soon for fear of being felled by their own virus," Sycor replied with an amused grunt. "Your plan is working better than anticipated."

Chapter Twenty-One

"You are being unfair, Zorroc called it exactly right. The fact that the Dargons have not yet attacked lends proof of his sound recommendations," Rosik pursued, not sure why it had become suddenly so important to bring Sherem around to his point of view.

"So he got lucky, he still remains a pampered, spoiled, ineffectual boy who was handed his power instead of earning it," Sherem fired back not willing to give ground when sure of his position.

The two had been embroiled in a spirited discussion for some time debating the merits and faults of Zorroc and his leadership abilities. Boredom, the underlying force of their conflict, guided their debate. The Dargons had been quiet now for a week following the misting, causing unrest between the starships wanting confrontation not complacency. Sherem had taken the position that Zorroc was not fit to rule because of his inexperience in battle and honing that only years in the field could provide. Rosik sighted that the current strategy had been put into place primarily by Zorroc and with the contention that, to date, it had worked better than anyone could have anticipated. The proof, he pointed out, resided in the results.

"You say pampered and spoiled; let me propose the following scenario. A boy at the age of fifteen is faced with the fact that his father is dying, having already lost his mother only two years before. As a result, although just barely past puberty, he begins assuming the responsibilities of running an empire, in support of his father. At the age of seventeen, while we freely cavorted, garnering sexual exploitations and stretching our warrior wings, Zorroc assumed responsibility for running an entire province, working with a council who had been in power for more years than he had been alive. Add to that, the responsibility of raising a baby girl. We, my friend, had the opportunity to grow up; Zorroc was not afforded that luxury. And so I would ask you to reevaluate your suppositions," he challenged while pouring both himself and Sherem another shot of Jive.

"You never voiced your support before, what happened to change your mind?"

Rosik shrugged and admitted, "The Miramid picked up a distress call from his party some months back when they had been ambushed by the Dargons on their way back from Earth. It turned out a traitor on the High Council set a trap for Zorroc and his mate. Zorroc proved astute, clear headed and had a surprising lack of ego for one in his position and I have grown to admire his poise and selfless dedication to his people."

Sherem mulled over his answer for a minute while savoring the superior Jive that Rosik had provided. "Why do you think the Dargons targeted Gattonia?"

"Maybe we were perceived as the weak link of the four provinces. It is their usual method when overtaking a planet; however, in this case they miscalculated and will pay dearly if the Miramid has anything to say about it."

"Tell me about the sister," Sherem yawned and scratched his beard, changing the subject abruptly. "Nadia, is that what she is called?"

"Yes, but there is not much to tell. She is young and beautiful and Zorroc guards her like a sphinx. His childhood may have been stolen from him but he protects his sister's fiercely. If anyone is spoiled and pampered, my friend, it is she."

Sherem grunted and prepared to continue his probe into Zorroc's sister when the alarms sounded the long awaited attack on Gattonia.

A grin slashed Sherem's features. "Time to get to my ship. Good hunting, my friend."

"And to you."

Weeks before the Dargons entered the air space of Ganz, all Pods, Starships and Cruisers slowly slipped from Gattonia and positioned themselves across the other three provinces. Part of Zorroc's plan was to let the Dargons enter Gattonia unmolested and then follow with their own ships slowly forcing them toward Ra. Civilians were told to remain in underground shelters for their protection and to maintain the possum ruse. Ground forces in all locations prepared to go on the offensive, supported by incoming air power. Their off-world allies would neutralize the Dargon's Mobil Space Station when signaled by the House of Ra. They wanted the fighting force of the enemy trapped and unable to retreat to defend their station. Timing remained the most intricate part of their plan.

The Dargons descended into Gattonia with confidence and the arrogant assumption they would find a crippled and dying population. It took them little time to realize their true situation. Their sonics showed incoming ships from all directions, surrounding them, and their efforts to break through the closing grid proved impossible. They were being blown out of the sky systematically by both ground and air forces. They were neatly trapped.

Considering the alternatives available, ground deployment of their troops to go hand to hand with the Gattonians won out over an air confrontation they would lose. And it held several advantages. One—although the Gattonians moved with more agility, they did not have the advantage of being able to fly, giving the Dargons superior mobility. Two—the Gattonian air force would be less likely to fire on them for fear of hitting their own forces. Three—the Dargons had no such weakness; it did not matter whether they forfeited their own warriors while blasting the Gattonians, so long as they exterminated the enemy and won the battle.

As the allied forces clashed with the Dargons, it took on the earmarks of a chaotic free-for-all. But with the great lengths the allied forces exerted to preserve their male-power and the Dargons strategy of taking out anyone who got in the way of their blazers, the tide slowly turned in favor the Gattonian forces, though casualties soared.

The Dargons, aware of their situation, searched desperately for an advantage that would turn the current probability of defeat into victory.

Assistance came in the form of Sandra.

The sun had begun to cast muted rays on the landscape of Gattonia as Sandra continued her surveillance of the area surrounding the dorm grounds. Then she spotted them. A small contingent of Dargons heading in her direction, some flying low while others lumbered on foot. She crept out to greet them.

"*Pssst*, over here," she whispered, unaccountably excited by what she intended. Of course, they could just kill her outright but either way her life had ended with the termination of Zana's. Now a searing hatred for Cat and a burning desire to see the House of Ra fall remained her only reasons for existence.

As they approached fully armed and wary, she raised her hands to show them she was unarmed and maintained her position as they closed in around her. She found something erotic about being helpless and at mercy of the enemy. Maybe they would tie her up and play with her after she had gained their trust. She cleared her throat and licked her lips before proceeding. "The building behind me is large and vacant but for a few women sequestered in a shelter on the ground floor. It would be a safe place to discuss the defeat of Gattonia."

The leader put a blazer to her throat and grunted, "Why would you assist us, Earth woman?"

"I want to see the leader of Gattonia and his whore fry in hell. They killed my lover so my time here is done. In exchange for helping you, I'd like safe passage off this cursed planet. Together, I believe we can bring down the House of Ra and possibly all of Gattonia." After a thorough search found her unarmed, they decided to proceed to the building she indicated and take the chance it was not a trap. Sandra led them up to the second floor that consisted of a large dining hall where their movements would go undetected from the occupants below.

The thirteen Dargons headed straight for the food and drink dispensers where they proceeded to gorge themselves as fast as the food appeared. Sandra was both repelled and drawn by their voracious appetites. At the conclusion of their meal, five of them approached and sat facing her. They eyed her carefully and she grew nervous under their attention. "Tell us why we should spare your life, child?" Gorn inquired sniffing her.

Sandra caught the interested signals he sent and relaxed into her chair and smiled knowingly. Men, after all, were men. "I know the layout of the House of Ra and the guards surrounding it. I believe I can get you inside, where we will take Zorroc's whore hostage and force him to surrender or watch her slowly die in front of him."

"What is so special about a whore? Surely she can be easily replaced, or is that what you intend?"

"The Gattonian holds no interest for me," she

paused to wet her bottom lip with her tongue. "I find that I am more interested in larger meatier game," she opted as she uncrossed her legs and held her knees apart inviting a tempting glimpse up her dress.

Gorn's eyes gleamed as the appendage between his legs began to make itself known. Sandra smiled. As the talk continued, there were two languages being spoken, one verbal, and one of the body.

Gorn wondered how long it would take her to die once he had sated himself in her. He would time things carefully...first drawing from her the pertinent information needed to defeat the leader of Gattonia, then teaching her the ways of Dargon passion.

"Catarina, his whore, is most likely carrying his child, which makes her valuable to him. That is why he will surrender to save her."

His attention caught at the mention of Cat's name. "Catarina, that name is familiar to me," Gorn mused, wondering what had become of Dyfainius and his plans concerning his daughter.

"It should be familiar; some of your people grabbed her on Zeba II, though she was later rescued. That woman has the damnedest luck." A quick flit of malice crossed her face.

"Yesss." No wonder they sent such a determined force to steal her back, it answered yet another of his questions, as he proceeded to troll the Earth female. It would be a pleasure to retake the woman stolen from him and guarantee her a slow rending death. "Are you familiar with the name Dyfainius?" he ventured as the others surrounding Sandra began to grow bored and drift away.

Sandra started. "Yes, he was the father of my lover. Then it's true; he did have dealings with your people. They executed him for being a traitor and then killed my lover."

"I thought his only child, a female." The question visible in his countenance.

"You thought correctly, I don't limit my sexual liaisons by gender or...species," she murmured while draping her arms across the back of her chair accentuating her generous breasts.

Gorn grunted and probed, "How will we gain access to this House of Ra, surely it is well fortified and guarded from unwanted intruders."

Sandra re-crossed her legs, letting her skirt inch further up her thigh before responding. "One of the Royal House Guards comes to visit me when he is both off duty and on. He uses a hidden pathway to slip away. I got him to reveal its location. We will not be detected." She proceeded to describe her plan.

"I am finished with you until full dark," he rumbled some time later. "I must prepare for our attack. Stay out of sight, I will come for you well before we depart to take care of your more immediate needs."

She left him with a full view of her most provocative walk. The meeting had gone perfectly.

****

"You look exhausted; can I get you something to eat or a strong dose of choc-tea?" Cat addressed her weary mate as he entered their chambers. The days had moved silently until the attack and then the sky exploded into a marathon light show, reminding her of the final scene from Independence Day. Cat found herself wondering how anything so beautiful could be so deadly. The Gattonian forces dominated, taking advantage of the element of surprise and their battle ready status. When the Dargons later took to the ground to engage the forces in hand-to-hand, things had looked bleak for a time but they gradually gained the upper hand, clearly in control of the outcome. The fighting in and around Ra had grown fierce, the Gattonians wanting a swift end and the Dargons desperate to revive their flagging victory.

"That would be fine. You should be down in the shelter; this area is far from secure." Hollow-eyed and drawn from too many hours of issuing orders and not enough sleep, he still looked like water to her desert.

"I am perfectly safe here and prefer our own chambers and mat infused with your scent," she murmured, snaking her arms around his neck to sniff and nip at his ear lobe. He lifted her off the ground and crushed her to him. "Besides, this place is guarded better than Fort Knox. No one could get within two miles of the place without a hundred people knowing about it. How's it going out there, anyway?"

He let her down but kept her in the circle of his arms. "It is going well. Our off-world allies have neutralized the Mobil Space Station so they can pose no threat in coming to the defense of their militia. We have suffered more casualties than I would like but we dispensed the virus almost twelve hours ago and are starting to see a change in the Dargon's effectiveness. They are growing weak but so far seem unaware of being misted. Apparently it does not occur to them that what they have done to others may be visited on them."

"What symptoms will they experience?"

He ducked his head and hid a smile. "Mainly flu like; nausea, some vomiting and diarrhea, weakness, fatigue...and impotence," mumbling the last word unintelligibly as he reached down to snag her thigh and buttocks in order to pull her more fully to him.

"I don't think I caught that last word," she commented suspiciously.

"Impotence, their member will no longer work, which they will no doubt discover on their way home."

"Talk about divine justice. Are you sure it will not have the same effect on you?"

"There is but one way to find out, my one." He, scooped her up, and proceeded to their platmat.

It had been a disastrous week, Gorn admitted. Nothing had gone according to form and now his warriors showed signs of sickness and he himself felt odd. For one, thoughts of the female waiting to pleasure him failed to stimulate his male tool. Expectant thoughts of taking and breaking her insides, erupted more repellant than reward, and the constant trips outside by him and his troop, to defecate, soon would catch the attention of the enemy, he worried. He hated depending on the woman for assistance but trusted that the outcome would win them Ganz. He knew now that the battle lay not with Gattonia but the entire planet and the reward to himself would be all the greater for a victory. He would crush them all by any means necessary. He had endeavored to contact the Station for permission to simply level Gattonia and leave the other provinces unmolested but so far, his efforts to reach them had failed. With every fighting force that the planet had in one concentrated area, the plan proved almost irresistible but he did not dare act on his own or his life, lands, and family would pay the price.

Men! Two of the Dargons had come for her just minutes before and already they were setting out for the House of Ra. The leader had not hazarded a glance in her direction though she had been positive he found her attractive. Nevertheless, true to her word, she led them to the south entrance of the lower level, guarded by three familiar males, one of whom, she knew by name. Jemi, young and enthusiastic, had a habit of enhancing his importance by spouting information concerning the defense of the House of Ra.

"Jemi, is that you? It's Sandra, my handsome hunk, I am so happy to see you."

The three Gattonians, who had been restless and bored for days, leapt to attention at the sound of her greeting. "What are you doing here, woman, it is well past curfew and this is not the front entrance you have approached," Jemi challenged while combing the area for more intruders.

"Don't be angry with me, baby, I've been lonely at the Women Dorm and starving for male companionship, so I took advantage of your secret path to surprise you. Please don't turn me away." She sauntered slowly toward the entrance flipping her hair to catch the breeze. "I could take all three of you at once and you wouldn't have to leave your station, now tell me that would be more interesting than your previous duties these last weeks." She reached down to the hem of her dress and slowly worked it up her thighs. Three sets of stares galvanized to her thatch...as they incinerated before her. She smiled, pleased that it had been their last vision before perishing.

"Now what, child?" Gorn asked quietly, feeling worse by the minute. Looking at his comrades, he knew they felt no better. Had there been something in the food? Was this an elaborate trap set into motion by the leader of Gattonia?

"We knock, what else," she smiled sweetly and rapped lightly on the panel. At the lack of response, she knocked louder and was answered immediately by a voice over the COM demanding her identity.

"It's just Sandra; I've come for a visit. I would have been here an hour ago if I hadn't got lost. Please let me in, it's dark and creepy out here." The panel slid open but before the Dargons could react, a guard pulled Sandra inside and the panel shut. Two sentinels threw Sandra against the wall and began firing questions at her. She answered innocently and when the two turned to confer on how to proceed, she pressed the panel pad instantly admitting the enemy. No alarm sounded, it happened too fast. Sandra, mildly surprised they had gotten this far, led them cautiously down the hall listening for approaching footsteps.

"Twill, you and Zog remain here and guard this exit to ensure our escape," Gorn ordered. "The rest follow me."

They proceeded down the corridor and up the stairs to the main level and opened the panel revealing the deserted hall. "Where do we go from here? You will lead."

Sandra nodded. "The master sleeping chamber is supposed to be in the right wing," she whispered, creeping down the hall. She led them unerringly toward Cat, recalling the layout Zana had described in detail. The closer they got the faster Sandra's blood coursed. She could almost feel Cat's neck beneath her hands, slowly squeezing the life from her. Finally, she would come out the victor.

The panel slid silently open revealing Cat sound asleep on a huge bed. Gorn stunned her, not wanting to give her a chance to alert others. He lifted her like a sack of potatoes under his arm and then backtracked.

"What is wrong, Zorroc," Prolinc asked, noting his friends still countenance. He had not moved for a few moments and seemed to be focused on something beyond himself.

"Catarina is not conscious, there is something wrong," he stated with growing panic. "I am going to our chambers and check on her."

"She is probably just deeply asleep, carrying your offspring must be a very tiring experience," Prolinc noted with a shade of humor.

"She is not asleep, I am going."

"Well, then I am coming as well," he sighed. The

two ran toward Zorroc's chambers. Which were empty.

Zorroc went right to the COM and ordered the immediate electronic sealing of the house and grounds and a physical check of each entrance. It was carried out in seconds.

The Dargons and Sandra rushed quietly toward the lower level and their exit. When Twill spotted them, he pushed the panel's exit button but nothing happened. He tried again, nothing.

Sandra rushed forward and pressed the keypad but still the panel refused to budge. Screeching her frustration she demanded, "What is wrong with this damned thing, it worked for me before. Did one of you do something?"

Suddenly, alarms began to sound. "How did they detect our presence? Come, we will hide ourselves in one of the shelters we passed," Gorn thundered, systemically opening the panels lining the hall until he came to living quarters that would adequately suit their needs. After entering, Gorn fired upon the keypad preventing unwanted company. Maybe they would think the panel had simply malfunctioned and move on. He entered one of the sleeping chambers and dumped Cat on the mat ordering Sandra to watch her.

Several minutes passed before Cat groaned and sat up, "Spit, what happened, I feel like I've been run over by a Pod." She surveyed her surroundings and hit the mat. "And why am I constantly waking up in a different location, from the one I went to sleep in," she groaned, not expecting an answer. She looked around and noticed Sandra seated in the corner across the room smiling maliciously.

"Surprised to see me, bitch?" Sandra cooed looking like the canary that swallowed the Cat. "So sorry you're feeling under the weather but trust me, it will only get worse. I'd enjoy the discomfort, if I were you, before it turns into torturous agony, and death. How does it feel to know that you will be the instrument that destroys the House of Ra, Gattonia, and your precious mate? Quite an accomplishment for one so...small," she taunted, enjoying the feeling of power over her archenemy. "The Dargons and I planned this little party..."

"The Dargons are here in this apartment? Sandra what were you thinking, they will either slice you up for food or rip you from the inside out taking turns with your body."

"I made a deal with them; you on a platter in exchange for me off this planet where I can work my way back to Earth. So, I'd be worrying about your own body, if I were you. I can take care of my own.

"And now if you will excuse me I'll alert them to your wakeful state, I'm sure they'll enjoy some fun with you before you get on the COM and do our bidding."

As soon as Sandra left the room, Cat bee-lined for the hidden panel leading to the caverns thanking the gods, the fates, and every force she could think of that they picked this particular shelter and room.

She moved quickly and quietly through the maze of trails, reaching out to communicate with Zorroc. He answered instantly and she warmed at the connection.

"Where are you?" he demanded.

"I'm in the caverns. The Dargons kidnapped me with the assistance of Sandra. They plan to use me as a hostage in order to get you and then Gattonia. They came right into the house and stunned me while I was asleep. How did they get in?"

Zorroc shoved his hands into his hair, cursing the breach in security that led to their current situation. And he was so incredibly frightened for her. It was not over. What would he do if they found her before he could get to her...but he must remain calm...to calm his mate. *"The guards covering the south lower level were neutralized. We are on our way, get as far into the caverns as possible, there is a chance they could find the entrance and come after you. We have arrived at the shelter. I will keep you informed."*

Sandra had just finished murmuring of Cat's conscious state when the internal COM announced the arrival of Gattonian troops led by Zorroc.

"I am Zorroc, Leader of Gattonia, you are defeated. We will allow you to surrender and leave our planet provided you give yourselves up within the next sixty-seconds. If not we will melt the panel and snuff anything we find," he said in an unemotional straightforward manner.

"Check your sleeping quarters, Leader, and you will see something belonging to you is missing and if you desire to see her again you will surrender Gattonia to me—Gorn, High Commander to Dargon." There were distinct grunts and shuffling behind the panel that accompanied his words.

"And if I were you, High Commander, I would check on your hostage because unlike you, I know exactly where my mate resides and it is not with you. Time is running out."

Gorn looked at Sandra and she wordlessly went to the sleeping chamber to confirm Cat's whereabouts. She had vanished. Sandra began to tear the room apart looking in any space that could hold their hostage. She turned and faced Gorn. "She's disappeared, she is no where. I left her on the mat." She noticed a distinct quiver in her voice as she nervously glanced back into the room, willing her captive to reappear. Gorn followed her into the room, searched with his eyes, then turned to Sandra.

"What have you done with her you useless spreader? Why did you let her escape?" He lumbered toward her, the threat palatable in his black, beady eyes.

"I didn't do anything for that worthless bitch! I've risked everything to help you, you must believe me..." Gorn advanced on her, grabbed her throat and snapped it loudly. She slumped to the floor.

He turned to his warriors. "There has to be a hidey hole of some sort, she is a puny Earth woman, not a spirit. Tear the place apart, and find it or you will meet a similar fate to the woman at your feet." Gorn went back to the panel and tried to bluff, "Your female remains right where we left her, I would let you talk to her if she were conscious but unfortunately the stun blow I inflicted has damaged her in some way."

"Cat, where are you?" he messaged.

"I see you have a sense of humor after all. I have no idea where I am," Cat replied, as she moved swiftly forward, turning from one path onto another, hopelessly disoriented. *"Geez, honey, what if I'm going in circles and wander close enough to the entrance for them to grab me? They have to know I'm missing by now."* Don't panic! Don't panic! She kept repeating to herself. Yeah, yeah she answered, she might as well be saying don't breathe, don't breathe.

"Stand still for a few moments and I will discern you location," he gently stated and then activated the search monitor on his wristband.

She liked his inner voice a lot better than her own at the moment, silently cursing the ancestor responsible for her directional guidance gene.

He advised that she stood almost a half mile from the entrance and told her to find the nearest cove and stay there until he could come for her. She took three steps and fell seven feet into an unlit hole slamming her right arm and thigh and landing on her left foot, which twisted underneath her. She groaned and patted her belly asking, "You all right in there, sweetie? Mama's a navigationally challenged, klutz." She curled herself into a ball and begged Zorroc to hurry. She could feel her ankle begin to swell.

"Cat fell into one of the pits, we need to speed this up," he told Prolinc and then to the panel, he advised them to stand back. He received no reply.

They blasted through in less than twenty-seconds and flooded the shelter finding it empty except for Sandra's dead body. The Dargons had found the caverns. Leaving twenty soldiers behind, Prolinc and Zorroc led the remaining team toward Cat's homing signal. They would retrieve her first and then go after the Dargons.

Sniffing Cat's scent, the Dargons located her within minutes after her fall but they could not determine a way to extricate her. The crevice that she fell into proved too narrow for their trunk like bodies to descend and she hunkered too far down to grab. Gorn came up with the solution. "You will stand and give me your hand so that I can lift you out, child. You will not be harmed if you do as I ask."

"No offense there, Gorn, 'cause I know what a sweet guy you are underneath all those slimy, stinky scales; but I would just as soon neck with Jaba the Hut."

"Javthut is not here but if you refuse to co-operate, there is no further reason for your existence. I will simply kill you. The choice is yours, of course." He gave her a sinister Dargon smile.

They came upon them from above and what Zorroc saw stopped him in his tracks. If they succeeded in grabbing her, they would be unable to protect her with a force field. He and Prolinc, most likely, had a strong enough bond to keep a blazer blast from disintegrating her, though three guardians in tripod formation would certainly have been safer. But if they took the time to summon another...

"There is no time to improve our position or numbers, you must tell her not to touch the slimy hand that reaches for her, our power will have to suffice," Prolinc mind-thought, grimly beginning to focus his power to link with Zorroc.

"Not necessarily. Old habits die hard, my friends. Let's do this," Bandoff appeared beside them smiling at their twin expressions of incredulity.

Zorroc let out a relieved breath. *"Do not touch him Catarina, pretend you cannot reach that far with your injuries then remain absolutely still; we will form a protective field over you, do you understand,"* Zorroc telepathed, garnering all of his massive power to protect her.

"All right Gorn, you win, I'll try to reach your hand, but I've injured both ankles and am not sure I can stand. Just give me a minute to prepare," and then she knelt and froze in place.

Gorn sniffed the air, as if sensing something awry, but disintegrated before the thought fully formed. They snuffed the rest of the party allowing them no time to fire on Cat.

Epilogue

The commotion was deafening. The south wing; cleared and reset for the festivities and chambers readied, welcomed the Gattonian allies from Ganz, Mesper and Jasper. The celebration spilled into every cranny of the House of Ra and out into the streets for miles. The Dargons, after losing seventy-five percent of their troops and one hundred percent of the starch between their legs, turned tail and fled. The allies did not bother to deter them.

Zorroc had saved his people, his planet and his mate.

The weeks following her brief respite in the pit were exuberant. Her injuries healed and she began to take on the proportions of a baby whale. Zorroc rejoiced in every inch and behaved worse than a mother hen protecting an only chick. Being smothered, however, did have its rewards. Cat fairly hummed with sensual overload both day and night. The brooding intensity that had been like a cloak surrounding her cat man had dissipated to reveal a playful, mischievous, and joyful side. Nadia was maturing into a lady as beautiful and passionate on the inside as the outside. The aunts remained the same and her two friends were every bit as addicted to their males as Cat was to hers. Long Live Co-dependency.

Of course, not everything was perfect. China and Rosik had been injured in battle and though both would recuperate, China lost the child she'd been carrying. Cat's parents had surfaced and now wanted to be a part of her life. They'd resigned their positions with the Earth space program and were apparently ready to settle into the role of parents and grandparents. They were only twenty-something years too late. Zorroc told her he would not encourage or discourage her involvement with them. He'd support her in whatever path she chose. And lastly, some of their allies, namely Sherem lingered on at the House of Ra, seemingly in no rush to leave.

The panel to their chambers slid open to reveal her very own dream come true...frowning ferociously. "You are supposed to be resting and yet I feel your mind working feverishly. What troubles you, my Divitta?" Zorroc purred, underlain with steely intent.

"I'm confused. Why is Sherem still here? Before the Dargons decided to visit, I got the distinct impression, things between the two of you rated somewhere between tolerance and antagonism. Is everything all right?"

"Everything is fine, the prince would like our two provinces to be closer, become stronger allies, if you will. I have agreed with the sentiment but not in the manner he intends to accomplish it," he murmured bemusedly, stripping slowly keeping his gaze fastened to hers until he wore nothing but a smile and a gleam.

Cat flushed hotly at the sight of Zorroc stalking her. Would she ever get used to the overpowering eroticism he exuded that sucker-punched her with electricity igniting every nerve-ending in her body? What had they been discussing anyway? She paused, transfixed...*transported*...to a world of pookas, feline predators, erotic adventures and all consuming love. And he filled her full.

It wasn't until much later, temporarily sated, that she remembered her derailed train of thought. "Zorroc?"

"*Hmm...*"

"What does Sherem want?"

"Nadia."

"Nadia? He can't have Nadia, she's betrothed to Prolinc."

"The betrothal is not the obstacle. Prolinc has asked permission to lifemate with Dee, and I granted it."

"When did that happen?" Cat screeched and sat up baring her increasingly plump breasts.

Zorroc leaned over her suckling first one breast then the other before softly growling his response, "This afternoon while you were sleeping."

"Uh...Uh..." Now what was she going to say? "Oh," she mind-stumbled, remembering. "So what is the obstacle?"

"She hates him."

"Hates who?"

Zorroc chuckled knowingly; his mate was short-circuiting again. "Nadia hates Sherem."

"Nadia can't hate Sherem, my God, the girl can't even hate the Dargons, she told me she felt sorry for them; how can she hate Sherem?"

"It poses a mystery, but there is another mystery much more important that I would solve. The one of my offspring."

"He's fine."

"It is not a he."

"But I thought you said...it's a she?"

"It is not a she."

"It's an it?" Oh no, were they dealing with a new species here? The ramifications were staggering. Oh yeah, now she remembered. In *Enemy Mine* the alien didn't have to have a partner to become pregnant, he was both male and female and would just drop a baby periodically. Oh My God—her last coherent thought, before Zorroc began to laugh...and laugh...and laugh. He roared...and cried...and howled...he'd become hysterical. This was just terrible. His mind had sprung. Well whose wouldn't with news like this!

She grabbed her belly, silently reassuring the, uh, little thing, that she loved it anyway. Her protective action brought Zorroc around.

"It is not an it, it is a them," he clarified, gasping for air and sanity.

Them—like the horrifying creatures in the movie Them? Cat visibly shuddered. Zorroc started cracking up again.

"Tri—tri—triplets," he spurted. "One boy and two girls, triplets."

"Triplets," she repeated, "triplets...well," her voice clogged, "well," she croaked again and then began to cry with joy and relief, and with overpowering love for all of them—She was having a litter.

"Thank you," she hiccupped, launching herself at him. *Whew*, she thought, there for a minute science fiction had taken on a whole new concept.

About the author...

Lil spends her time at the mercy of her fertile imagination, which garnered her a nomination for Best Erotic Paranormal Romance from Romantic Times Book Reviews along with many other, very much appreciated, superlative accolades from premier review sites.

She now lives in Weeki Wachee, Florida, enjoying the "big birds," mermaids and manatees—and ruled by her demando cats: Katu, China Cat Sunflower and Mad Max.

Lil loves to hear from her readers at lgibsn@tampabay.rr.com and has this to say to them:

Dear readers, a short note to let you know why I dropped from the face of the writing world. My husband, John, passed away in his sleep November of 2007. He captured my heart twenty-four years ago and holds it still. He was my soulmate, best friend, lover and lifemate. His loss is difficult, to say the least, but to compound it all, I also lost both parents, five months after John, whom both of us were very close to.

I am happy to report that I began writing again in October of 2008 and hope to create many more stories to entertain and amuse you. Please look for soon-to-be-released *Sherem*, Book 2 of Feline Predators of Ganz. Followed by the much awaited Book 3, *Rosik*.

I thank The Wild Rose Press and my editor, Amanda Barnett, for their patience and support during this time of great strife and hope you continue to enjoy my present and future heroes and heroines.

I love to hear from my readers.
Kindest regards, Lil.

LaVergne, TN USA
14 October 2010
200755LV00001B/3/P